NEW STORIES
FROM THE SOUTH

The Year's Best, 1992

edited by
Shannon Ravenel

NEW STORIES
FROM THE SOUTH

The Year's Best, 1992

Algonquin Books of Chapel Hill

published by
Algonquin Books of Chapel Hill
Post Office Box 2225, Chapel Hill, North Carolina 27515-2225
a division of Workman Publishing Company, Inc.
708 Broadway, New York, New York 10003

ISSN 0897-9073
ISBN 1-56512-011-6

CONTENTS

PREFACE

This is the seventh annual edition of *New Stories from the South*. In the last six editions, I've used this space to try to define the two operative words in our anthology's title: "New" and "South." Meanwhile, Roy Blount, Jr., was at work on this problem, and he seems to have solved it:

> There's Southern new and Northern new,
> And one is warmer and funkier too,
> And one has no fried okra at all.
> And I know which, and so do y'all.

Thus freed from the obligation to ruminate on the borders of the "new" South, this year I want to talk about the periodicals from which the stories here have come.

Of the seventeen short stories gathered here, fourteen first appeared in what are familiarly called "little magazines." The other three stories were originally published in two of the handful of "slick magazines" that still regularly publish good short fiction. Several of the small magazines represented this year are older and more established than others; *The Antioch Review, The Georgia Review, The Kenyon Review, The Paris Review, The Southern Review,* and *The Virginia Quarterly Review* are well known to readers familiar with this corner of the American literary map. Others are probably not so well known: *Black Warrior Review, The Cres-cent Review, The Missouri Review, New England Review/Breadloaf Quarterly, Ontario Review,* and *Pembroke Magazine.*

Those first six are actually giants among the little magazines. But the paragon of these giants, *The Paris Review,* could none-theless fit all its subscribers into a small college's football sta-dium. The subscribers to *Pembroke Magazine* would probably rattle around in a high-school gym.

Almost none of these literary magazines can afford to pay their writer-contributors more than a token amount plus free copies of the issue in which their work appears. And while the editor of *Zyzzyva,* a West Coast journal, boasts in his preface to the spring 1992 issue that his current print run "happens to be slightly more than the number of unsolicited manuscripts we receive each year," the number of submissions most of these magazines receive each year is double, triple, perhaps even quadruple the number of their subscribers.

What's the deal?

The deal is that there are, in America, more than three hun-dred graduate and undergraduate writing programs turning out writers who need someplace to expose their work. America's best fiction writers not only establish themselves first in the liter-ary journals, they continue to publish much of their finest work there. In fact, the only real market for first-rate new short fiction exists in the little magazines.

If it's true that there are so few paying subscribers, who in the world is the audience for this wealth of creativity? Who is reading the new writers' first published stories? Who is keeping up with the latest poetry from John Updike, the newest excerpt from Reynolds Price's novel-in-progress? I'm reading these maga-zines. The series editors of *The Best American Short Stories* and *The Best American Poetry* and *The Best American Essays* are read-ing them. The editors of the *O. Henry Awards* and *Pushcart Prize* anthologies are reading them. But except for anthologists and a few literary agents on the prowl and maybe a young fiction editor here and there, who else? You don't see commuters reading *The Georgia Review* or subway straphangers clutching copies of *The Kenyon Review*. Anybody know who does subscribe to *Black Warrior* or *Antioch*? To any literary journal at all for that matter?

The obvious answer is that there are precious few subscribers and that the magazines' mailing lists share the same names. This pool of subscribers is shallow, barely enough to water the two thousand American litmags listed in *The International Directory of Little Magazines and Presses*. Nevertheless, new literary journals keep springing to life and refusing to wither away.

We regret that this issue is several months behind schedule. Most of our funding comes from the College of Arts and Sciences and due to the precarious state of funding for education our budget has been drastically reduced, and may be further curtailed in the coming fiscal year. While we're attempting to amend this situation with grant money and other outside funding, we can't guarantee that our publication schedule will be as consistent as it has been in the past . . . We appreciate your patience and continued support, and trust that the wait will be worth it.

Those words are taken from an all-too-familiar notice addressed to "Our Subscribers" slipped into the pages of one of the literary journals I read in 1991. Little magazines are famous for their grit and for proving again and again the romantic notion that hunger stirs creative determination. Now that recession has bitten deeply into state and national treasuries, everybody's determination will have to intensify. Some of the shakier publications won't manage to hang in. The magazine whose apology is quoted above has not, to date, sent a subsequent issue.

Yet I'm betting the next number will arrive before another year is out. Someone on the staff (probably unpaid) will find funding, will reassemble the volunteer readers, will unlock the one-room office in the basement of the English building, blow the dust off the heaps of unopened manila submission envelopes, roll up her sleeves, and begin again to read, sift, select, reject (kindly), edit, and copy-edit. She will set the next issue into type on a borrowed Mac, will proofread, will badger a graphics designer acquaintance into creating a cover, will haggle with a printer, will run labels off on her own PC, will address the envelopes, stuff and seal them, haul them to the post office in the trunk of her car, count out the postage, and feel a surge of pride that, once again, the magazine goes out to the faithful.

That surge of pride is well deserved. And though the subscribers are few, their gratitude is great because, for the most part, the faithful few are the contributors themselves, the writers whose work appears on those hard-won pages. Included among them, I am also willing to bet, are the seventeen writers represented in this edition of *New Stories from the South*. From all of us, then, a heartfelt thanks to the magazines listed in the back of this book— with their addresses and subscription rates. Join the faithful!

Shannon Ravenel
Chapel Hill, North Carolina
1992

PUBLISHER'S NOTE

The stories reprinted in *New Stories from the South, The Year's Best, 1992* were selected from American short stories published in magazines issued between January and December 1991. Shannon Ravenel annually consults a list of 85 nationally distributed American periodicals and makes her choices for this anthology based on criteria that include original publication first-serially in magazine form and publication as short stories. Direct submissions are not considered.

NEW STORIES
FROM THE SOUTH
The Year's Best, 1992

Lee Smith

THE BUBBA STORIES

(from *The Southern Review*)

Even now when I think of my brother Bubba, he appears instantly just as he was then, rising up before me in the very flesh, grinning that one-sided grin, pushing his cowlick back out of his tawny eyes, thumbs hooked in the loops of his wheat jeans, Bass Weejuns held together with electrical tape, leaning against his little green MGB. John Leland Christian III—Bubba—in the days of his glory, Dartmouth College, c. 1965. Brilliant, Phi Beta Kappa his junior year. The essence of cool. The essence not only of cool but of *bad,* for Bubba was a legendary wild man in those days; and while certain facts in his legend varied, this constant remained: Bubba would do anything. *Anything.*

I was a little bit in love with him myself.

I made Bubba up in the spring of 1963 in order to increase my popularity with my girlfriends at a small women's college in Virginia. I was a little bit in love with them, too. But at first I was ill at ease among them: a thistle in the rose garden, a mule at the racetrack, Cinderella at the fancy dress ball. Take your pick—I was into images then. More than anything else in the world, I wanted to be a writer. I didn't want to *learn to write,* of course. I just wanted to *be a writer,* and I often pictured myself poised at the foggy edge of a cliff someplace in the south of France, wearing a cape, drawing furiously on a long cigarette, hollow-cheeked and haunted, trying to make up my mind between two men. Both of them wanted me desperately.

But in fact I was Charlene Christian, a chunky size twelve, plucked up from a peanut farm near South Hill, Virginia, and set down in those exquisite halls through the intervention of my senior English teacher, Mrs. Bella Hood, the judge's wife, who had graduated from the school herself. I had a full scholarship. I would be the first person in my whole family ever to graduate from college unless you counted my Aunt Dee, who got her certificate from the beauty college in Richmond. I was not going to count Aunt Dee. I was not even going to *mention* her in later years, or anybody else in my family. I intended to grow beyond them. I intended to become a famous hollow-cheeked author, with mysterious origins.

But this is the truth. I grew up in McKenney, Virginia, which consisted of nothing more than a crossroads with my father's store in the middle of it. I used to climb up on the tin roof of our house and turn slowly all around, scanning the horizon, looking for . . . what? I found nothing of any interest, just flat brown peanut fields that stretched out in every direction as far as I could see, with a farmhouse here and there. I knew who lived in every house. I knew everything about them and about their families, what kind of car they drove and where they went to church, and they knew everything about us.

Not that there was much to know. My father, Hassell Christian, would give you the shirt off his back, and everybody knew it. At the store, he'd extend credit indefinitely to people down on their luck, and he let some families live in his tenant houses for free. Our own house adjoined the store.

My mother's younger brother Sam, who lived with us, was what they then called a Mongoloid. Some of the kids at school referred to him as a "Mongolian idiot." Now the preferred term is Down syndrome. My Uncle Sam was sweet, small, and no trouble at all. I played cards with him endlessly, all the summers of my childhood—Go Fish, rummy, Old Maid, Hearts, blackjack. Sam loved cards and sunshine and his cat, Blackie. He liked to sit on a quilt in the sun, playing cards with me. He liked to sit on the front porch with Blackie and watch the cars go by. He loved it when I told him stories.

My mother, who was high-strung, was always fussing around after Sam, making him pick up paper napkins and turn off the TV and put his shoes in a line. My mother had three separate nervous breakdowns before I went away to college. My father always said we had to "treat her with kid gloves." In fact, when I think about it now, I am surprised that my mother was ever able to hold herself together long enough to conceive a child at all, or come to term. After me, there were two miscarriages, and then, I was told, they "quit trying." I was never sure what this meant, exactly. But certainly I could never imagine my parents having a sexual relationship in the first place—he was too fat and gruff, she was too fluttery and crazy. The whole idea was gross.

Whenever my mother had a nervous breakdown, my grand-mother, Memaw, would come over from next door to stay with Sam full time, and I would be sent to South Hill to stay with my Aunt Dee and my little cousins. I loved my Aunt Dee, as different from Mama as day from night. Aunt Dee wore her yellow hair in a beehive and smoked Pall Mall cigarettes. After work she'd come in the door, kick off her shoes, put a record on the record player, and dance all over the living room to "Ooh-Poo-Pa-Doo." She said it "got the kinks out." She taught us all to do the shag, even little Tammy.

I was always sorry when my dad appeared in his truck, ready to take me back home.

When I think of home now, the image that comes most clearly to mind is my whole family lined up in the flickering darkness of our living room, watching TV. We never missed "The Ed Sullivan Show," "Bonanza," "The Andy Griffith Show," or "Candid Cam-era"—Sam's favorite. Sam used to laugh and laugh when they'd say, "Smile! You're on Candid Camera!'" It was the only time my family ever did anything together. I can just see us now in the light from that black-and-white Zenith TV, lined up on the couch (me, Sam, Memaw), with Daddy and Mama in the recliner and the antique wing chair, respectively, facing the television. We always turned off all the lights in order to watch TV, and sat quietly, and didn't eat anything.

No wonder I got a boyfriend with a car as soon as possible, to get out of there. Don Fetterman had a soft brown crew cut and wide brown eyes and reminded me, in the nicest possible way, of the cows that he and his family raised. Don was president of the 4-H Club and the Tri-Hi-Y Club. I was vice president of the Tri-Hi-Y Club (how we met) and president of the Glee Club. We were both picked as "Most Likely to Succeed."

We rubbed our bodies together at innumerable dances in the high school gym while they played "our" song—"The Twelfth of Never"—but we never, never went all the way. Don wouldn't. He believed we should save ourselves for marriage. I, on the other hand, having read by this time a great many novels, was just dying to lose my virginity so that I would mysteriously begin to "live," so that my life would finally *start*. I knew for sure that I would never become a great writer until I could rid myself of this awful burden. But Don Fetterman stuck to his guns, refusing to cooperate. Instead, for graduation, he gave me a pearl "preengagement" ring, which I knew for a fact had cost $139 at Snows Jewelers in South Hill, where I worked after school and on weekends. This was a lot of money for Don Fetterman to spend.

Although I didn't love him, by then he thought I did; and after I got the ring, I didn't have the nerve to tell him the truth. So I kept it, and kissed Don good-bye for hours and hours the night before he went off to join the marines. My tears were real at this point, but after he left I relegated him firmly to the past. Ditto my whole family. Once I got to college, I was determined to become a new person.

Luckily my freshman roommate turned out to be a kind of prototype, the very epitome of a popular girl. The surprise was that she was *nice,* too. Dixie Claiborne came from Memphis, where she was to make her debut that Christmas at the Swan Ball. She had long, perfect blond hair, innumerable cashmere sweater sets, and real pearls. She had lots of friends already, other girls who had gone to St. Cecilia's with her (at first it seemed to me a good two-thirds of all the girls at school had gone to St. Something-or-other). They had a happy ease in the world and a strangely uniform appearance that I immediately began to copy—spending my whole semester's money, saved up from my job at the jeweler's, on several A-line skirts, McMullen blouses, and a pair of red Pappagallo shoes. Dixie had about a thousand cable-knit sweaters, which she was happy to lend me. In addition to all the right clothes, Dixie came equipped with the right boyfriend, already a sophomore at Washington and Lee University, the boys' school just over the mountain. His name was Trey (William Hill Dunn III). Trey would be just so glad, Dixie said, smiling, to get us all dates for the Phi Gam mixer. "All of us" included our whole suite—Dixie and me in the front room overlooking the old quadrangle with its massive willow oaks, Melissa and Donnie across the hall, and Lily in the single just beyond our little study room.

Trey fixed us up with several Phi Gams apiece, but nothing really clicked; and in November, Melissa, Donnie, Lily, and I signed up to go to a freshman mixer at UVA. As our bus approached the university's famous serpentine wall, we went into a flurry of teasing our hair and checking our makeup. Looking into my compact, I pursed my lips in a way I'd been practicing. Unfortunately I had a pimple near my nose, but I'd turned it into a beauty spot by covering it up with eyebrow pencil. I hoped to look like Sandra Dee.

Freshman year, everybody went to mixers, where freshman boys, generally as ill at ease as we were, stood nervously about in the social rooms of their fraternity houses, wearing navy blue blazers, ties, and chinos. Nobody really knew how to date in this rigid system so unlike high school—and certainly so unlike prep school, where many of these boys had been locked away for the past four years. If they could have gotten their own dates, they would have. But they couldn't. They didn't know anybody either. They pulled at their ties and looked at the floor. They seemed to me generally gorgeous, entirely unlike Don Fetterman with his feathery crew cut and his 4-H jacket, now at Camp Lejeune. But I still wrote to Don, informative, stilted little notes about my classes and the weather. His letters in return were lively and real, full of military life ("the food sucks") and vague sweet plans for our future—a future that did not exist, as far as I was concerned, and yet these letters gave me a secret thrill. My role as Don Fetterman's girl was the most exciting role I'd had yet; and I couldn't quite bring myself to give it up, even as I attempted to transform myself into another person altogether.

"Okay," the upperclassman in charge announced casually, and the St. Anthony's Hall pledges wandered over in our direction.

"Hey," the cutest one said to a girl.

"Hey," she said back.

The routine never varied. In a matter of minutes the four most aggressive guys would walk off with the four prettiest girls, and the rest of us would panic. On this particular occasion the social room at St. Anthony's Hall was cleared in a matter of minutes, leaving me with a tall, gangly, bucktoothed boy whose face was as pocked as the moon. Still, he had a kind of shabby elegance I already recognized. He was from Mississippi.

"What do you want to do?" he asked me.

I had not expected to be consulted. I glanced around the social room, which looked like a war zone. I didn't know where my friends were.

"What do *you* want to do?" I asked.

His name (his *first* name) was Rutherford. He grinned at me. "Let's get drunk," he said, and my heart leaped up as I realized that my burden might be lifted in this way. We walked across the beautiful old campus to an open court where three or four fraternities had a combo started up already, wild-eyed electrified

Negroes going through all kinds of gyrations on the bandstand. It was Doug Clark and the Hot Nuts. The music was so loud, the beat so strong, that you couldn't listen to it and stand still. The Hot Nuts were singing an interminable song; everybody seemed to know the chorus, which went "Nuts, hot nuts, get 'em from the peanut man. Nuts, hot nuts, get 'em any way you can." We started dancing. I always worried about this—all I'd ever done before college, in the way of dancing, was the shag with my Aunt Dee and a long, formless *clutch* with Don Fetterman, but Rutherford was so wild it didn't matter.

People made a circle around us and started clapping. Nobody looked at me. All eyes were on Rutherford, whose dancing reminded me of the way chickens back home flopped around after Daddy cut their heads off. At first I was embarrassed. But then I caught on—Rutherford was a real *character*. I kept up with him as best I could, and then I got tickled and started laughing so hard I could barely dance. *This is fun,* I realized suddenly. This is what I'm *supposed* to be doing. This is college.

About an hour later we heard the news, which was delivered to us by a tweed-jacketed professor who walked up onstage, bringing the music to a ragged, grinding halt. He grabbed the microphone. "Ladies and gentlemen," he said thickly—and I remember thinking how odd this form of address seemed—"Ladies and gentlemen, the president has been shot."

The whole scene started to churn, as if we were in a kaleidoscope—the blue day, the green grass, the stately columned buildings. People were running and sobbing. Rutherford's hand under my elbow steered me back to his fraternity house, where everyone was clustered around several TVs, talking too loud. All the weekend festivities had been canceled. We were to return to school immediately. Rutherford seemed relieved by this prospect, having fallen silent—perhaps because he'd quit drinking, or because conversation alone wasn't worth the effort it took if nothing else (sex) might be forthcoming. He gave me a perfunctory kiss on the cheek and turned to go.

I was about to board the bus when somebody grabbed me, hard, from behind. I whirled around. It was Lily, red-cheeked and glassy-eyed, her blond hair springing out wildly above her blue sweater. Her hot pink lipstick was smeared. Lily's pretty, pointed face looked vivid and alive. A dark-haired boy stood close behind her, his arm around her waist.

"Listen," Lily hissed at me. "Sign me in, will you?"

"What?" I had heard her, but I couldn't believe it.

"*Sign me in.*" Lily squeezed my shoulder. I could smell her perfume. Then she was gone.

I sat in a backseat by myself and cried all the way back to school.

I caught on fast that as far as college boys were concerned, girls fell into either the Whore or the Saint category. All girls knew that if they gave in and *did it,* then boys wouldn't respect them, and word would get around, and they would never get a husband. The whole point of college was to get a husband.

I had not known anything about this system before I got there. It put a serious obstacle in my path toward becoming a great writer.

Lily, who had clearly given up her burden long since, fell into the Whore category. But the odd thing about it was that she didn't seem to mind, and she swore she didn't want a husband anyway. "Honey, a husband is the *last* thing on my list!" Lily'd say, giggling. Lily was the smartest one of us all, even though she went to great lengths to hide this fact. Later, in 1966, Lily and the head of the philosophy department, Dr. Wiener, would stage the only demonstration ever held on our campus; they walked slowly around the blooming quadrangle carrying signs that read GET OUT OF VIETNAM while the rest of us, well oiled and sunning on the rooftops, clutched our bikini tops and peered down curiously at the two of them.

If Lily was the smartest, Melissa was clearly the dumbest, the nicest, and the least interested in school. Melissa came from

Charleston, South Carolina, and spoke so slowly that I was always tempted to leap in and finish her sentences for her. All she wanted to do was marry her boyfriend, now at the University of South Carolina, and have babies. Donnie, Melissa's roommate, was a big, freckled, friendly girl from Texas. We didn't have any idea how rich she was until her mother flew up and bought a cabin at nearby Goshen Lake so Donnie and her friends would have a place to "relax."

By spring, Dixie was the only one of us who was actually pinned. It seemed to me that she was not only pinned but almost married, in a funny way, with tons and tons of children—Trey, her boyfriend; and me; and all the other girls in our suite; and all the other Phi Gams, Trey's fraternity brothers at Washington and Lee. Dixie had a little book in which she made a list of things to do each day, and throughout the day she checked them off one by one. She always got all of them done. At the end of first semester she had a 4.0 average; Trey had a 0.4. Dixie just smiled. Totally, inexplicably, she loved him.

By then most of the freshman girls who weren't going with somebody had several horror stories to tell about blind dates at UVA or W&L fraternities—boys who "dropped trou," or threw up in their dates' purses. I had only one horror story, but I never told it, since the most horrible element in it was me.

This is what happened. It was Spring Fling at the Phi Gam house, and Trey had gotten me a date with a redheaded boy named Eddy Turner. By then I was getting desperate. I'd made a C in my first semester of creative writing, while Lily had made an A. Plus, I'd gained eight pounds. Both love and literature seemed to be slipping out of my sights. And I was drinking too much—we'd been drinking Yucca Flats, a horrible green punch made in a washtub with grain alcohol, all afternoon on the night I ended up in bed with Eddy Turner.

The bed was his, on the second floor of the Phi Gam house— not the most private setting for romance. I could scarcely see

Eddy by the street light coming in through the single high window. Faintly, below, I could hear music, and the whole house shook slightly with the dancing. I thought of Hemingway's famous description of sex from *For Whom the Bell Tolls*, which I'd typed out neatly on an index card: "The earth moved under the sleeping bag." The whole Phi Gam house was moving under me. After wrestling with my panty girdle for what seemed like hours, Eddy finally tossed it in the corner and got on top of me immediately. Drunk as I was, I wanted him to. I wanted him to *do it*. But I didn't think it would hurt so much, and suddenly I wished he would kiss me or say something. He didn't. He was done and lying on his back beside me when suddenly the door to the room burst open and the lights came on. I sat up, grasping for the sheet that I couldn't find. My breasts are large, and they had always embarrassed me. Until that night, Don Fetterman was the only boy who had ever seen them. It was a whole group of Phi Gams, roaming from room to room. Luckily I was blinded by the lights, so I couldn't tell exactly who they were.

"Smile!" they yelled. "You're on 'Candid Camera!'" Then they laughed hysterically, slammed the door, and were gone, leaving us in darkness once again. But I was sobbing into Eddy's pillow because what they said reminded me of Sam, whose face would not leave my mind then for hours while I cried and cried and cried and sobered up. I didn't tell Eddy what I was crying about, nor did he ask. He sat in a chair and smoked cigarettes while he waited for me to stop crying. Finally I did. Eddy and I didn't date after that, but we were buddies in the way I was buddies with the whole Phi Gam house due to my particular status as Dixie's roommate. I was like a sister, giving advice to the lovelorn, administering Cokes and aspirins on Sunday mornings, typing papers.

It was not the role I'd had in mind, but it was better than nothing, affording me at least a certain status among the girls at school; and the Phi Gams always saw to it that I attended all the big parties, usually with somebody whose girlfriend couldn't make it. Often, when the weekend was winding down, I could be found down in the Phi Gam basement alone, playing "Tragedy," my favorite song, over and over on the jukebox.

> Blown by the wind
> Kissed by the snow
> All that's left
> Is the dark below.
> Gone from me,
> Oh, oh.
> Trag-e-dy.

It always brought me right to the edge of tears, because I hadn't ever known any tragedy myself, or love, or drama. *Wouldn't anything ever happen to me?*

Meanwhile, my friends' lives were like soap opera—Lily's period was two weeks late, which scared us all, and then Dixie went on the pill. Melissa and her boyfriend split up (she lost seven pounds, he slammed his hand into a wall) and then made up again.

Melissa was telling us about it, in her maddening slow way, one day in May when we were all out at Donnie's lake cabin, sunning. "It's not the same, though," Melissa said. "He just gets *too mad*. I don't know what it is; he scares me."

"Dump him," Lily said, applying baby oil with iodine in it, our suntan lotion of choice.

"But I *love* him," Melissa wailed, and Lily snorted.

"Well," Dixie began diplomatically, but suddenly I sat up.

"Maybe he's just got a wild streak," I said. "Maybe he just can't control himself. That's always been Bubba's problem." Suddenly the little lake before us took on a deeper, more intense hue. I noticed the rotting pier, the old fisherman up at the point, Lily's painted toenails. I noticed *everything*.

"Who's Bubba?" Donnie asked me.

Dixie eyed me expectantly, thinking I meant one of the Phi Gams, since several of them had that nickname.

"My brother," I said. I took a deep breath.

"*What*? You never said you had a *brother*!" Dixie's pretty face looked really puzzled now.

Everybody sat up and looked at me.

"Well, I do," I said. "He's two years older than me, and he stayed with my father when my parents split up. So I've never lived with him. In fact I don't know him real well at all. This is very painful for me to talk about. We were inseparable when we were little," I added, hearing my song in the back of my mind. "*Oh, oh . . . Trag-e-dy!*"

"Oh, Charlene, I'm so sorry! I had no idea!" Dixie was hugging me, slick hot skin and all.

I started crying. "He was a real problem child," I said, "and now he's just so wild. I don't know what's going to become of him."

"How long has it been since you've seen him?" Melissa asked.

"About two years," I said. "Our parents won't have anything at all to do with each other. They *hate* each other, and especially since Mama got remarried. They won't let us get together, not even for a day; it's just awful."

"So how did you get to see him two years ago?" Lily asked. They had all drawn closer, clustering around me.

"He ran away from school," I said, "and came to my high school, and got me right out of class. I remember it was biology lab," I said. "I was dissecting a frog."

"Then what?"

"We spent the day together," I said. "We got some food and went out to this quarry and ate, and just drove around. We talked and talked," I said. "And you know what? I felt just as close to him then as I did when we were babies. Just like all those years had never passed at all. It was great," I said.

"Then he went back to school—or what?"

"No." I choked back a sob. "It was almost dark, and he was

taking me back to my house, and then he was planning to head on down to Florida, he said, when all of a sudden these blue lights came up behind us, and it was the police."

"The *police*?" Dixie looked really alarmed then. She was such a good girl.

"Well, it was a stolen car, of course," I explained. "They nailed him. If he hadn't stopped in to see me, he might have gotten away with it," I said, "if he'd just headed straight to Florida. But he came to see me. Mama and Daddy wouldn't even bail him out. They let him go straight to prison."

"Oh, Charlene, *no wonder* you never talk about your family!" Dixie was in tears now.

"But he was a model prisoner," I went on. I felt exhilarated. "In fact they gave all the prisoners this test, and he scored the highest that anybody in the whole history of the prison had *ever* scored, so they let him take these special classes, and he did so well that he got out a whole year early, and now he's in college."

"Where?"

I thought fast. "Dartmouth," I said wildly. I knew it had to be a northern school, since Dixie and Melissa seemed to know everybody in the South. But neither of them, as far as I could recall, had ever mentioned Dartmouth.

"He's got a full scholarship," I added. "But he's so wild, I don't know if he'll be able to keep it or not." Donnie got up and went in and came back with cold Cokes for us all, and we stayed out at Goshen Lake until the sun set, and I told them all about Bubba.

He was a KA, the wildest KA of them all. Last winter, I said, he got drunk and passed out in the snow on the way back to his fraternity house; by the time a janitor found him the following morning, his cheek was frozen solid to the road. It took two guys from maintenance, with electrical torches, to melt the snow around Bubba's face and get him loose. And now the whole fraternity was on probation because of this really gross thing he'd made the pledges do. "What really gross thing?" they asked. "Oh, you don't want to know," I said. "You really don't."

"I *really do*," Lily insisted, pushing her sunburnt face into mine. "Come on. After Trey, nothing could be that bad." Even Dixie grinned.

"Okay," I said, launching into a hazing episode that required the KA pledges to run up three flights of stairs, holding alum in their mouths. On each landing they had to dodge past these two big football players. If they swallowed the alum during the struggle, well, alum makes you vomit immediately, so you can imagine . . . they could imagine. But the worst part was that when one pledge wouldn't go past the second landing, the football players threw him down the stairs, and he broke his back.

"That's just *disgusting*," Donnie drawled. "Nobody would ever do that in Texas."

But on the other hand, I said quickly, Bubba was the most talented poet in the whole school, having won the Iris Nutley Leach Award for Poetry two years in a row. I pulled the name "Iris Nutley Leach" right out of the darkening air. I astonished myself. And girls were just crazy about Bubba, I added. In fact this girl from Washington tried to kill herself after they broke up, and then she had to be institutionalized for a year, at Shepherd-Pratt in Baltimore. I knew all about Shepherd-Pratt because my mother had gone there.

"But he doesn't have a girlfriend right now," I said. Everyone sighed, and a warm breeze came up over the pines and ruffled our little lake. By then Bubba was as real to me as the Peanuts towel I sat on, as the warm, gritty dirt between my toes.

During the next year or so, Bubba would knock up a girl and then nobly help her get an abortion (Donnie offered to contribute); he would make Phi Beta Kappa; he would be arrested for assault; he would wreck his MGB; he would start writing folk songs. My creativity knew no bounds when it came to Bubba, but I was a dismal failure in my first writing class, where my teacher, Mr. Lefcowicz, kept giving me B's and C's and telling me, "Write what you know."

I didn't want to write what I knew, of course. I had no intention of writing a word about my own family or those peanut fields. Who would want to read about *that*? I had wanted to write in order to *get away* from my own life. I couldn't give up that tormented woman on the cliff in the south of France. I intended to write about glamorous heroines with exciting lives; one of my first—and worst—stories involved a stewardess in Hawaii. I had never been to Hawaii, of course. At that time, I had never even been on a plane. The plot, which was very complicated, had something to do with international espionage. I remember how kindly my young teacher smiled at me when he handed my story back. He asked me to stay for a minute after class. "Charlene," he said, "I want you to write something true next time."

Instead, I decided to give up on plot and concentrate on theme, intending to pull some heartstrings. It was nearly Christmas, and this time we had to read our stories aloud to the whole group. But right before that class, Mr. Lefcowicz, who had already read them, pulled me aside and told me that I didn't have to read my story out loud if I didn't want to.

"Of course I want to," I said.

We took our seats.

My story took place in a large unnamed city on Christmas Eve. In this story, a whole happy family was trimming their Christmas tree, singing carols, and drinking hot chocolate while it snowed outside. I think I had "softly falling flakes." Each person in the family got to open one present—selected from the huge pile of gifts beneath the glittering tree—before bed. Then they all went to sleep, and a "pregnant silence" descended. At three o'clock a fire broke out, and the whole house burned to the ground, and they all burned up, dying horrible deaths, which I described individually—conscious, as I read aloud, of some movement and sound among my listeners. But I didn't dare look up as I approached the story's ironic end: "When the fire trucks arrived, the only sign of life to be found was a blackened music box in the smoking ashes, softly playing 'Silent Night.'" By the end of my story, one girl had put her head down on her desk; another was having a coughing fit. Mr. Lefcowicz was staring intently out the window at the wintry day, his back to us. Then he made a sudden show of looking at his watch. "Whoops! Class dismissed!" he cried, grabbing up his book bag. He rushed from the room like the White Rabbit, already late.

But I was not that stupid.

As I walked across the cold, wet quadrangle toward our dormitory, I understood perfectly well that my story was terrible, laughable. I wanted to die. The gray sky, the dripping, leafless trees, fit my mood perfectly, and I suddenly remembered Mr. Lefcowicz saying, in an earlier class, that we must never manipulate nature to express our characters' emotions. "Ha," I muttered scornfully to the heavy sky.

The very next day I joined the staff of our campus newspaper. I became its editor in the middle of my sophomore year—a job nobody else wanted, a job I really enjoyed. I had found a niche, a role, and although it was not what I had envisioned for myself, it was okay. Thus I became the following things: editor of the newspaper; member of Athena, the secret honor society; roommate of Dixie, the May queen; friend of Phi Gams; and—especially—sister of Bubba, whose legend loomed ever larger. But I avoided both dates and creative writing classes for the next two years, finding Mr. Lefcowicz's stale advice, "Write what you know," more impossible with each visit home.

The summer between my sophomore and junior years was the hardest. The first night I was home, I realized that something was wrong with Mama when I woke up to hear water splashing in the downstairs bathroom. I got up and went to investigate. There she was, wearing a lacy pink peignoir and her old gardening shoes, scrubbing the green tile tub.

"Oh, hi, Charlene!" she said brightly, and went on scrubbing, humming tunelessly to herself. A mop and bucket stood in the corner. I said good night and went back to my bedroom, where I looked at the clock: it was 3:30 A.M.

The next day Mama burst into tears when Sam spilled a glass of iced tea, and the day after that Daddy took her over to Petersburg and put her in the hospital. Memaw came in to stay with Sam during the day while I worked in the jeweler's at South Hill, my old job.

I'd come home at suppertime each afternoon to find Sam in his chair on the front porch, holding Blackie, waiting for me. He seemed to have gotten smaller somehow—and for the first time, I realized that Sam, so much a part of my childhood, was not growing up along with me. In fact he would *never* grow up, and I thought about that a lot on those summer evenings as I swung gently in the porch swing, back and forth through the sultry air, suspended.

In August I went to Memphis for a week to visit Dixie, whose house turned out to be like Tara in *Gone With the Wind*, only bigger, and whose mother turned out to drink sherry all day long. I came back to find Mama out of the hospital already, much improved by shock treatments, and another surprise—a baby blue Chevrolet convertible, used but great looking, in the driveway. My father handed me the keys.

"Here, honey," he said, and then he hugged me tight, smelling of sweat and tobacco. "We're so proud of you," he said. He had traded a man a combine or something for the car.

So I drove back to school in style, and my junior year went smoothly until Donnie announced that her sister Susannah, now at Pine Mountain Junior College, was going up to Dartmouth for Winter Carnival, to visit a boy she'd met that summer. Susannah just *couldn't wait* to look up Bubba.

Unfortunately, this was not possible, as I got a phone call that very night saying that Bubba had been kicked out of school for leading a demonstration against the war. Lily, who had become much more political herself by that time, jumped up from her desk and grabbed my hand.

"Oh, no!" she shrieked. "He'll be drafted!" and the sudden alarm that filled our study room was palpable—as real as the mounting body count each night on TV—as we stared, Lily and Dixie and Donnie and I, white-faced at one another.

"Whatever will he do now?" Donnie was wringing her hands.

"I don't know," I said desperately. "I just don't know." I went to my room—a single, this term—and thought about it. It was clear that he would have to do something, something to take him far, far away.

But Bubba's problem was soon to be superseded by Melissa's. She was pregnant, really pregnant, and in spite of all the arguments we could come up with, she wanted to get married and have the baby. She wanted to have *lots* of babies, and one day live in the big house on the Battery that her boyfriend would inherit, and this is exactly what she's done. Her life has been predictable and productive. So violent in his college days, Melissa's husband turned out to be a model of stability in later life. And their first child, Anna, kept him out of the draft.

As she got in her mother's car to leave, Melissa squeezed my hand and said, "Keep me posted about Bubba, and don't worry so much. I'm sure everything will work out all right."

It didn't.

Bubba burned his draft card not a month later and headed for Canada, where he lived in a commune. I didn't hear from him for a long time after that, all tangled up as I was by then in my affair with Dr. Pierce.

Dr. Pierce was a fierce, bleak, melancholy man who looked like a bird of prey. Not surprisingly, he was a Beckett scholar. He taught the seminar in contemporary literature that I took in the spring of my junior year. We read Joseph Heller, Kurt Vonnegut, Flannery O'Connor, John Barth, and Thomas Pynchon, among others. Flannery O'Connor would become my favorite, and I would do my senior thesis on her work, feeling a secret and strong kinship, by then, with her dire view. But this was later, after my affair with Dr. Pierce was over.

At first, I didn't know what to make of him. I hated his

northern accent, his lugubrious, glistening dark eyes, his all-encompassing pessimism. He told us that contemporary literature was absurd because the world was absurd. He told us that the language in these books was weird and fractured because true communication is impossible in the world today. Dr. Pierce told us all this in a sad, cynical tone full of infinite world-weariness, which I found both repellent and attractive.

Finally I decided to go in and talk to him. I am still not sure why I did this—I was making good grades in his course, I understood everything. But one blustery, unsettling March afternoon I found myself sitting outside his office. He was a popular teacher, rumored to be always ready to listen to his students' problems. I don't know what I meant to talk to him about. The hour grew late. Shadows lengthened in the hall. I smoked four or five cigarettes while other students, ahead of me, went in and came out. Then Dr. Pierce came and stood in the door. He took off his glasses and rubbed his eyes. He looked tired, but not nearly as old as he looked in class, where he always wore a tie. Now he wore jeans and an old blue work shirt, and I could see the dark hair at his neck.

"Ah," he said in that way of his that rendered all his remarks oddly significant, although I could never figure out why. "Ah! Miss Christian, is it not?"

He knew it was. I felt uncomfortable, like he was mocking me. He made a gesture; I preceded him into his office and sat down.

"Now," he said, staring at me. I looked away, out the window at the skittish, blowing day, at the girls who passed by on the walkway, giggling and trying to hold their skirts down. "*Miss Christian,*" Dr. Pierce said. Maybe he'd said it before. Finally I looked at him.

"I presume you had some reason for this visit," he said sardonically.

To my horror, I started crying. Not little ladylike sniffles, either, but huge groaning sobs. Dr. Pierce thrust a box of Kleenex in my direction, then sat drumming his fingers on his desk.

I kept on crying. Finally I realized what he was drumming: the *William Tell* overture. I got tickled. Soon I was crying and laughing at the same time. I was still astonished at myself.

"Blow your nose," Dr. Pierce said.

I did.

"That's better," he said. It was. He got up and closed his office door although there was really no need to do so, since the hall outside was empty now. Dr. Pierce sat back down and leaned across his desk toward me. "What is it?" he asked intently.

But I still didn't know what it was. I said so, and apologized. "One thing though," I said. "I'd like to complain about the choice of books on our reading list."

"Aha!" Dr. Pierce said. He leaned back in his chair and made his fingers into a kind of tent. "You liked Eudora Welty," he said. This was true; I nodded. "You liked *Lie Down in Darkness*," he said. I nodded again.

"But I just *hate* this other stuff!" I burst out. "I just hated *The End of the Road*, I hated it! It's so depressing."

He nodded rapidly. "You think literature should make you feel good?" he asked.

"It used to," I said. Then I was crying again. I stood up. "I'm so sorry," I said.

Dr. Pierce stood up too and walked around his desk and came to stand close to me. The light in his office was soft, gray, furry. Dr. Pierce took both my hands in his. "Oh, Miss Christian," he said. "My very dear, very young Miss Christian, I know what you mean." And I could tell, by the pain and weariness in his voice, that this was true. I could see Dr. Pierce suddenly as a much younger man, as a boy, with a light in his eyes and a different feeling about the world. I reached up and put my hands in his curly hair and pulled his face down to mine and kissed him fiercely, a way I had never kissed anybody. I couldn't even imagine myself doing this, yet I did it naturally. Dr. Pierce kissed me back. We kissed for a long time while it grew finally dark outside, and then

he locked the door and turned back to me. He sighed deeply—
almost a groan—a sound, I felt, of regret, then unbuttoned my
shirt. We made love on the rug on his office floor. Immediately we
were caught up in a kind of fever that lasted for several months—
times like these in his office after hours, or in the backseat of my
car parked by the lake, or in cheap motels when I'd signed out to
go home.

Nobody suspected a thing. I was as good at keeping secrets as I
was at making up lies. Plus, I was a campus leader, and Dr. Pierce
was a married man.

He tried to end it that June. I was headed home, and he was
headed up to New York where he had some kind of fellowship to
do research at the Morgan Library.

"Charlene—," Dr. Pierce said. We were in public, out on the
quadrangle right after graduation. His wife walked down the hill
at some distance behind us, with other faculty wives. Dr. Pierce's
voice was hoarse, the way it got when he was in torment (which
he so often was, which was one of the most attractive things
about him. Years later, I'd realize this). "Let us make a clean
break," he sort of mumbled. "Right now. It cannot go on, and
we both know it."

We had reached the parking lot in front of the chapel by then;
the sunlight reflected off all the cars was dazzling.

Dr. Pierce stuck out his hand in an oddly formal gesture. "Have
a good summer, Charlene," he said, "and good-bye."

Dr. Pierce had chosen his moment well. He knew I wouldn't
make a scene in front of all these people. But I refused to take
his hand, rushing off madly through the parked cars to my own,
gunning it out of there and out to the lake where I parked on the
bluff above Donnie's cabin, in the exact spot where he and I had
been together so many times. I sat at the wheel and looked out
at the lake, now full of children on some kind of school outing.
Their shrill screams and laughter drifted up to me thinly, like the
sounds of birds in the trees around my car. I remember I leaned

back on the seat and stared straight up at the sun through the trees—just at the top of the tent of green, where light filtered in bursts like stars.

But I couldn't give him up, not yet, not ever.

I resolved to surprise Dr. Pierce in New York, and that's exactly what I did, telling my parents I'd gone on a trip to Virginia Beach with friends. I got his summer address from the registrar's office. I drove up through Richmond and Washington, a seven-hour drive. It was a crazy and even a dangerous thing to do, since I had never been to New York. But finally I ended up in front of the brownstone in the Village where Dr. Pierce and his wife were subletting an apartment. It was midafternoon and hot; I had not imagined New York to be so hot, hotter even than McKenney, Virginia. I was still in a fever, I think. I knocked on the door, without even thinking what I would do if his wife answered. But nobody answered. Nobody was home. Somehow this possibility had not occurred to me. I felt suddenly, totally exhausted. I leaned against the wall, and then slid down it, until I was actually sitting on the floor in the hall. I pulled off my pantyhose and stuffed them into my purse. They were too hot. I was too hot. I wore a kelly green linen dress; somehow I'd thought I needed to be all dressed up to go to New York. I don't even remember falling asleep, but I was awakened by Dr. Pierce shaking my shoulder and saying my name.

Whatever can be said of Dr. Pierce, he was not a jerk. He told me firmly that our relationship was over, and just as firmly that I should not be driving around New York City at night by myself, not in the shape I was in.

By the time his wife came home with groceries, I was lying on the studio bed, feeling a little better. He told her I was having a breakdown, which seemed suddenly true. Dr. Pierce and I looked at the news on TV while she made spaghetti. After dinner she lit a joint and handed it to me. It was the first time anybody had ever offered me marijuana. I shook my head. I thought I was crazy enough already. Dr. Pierce's wife was nice, though. She was pale with long, long blond hair, which she had worn in a braid at school, or up on top of her head. Now it fell over her shoulders like water. I realized that she was not much—certainly not ten years—older than I was, and I wondered if she, too, had been his student. But I was exhausted. I fell asleep on the studio couch in front of a fan, which drowned out the sound of their voices as they cleaned up from dinner.

I woke up very early the next morning. I wrote the Pierces a thank-you note on an index card that I found in Dr. Pierce's briefcase and left it propped conspicuously against the toaster. The door to their bedroom stood open, but I did not look in.

Out on the street I was horrified to find that I had gotten a parking ticket and that my convertible top had been slashed—gratuitously, too, since there was nothing in the car to steal. Somehow this upset me more than anything else about my trip to New York, more than Dr. Pierce's rejection—or his renunciation, as I preferred to consider it—which is how I did consider it, often, during that summer at home while I had the rest of my nervous breakdown.

My parents were very kind. They thought it all had to do with Don Fetterman, who was missing in action in Vietnam, and maybe it did, sort of. I was "nervous" and cried a lot. Finally my Aunt Dee got tired of me mooning around, as she called it. She frosted my hair and took me to Myrtle Beach, where it proved impossible to continue the nervous breakdown. The last night of this trip Aunt Dee and I double-dated with some Realtors she'd met by the pool.

Aunt Dee and I got back to McKenney just in time for me to pack and drive to school, where I was one of the seniors in charge of freshman orientation. Daddy had gotten the top fixed on my car; I was a blonde; and I'd lost twenty-five pounds.

The campus seemed somehow smaller to me as I drove through the imposing gates. My footsteps echoed as I carried my bags up to the third floor of Old North, where Dixie and I would have the coveted "turret room." I was the first one back in the whole dorm, but as I continued to haul things in from my car, other seniors began arriving. We hugged and squealed, following a script as old as the college. At least three girls stopped in midhug to push me back, scrutinize me carefully, and exclaim that they wouldn't have recognized me. I didn't know what they meant.

Sweaty and exhausted after carrying everything up to our room, I decided to shower before dinner. I was standing naked in our room, toweling my hair dry, when the dinner bell began to ring. Its somber tone sounded somehow elegiac to me in that moment. On impulse, I began rummaging around in one of my boxes, until I finally found the mirror I was looking for. I went to stand at the window while the last of the lingering chimes died on the August air.

I held the mirror out at arm's length and looked at myself. I had cheekbones. I had hipbones. I could see my ribs. My eyes were darker, larger in my face. My wild damp hair was as blond as Lily's. I looked completely different.

Clearly, *something had finally happened to me.*

That weekend Dixie, Donnie, Lily, and I went out to Donnie's cabin to drink beer and catch up on the summer. We telephoned Melissa, now eight months pregnant, who claimed to be blissfully happy and said she was making curtains.

Lily snorted. She got up and put Simon and Garfunkel on the stereo, and got us all another beer. Donnie lit candles and switched off the overhead light. Dixie waved her hand, making the big diamond sparkle in the candlelight. Trey, now in law school at Vanderbilt, had given it to her in July. Dixie was already planning her wedding. We would all be bridesmaids, of course. (That marriage, oddly, would last for only a few years, and Dixie would divorce once more before she went to law school herself.) Donnie told us all about her mother's new boyfriend. We gossiped on as the hour grew late and bugs slammed suicidally into the porch light. The moon came up big and bright. I kept playing "The Sound of Silence" over and over; it matched my mood, my new conception of myself ("In my dreams I walk alone, over streets of cobblestone . . ." I also liked "I Am a Rock; I Am an Island").

Finally Lily announced that she was in love, *really in love* this time, with a young poet she'd met that summer on Cape Cod, where she'd been waitressing. We waited while she lit a cigarette. "We lived together for two months," Lily said, "in his room at the inn, where we could look out and see the water." We all just stared at her. None of us had ever lived with anybody, or known anyone who had. Lily looked around at us. "It was wonderful," she said. "It was heaven. But it was not what you might think," she added enigmatically, "living with a man."

For some reason I started crying.

There was a long silence, and the needle on the record started scratching. Donnie got up and cut it off. They were all looking at me.

"And what about you, Charlene?" Lily said softly. "What happened to you this summer, anyway?"

It was a moment that I had rehearsed again and again in my mind. I would tell them all about my affair with Dr. Pierce, and how I had gone to New York to find him, and how he had renounced me because his wife was pregnant. I had just added this part. But I was crying too hard to speak. "It was awful," I said finally, and Dixie came over and hugged me. "What was awful?" she said, but I couldn't even speak; my mind filled suddenly, oddly, with Don Fetterman as he'd looked in high school, presiding over the Tri-Hi-Y Club. He held the gavel firmly in his hands; he could call any group to order.

"Come on," Dixie said, "tell us."

The candles were guttering; the moon made a path across the lake. I took a deep breath.

"Bubba is dead," I said.

"Oh, God! Oh no!" A kind of pandemonium ensued, which I don't remember much about, although I remember the details of my brother's death vividly. Bubba drowned in a lake in Canada, attempting to save a friend's child that had fallen overboard. The child died, too. Bubba was buried there, on the wild shore of that northern lake, and his only funeral was what his friends said as they spoke around the grave one by one. His best friend had written to me, describing the whole thing.

"Charlene, Charlene, why didn't you tell us sooner?" Donnie asked.

I just shook my head. "I couldn't," I said.

Later that fall I finally wrote a good story—about my family, back in McKenney—and then another, and then another. I won a scholarship to graduate school at Columbia University in New York, where I still live with my husband on the West Side, free-lancing for several magazines and writing fiction.

It was here, only a few weeks ago, that I last saw Lily, now a prominent feminist scholar. She was in town for the MLA convention. We went to a little bistro near my apartment for lunch, lingering over wine far into the late December afternoon while my husband baby-sat. Lily was in the middle of a divorce. "You know," she said at one point, twirling her tulip wineglass, "I have often thought that the one great tragedy of my life was never getting to meet your brother. Somehow I always felt that he and I were just meant for each other." We sat in the restaurant for a long time, at the window where we could see the passersby hurrying along the sidewalk in the dismal sleet outside, each one so preoccupied, so caught up in his own story. We sat there all afternoon.

———————

Lee Smith lives in Chapel Hill, North Carolina. She teaches full time at North Carolina State University. She is also working at the Center for Documentary Studies at Duke University. Her new novel, *The Devil's Dream*, was published by Putnam in June 1992.

PHOTO CREDIT: JIM STRICKLAND

Although all people and events in "The Bubba Stories" are fictitious, it is true that I was a chronic, no-holds-barred, flat-out liar from the time I could talk until I started writing fiction seriously. My father liked to say that I'd climb a tree to tell a lie when I could stand on the ground and tell the truth. I never made up a brother. But for years I have wanted to write a story about that old complicated love triangle: real life, truth, and fiction.

Abraham Verghese

LILACS

(from *The New Yorker*)

B obby sits up on the side of the bed. He feels weak, spinny-
headed, and hollow. In a little while he tugs at the bedspread and wraps it around himself. Using the chest of drawers
and the television for handholds, he stumbles to the air-condi-
tioning unit below the window. He leans over the gray box, turning his head away from the cold blast, fumbling till he finds the
concealed door to the control panel, and then blindly punches
buttons till it turns off.

He draws the curtain back cautiously. He stares out at the
motel parking lot for several minutes, focusing on any movement that might suggest he is being watched. Over the high
wall behind the parking lot he sees the blue-green span of Tobin
Bridge and, beyond that, the Boston skyline. The parking lot has
filled up overnight. He sees Massachusetts plates, New Hamp-
shire plates—an Indiana plate on a jeep reads HOOSIER HOSPI-
TALITY.

FIRST IN THE WAITING ROOM. That would be on his license
plate. If he had a car. When he walked into the motel lobby
the previous night, it had smelled of coriander. The manager,
an Indian, had stared at him with alarm. "No vehicle?" he said.
Behind the counter, a door stood open, revealing a woman's fat
leg on a recliner; a silver toe ring looked welded onto her sec-

ond toe. There were the murmurs of a TV and the shrill voices of children speaking in another language. Bobby peeled three hundred-dollar bills from his roll, and the man's manner softened considerably. "What it is happened to your face?" the man asked, coming close to Bobby. The woman in the recliner stuck her head around to look.

"Oh, I was born this way," Bobby had answered. He had smiled at the fat woman, who quickly retracted her head.

The bathroom is cold. He brushes his teeth with the bedspread still wrapped around him. He tries not to look into the mirror. Why look? Better to remember himself as he used to be. As he is in the photograph in the briefcase—a photograph Primo took. It is from Myrtle Beach, the summer of 1973, when he was twenty-one years old. In the photograph his hair comes down to his shoulders. He is bare-chested, sitting sideways on Primo's '64 Harley, one hand on the tank and the other resting lightly on his thigh—his own thigh. He is smiling—a strong smile, a smile of certainty. Primo had said something to make him smile, something flattering, and his Fu Manchu mustache looks innocent, young. In the background is Primo's airplane, and beyond that, faintly, the sea, though in the photograph it blurs with the blue of the sky. Carolina blue.

In those days, Bobby worked as a manager in the Myrtle Mystery Mall, selling tokens for the peephole dioramas, supervising the soda and trinket concessions, keeping the lines flowing through the Dinosaur Cyclorama, shooing out the couples who lingered in the dark recesses of the Polynesian Fire-Walk of Love. He was ten years old the first summer his parents brought him to Myrtle Beach. They drove down from Spartanburg and rented a "cottage" (in reality, a double-wide trailer) for two weeks in late July, in what became an annual family ritual. Bobby, an only child, distracted, suffering again that summer with bad eczema, spent most of his time and all of his allowance in the Myrtle Mystery Mall. He thrilled to its dark, paneled interiors, the dim, red glow of the Chinese lanterns, the labyrinth of doors and corridors leading to exhibits, but most of all he thrilled to being part of the clique of boys who hung around in their flowery sports shirts and shades and seemed unofficially to preside over the whole phantasmagoria. They encouraged him to disobey the HANDS OFF sign on the Iron Maiden in the Gallery of Torture; they laughed when he tested the blade edge of the guillotine with his tongue; and later, sitting in a prop room, they let him sip from the silver hip flask that they were passing around—a mark of his acceptance. He much preferred their company to baking on the beach with his parents or sitting mute in the backseat while his father, talking nonstop, inched the Buick into the family cavalcade that went up and down the strip in search of a different fast-food joint for the evening.

The year his father died, Bobby dropped out of the English honors program at Appalachian State and moved to Myrtle Beach, landing a job in his old hangout. Every day, Bobby caught triptychs of himself in the Distortion Gallery; Bobbys were catapulted out of one mirror and reeled back into another: thin Bobbys, fat Bobbys. In the evenings, Bobby went to the Connection, and there he saw himself reflected in the eyes of guys from Johnson City, Fayetteville, Raleigh, wherever. They would cluster around him, buy him drinks, while he looked over the tops of their heads. One night he saw Primo come in, look around, and leave before Bobby could get near him—it was the only time Bobby had seen a better-looking man than himself in the place. Primo had returned in an hour, dressed in leather. This time Bobby walked over, scattering the people around them.

"If I had known," Bobby said, fingering the straps on Primo's shoulders, "I would have worn my skins."

"It's not too late," Primo said. They didn't make it out of the parking lot.

He rinses off the toothbrush. He has no razor, and, in any case, his beard barely grows anymore. He runs a washcloth over his face and works the corners of his eyes. His eyelashes have grown long and translucent and have curled up at the ends—a side effect of AZT, according to Dr. Chatupadia. Of the six doctors in the clinic at Boston Metropolitan, four are from India, one is from Pakistan, and one is a Palestinian. Chatupadia, who has been Bobby's physician ever since Bobby moved to Boston nine years ago, took a photograph of Bobby's closed eyelids with the eyelashes dangling and sent it to *The New England Journal of Medicine*. Chatupadia was disappointed when they sent the photograph back, saying that what it showed was now a well-described side effect of AZT. He showed the letter to Bobby. "'Well-described,' they are calling it, Bobby!" he said, pronouncing it *Boobee*. "These people," Chatupadia said, and he wagged his head from side to side, letting the silence stand for all the injustice in his life and Bobby's life. Bobby agreed. *These people . . .*

These people had no place for Bobby. These people were waiting for him to die. Even Chatupadia seemed to regard his longevity, his hanging on despite plummeting weight and daily fevers, as an aberration. He was a bird without wings, suspended in midair, defying the ground below. His Social Security supplement, even with Medicaid, could not support him. It didn't cover the medications for the infections—the opportunists—that threatened to kill him before the AIDS virus did. Five days earlier, after waiting for three months, Bobby was turned down from the only multicenter interferon trial in Boston. Because his white-blood-cell count was too low, Chatupadia said.

"But my count is low *because* of the AIDS!"

"So sorry, Boobee. They won't allow it."

The other interferon trial in the United States was in Durham. He didn't have the money to go to Durham, but he called anyway, not telling them his white count. "Sorry, we are fully enrolled," a tired male voice had said. "And the study protocol only allows our own patients—our own AZT failures—to be enrolled."

"What if I came down there and waited on your doorstep?" Bobby asked.

They had a waiting list of three hundred. The doorstep was full.

"Just give me *some* of the drug! You don't understand—I have no more rope to hang on to."

But they couldn't. Protocol.

These people . . . But Bobby cannot give up. He cannot. He will not give them that satisfaction. He will go to the clinic today, as he has done every Wednesday these nine years. He will be first in the waiting room, as always. He will sit there and show everyone that he lacks neither determination nor, as of last night, money. And he will remind them of their impotence.

"We are an army of Boobees, an army with overgrown eyelashes," Bobby says to the shrouded figure in the mirror. His voice echoes in the bathroom, and he speaks even louder: "Across this great country, our army is converging on city hospitals. We will assemble in the waiting rooms. We will wait for the clinics to open. We will be treated—we Americans—by our Indian, our Pakistani, our Filipino, our Palestinian doctors: the drones. Upstairs, the queen bees will be working on the cure, appearing on television, writing for the journals."

Someone bangs on the wall next door. "Fuck you!" Bobby shouts, but he has lost enthusiasm for his speech.

He pulls his T-shirt on, trying not to snag it on his Hickman catheter. The catheter enters above his right nipple and then tunnels under the skin to pierce the large vein beneath his collarbone and extend through it till it reaches the vein just above his heart. For two years the Hickman has been his lifeline. It has spared him countless needles; blood for testing has been drawn out of it, and all his intravenous medicine, at home and in the hospital, administered through it. He has not used the catheter in two days; the solution he injects to keep it open is in the refrigerator in the South End apartment he abandoned in such haste the previous day. The catheter has probably clotted off, he thinks.

He turns on the TV as he dresses. He flips past the local news stations, half expecting to see his mug flash on the screen, and stops at CNN. He presses the mute button as Miss Cheekbones talks. He speaks for her: "An overgrowth of eyelashes is being described among persons infected with the AIDS virus who are on the anti-AIDS drug AZT." Here she flashes her dimples, and Bobby continues. "Concern is being expressed by advocates that this will result in people being identified in their workplace as infected with the AIDS virus. . . ." He remembers his father watching boxing on television with the volume turned off, providing ringside commentary in his loud voice: "Muñoz, once again pounding the body, coming straight ahead, hooking to the ribs— Styles make fights, wouldn't you say, Marv? You couldn't find two more different fighters. Concinni hasn't stopped moving, dodging, backpedaling, weaving—Oh! Concinni is tagged with a left! He's in trouble! He's down! Good night, sweet prince!"

He picks up the briefcase. It is burgundy and made of soft leather; it belonged to Michael. Michael moved into the apartment soon after Primo moved out. Michael did research on mice at the Genecor Research Center— mice with heart disease. He got sick and moved back to Iowa, leaving everything: his medicine, his furniture, his briefcase.

The bag has handles that slide out. In the outer, zippered pocket is Bobby's birth certificate, his living will, his prescriptions, a yellow pad, and a pen. Inside the bag is the gun. And thick wads of hundred-dollar bills. He takes the gun out—Primo's gun. In his hand it looks animate and repulsive. He regrets having it; he regrets having needed it. He walks around the room, looking for a place to hide it. He has a vision of a child discovering the gun, examining it, playing with it. Reluctantly, he puts it back in the briefcase.

He leaves the motel after a last look around. He takes a bus and gets off near MIT, near the hospital. A mist is rising off the river. He walks onto the bridge on Massachusetts Avenue. Halfway across, the muscles of his calves begin to hurt. These are not my muscles, he thinks as he reaches down to touch them. This is not my pain. He leans over the railing and looks down at the water. A purple reflection of his face flashes at him, and he pulls away from the railing.

He starts walking again, watching his feet: one boot with silver chain, the other plain; left, right, left, right. This is the only way to do it, he thinks—something Primo never understood. He is angry when he thinks of Primo, and Michael. Primo gave up almost at once. Primo had made the move to Boston with Bobby, in search of better AIDS care, but had bolted from the clinic after the first visit, terrified by the sight of a cachectic young man in the waiting room. Primo's only fight—before he was hospitalized—was to take wild risks in his plane. He tried Dead Man's Stalls and Cuban Eights in the Cessna until they took away his license. Later, Bobby heard from others—because they had separated by then; the path Bobby had chosen to deal with the disease made Primo and his fatalism impossible to be around—that Primo began to cruise, spreading it, poisoning as many others as he could, as if it would ease his own pain. This had enraged Bobby so much that he did not attend Primo's funeral. Primo's mother called him afterward, screamed at him, accused him of killing her son. Michael gave up in a different way: he left one morning, saying that the magic of being in Waterloo, Iowa, eating his mama's cooking, going to the high-school ballgames, doing whatever one did in Waterloo, Iowa, would somehow save him. It didn't.

Meanwhile, Bobby had tried it all: AZT, then DDI, now DDC. And ganciclovir. And the underground Compound Q. And intravenous protein feeds. And aerosol pentamidine. He had meditated—he still did. He had gone macrobiotic until he could no longer swallow. "Oh, I may die," he shouts at a car that passes by, "but not without a goddamn fight!"

Near the Christian Science Building, Bobby jams one toe between the stones of the retaining wall and climbs up to reach some lilacs that hang from a bush. It is more effort than he thought it would be. He gets the flowers, but his shoulder hurts.

He hears the woman's voice before he sees her. "Those are pretty flowers. But you should leave them on the tree."

She wears a track suit and tennis shoes; her gray hair peeks out from under a scarf. A handkerchief is tightly wadded in her hand, and she is breathless. Bobby holds the flowers out to her; it freezes whatever else she was going to say, and she breaks into a shy smile. He drops slowly to one knee. He imagines he catches the scent of her perspiration, sees the steam rising off her body. "The official flower of our state, ma'am."

"You shouldn't have done that," she says, her hands reaching for one cluster, "but they are beautiful."

"Aren't you going to ask me what state?"

"Are you all right?"

He gets up and rubs his shoulder. It is on his tongue to say "the State of Immunodeficiency." Instead, he says, "No, I'm not all right."

Her smile melts into an expression of concern. She moves her feet, conscious that she has tarried too long already, but feels obliged to ask: "Can I do anything?"

"Are you a magician?" Bobby asks. "Never mind. No, you can't do anything. Thank you for stopping, though. Thank you."

She waves and walks away briskly, her elbows pumping high, her lockstep gait quickening; she turns when she nears the bridge, and smiles.

Bobby watches her till she is out of sight; he feels the anger return again. It comes in waves and crashes over him. Yesterday, rage at the mindless bills, the dunning letters, and—finally—the cutting off of his telephone and electricity had carried him downtown. He had seen his reflection as he tore into the Bank of Boylston—a whirling dervish in a black coat, with gun drawn. He almost shot at the reflection. Could a face really be that purple? He braced himself, expecting to be challenged at any moment. Instead, they pushed money bundles at him, even gave him a bag to stuff them in. When the bag was full, he shouted, "What now?

What now?" but none of the prone figures would move. "What now?" he cried to the camera on the ceiling.

Too late he remembers that he could have given the woman some of the money.

He rests outside the hospital by the dry fountain that is full of butts and matchsticks. Then he starts walking again, against the flow of traffic as the eleven-to-seven nurses head for the parking lot. He bypasses the main entrance and goes into the tunnel and walks down it to the Kass Memorial Building and then takes the elevator to the fifth floor. He walks past patients' rooms smelling of Lysol and bacon. In the nurses' lounge the coffee is fresh, and he pours himself a cup, then snaps open drawer after drawer until he finds some sugar. He empties six packets into his cup.

Two people in white come in. One male, one female. One black, one white.

"Who are you?" one asks.

"Who are you?" he replies.

"We work here."

"*We work here*," Bobby says. Such complacency, such arrogance, he thinks. "And I am a walking skeleton. I'm a voodoo doll. I own this hospital." They look confused. He explains: "I'm your three square meals a day."

His hands are full now, what with the lilacs and the coffee and the briefcase. He moves toward the nurses and they step quickly aside.

Bobby goes down the stairs to the second floor and then through a long hallway, past dark labs and locked offices, until he reaches the clinic waiting room. Before the first sip of coffee is past his throat, before he can even sit down, he feels his intestines start to writhe, and he hurries for the men's room.

Back in the waiting room, he takes one lilac stalk and leans over the counter, over the patient-register book, and wedges the stalk between the printer stand and the printer. Laurelei will keep it there all day. She says that whenever she thinks of lilacs or smells them she thinks of him.

He tries breathing and meditation. He wants to feel the prana ebb and flow. *Ommmmm*. His mind strays and he brings it back. *Ommmmm*. But there is only anger. *Ommmmm*. He thinks of his job as a short-order cook in Hoboken, ten years ago, while Primo was enrolled in a six-month course for his commercial license. It was fluid motion for Bobby—a moving line walked past him and they called the tune while he danced. He was the ballerina of Niko's in Hoboken, cracking eggs, flipping hotcakes, buttering toast, sliding the dishes down the counter. Oronfrio, the manager, said he didn't know why Bobby bothered with the men when he could have had any of the women. "Because I can have any of the men," Bobby would say, flipping a morsel of scrambled egg into the air and catching it on his tongue, all the while looking into Oronfrio's eyes. *Ommmmm*. He thinks of his mother in Spartanburg and how she must shudder when she thinks of him with Primo. *That's right, Mama. I was his blushing bride. He did to me more or less what Dad did to you.* She will be surprised when she gets the money he sent her. She will draw the shades and walk around the living room talking to herself, tormented by the knowledge of where the money came from and what she ought to do, and by her greed for the money and her wish to burrow in her house and deny his existence. He laughs aloud, and gives up the idea of meditation.

Three guys come in; two of them are a couple he knows from the waiting room. They run a bar in the South End. Bobby remembers buying some dope from one of them a year ago. The third one—the new one—is not quite with them. He signs in and sits two seats away from Bobby while the couple sign in. Bobby smells after-shave on the new guy, but beneath it is a sour, unwashed smell. It is the smell of fear, Bobby thinks; it irritates him. Laurelei arrives behind the desk and turns pale when she sees

Bobby. "Thanks," she stammers when the dope dealer comments on the flowers. "Bobby brings them in," she adds, and looks at Bobby fearfully. Bobby waves back and points at the rest of the flowers, which he has arranged in a soda can on the windowsill, but Laurelei runs into the inner office.

"The official AIDS flower," Bobby says to the new guy, pointing to the lilacs. The new guy looks at the lilacs and then at the purple growths on Bobby's face. "Get it?" Bobby asks, touching the biggest growth, over his right eyelid. "Lilacs out of the dead land. Get it?"

The new guy just blinks. The disease is not choosy, Bobby thinks; this kid is dumb as a coal bucket.

The new guy tries to ignore Bobby. He shakes out a cigarette with trembling fingers. There is a ring with a turquoise stone on his pinky, and his nails are long. They would be elegant in a different setting from the Metropolitan Hospital clinic. His brown hair is slicked back in a "wet look"—a style that Primo favored years before it became commonplace. Bobby moves over to sit next to him.

"You didn't really have a bath, did you?" Bobby asks. "Your hair looks like you had a bath, but you didn't. And you hurried with your breakfast—doughnuts on the way? How did I know? The powdered sugar on your mustache. I'm Bobby, by the way." The new guy has the cigarette in one hand and a lighter in the other. "You can't smoke here. You can shake my hand, though. You can't get it by shaking my hand. Besides, you already got it."

The new guy puts the lighter away and Bobby shakes his hand. The hand feels crumbly, fragile, but it is its sweatiness that primes Bobby, forces him to take more interest in this boy.

"You must be Clovis," Bobby says. "I saw the register. 'Clovis: Forty-five.' Forty-five minutes is for new patients. Must be you. Let me guess. You tested positive—what, two years ago? And you were positive before that but didn't want the test. And now you wake up in the night and you feel cold and you put on socks and wrap your head up, and then in an hour you drench the sheets. And then you feel cold again. That's why you didn't shower, right? You were cold when it was time to have the shower. Am I right? You're shit scared, am I right?"

Clovis tries to get up. "Sit down," Bobby says to him. "You can't afford not to listen to me. You need to listen to me. I'm a survivor—nine years. If you don't want to live, just keep walking. That's better. Let's begin." Bobby puts both his hands round Clovis's forearm and twists the skin in opposite directions; Clovis yelps. "That's called a barber's twist, Clovis. Keep your eyes on the skin." A shower of fine red dots makes a bracelet on Clovis's forearm. "Oh, oh! You know what that means, don't you? Your platelets are low. You're farther along than you thought, Clovis. Good thing you came today." Clovis's face shrivels.

Clovis's acquaintances are getting out. Clovis tries to rise again. His eyes plead with the couple, who are standing at the door, but Bobby takes the gun out of the briefcase and sets it on the chair. "Clovis is with me," Bobby tells them. "And don't roll your eyes at me, honey. You guys don't look so hot yourselves. You got a way to make him live? I can make him live. What have you got?" The couple hurry out.

Bobby looks at Clovis; he wonders why he is bothering with this kid. Has Clovis become his hostage? In return for what? Bobby gets up and bolts the door. He paces around and then sits down. He has no doubt the police will be here soon. He takes one of Clovis's cigarettes and lights it and hands it to Clovis. "You can smoke now, Clovis. Everything has changed." He sits down and thinks awhile and then picks his words carefully.

"You don't know how special I am, Clovis. I am a nine-year survivor. I've beaten the odds; I am way over the median survival. Look it up, if you want. I'm the only nine-year guy in this clinic. And it wasn't luck either, Clovis. I fought for every fucking bit of it; I *scrapped* for it; I *took* all the responsibility."

Clovis is listening; the fear and gloom that were on his face are momentarily erased.

"Level with me, Clovis. What is the scariest thing about this whole business? That you can die from it? Death? Bang, bang? You probably will die from it, right?" Clovis's eyes get big. "And that fear is what kept you from being tested? And that fear is still there—right?" Clovis's eyes get even wider. Bobby takes out his yellow pad and pencil. He pats Clovis's hand. "The only way to beat this is to lose your fear, Clovis," he says kindly. "The fear doesn't do you any good. In fact the fear can kill you before the disease does. It's like most anything else in life: lose your fear and it can't touch you."

Bobby massages Clovis's hand, trying to imagine what it is like to be a Clovis. What does a Clovis really feel? He sees a LOSER, LOSER, LOSER sign flash across Clovis's face. Clovis is giving up, retreating again. Clovis is ugly, Bobby thinks. The dimples are really pimples, he has dandruff on his eyelashes, his face is oily. Clovis tries to withdraw his hand. Bobby considers stopping but feels obliged to continue; let the kid have the message, for what it's worth.

"It's not illegal to hold hands—is it, Clovis? Okay, I'm going to let go of your hand. I want you to answer a series of questions for me. I'll write down your answers on paper, and then you put that paper in your pocket and carry it with you. Then—trust me—you will have conquered death. It worked for me. Okay? First of all, where do you want to die?"

Clovis's chin is quivering. Bobby makes lines and draws columns on the paper. He is aware of the absolute silence in the building. "I'm asking you where you want to die. In the hospital? At home? On the street? You live with those guys, right? You all came in the same car, right? You work in the bar for them, right? A little dope, a little head—Hey, *I* know. So, you ready to die with them, in their apartment? In the South End? Or you want to die at your own house, in your mama's arms? Or do you want to die with me?" Clovis begins to open his mouth, but no answer seems forthcoming. "With Mama," Bobby whispers for him. He uses a southern accent. Childlike and *very* southern.

"With Mama? Let me guess—Alabama? Tennessee? Okay, you want to die with Mama? You need to write that down, Clovis. Get that down on paper. Otherwise they'll dump you in Roxbury Cemetery. Okay, so you want to die at home. Now, what do you want them to do with your body?"

Clovis is weeping now, his face in his hands, and Bobby strokes the ducktail, his fingers coming away greasy. "It boils down to do you want to be cremated or buried?" Bobby busies himself writing on the yellow sheet. He is aware of the sirens approaching the parking lot outside, but he concentrates on the paper:

BODY	Home	x	Away	
DISPOSAL	Bury		Cremate	x
SERVICE	Yes	x	No	
MUSIC				
TOMBSTONE				

"I personally can't stand the thought of waking up one day to find I'm locked in a pine box with rats nibbling at my eye sockets. If I was you I would go for cremation. It's cheaper, easier for your family."

Clovis is sniffling and carrying on. Bobby lets the X remain where it is. Cremation for Clovis.

"Music? I assume you want a service—so, music. See, that's something you can control. Music: what do you want them to play? Come on, Clovis—music?

"'Rocky Top,' Clovis? 'Rocky Top you'll always be, Home sweet home to me, Good old Rocky Top, Rocky Top, Tennessee.'" Singing the song makes Bobby laugh. He gets up and tries to clog but can't move his feet quickly enough. "Good choice, Clovis! 'Rocky Top' it shall be." He writes in "Rocky Top." He lets go of the pad to hold Clovis's hand again, because Clovis is trying to get away. Clovis sits down on the floor, his hand in Bobby's grasp.

"The eulogy, Clovis! Don't forget the eulogy. What do you

want them to say? Okay, okay, you can think about that. But the tombstone, the grave marker. That *has* to be your choice. 'Clovis. Our beloved son—' "

Clovis breaks loose. He unbolts the door, pulls it open, and runs around the corner.

"Wait, Clovis! Put this paper in your pocket."

Bobby picks up the gun but then tosses it out the window. He sits on the floor and carefully folds the paper into an airplane. His body is rocking back and forth with concentration. When he is done, he stands up and looks out the window. He is astonished by the crowd below. He sees Chatupadia and waves. He slowly pushes the window wide open and stands on a chair. With a flick of the wrist he sails the plane out. It is a wonderful plane—the best he has ever made. It catches an updraft and rises in a tight spiral. Bobby is drawn to the window: the yellow plane is still climbing. Bobby steps out on the sill and cranes his neck to follow it. Finally, when it can climb no more, it banks into a lazy left turn. He is aware of voices yelling at him, but they are drowned out by the roar of the plane's engine. He imagines himself as the pilot. The plane finds another updraft. Bobby increases the power to full throttle and points the nose straight up. Gravity works against him, and he watches the airspeed indicator drop rapidly. Just before the plane shudders to a stop, he applies full rudder. He has timed it exactly, and his plane makes a perfect Hammerhead turn, rotating on the tip of one wing. Now he points the nose at the crowd below. He sees his airspeed rise again. The wings shudder and the wind whips at his face. He puts his finger on the fire button. "Coming at you!" he shouts.

———————

Abraham Verghese is a physician and writer and lives with his wife and two children in El Paso, Texas, where he is Professor of Medicine and Chief of Infectious Diseases at Texas Tech Medical Center at El Paso. He is a graduate of the Iowa Writers Workshop and his stories have appeared in *The New Yorker*, *Black Warrior Review*, and elsewhere. His essays have appeared in *Granta*, *Sports Illustrated*, and *The North American Review*. His first book, a literary memoir about coming of age as a physician and infectious disease specialist in the rural South during the era of AIDS, will be published by Simon and Schuster in 1993.

PHOTO CREDIT: JAMES FARNUM, M.D.

"Lilacs" was inspired by a patient with AIDS whom I took care of in Johnson City, Tennessee. He had monstrous lesions of Kaposi's sarcoma on his face and a manner so obnoxious and so deliberately antagonistic that it made it tricky to see beyond this and recognize his particular form of bravery. Other elements of the story borrow from my experience with HIV clinics—particularly the waiting rooms—in Boston and Iowa. I began with the character and his anger and went along for the ride. Bobby's endurance and determination were all that he had left that was of any value to him; he had no medical options, and no amount of money could buy him more time. His diatribe with Clovis surprised me as much as it must have Clovis; it was, however, despite being cruel, also an act of love, a legacy to another young man from the rural South who had escaped to the big city to find anonymity and freedom only to encounter this unforgiving virus. Bobby's actions in the story exceeded all permissible boundaries. But what are permissible boundaries when you are dying of AIDS? The story came out in one quick rush and then underwent several revisions, the most significant of which was I changed to the present tense the better to convey a sense of urgency. Mary Evans, who is my agent, and

Daniel Menaker at The New Yorker, *helped me considerably through numerous revisions. I think we all were cautious about tinkering with Bobby, fearful that in his testy, irascible state, Bobby would tell us to butt out.*

Mary Ward Brown

A NEW LIFE

(from *The Atlantic Monthly*)

They meet by chance in front of the bank. Elizabeth is a recent widow, pale and dry-eyed, unable to cry. Paul, an old friend, old boyfriend, starts smiling the moment he sees her. She's never seen him look so happy, she thinks. Under one arm he carries a wide farm checkbook, a rubber band around it so things won't fall out.

"Well. This is providential." He grips her hand and holds on, ignoring the distance he's long kept between them. Everything about him seems animated. Even his hair, thick, dark, shot with early gray, stands up slightly from his head instead of lying down flat. In the sunlight the gray looks electric. "We've been thinking about you," he says, still smiling. "Should have been to see you."

"But you *did* come." Something is different about him, she thinks, something major. Not just the weight he's put on.

"We came when everyone else was there and you didn't need us. We should have been back long ago. How are you?"

"Fine," she says, to end it. "Thank you."

"You don't look fine." He frowns. "You're still grieving, when John is with God now, and well again. Happy."

So that's it. She's heard that Paul and his wife, Louise, are in a religious group just started up outside the church. They call

themselves Workers of the Vineyard. Like a rock band, someone said.

Elizabeth turns toward the bank as if she hasn't heard what
Paul said. Behind her, small-town traffic moves up and down the
street, a variety of midsize cars and pickup trucks, plus an occasional big car or van. In front, the newly remodeled bank updates
a street of old brick buildings. Some are painted white, green,
gray. Around the corner the beauty shop is pink.

This is the southern Bible Belt, where people talk about God
the way they talk about the weather, about His will and His bless-
ings, about why He lets things happen. The Vineyard people say
also that God talks to them. Their meeting place is a small house
on Green Street, where they meet, according to neighbors, "all
the time."

Their leader is the new young pastor of the Presbyterian
church, called by his first name, Steve.

Regular church members look on the group with suspicion.
"Crazy" is the word that reaches Steve.

"Some thought Jesus was a little crazy too," he has countered,
with a smile. He is a spellbinding preacher, and no one moves or
dozes while he speaks, but his church congregation is split in two.
Some are for him and some against him, but no one is neutral.
He is defined by extremes.

Paul opens the door to the bank for Elizabeth. "What are you
doing tonight?" he asks, from behind her.

She whirls about to face him.

"Louise and I could come over after supper. How about it?"
He winks.

He couldn't get along without the winks and jokes, Elizabeth
had decided years ago. They were to cover up all he meant to
hide—new hurts, old wounds, the real Paul Dudley. Only once
had she ever seen him show pain. When his favorite dog, always
with him, had been hit by a truck, he'd covered his face with his
hands when he told her. But the minute she'd touched him, ready
to cry too, he'd stiffened. "I'll have to get another one," he'd said,

more to himself than to her. And right away he had. Another liver-spotted pointer.

"You're turning down a good way of life, though," her mother had said a little sadly, when she didn't take the ring. It had been his mother's diamond. He'd also inherited a large tract of land and a house in the country.

Among Elizabeth's reasons was one she'd never mentioned, for fear that it might sound trivial. He had simply made her nervous. Wherever they'd gone, to concerts, plays, movies, he hadn't been able to sit still and listen but had had to look around and whisper, start conversations, pick up dropped programs. Go for more popcorn. He had rummaged through his hair, fiddled with his tie, jiggled keys in his pocket, until it had been all she could do not to say, "Stop that or I'll scream!"

He hadn't seemed surprised when she told him. Subdued at first, he had rallied and joked as he went out the door. But he'd cut her out of his life from then on and ignored all her efforts to be friendly. Not until both were married had he even stopped on the street to say hello.

Back home now in her clean, orderly kitchen, Elizabeth has put away groceries and stored the empty bags. Without delay she has subtracted the checks she wrote downtown. Attention to detail has become compulsive with her. It is all that holds her together, she thinks.

Just before daylight-savings dark Paul and Louise drive up in a white station wagon. Paul is wearing a fresh short-sleeved shirt, the tops of its sleeves still pressed together like uncut pages in a book. In one hand he carries a Bible as worn as a wallet.

Louise, in her late forties like Elizabeth, is small and blond. Abandoned first by a father who'd left home, then by a mother his leaving had destroyed, she'd been brought up by worn-out grandparents. Her eyes are like those of an unspoiled pet, waiting for a sign to be friendly.

When Elizabeth asks if they'd like something cool to drink,

now or later, they laugh. It's a long-standing joke in Wakefield. "Mr. Paul don't drink nothing but sweet-milk," a worker on his place said years ago.

"Now would be nice," he says, with his happy new smile.

Elizabeth leads the way to a table in her kitchen, a large light room with one end for dining. The table, of white wood with an airy glass top, overlooks her back lawn. While she fills goblets with tea and ice, Paul gazes out the window, humming to himself, drumming on the glass top. Louise admires the marigolds, snapdragons, and petunias in bloom. Her own flowers have been neglected this year, she says. Elizabeth brings out a pound cake still warm from the oven.

"Let's bless it," Paul says, when they're ready.

He holds out one hand to her and the other to Louise. His hand is trembling and so warm it feels feverish. Because of her? Elizabeth can't help thinking. No, everyone knows he's been happy with his wife. Louise's hand is cool and steady.

He bows his head. "Lord, we thank You for this opportunity to witness in Your name. We know that You alone can comfort our friend in her sorrow. Bring her, we pray, to the knowledge of Your saving grace and give her Your peace, which passes understanding. We ask it for Your sake and in Your name."

He smiles a benediction, and Elizabeth cuts the cake.

"The reason we're here, Elizabeth"—he ignores the tea and cake before him—"is that my heart went out to you this morning at the bank. You can't give John up, and it's tearing you apart."

He's right, she thinks. She can't give John up and she *is* torn apart, after almost a year.

"We have the cure for broken hearts," he says, as if stating a fact.

Louise takes a bite of cake, but when Paul doesn't, she puts down her fork. On her left hand, guarded by her wedding band, is a ring that Elizabeth has seen before.

"I have something to ask you, Elizabeth." He looks away tactfully. "Are you saved?"

"I'm afraid not, Paul," she says, in a moment. "What happened to John did something to my faith. John didn't deserve all that suffering, or to die in his prime. I can't seem to accept it."

"Well, that's natural. Understandable. I was rebellious myself at one time."

Strange, she thinks. She didn't remember him as being religious at all. On the contrary, he'd worked all day Sunday on a tractor while everyone else went to church.

"But I had an encounter with Jesus Christ that changed my life," he continues. "I kept praying, with all my heart, and He finally came to me. His presence was as real as yours is now. You have to really want Him, though. Most people have to hit rock bottom, the way I did, before they do. You have to be down so low you say, 'Lord, I can't make it on my own. You'll have to help me. *You* take over!'"

When was that? She tries to think. Things had gone so well for him, it seemed. He had all he'd ever wanted out of life—all he'd wanted when they were dating, at least—a big family, and to live on his land. He'd been an only child whose parents had died young. Louise had been orphaned too, in a way. So they'd had a child every year or two before they quit, a station wagon full of healthy, suntanned children. All driving themselves by now, Elizabeth had noticed.

As for herself, rock bottom was back in that hospital room with John, sitting in a chair by his bed. Six months maybe, a year at the most, they'd just told her in the hall. She'd held his hand until the Demerol took effect and his hand had gone limp in hers. Then she'd leaned her head on the bed beside him and prayed, with all her heart. From hospital room to hospital room she had prayed, and at home in between.

"I've said that too, Paul, many times. I prayed, and nothing happened. Why would He come to you and not me?"

"Because you were letting something stand in your way, my dear." His smile is back, full force. "For Him to come in, you have to get rid of self—first of all your self-will! 'Not my will but Thine be done,' He said on the cross."

He breaks off, turns to the tea and cake before him. With the first bite of cake he shuts his eyes. A blissful smile spreads over his face.

"Umh, umh!" He winks at Louise. "How about this pound cake, Mama!"

Late the next afternoon Elizabeth is watering flowers in her backyard. Before, she grew flowers to bring in the house, zinnias for pottery pitchers, bulbs for clear glass vases. Now she grows them for themselves, and seldom cuts them. She has a new, irrational notion that scissors hurt the stems. After what she's seen of pain, she wants to hurt nothing that lives.

From where she stands with the hose, she watches a small red car turn into her driveway. In front of the house two young girls in sundresses get out.

"Mrs. North?" the first girl says, when Elizabeth comes up to meet them. "You probably don't remember me, but I'm Beth Woodall, and this is Cindy Lewis. We're from Workers of the Vineyard."

Beth is blond and pretty—a young Louise, Elizabeth thinks. Her smiles spin off like bubbles, but Cindy has a limp and something is wrong with one arm. Elizabeth doesn't look at it directly.

"What can I do for you girls?"

"Oh, we just came to see you," Beth says. "Paul and Louise thought we might cheer you up."

In the living room Beth is the speaker. "We all knew your husband from the paper, Mrs. North. He was wonderful! My dad read every line he ever wrote, and says this town is lost without him." She pushes back her hair, anchors it behind one ear. Her nails, overlong, pale as seashells, seem to lag behind her fingers. "We've all been praying for you."

The hose has made a wet spot on the front of Elizabeth's skirt. To avoid looking up, she rubs it with her hand.

"I know how you feel, though," Beth says quickly. "Remember Billy Moseley, who was killed in that wreck last year? He was my boyfriend since grammar school, and we'd have gotten married someday, if he'd lived. We were just always . . . together." Her eyes fill up with tears.

Elizabeth remembers Billy, handsome, polite. A star athlete killed by a drunk driver. She feels a deep stir of sympathy, but like everything painful since John died, it freezes before it can surface. Frozen, it seems packed in her chest, as in the top of a refrigerator so full the door will hardly shut. She looks back at Beth with dry, guilty eyes.

"Well, I'm all right now," Beth says. "But I thought for a while it would kill me. I didn't want to live without Billy, until I met the people at The Vineyard. They made me see it was God's will for him to die and me to live and serve the Lord. Now I know Billy's waiting for me, and it's not as bad as it was." She shrugs. "I try to help Billy's mother, but she won't turn it over to the Lord."

The room is growing dark. Elizabeth gets up to turn on more lights, which cast a roseate glow on their faces, hands, feet in open sandals "Would you girls like a Coke?"

"Yes, ma'am." Beth blinks her eyes dry. "A Coke would be nice."

They follow Elizabeth to the kitchen, where she pours Coca-Cola into glasses filled with ice cubes.

"You must get lonesome here by yourself," Cindy says, looking around. "Are your children away from home or something?"

"I don't have children, Cindy." Elizabeth hands her a glass and a paper napkin. "My husband and I wanted a family but couldn't have one. All we had was each other."

"Ah!" Beth says quickly. "*We'll* be your children, then. Won't we, Cindy?"

It is seven o'clock in the morning and Elizabeth is drinking coffee, staring dejectedly out the kitchen window. During the night she had a dream about John. He was alive, not dead.

John had been editor-publisher of the Wakefield *Sun*, the town's weekly paper, had written most of the copy himself. In the dream he and Elizabeth were in bed for the night.

John had liked to work in bed and she had liked to read beside him, so they'd gone to bed early as a rule. Propped up on pillows, he had worked on editorials, for which he'd been known throughout the state. At times, though, he had put aside his clipboard and taken off his glasses. His eyes, blue-gray and rugged, like a tweed jacket he'd worn so many winters, would take on a look that made the book fall from her hand and later, sometimes, onto the floor.

In the dream, as he looked at her, the phone by their bed rang. He'd forgotten a meeting, he told her, out of bed at once. He had to get down there. It had already started, a meeting he was to cover for the paper. He hurried into clothes but stopped at the bedroom door.

"I'll be right back," he said, like a mischievous boy.

But he wasn't back and never would be, she was reminded, wide awake. In the dark she checked the space beside her with her hand to be sure, and her grief seemed new again, stronger than ever, reinforced by time. If only she could cry, she thought, the way most widows do! *Cry,* people told her, over and over, but she couldn't. That part of her seemed to freeze up and go numb every time.

She woke from the dream at two o'clock in the morning, and hasn't slept since. Now she's glad to be up with something to do, even if it's only an appointment with her lawyer. She has sold John's business but kept the building, and the legalities are not yet over. She wants to be on time, is always on time. It is part of her fixation on details, as if each thing attended to were somehow on a list that if completed could bring back meaning to her life.

In the fall she will go back to teaching school, but her heart is not in it as before. For twenty years she was John's wife first of all, from deadline to deadline, through praise, blame, long stretches of indifference. He couldn't have done it without her, he'd said, with each award and honor he'd been given. Now no other role seems right for her, which is her problem, she's thinking as the front doorbell rings.

Louise is there in a fresh summer dress, her clean hair shining in the sun. She smells of something lightly floral.

"May I come in?"

Still in a nightgown and robe, aware of the glazed-over look in her eyes, Elizabeth steps back, opens the door wide. "How about a cup of coffee?" she says, forcing herself to smile in return.

At the white table Louise takes the place she had before. "I won't stay long," she says.

Elizabeth puts on a new pot of coffee, gets out a cup and saucer and a cloth napkin. Outside all is quiet. Stores and offices won't open until nine, so why is Louise in town at this hour?

"I was praying for you," she says, as if in answer. "But the Lord told me to come and see you instead."

Elizabeth turns to look at her. "God told you?"

Their eyes meet. Louise nods.

"He wanted you to know that He loves you, that's all. He wanted me to bring you His love." Her face turns a sudden bright pink, which deepens and spreads.

At a loss, Elizabeth goes for the coffeepot, pours a cup for Louise and one for herself. She has learned to drink hers black, but Louise adds milk and sugar. Both wait for the coffee to cool.

"Come with us to The Vineyard next time, Elizabeth," Louise says, all at once.

This is what she really came for, Elizabeth thinks, and it's a plea, as from someone safe on the bank to a swimmer having trouble in the water.

"It could save your life!" Louise says.

The Vineyard meeting place is a narrow, shotgun-style house of the 1890s, last used as a dentist's office. It has one large room in front and two small rooms in back. Having been welcomed and shown around, Elizabeth stands against the wall of the front room with Paul and Louise. The group is smaller than she expected, and not all Presbyterian. Some people are from other churches as well, all smiling and excited.

Everything revolves around Steve, a young man in jeans who looks like a slight blond Jesus. When Elizabeth is introduced, he looks deep into her eyes.

"Elizabeth," he says, as if he knows her already. "We were hoping you'd come. Welcome to The Vineyard!"

To her surprise, he says no more and moves on, but she has felt his power like the heat from a stove. She finds herself following him around the room with her eyes, wanting to know what he says to other people. Like a salesman sure of his product, he puts on no pressure.

The night is hot and windows are open, but no breeze comes through. Rotary fans monotonously sweep away the heat in front of them, in vain. Someone brings in a pitcher of Kool-Aid, which is passed around in paper cups.

"Okay, people." Steve holds up his cup, raises his voice for attention. "Let's have a song."

Everyone takes a seat on the floor, in a ring shaped by the long, narrow room. A masculine girl with short dark hair stands up. She tests one key, then another, low in her throat, before leading off. "We are one in the Spirit, we are one in the Lord . . ."

Most of the singers are young, in shorts or jeans, but some are middle-aged or older. Of the latter, the majority are single women and widows like Elizabeth. The young people sit with folded legs, leaning comfortably forward, and the men draw up one leg or the other. But the women, in pantsuits or sleeveless dresses, sit up straight, like paper dolls bent in the middle.

The song gains momentum for the chorus, which ends, "Yes, they'll know—oh, we are Christians by our love!"

"All *right*," Steve says. "Time to come to our Lord in prayer."

Someone scrambles up to turn off the light switch while someone else lights a candle on the Kool-Aid table. In the semidarkness Steve reaches out to his neighbor on each side, and a chain of hands is quickly formed.

Elizabeth, without a hand to hold in her new single life, is glad to link in. She could be joining the human race again, she thinks, smiling at the young woman on her left and Paul on her right. Paul's hand no longer trembles but feels as it did in high school— not thrilling but dependable, something to count on.

The room is suddenly hushed. "For the benefit of our visitor," Steve says, "we begin with sentence prayers around the circle, opening our hearts and minds to God." He bows his head. "We thank You again, Heavenly Father, for the privilege of being here. Guide us, we pray, in all we say and do, that it may be for the extension of Your kingdom. Thank You as always for each other but above all for Your blessed son, Jesus, who is with us tonight, here in this circle."

Oh, no, Elizabeth thinks. *I can't do this. How did I ever get here?* She's never prayed out loud in her life except in unison.

But a thin boy on Steve's left is already speaking. "You turned me around, Lord. Before You, all I lived for was that bottle. I didn't think about nobody but myself . . ."

Eagerly, one after the other, they testify, confess, ask help in bringing others to Jesus as Lord and Savior. They speak of the devil as if he's someone in town, a troublemaker they can't avoid.

A checkout girl from the supermarket starts to cry and can't stop. From around the circle come murmurs of "God bless you" and "We love you," until her weeping begins to subside.

"My heart's too full tonight," the girl sobs at last. "I have to pass."

The room begins to feel crowded and close. On each side Elizabeth's hands are gripped tighter. The back of her blouse is sticking to her skin.

"Praise God!" a man cries out in the middle of someone's prayer.

"Help me, Lord," a woman whimpers.

A teenage boy starts to pray, his words eerily unintelligible. Tongues? Elizabeth wonders, electrified. They do it here, she's heard. But something nasal in his voice gives the clue, and she has a wild impulse to laugh. He's not speaking in tongues but is tongue-tied from a cleft palate.

Too soon Elizabeth hears Paul's voice beside her, charged with emotion. He's praying about the sin of pride in his life, but she can't pay attention because she will be next. Heavy, galloping hoofbeats seem to have taken the place of her heart.

When he's through, she says nothing. She would like to say "I pass," or something, anything, but is unable to decide on, much less utter, a word. Her hands are wet with cold perspiration. She tries to withdraw them, but Paul on one side and the young woman on the other hold on tight. Fans hum back and forth as her silence stretches out.

At last someone starts to pray out of turn, and the circle is mended. As the prayers move back to Steve, Elizabeth gives a sigh of relief and tries to ease her position on the floor without being obvious. Steve gives a new directive.

"We'll now lift up to God those with special needs tonight." He allows them a moment to think. "I lift up Jane, our choir director, in the medical center for tests and diagnosis. Her tests begin in the morning."

They pray in silence for Jane, for someone in the midst of divorce, for a man who's lost his job. An unnamed friend with an unidentified problem is presented.

Louise clears her throat for attention, and then hesitates before speaking out. When she does, her voice is girlish and sweet, as usual.

"I lift up Elizabeth," she says.

Elizabeth has avoided the telephone all day, though she's heard it ring many times. The weather is cloudy and cool, so she has spent the morning outside, weeding, hoeing, raking, and has come to one decision. She will not see the soul-savers today.

Tomorrow, perhaps, she can face them. Today she will do anything not to. They were holding her up not for her but for them, she believes. They refuse to look on the dark side of reality, and they want her to blink it away too. If she can smile before loss,

grief, and death, so can they. They're like children in a fairy
tale, singing songs, holding hands. Never mind the dark wood,
wolves, and witches. Or birds that eat up the breadcrumbs.

During lunch she takes the phone off the hook, eats in a hurry,
and goes back out with magazines and a book. For supper she
will go to Breck's for barbecue and visit with whoever's there.
When she comes back, the day will be over. "One day at a time"
is the new widow's motto.

She is drying off from a shower when the front doorbell rings.
She doesn't hurry, even when it rings again and someone's finger
stays on the buzzer. The third time, she closes the bathroom door
carefully, little by little, so as not to be heard. Gingerly, as if it
might shock her, she flips off the light switch.

Soon there is knocking on the back door, repeated several
times. She can hear voices but not words. When she continues to
do nothing, hardly breathing for fear they will somehow know or
divine that she's there, the knocking stops and the voices, along
with retreating footsteps, fade away. Through a sneaked-back
window curtain she can see the small red car moving off.

Suddenly, in her mind's eye, she can also see herself, as from
a distance, towel clutched like a fig leaf, hiding from a band of
Christians out to save her soul!

For the first time in her widowhood she laughs when she's
alone. It happens before she knows it, like a hiccup or a sneeze.
With abandon, such as she'd thought lost to her forever, she
draws out the laugh as long as possible, winding up with a
chuckle.

Smiling for a change, as if playing a game, she dresses in a
hurry and picks up her purse. She's about to walk out the back
door when the front doorbell rings.

This time, keys still in hand, she goes at once to open her
front door.

Beth and Cindy, plus Steve and two policemen, stare back at
her. The policemen are in uniform, dark blue pants and lighter

blue shirts, with badges, and insignia, and guns on their belts. Obviously they've been deciding how to get into the house without a key.

For a moment no one speaks. Then Beth, wide-eyed, bursts out, "You scared us to death, Mrs. North! We thought you had passed out or something. We knew you were in there because of your car."

"I didn't feel like seeing anyone today." Elizabeth's voice is calm and level. Where did it come from, she thinks, that unruffled voice? She should be mad or upset, and she's not.

"Sorry to bother you, Mrs. North," the older policeman says. "Your friends here were worried."

And suddenly, out of the blue, Elizabeth is suffused with what seems pure benevolence. For a split second, and for no reason, she is sure that everything is overall right in the world. And not just for her but for everyone, including the dead.

"No bother," she says, half-dazed, to the policeman. "I thank you."

Steve has said nothing. His eyes are not innocent like Beth's and Cindy's. They are the eyes of a true believer, blessed or cursed with certainty. His focus has been steadily on her, but now it breaks away.

"Let's go, people," he says lightly. "God bless you, Elizabeth. Glad you're okay."

Elizabeth has slept all night, for once. As she sits down to cereal and coffee, she is sure of one thing. She has to start what everyone tells her must be "a whole new life" without John, and she has to do it now. Though still frozen and numb inside, she has found that she can at least laugh. And she has experienced, however fleetingly, what must have been grace.

When she hears a car door slam out front—not once but twice—she gets up without waiting for anyone to ring or knock. It is Paul and Louise, for the first time not smiling. Paul has on khaki work clothes. Louise has brushed her hair on top, but underneath sleep tangles show.

On the living-room sofa they sit leaning forward. Paul rocks one knee from side to side, making his whole body shake from the tension locked inside him.

"They should have come to us instead of going to the police," he says at once. "They just weren't thinking."

"No, it was my fault," Elizabeth says. "I should have gone to the door."

"Why *didn't* you?" Louise wants to know.

"Well . . ." She looks down, falls silent.

"Our meeting upset you?" Paul asks in a moment.

Elizabeth's housecoat is old and too short. She starts checking the snaps down the front. They catch her like this every time, she thinks. Why can't they call, like everyone else, before they come?

"Level with us, honey," he says. "We're your friends. What upset you so much?"

Except for the sound of her fingertips on the cloth, the room is utterly quiet.

"We need to pray about this," Paul says. "Let's pray . . ."

"No!" Elizabeth is on her feet without meaning to be. "No, Paul. I can't, I'm sorry." She's out of breath, as from running. "This has got to stop! I can't be a Worker of the Vineyard. You're wasting your time on me. You'll have to find somebody else."

He says nothing for so long that a countdown seems to start up inside her. But then he stands up slowly, followed by Louise. At the door, with his hand on the knob, he turns to face her.

"Well, Elizabeth," he says, "I guess it's time to say good-bye."

Her heart slows down as if brakes had been applied. The beats become heavy, far apart. She can feel them in her ears, close to her brain.

"I'm sorry, Paul!" she says quickly. Before his unforgiving eyes she says it again, as if holding out a gift she knows to be inadequate. "I'm *sorry*!"

But this time he has no joke or smile. Without a word he takes Louise by the arm and they turn to go.

She watches them walk to the car side by side, not touching. Paul opens the door for Louise, shuts her safely in, and gets behind the wheel. The station wagon moves out of sight down the driveway.

Elizabeth's cereal is soggy, her coffee cold. She pushes it all away, props her elbows on the table, and buries her face in her hands. Suddenly, as from a thaw long overdue, she's crying. Sobs shake her shoulders. Tears roll down her cheeks, seep through her fingers, and run down her wrist. One drop falls on the glass top and sparkles like a jewel in the morning sunlight.

Mary Ward Brown lives on a farm in Alabama, twenty miles from Selma. Her collection of short stories, *Tongues of Flame*, received the 1991 Lillian Smith Award for fiction.

PHOTO CREDIT: JERRY SIEGEL

The germ of "A New Life" was a statement I once heard, made with stunning conviction, "God told me . . ." I'd known small-town groups like the PTL, had been interested in their effect on the people involved, also the people they chose to affect. For the story, I think the group took shape first, then Paul. The trouble was, I didn't like Paul and kept withholding the understanding he was due. So I had to rewrite many times, worked on the story for more than a year. Back of it all, I think, was my awareness of the presence and power of religion in the South. Most people go to church. A majority of the daytime radio stations are Chris-

tian. On the outskirts of every town, new churches keep springing up. In no time, they're adding Sunday School rooms and a Fellowship Hall. A Southerner's church denomination is part of his identity, like his family and hometown. I felt driven to get some of this into a story.

Nanci Kincaid

A STURDY PAIR OF SHOES THAT FIT GOOD

(from *The Crescent Review*)

It has to do with your blood and how it is changed after he just walks out late at night, letting the screen door slam behind him, thinking you are probably asleep, but not thinking enough about it to look in and see. He doesn't say good-bye. You hear him go, but don't believe it and pray to God it's a dream, like you are paralyzed in your too hot little bed with your brother, who is paralyzed too. And neither of you gets up to go see, because then it might be true. So me and Roy laid in bed like we are dead, and we wished it, while we listened to the sounds Mother made. She didn't scream. So we didn't. And in the morning we unparalyzed and Mother's eyes were gone, swollen off her face like two slits someone has stuffed large marbles into and sewn closed with catgut. She was ugly-faced, our own mother, and something inside us broke at the sight of her and spilled into our blood like splinters, tiny sharp points of glass, and it stayed that way, making it hurt to breathe, making it hurt to have a pumping heart. But we didn't cry.

This was before Mother found God. Back when she *was* God. Mother was not like any other mother, even later, after she married Walter, who was a normal man.

We didn't have a mirror in our house until Mother married

Walter and he couldn't find anyplace to look while he parted his hair in the mornings, and he mentioned it and then we all knew for the first time. No mirrors. How did me and Roy know what we looked like? How did Mother know if her lipstick was on straight? Walter was amazed, but thought it was a nice quality, a woman who wasn't busy looking at herself, fixing, painting, and curling. But the truth was Mother didn't need a mirror to see herself, because she saw herself in every other person she looked at. It was like she went inside them, felt what it was to be them, and then came out shining and knowing, looking good. At least in our eyes. I think she wanted to raise me and Roy and Benny to do the same, see ourselves in everybody we ever looked at, but we weren't good at it.

It was the first week in September, still hot as blazes. School was getting ready to let in and Mother loved getting us ready, getting Roy new dungarees and me plaid dresses and a couple of writing tablets and pencils, and always new shoes. She made a to-do of it, which we liked. But Melvina's kids weren't going too, which drove Mother crazy—she couldn't stand for us to carry packages into the house in front of Melvina, our new Sears saddle oxfords and the J.C. Penney's bag with my back-to-school dresses in it and our school supplies from Woolworths. She made us leave everything out in the trunk of the car until evening, after Melvina had gone home. Then she slipped the stuff into the house and put it all away like a reverse criminal.

When Melvina found things she said, "I see you got Roy and Lucy they new school clothes. How many dresses you get Lucy? Roy been needing socks." She wanted to see everything, she wanted to know what it cost, and she went looking through the drawers and closets to see what all Mother had bought us. Sometimes she laid everything out on the bed, just to look it over. Sometimes she carried each individual thing into the kitchen, where she commented and arranged it on the kitchen table, making a display. "Let's see," she said, "two dresses with a sash and one with a buckle belt. When did Roy grow to a size eight? Look at these underpants—what's this?"

"It's the days of the week," Mother said.

"You don't mean it?" Melvina looked at the panties closely. "Seven pair," she said. "You mean each day has its own panty?"

"You don't have to stick to it," Mother said.

"Wait," Melvina said, laying the panties out side by side. "They ain't seven. They's just five pair. What days is missing?"

Mother looked at the panties. "It's just Monday through Friday," she said, "school days." She talked like the idea was stupid, but at J.C. Penney she thought it was cute.

"That don't make sense," Melvina said. "What's a child supposed to do on Saturday and Sunday—go bare-bottomed? They ought not to leave none the days out, most especially Sunday. I wouldn't of bought none of these unless it was a full set."

But Mother was hardly listening because she was going inside Melvina—me and Roy knew it—and she was feeling things.

If you knew her, you could see it happening. She could be Skippy's mother as easy as ours. She can be Annie's mother, and Orlando's, and Nappy's and Leroy's, and even hateful Alfonso Junior's mother. She could go into Melvina and be a colored woman with eleven kids—which, as Walter said, was eleven too many—and she could live in Melvina's fall-down house and see how it was to sweep a dirt yard day after day and look at her delicious children knowing full well this world was going to eat them right up first chance it got. Mother would be Melvina and love Melvina's kids every bit as much as she loved me and Roy and Benny. In fact, we suspected she could love them more. She looked out into the yard, the patch of woods where our yard joined Melvina's yard, and she saw Melvina's boys all over the place. She saw Annie giving orders nobody was minding and the boys bare-chested and as brave as long sticks can make boys. They played swords. And they were pop-bellied just like Roy and Benny, skinny-legged that way.

Melvina was saying, "How much these tablets run?" but

Mother couldn't hear Melvina because she was Melvina. "They're . . ." She paused. "They're. . . ."

"What?" Melvina said, realizing Mother was talking about her very own children.

"Shoeless," Mother said.

"Oh, that," Melvina said, disappointed, wanting more, wanting beautiful, or strong. "Don't need shoes in the summertime."

But Mother got it in her head that shoes were the answer. Shoes were what would get Melvina's kids a good education. Then they could change the world. Shoes would save them. Skippy and Orlando would give up fishing if they had good school shoes. Alfonso Junior would give up dancing with his sweetheart Virginia at the Blue Bird and running whiskey both, if he had new shoes to wear. Annie could learn to read, old as she was, if she just had good shoes. The idea got into Mother's head like that, which was crazy because Mother never wore shoes herself. She only put on shoes if she was going to the grocery store.

But suddenly she believed in shoes like some people believe in the Bible and some people believe in telling the truth. Mother said there were people so poor they had to join the army to get a pair of shoes. You couldn't join the human race without them. Life, liberty, and a sturdy pair of shoes that fit good.

Me and Roy hated it when Mother got like this, when she tried to make us ashamed of having something that we didn't even particularly want. Like Roy'd wanted boots and I begged for Mary Janes, but no, we got saddle oxfords. And then Mother got mad at us and said, "Just look next door at Melvina's kids and think what they wouldn't give for new shoes." We didn't even try to argue with her. "I bet they know how to appreciate shoes," she said.

And the next we knew Mother put the September grocery money Walter gave her in her purse and took Melvina and all her kids to buy new shoes. "Buy them a little bit big so they'll last," she said. Mother herself drove Melvina and that carload to Sears.

She had to make two trips. Me and Roy went both times. And Melvina didn't argue with her. In fact, she got herself a new pair of black Sunday shoes while she was at it.

Skippy got red tennis shoes. The rest of Melvina's kids got those black shoes that Melvina said wouldn't get too dirty too quick. But not Skippy. Fire-engine red. Seeing him in those shoes was like seeing somebody with a couple of red people on his feet—alive like that.

I knew it wasn't going to be good from the minute I saw Walter's truck pull up in the yard, his wet hair creased where he wore a hat all day. It was too hot for Mother to be telling Walter any news he wasn't expecting. I could tell by the way he walked into the house and let the screen door slam.

Mother fiddled with her hair, putting her bobby pin in her mouth, then back in her hair again. "You have a good day?" she said, but her voice didn't sound right. My blood started rocking. And then she told him. "Guess what?" she said, and her voice did like a bird flitting from branch to branch, too high up.

"You think I'm out there busting my butt for the month of August so I can buy half the niggers in Tallahassee damn shoes?" Walter said, his eyes fixed, his voice with a shake to it. Mother looked at me and Roy, who had gone stiff, listening. Walter's voice rattled like a snake's tail and Mother stood like a woman who was watching it coil, and waiting.

"Do you and the kids ever want for anything?"

"No," Mother said. She was squinting.

"You're damn right you don't. But I ain't going to be daddy to that litter next door, Sarah. God damn it. Do you understand me?"

"Walter . . . ," she said, but he cut her off.

It wasn't like the time Mother bought Walter those button-down-collar shirts he said he didn't like, but she bought them anyway because she thought he would look nice in them, and even now he never would wear them. He was aggravated then, but not pure spitting mad. It wasn't like that time she tore up some of Walter's worn-out pants to make Melvina dust rags, or the time she volunteered Walter and his truck to take some church chairs out to Killian Gardens for a picnic that Walter was no way in hell going to. Had to be at the church at six o'clock in the morning to load those chairs, on a Saturday, Walter's sleeping-late day. He was cussing. Mother had to hug and kiss him all week to get him to go. She told him God would appreciate it, Walter helping with a church thing. It seemed to me and Roy like one more thing God couldn't get done without Mother's help. God was just some floating idea in the air, but Mother was the real thing, with two feet on the ground. So Walter did it, carried those chairs for the church, but he did it the way a chain-gang convict digs a ditch. After he left, Mother told us she didn't think God was going to count it as one of Walter's good deeds after all, since he did it so mean-spirited. But me and Roy made her swear she wouldn't tell him so.

But all of that was nothing like now, Walter's voice rattling at Mother, getting ready to strike, all because she bought a bunch of shoes that he said would every one be lost or torn up inside a week. "I'm sick to death of this do-gooding mess, Sarah. You hear me? One more stunt like this and that's it, I swear. I'm through messing with it."

"Walter . . . ," Mother said.

"Don't talk to me. There's nothing you can say that I want to hear." He turned to leave, walked through the living room where me and Roy and Benny sat frozen, slapped his hat back on his head, and tugged hard on it, pulling it low over his eyes.

"What are you looking at?" he said. We could not get up enough sound to answer.

Hollow-headed, I watched Walter walk across the room and out the door. He didn't slam the screen door: he closed it slow. It had a screech to it. Then Walter got into his truck and peeled out the driveway like a police car on its way to a crime. Mother hurried over to the picture window and watched his highway truck roar off down California Street.

I looked at little Benny sitting still as a rock. His face looked like somebody had erased part of it, like his face was a piece of lined paper with all the words gone.

Walter didn't come back for supper, so we finally ate without him. Had a quiet supper because Mother seemed like she wanted it that way.

By our bedtime Walter still wasn't home. Like a robot Mother got Roy and Benny bathed and into their pajamas—like a robot, like she was doing it but had no idea what it was she was doing. She tucked them into bed and got their prayers said for them because they were no good at it and taking too long. She kissed me and got the lights off and the doors closed to our rooms so she could go sit alone in the living room until Walter came home. She wasn't going to get into a lonely bed in the dark and worry herself into crying like she used to do with our real daddy. No. She was sitting up in the living room all night if she had to. Forever if she had to. Mother sitting on the sofa with her legs folded beneath her, hugging a pillow on her lap.

I couldn't get to sleep.

I'd always thought Walter was like a mountain the same as our real daddy was like a valley. A valley is green and deep, with streams twisting and floating through, a valley can be very nice, but to some people it just seemed low-down. Walter was like a mountain the way mountains don't move around, just sit there and let people move around them. All this time me thinking Walter was a peaceful mountain when really he was a volcano—a volcano looks like a mountain in every way, except it's got boiling insides.

I wondered if Mother was doing something wrong when it came to men, if there was something about being a wife that she didn't know and never had.

If Walter didn't come back, what then? Would we move back to the trailer court? Go live with Granddaddy on his farm in Alabama? Be some of those people that line up at the Salvation Army?

Melvina would say, "Lord, Mrs. Sheppard, you can't keep a husband, can you?" She would say that, and it half her fault in the first place. Walter gave up on us because stupid Melvina couldn't get her own dumb kids any shoes. Had one hundred kids, then acted pitiful because she couldn't get enough shoes. She dragged out every new thing Mother bought, laid it out on the table, so Mother had to go inside Melvina to get away from herself—then Mother felt things. I was tired to death of it too, like Walter. I was. I was tired of them next door never having one thing they needed, hardly had nothing, and us having to watch them do without until we got to hating what it is we had because it was better and plenty and we ought to be enjoying it but we couldn't. Melvina wouldn't let us. Skippy wouldn't let us. No colored people anywhere would let us enjoy ourselves because they were always sitting around somewhere having nothing. Waiting for some check in the mail that never came. Waiting on nothing. Nothing. Nothing. I had a low opinion of God because of it.

Walter was still not home. I would hear his truck drive up in the yard, would hear old George scramble up out of the flower bed or scratch on the screen. I would hear the keys rattle in Walter's pocket, all those keys he kept on a chain so when he walked it sounded like he had a hundred dollars' worth of spending change. It was like bells ringing, and it would be music to my ears now, some here-comes-Walter-home-again song. But Walter didn't come.

I thought Walter understood Mother better, like me and Roy, and probably even Benny. We knew she was not an ordinary mother. Not like Karen and Bubba got, a secretary mother who was always too worn out for any kid foolishness, who stayed at the beauty parlor all day Saturday and painted her long finger-nails romance red. And not like Jimmy and Donald's mama, who was nice but didn't do anything but clean up her house all the time and spray for roaches. And all those mothers that mostly minded their own business—and their own kids' business—and didn't worry that much about the entire world.

Sometimes me and Roy wished Mother would grow African violets in the windowsills and crochet toilet-paper covers. We wanted Mother to be regular, but she never would do it. Couldn't do it. And we thought Walter knew that. I thought he understood. Karen and Bubba's mother would take the grocery money and buy her own self fifty pairs of shoes and line them up in her closet like something to be proud of, which seemed like a thing that could make a husband mad. Mother never would do that. But Walter was mad anyway.

Like Miss Margaret Ann next door, who cried every day for a week when she lost the gold cross off her necklace and she was scared to tell her husband Jake. "The only piece of good jewelry I got to my name—lost," she said. "Jake's going to kill me," she kept saying. "He's going to kill me." She had us on our hands and knees combing through the grass in her yard, searching for it, promising us everything if we'd just find it for her. Saying it was the only nice present Jake had ever given her. She made herself sick over losing it. And when she told Jake it was gone, what did he do? Hit her? More than once? We didn't see her for two days afterward.

Keeping a man must be a hard thing, the hardest thing a woman had to do—keeping a man satisfied, keeping him from running off because he's mad about something or nothing. It seemed like women had this natural stay in them, like Mother did, but men had a come-and-go quality. I didn't want to grow up and do it—belong to a daddy or a husband or be looking for one to belong to, live in a man's house, drive his car, iron his work shirts, hug him a bunch so he'd take some church chairs out to the picnic grounds. I was not going to do it.

I'd listened to Mother and Melvina talk. There was a science to it, like a pinned-down frog getting cut up and studied—peel back the skin and look underneath. Their talking was like somebody with a sharp knife cutting off a fish's head, scooping out his guts, scraping off his scales, cleaning the thing. Mother said you could be honest with a colored woman and she wouldn't faint or put your name on the prayer list at the Methodist Women's League, because the truth was, she probably knew it before you told her, probably done it herself or knew somebody who did. Mother said you could trust a colored woman and she said she owed Melvina something over that. And we were back to those shoes again, like Skippy was stomping through my head in his hateful red high-top tennis shoes, stomping on my head with his new shoes that made Walter leave tonight. I hoped Skippy was happy.

When Mother was putting us to bed, Benny said, "Why is Walter mad?"

"Just because," Mother said.

"Is he going to stay mad?"

"I don't think so," she said. "Maybe Walter was mad about me giving away the grocery money—for sure he was—but God was very happy about it. Walter is just a man," she said, "but God is God."

She made Benny cry, saying it. We didn't like for Mother to talk about God like he was something above what she was. We didn't believe it. We thought God would be nothing without Mother.

"I don't know what else a woman can do," she said, "God whispering a clear message in one ear, and Walter in the other ear saying 'What's for supper?'"

I was glad God didn't talk to me like he did Mother. Give me tear-the-family-apart messages. I had tried talking to him, but he never answered me. It would not surprise me if he wrote Mother letters or sent telegrams or called her on the telephone. But I was glad he didn't do me like that.

Would Walter come back or not? Would he quit loving Mother since she do-gooded so much nobody could stand it? Would he go up to Melvina's and snatch those shoes off those kids' feet, throw them in a sack, take them back to the Sears store, and demand his money back? Would he sell this green California Street house and move back to his peaceful blue trailer, alone? Would he just never be seen again, like Melvina's husband, old Alfonso, next door? Then we'd hear he was off dancing with some good-looking woman at the Elks Club? What would Walter do?

I had no control over myself when I was worried like this. I prayed before I noticed I was doing it. I offered God deals, swearing to be perfect for the rest of my life if he'd just make Walter come home. I talked God's ears off. Begged. And then I wondered how I was supposed to know for sure God was listening to me. I wanted a little proof, like a bolt of lightning out my window or a voice in the darkness. Finally I settled on a plan where I would lie with my hand up in the air, like when you want to get called on to answer the question, except I was lying in bed, eyes closed, and just my hand straight up in the air. I wanted God to touch it. That was all. I wouldn't look. I wouldn't ask for more. Just wanted him to touch me so I knew he heard me. I knew he'd do it if I waited long enough. He must have known who my mother was. He would touch me if I just didn't give up. So I reached. And kept on reaching. And with my eyes closed and a long time passing, I got tired. And finally I fell asleep and my arm dropped down, and I forgot.

Walter was still not home.

Maybe that was God's idea of a miracle, letting you fall asleep and forget for a while, which was a miracle of sorts, I guess.

But the next morning I remembered instantly, because the air was not good to breathe, like there was something bad floating around, and every breath I took I was sucking in the bad. It wasn't like a morning when you were little and you jumped out of bed and ran through the house yelling, "Did Santa Claus come?" We didn't get up and run through the house screaming, "Is Walter home?" We got up quietly and walked toward the kitchen, wanted to see if Walter was home but be calm about it. Roy was like me about that, Benny too. We walked silently into the kitchen with our pajamas on. Mother already had our breakfast on the table. "Good morning," she said. "Sit down and eat while it's hot."

She had on yesterday's shorts and shirt, no nightgown or housecoat like a person had on if she just got up from bed. Me and Roy and Benny sat down to eat our oatmeal. We hated oatmeal. Mother almost never fixed it since we hated it so much. Slimy oatmeal with sugar and milk on it. Even Walter said it was Yankee food. What he liked was grits. Us too. But on this day we didn't complain, just ate the sugar off the top and that was all. It wasn't no time to be saying we hated oatmeal.

The living room was cleaned up, the magazines arranged neatly on the coffee table, the pillows arranged on the sofa, the furniture polished with that greasy lemon smell, no toys lying around. It was like company was coming. Me and Roy and Benny listened to Mother rattle dishes in the kitchen. The shower wasn't running, so Walter wasn't in it. The look on Mother's face said what we wanted to know.

It was the first day of school. Me and Roy got on our new school clothes, Mother saying cheerful stuff—we looked so nice, have a wonderful day at school, two smart kids like me and Roy. Benny was practically crying about not going too and Mother told him his turn was coming. She said she would get Melvina to bring Nappy and Leroy with her today, since the rest of her kids were supposed to be going to school now that they had new shoes to wear, and nobody was left to look after Nappy and Leroy. She said they could play outside with Benny all day on his pedal tractor, load up the wagon with pine straw and pull each other all over the yard, get Benny's little plastic army men and his toy cars and make little towns with sand roads and shoebox houses.

Benny, Leroy, and Nappy had spent all summer messing around in the dirt like that, turning on the water spigot and drinking out of the hose, squirting each other in the face. It worked good, the three of them playing together. It kept Benny from worrying Mother to death about how long until Roy got home, and made it so Melvina could work at our house and look after her own kids at the same time. Make three peanut-butter sandwiches for lunch instead of one. Yell out the screen door "Hush that racket" and "Stop that throwing sticks before I come out there and throw a stick myself, right on your behinds." It worked good, not much trouble to it.

Me and Roy trooped off to school. I had my hair long now. It would reach in a ponytail. And I had a new school dress that didn't look so babyish—Patricia said where did I get that dress because it was a sharp-looking dress—so me and Roy went off to school and I looked pretty good, but didn't feel that good. I hated to leave Mother when I knew she was going to stew over Walter all day.

Then me and Roy saw Skippy and Orlando and them going up the dirt road the opposite way from us. Saw them in their shoes. I waved at them, since I don't mind waving at somebody going off to school like they should be instead of doing a bunch of Huckleberry Finn fishing, but they didn't wave at me. Skippy just did this dance in the road, one of them crazy-looking colored dances, him in his shoes, twirling around and jerking, those feet going. It was nice. It was nothing to Skippy that his no-good daddy stayed gone. He probably liked it that way.

And Roy didn't say a thing about Walter being gone. But I knew he was more mad at Mother for making Walter mad than he was at Walter for being mad. Roy was like that. I knew what that boy thought without him saying so. Usually it was whatever I didn't think.

I told myself when I got to school I was putting on some of Patricia's red lipstick.

You don't have to hurry up for bad news. Our real daddy taught us that. Bad news would wait for you. After school we couldn't wait to pull off our school clothes and get into shorts and bare feet. We saw Leroy and Nappy out underneath the picnic table where there was shade. Usually Benny came running when he saw Roy was home. Me and Roy banged on in the house to deschoolify.

The house was clean. Mother was fixed up. She still had pin curls in her hair, but she was just out of the tub clean and wearing White Shoulders powder that smelled like magnolia trees. She came out of the bathroom with a hairbrush in her hand and said, "Don't make a mess, you two. Me and Melvina have not cleaned this house all day for the two of you to run through it like a couple of hurricanes."

We could smell Melvina was making vegetable soup with a beef bone for flavor. It smelled like fall, when you started back to school and made homemade vegetable soup and cheese bread, saying summer was officially over, although it was every bit of ninety heavy wet degrees, even with the fans going.

If Walter came home, then everything would be just right. He would smell that good soup cooking on the stove and see how pretty Mother could be when she wanted to, and he would know that grocery money was nothing important. We could get along good without it, just this one time. Mother would probably say, "Never mind about that grocery money, because we are rich in the important things, Walter Sheppard." I could hear her say that because she said it to me and Roy and Benny whenever we begged for some fancy thing that cost too much. I didn't want her to say it to Walter, though. Thought if she had good sense, she wouldn't.

Melvina sent me and Roy outside with peeled oranges. We sat up on the picnic table to eat them. "Where's Benny?" I said.

"Don't know," Leroy said. "He's gone."

"Gone where?"

"Don't know."

"Nappy, where's Benny?" Nappy only shrugged his shoulders.

"He's got to be somewhere," I said. Me and Roy started calling him, but he didn't come. "You guess he's hiding?" asked Roy.

Melvina came outside yelling for him, but it was useless. Mother said for Roy to look in the woods and for me to look under the house and for Leroy to go ask Miss Margaret Ann. Then she started calling him.

There was no sign of him. It was not like Benny to go off this way. Mother said for Melvina to get Skippy to scout the woods. Her tone of voice said, Dear goodness, what if he wandered away and fell into the deep part of the stream or got bit by a poison snake? "Find him, Skippy," she said. "See if you can find him." He and Orlando took off running, Skippy's red feet blurring as he jumped over briars and wove through the trees leaving specks of red imprinted in the air. His shoes would get torn up.

Then Mother sent me and Roy down California Street, house to house, to see if anybody down there had seen Benny. We took off. We could hear Mother calling him, her voice floating through the neighborhood. It sounded like a suppertime voice, with alarm in it. We were more than halfway down California Street, been to every house, and not a soul had seen Benny. The mothers hollered to their kids, "Any of y'all seen little Benny Sheppard?" "No, ma'am," they every one said. So me and Roy kept on.

Karen and Bubba came outside and went house to house with us. It wasn't dark yet, but it was thinking about it. Me and Roy hoped Mother had found Benny by now, or Skippy had, so we left Karen and Bubba still going down the street looking for him, because they were enjoying the heck out of having a good reason to ring doorbells. They kept at it with the vengeance of a posse, and me and Roy started home, ran the whole way.

Benny was not found. Mother and Miss Margaret Ann and Jake were in the yard with Melvina, Skippy, Leroy, and Nappy. They were all gathered up in a crooked circle. Skippy said, "Benny is not in the woods and it's wanting to get dark." We said nobody had seen a sign of him down California Street. Mother was past regular worrying now, she was thinking. What if somebody came by and picked him up, same as people came by and threw out puppies and cats—they could come by and snatch up a little boy. "Don't go imagining stuff," Jake said.

Melvina said to Nappy and Leroy again, "How come you didn't see that boy go off?" Their shoes were so scuffed, I thought she would spank them when they got home. Miss Margaret Ann was patting Mother's arm—Mother, all fixed up, planning on having things perfect.

"I'm going inside to call Walter, because Walter ought to know," Jake said to Mother. "I'm calling him at the highway department."

Mother didn't say don't. She didn't tell about Walter being gone. She stood with her arms crossed, biting her bottom lip. If you looked in her eyes, you could see all the things she imagined in there—where Benny was and what might have happened to him. It was clear she would cry any minute because she was running out of anything else to try.

"We got to call the police," she said.

Melvina hated the way Mother would call the police at the drop of a hat. "No matter how bad things gets, the police can always make it worse," she said. "It's like when those little nasty mealy bugs get into a sack of flour   can't do nothing but throw it out, It's the same with the police. Make a mess impossible to fix."

"Oh, Melvina," Mother said.

"Don't talk to me about it. I'm going home if you calling the police. I mean that thing."

"Yes," Miss Margaret Ann said. "Call the police. It would make everybody feel better. Let the police find Benny."

"We have to," Mother said. "It's been more than two hours."

Jake came back outside and said, "Walter is not at the highway department." And there went Mother, her face. Of course Walter was not at the highway department. He was clear up in Valdosta with his brother Hugh, or down at Panama City eating seafood in an oceanside restaurant, checked into a pink stucco hotel with cement flamingos stuck here and there in the courtyard. Walter was gone. No need for anybody to call Walter.

"I'm calling the police," she said and turned to go inside. The mosquitoes were out. Jake was shaking his head saying, "Ain't like Benny to disappear this way." Melvina said she felt bad because when she looked out after the boys this afternoon and saw her two, she assumed Benny, like he was under the picnic table so she couldn't see him good. Just saw two and counted three.

And here came Karen and Bubba. And Donald's mama in the car. And one-half the neighborhood coming to gather in our yard—see what was happening. Wait with us because waiting was always better in a crowd. Gathering up is what neighborhoods did with something wrong. Annie came down with more of her brothers, her black shoes looked like she'd shined them with Vaseline, and Melvina said, "She gone to call the police." Annie said, "That woman love the police." It looked like there was going to be a meeting. Melvina's kids chased each other. Every child in the yard barefooted, but not Melvina's kids—they scrambled around after each other, big-footed in their new shoes. Skippy's feet looked like a set of taillights moving about the yard, shining in my face. Karen was sucking her thumb, and some kids we didn't hardly know or like were playing pitch with gumballs off our gumball tree. Miss Margaret Ann cut on the porch light. Me and Roy felt nervous. We were thinking how nice we would be to Benny when he got home. Roy was going to let him sleep with him, both of them on the top bunk.

Then somebody hollered, "Here comes Walter." Everybody looked up California Street, up the dirt road past Melvina's, and we saw that highway truck throwing up a little dust cloud, but not much of one because the truck went slow, it had its lights on. Me and Roy ran to the edge of the street with everybody else. "Here comes Walter." He saw the bunch of us standing out in the yard and tooted his horn, flashed his headlights, and tooted his horn again. He waved like he was in a parade.

And we saw Benny. He had Benny.

"Thank the crazy Lord," Melvina said. She swatted Leroy, who was stepping on Nappy's feet, making him cry.

Benny was in the back of Walter's truck, not the cab. Mother's going to have a fit, I thought at first, and then I saw that he was on his pedal tractor. Benny was sitting on his little orange tractor in the back of Walter's truck. That boy was smiling.

Mother saw them out the picture window and ran out to the truck and as Jake lifted Benny out Mother grabbed him, hugged him, kissed all over his face, couldn't even talk, couldn't even fuss. Tears were going down her face. Walter walked around to where she was and she looked at him. Just looked at him. Couldn't say a word. Carried Benny into the house.

People gathered around Walter and said, "Where was that boy?" They said, "Thank goodness he's safe, because there isn't no telling what might could happen."

"You ought to whip him," Melvina said. "I'd whip one of mine that run off that way."

Walter lifted the toy tractor out of the back of his truck and set it down. Leroy and Nappy both made a run for it. "Take turns," Melvina said, yanking the tractor to the edge of the crowd. "Get out from under people's feet."

Walter leaned against the truck and answered questions. "I was driving home from work," he said. "I went by the Snack Shack like I always do, not paying any attention, and I see this little child driving his toy tractor up to one of the gas pumps out front. I laughed until I looked close and seen it was Benny—clear up in French Town. All that long way. So I stop to get him, says, 'Benny, what in the world are you doing way up here?' and Benny says he come to get gas because he was about to pedal all the way out to the highway department." Walter laughed telling it, but he didn't tell it all—that Benny was coming after him, to bring him home to Mother. He only told that part later.

He bought Benny a candy bar, said he bet his mama was fit to be tied, a little boy in colored town by himself, so he loaded Benny in the truck and came home.

He was not mad. Me and Roy certainly noticed that Benny was riding in the back of the truck, where we always wanted to ride, but Walter never would let us.

So the people went home. Melvina and Annie lingered until last, then rounded up Nappy and Leroy, who ran through the woods home, whooping like two wild Indians. Skippy was standing at the edge of the yard, leaning against a tree, with his arms folded, his shoes glowing like two embers. Walter glanced at him. "Skippy," he said. "Too bad you couldn't get red shoes."

Me and Roy went inside with Walter, that soup smelling good.

I don't know what got wrong with me. I spent almost the whole night praying for Walter to come home, then there he was—home. I should have said, "Walter, I'm glad you're home. So glad." A simple thing like that.

I walked to the house with Walter in dead silence. So did Roy. We acted like we hadn't noticed Walter was gone all night, we acted like all we cared about was that soup cooking and how fast we could get to it. And ordinarily I would have fussed about Walter letting Benny do what he never let me and Roy do—and Benny younger than us. I would have made a fuss out of it, said it wasn't fair, but because of how things were, I didn't. Walter could have let Benny drive the truck and I wouldn't have said a word.

Mother was quiet. She got Benny bathed and into his pajamas. If she got mad at him we didn't hear her. Then we sat down to eat. Walter was quiet too. He just ate. Mother hardly looked at him. Me and Roy didn't like how tears kept going down her face and she couldn't do one thing to stop them, just wipe them away with her napkin. Me and Roy ate our soup as fast as we could— we wanted out of that quiet room.

After supper Walter sat in his chair and read the paper. Me and Roy and Benny watched some TV. Mother cleaned off the table and washed the dishes. We could hear them. Walter cleared his throat and turned his newspaper page. It was a bad feeling, the tension in the house. Mother and Walter were ignoring each other, acting like they didn't even know each other, but they were two magnets and there was this pull between them. We could all feel it. If I stood between Walter in his chair and Mother in the kitchen, it was like when the rains came and the ditches flooded and that strong water rushed downhill, pulling you with it. But it was not about water. It was in the air, that pull.

I don't think Walter knew one word he read in the *Tallahassee Democrat*. I don't think Mother knew what dishes were washed and not washed and she just opened a cabinet and put any dish anywhere. Because Mother was a magnet and Walter was one. And they didn't know what to do about it. That pull.

Mother should have been finished in the kitchen, but she didn't come out. We didn't know what she was doing but suddenly we heard a crash like a dish breaking, shattering on the hard linoleum floor, and we heard Mother say, "Damn," which Mother never said. Walter got up and walked into the kitchen where Mother was stooped down with a whisk broom. She didn't look up.

"You okay?" Walter said. He stood there and looked at Mother picking up broken pieces. He looked at her shiny curled hair and those bare feet with that light pink polish on her toes.

It was so much like Mother, squatted down in the middle of something broken. Dealing with a mess and blaming herself for it. Trying to clean up things that were not right. Like if that plate was a person then Mother would save all those little splintered pieces and get out the glue. Everybody would say to her, "Forget it. You'll never get that fixed. It's ruined. Throw it out." And Mother would sit up half the night with the glue and a million pieces that didn't fit anymore and try to put that plate back together. If a person was a plate she would do that, because that's how Mother was. And maybe Walter knew that.

"Don't step on that glass," he said.

Mother stood up with a dustpan of glass bits and took a couple of steps to the trash can, near where Walter stood. She dumped the broken pieces into the trash.

"Sarah," Walter said.

She looked at him like it was a hard thing to do and it hurt to do it.

"It's only a plate." He smiled at her, not a smile with any teeth in it, but a smile that only showed in his eyes. A smile that Mother recognized. "It's not the end of the world," Walter said.

Mother laughed. She was a wreck, crying and laughing together. Walter reached out and put his hands on Mother. He pulled her close to him and it was like she melted into a puddle in his arms. He held her the way you squeeze an orange—the more you squeeze the more juice you get—Mother cried hard, those tears rolling down her face, and her arms went up around Walter's neck, her making sobs someplace between laughing and crying. Walter lifted Mother up, twirled her around the kitchen—her feet didn't touch the floor. His head was bent down and resting on Mother's wet neck. He was holding her like she couldn't get loose if she wanted to—and her, like she never did want to.

It made me cry to see them.

I'm like Mother about crying over a happy thing just like it was something sad. To see Walter love Mother in the kitchen, hug her like that, her lifted off the floor, held up high like she should be. Mother and Walter wrapped around each other, twirling, and they didn't care who saw them. Mother was happy crying.

My insides melted and I went to them, wrapped myself around them too. Then Roy came. And Benny. And me and Roy were crying just as hard as Mother. Crying so hard we were shaking, all of us, our crying coming in waves, all of us tangled together. Us, like a wad of paper clips on some magnets. That good pull.

Walter didn't cry, but he couldn't get us to stop. He said, "Ain't nobody died and y'all forgot to tell me, did they?" And we laughed in the middle of our crying. Walter said, "Who turned your spigots on?" but he knew who did. He knew everything was about him. We were all soaking wet—it a too-hot night, and us in a too-hot kitchen.

Mother said, "I love you, Walter." So then me and Roy and Benny said it too. And he hugged us all, put his face up against Mother's and was quiet. In a minute he said, "You're all right yourselves." His arms were pressing me and Roy and Benny hard against Mother's leg and his, squeezing us together into one tangled thing.

That night after we were in bed, supposed to be asleep, I heard Mother and Walter in the living room talking quietly for a long time. I heard them like a humming motor, like machinery that was fixed again and working so good it purred. They sounded as good as a window fan, drowning things out. I think Mother was promising Walter things. I think she was thanking him for hanging mirrors in the house, she was promising to look in them instead of going inside Melvina, even for a few seconds, when she wanted to see herself. She was saying that she was wrong about shoes—that she had stopped believing in them. I bet she was asking him for forgiveness right that minute. I was glad I couldn't hear her.

In a little bit they went down the hall to bed. They put on the radio in their room. It played a love song, but I couldn't clearly hear the words. They closed the door. I heard it click. And they locked it.

Born in Tallahassee, Florida, Nanci Kincaid has lived in Virginia, Wyoming, and Alabama where she recently received her MFA from the University of Alabama. Presently she teaches fiction writing at the University of North Carolina at Charlotte. Her first novel, *Crossing Blood*, was published by Putnam this year. She has published her short stories in many magazines and several anthologies. She is a recipient of an NEA grant and is presently completing her second book, *Pretending the Bed is a Raft*.

PHOTO CREDIT: CHIP COOPER

This story began with a memory that I wanted to capture on the page. As I began to put the words down the memory joined with other memories—not necessarily related—and escalated into a story.

There is a fine line between memory and fiction—and I love the moment when the writer releases a memory from the confines of its historical place and allows it to float through the imagination attracting and collecting whatever extraneous substance it will. The most satisfying stories, I think, are those that skillfully blend memory and imagination in ways that surprise even the writer.

Robert Morgan

DEATH CROWN

(from *Pembroke Magazine*)

I had no sooner walked into the room, maybe into the house, than I saw what the truth was. It was like a smell in the air, or a sound you can't really hear but know is there. It was a feeling in that old house and it hit me as soon as I stepped through the door. I didn't even pay much attention to Myrtle or to Annie where they set by the fire. I must have spoke to them but I don't remember it. It wasn't Myrt and Annie I was concerned with anyway. They didn't seem to realize what was happening though it was taking place right in their own house. And they were just setting there hunched up by the fire.

"Harold," I said soon as we walked in, "you might as well go back home. I'm staying here to the end." And I don't know what he did after that. He must have stood around the fire with his hat in his hands talking to Myrt and Annie as he always did about the weather and about their cow and about the terrible people running the government. But I didn't notice. And I guess he eventually walked back down the hill to that little pickup and drove home by hisself. I don't know. I had other things on my mind.

We had come out on a drive to the old place to see how Alice was. It was just a hunch I had, to see how she was doing. It was one of those cold clear days in November, the first real cold day we'd had. The leaves was finally all gone, after about a week of

rain, except a yellow one hanging here and there on a branch willow. But it looked like winter and the country had been scrubbed
and polished by the rain. It was cold enough so the hemlocks got
that black look they have in freezing weather. The ground in the
yard was beginning to freeze.

When I stepped through the door into Alice's room the first
thing I saw was the ball of white light on her pillow. It looked
like the sunlight from the window had poured itself into a little
cloud. There was a crack in the blind and the light had found its
way right to the pillow and just seemed to hover there. It looked
like a puff of breath had just stayed and caught fire.

But it was just Alice's hair. She had the purest white hair you
ever saw. As she got older it just got whiter, not yellow and tired
the way some old people's hair gets. It had a snowy look that
almost startled with its whiteness.

I couldn't see her face at first. You could smell the change in
the room, but it wasn't anything you could describe. Myrt and
Annie had kept her clean and it wasn't anything like a bad smell,
and it wasn't just the smell of camphor and the old wood smell
of the house. The house had been there so long it had its own
scent of leather and smoke and coffee mixed with must in the
attic. And sometimes I thought I could still smell the smoke of
Great-Grandpa's pipe, though he had been dead for twenty years.

This smell was different from them all. It was something in the
air like the heat of a hot electric wire, or the feeling there's just
been a loud noise that disturbed the elements but wasn't heard
by humans. I expected to hear a rustling, or see a curtain move,
but the air was absolutely still, even when wind outside pressed
the house and shook it a little.

Her hair was so bright you couldn't see Annie's face at first.
But when I bent closer I saw there was a new expression there. It
was not a look of pain so much as struggle. The look confirmed
the feeling I'd had. I'd seen that look before on Grandma and on
Aunt Mary's face before they passed away.

So I just got a chair out of the corner. It had a blanket and a hot-water bottle and a pile of papers on it. But I set all that aside and brought the chair close to the bed. If I was going to stay I might as well make myself comfortable. I was wearing my Sunday clothes with my old gray coat. We'd come over after church and I had on earrings and a necklace. But it didn't matter because I wasn't thinking of myself.

I pulled the chair right up to the bed and took Alice's hand. Even though it was under the covers it was a little cold. I held her hand in both of mine and said, "Alice, you know who this is?"

Her head rolled on the pillow and she opened her eyes and looked at me. But she had that wild look, the way she sometimes did. Most of the time she had the mind of a child and was sweet as a little girl. But sometimes she'd get this look in her eyes like she was going to hurt somebody or run away, or no telling what. And then she would quiet down and be herself again. It would scare you to see that look on such a little woman with all that white hair.

She looked at me and then she closed her eyes again. I couldn't tell if she knowed me or not. When she was having a bad spell it was like she didn't know anybody.

"Alice," I said, squeezing her hand, "I've come to stay with you; I'm not going to leave you."

And I could feel her hand squeeze back. It was just a faint squeeze, but I could feel it for sure. She never opened her eyes, but I could tell she knowed who I was.

"I'll be here if you want me," I said.

The sun had moved a little bit off her hair, and I couldn't see her face well. But the shaft of light was still on the pillow, blinding me a little. My eyes would have to get adjusted to the dark.

Ever since I was a little girl I was Alice's favorite in the family. We just naturally enjoyed each other. They never let her go to church or to school, and most kids was afraid of her. I remember once Mama brought me over there for Sunday dinner and I took my doll. It was a new doll, a china doll, with long blond hair, and I carried it everywhere with me. Alice seen me holding it as we stood around on the porch before dinner and she pulled me into her room and showed me her doll. It didn't even strike me as strange that this old woman, who was really Mama's aunt and whose hair was already getting white, was playing with dolls. I thought, She doesn't have any children but she has dolls instead.

Her doll was just a rag doll, and it was kind of worn out and dirty. But she held it in her arms the way I held my new doll.

"My baby," she said, and rocked it. She had a laugh I liked. We talked about the dolls till dinnertime when they brought her a tray from the kitchen and I had to go set at the table.

And everytime I went over to Grandma's house I'd see her and we played hopscotch or run in the meadow below the spring.

Her job was to carry water for the family. She loved to carry water, bucket after bucket, up the hill from the spring. She felt useful doing it, and would sometimes empty a bucket off the back porch just so she could go back to refill it.

"I've carried six buckets," she'd say and smile, though I don't think she could count and would just choose a number she had heard.

And when Myrt was doing the washing, Alice carried buckets to fill the washpot, and to fill the tub where the washboard was.

But soon as I come over she'd want to play, and set her buckets down on the trail and run to the meadow. We'd run and laugh so hard we'd fall down and roll in the grass. Then Myrt would find us and tell her to quit footercootering and bring the water on up to the house where they was about to boil some corn. That's the word Myrtle always used, "footercootering." I never heard anybody else use it. And I'd help her carry a bucket, though looking back I wish I'd helped her more.

"She's been going down since Wednesday," Myrt said when I went back to the fire to warm my hands. "We called the doctor and he come out and listened to her heart, but he didn't know hardly what to do. He said if we brought her to the hospital he could run some tests."

"Did he give her anything?"

"He give her some pills, but I don't think they do no good. And there's no way we could get her to the hospital. I think she'd die before she'd go. She ain't left this place in seventy years."

Myrt was right about that. And besides, it was too late for the hospital to do any good.

I told Annie to start a fire in the cookstove and heat a kettle of water. I was going to wash Alice off. I thought she might feel better if she was cleaned up a little.

"No, no, I'm going to freeze," she said when I pulled back the bedcovers a little. She held on to the quilts right over her throat.

"Now Alice, I'm not gonna hurt you. I'll just wash a little bit at a time and dry you off. You'll feel better."

She had that wide wild look in her eyes again. I put my hand on her forehead to calm her down.

"You're gonna be all right," I said. "This is Ellen. You remember Ellen."

She rolled her eyes and come back to herself a little. "How's Evie?" she said.

"Evie's fine," I said.

My mama, her niece, had been dead for twenty years, but I didn't want to upset her. Time had stopped for her long ago.

"I'm going to wash you a little," I said. "And then you'll feel better."

I pulled back the bedclothes a little at a time and washed her feet and ankles and then her legs and upper body. It was pitiful to see how thin she was, just a skeleton with skin, like she hadn't eat anything in months, which she hadn't. I was careful not to drip any water on the sheets. And when I finished I tucked her in again. I was going to empty the pan off the back porch.

"I'll be back," I said, and patted her shoulder.

"I can't breathe," she said. "They ain't no air in here."

"They's plenty of air," I said. But there was terror in her eyes. She fought back at the quilts I had tucked around her.

"Open the window," she said.

"You can't open a window," I said. "It's winter outside."

She tore the quilts almost off the bed and rassled to get up.

"You can't get up, Alice," I said. "You're too weak."

"Open a window," she said.

"All right, stay in bed and I'll open a window."

I wrapped the quilts back around her and raised the window a crack. Wind cut through even that and chilled the room. It was getting late in the afternoon by then and the sun had moved away from the window. Wind rattled the sash and stirred the papers on the night table. I closed it down to the finest crack, as the counterweights knocked in the walls.

"Open the window," Alice said. "I can't breathe."

I reopened it so she could hear the whistle in the slot. The room was already cool, but it got colder quickly with the fresh air. You could smell the air off the pasture and the sour of the new-fallen leaves in ditches. I got a blanket and put it around my shoulders, and moved my chair far as I could from the window and still be able to reach Alice.

But the wind seemed to make her feel better. She began to breathe more regular and she closed her eyes. I thought she was going to sleep. But then she opened them again, to make sure I was still there.

"Alice, are you hungry?" I said because it was getting on toward suppertime and I could smell cooking in the other end of the house.

"Would you like some soup?" I said. "Smells like Myrt's cooking some hog sausage."

I thought she was gonna nod her head yes, but no sooner had I asked than she closed her eyes and just seemed to go to sleep. She must have been tired from the struggle to breathe. Her breath was not regular. I eased the window down so as not to disturb her.

While Alice was sleeping I wondered what my duty was. Was she a Christian? Was she ready to die? She never had been to church since she was a little girl. Had she ever in her mind reached the age of accountability, as the preachers say? Was she responsible for herself?

My daddy, who was a preacher, used to argue with the deacons about who would be saved. "Ain't nobody going to heaven that's not been baptized," one said.

"But how about the Indians that died here before the white men came and brought the Word?"

"They will die in their sins," Carl Evans said.

"And how about all the people in China that never heard of Jesus?" Daddy said.

"I've heard they will be given a second chance," another deacon said.

"You must be born again," Charles Whitby said.

"And how about the little babies that die before the age of accountability?" Daddy said.

"You must be washed in the blood," Carl Evans said.

But Daddy said later they was just ignorant. It didn't make sense to condemn people that never had a chance to believe. What kind of God would do a thing like that? All the little children that had died early would be in heaven. And Alice in her mind was still a little child.

It put my mind to rest to think about Alice as a little girl, even though her hair was white and her face wrinkled. As it got dark in the room you couldn't see nothing but her hair, which seemed to glow against the pillow. It was like a shiny little cloud that just floated there.

"Do you want some supper?" Myrt said, and light shot from the opened door on Alice's face.

"She's resting now," I said.

"Poor thing, she needs some rest," Myrt said. "The last three nights she kept us awake with her raving. You'd think she had a demon in her the way she carries on."

"She's sleeping now."

"Annie's cooked up some sausage and taters," Myrt said. "You better come eat if you're going to stay with her."

"I can't leave her," I said. "Not now."

Myrt brought me a plate of sausage and potatoes and a glass of iced tea. I lit the lamp on the night table by the bed hoping it wouldn't wake Alice up. In the shadows from the lamp the room looked even bigger than it had before. The shadows pulled at the light, drawing it away from the shiny chimney.

It seemed strange to be eating in the room there with Alice, but I went ahead anyway. The belly don't know any shame or any rules except its own. Annie's sausage was hot and filling.

Alice shifted in her sleep and I wondered if she was awake and keeping her eyes closed. Maybe the smell of the sausage woke her up. But her breathing continued regular and I put the empty plate on the night table and leaned closer. The fuzz on her chin sparkled in the light. But her skin was still very fair.

Mama told me that when Alice was a teenager she was the prettiest girl in the valley. Her hair was blond and her skin perfect and glowing. Boys would come by on Sunday afternoons just to sit by the fire and look at her. They pretended to be visiting her brother or be courting her sisters. If she was feeling good she would sit in her corner and smile. If she was upset she run off to her room and slammed the door. Nobody seemed offended by her doings.

One boy, Otho Jarvis, was stuck on her more than the rest. He come every Sunday for a year, and had dinner and stayed to talk to the family. One time he took Great-Grandpa aside and asked if he could marry Alice.

"She ain't no woman to marry," Great-Grandpa said.

"Mr. Jackson, my intentions are honorable," Otho said.

"But you see what she is. In her mind she's just a child, less than a child."

"But she's a woman also. I'll marry her and take care of her, just like she is, and be kind to her."

But Great-Grandpa wouldn't agree to it. He said it wouldn't be fair to nobody. That Alice in her childish mind wouldn't be able to take care of children and look after them and raise them. And it wouldn't even be fair to Otho when he got older, trying to look after a place, and the children, and Alice. So Great-Grandpa put a stop to it. And one by one the other children married and left home and Alice stayed with the old people, carrying water from the spring and playing with her doll. But later Grandma took her in after she heired the old place and that's why Mama growed up with Alice in the house.

The wind picked up again, after it was dark, and rattled the window sash. You could feel the air seeping in through cracks of the old house. The lamp flame fluttered a little in its chimney. I pulled the blanket tight around my shoulders and wondered if it was going to snow. If the wind died down it was certainly going to come a hard freeze. I must have dozed a little.

"Open the window," Alice said. She was awake, and her eyes rolled in terror. "I can't breathe," she said.

"It's cold out there," I said. "Hear the wind?"

She fought at the covers and was working to get up.

"I'll open the window just a crack," I said. I raised the window just enough so you could feel the cold air slicing through the room but things wasn't blowing around.

She relaxed again, and lowered her head on the pillow. Her hair had been flattened behind and stood straight up. Her eyes wandered around the room.

"Where's Mama?" she said.

"Mama's all right," I said. "She's in the next room." There didn't seem to be any point in telling her that Great-Grandma had been dead thirty-five years.

"Everything's just fine," I said. I looked at my watch. It was almost ten.

"Would you like some coffee, Ellen?" It was Annie at the door. "I just made a fresh pot," she said.

"I'll have a cup," I said. "And maybe Alice will have some too."

Alice was looking toward the door. She had always loved coffee, and the smell of the fresh pot was strong through the open door.

"Bring me two cups and I'll try to feed her some," I said.

Annie returned with two steaming mugs, and took the supper plate away.

"Here's some coffee for you," I said to Alice, blowing on the cup to cool it off.

She was too low in the bed to even sip from the full mug. She seemed lost among the quilts except for the luminous hair.

"I'll have to pull you up," I said, and put my hands under her arms. It's always astonishing to find how hard it is to move someone. Leaning over her I had no way to get any leverage.

"Can you push with your feet?" I said, but she didn't seem to understand me. "Push against the end of the bed," I said.

But I don't think she even understood me. Bracing myself against the bedpost I dragged her up and put a pillow behind her back. I blowed on the coffee again and held the mug to her lips.

"It's hot," I said, but she didn't listen. She took a sip, a big sip, and then spit and shook her head.

"You scalded me," she said, and glared.

"I told you it was hot, to go slow," I said. But she shook her head like a two-year-old.

"Too hot," she said, and looked at me with that wild look.

"We'll just take it slow," I said.

She shook her head and slapped at the cup. "No," she said, and knocked half the coffee down her shoulder and on the pillow.

Ey, ey, ey!" she screamed.

I put the mug down on the night table and tried to sponge up the coffee with a Kleenex.

"It's okay, it's okay," I said, and put my left hand on her forehead as I tried to soak up and wipe away most of the coffee. The skin on her shoulder was not even red, so I doubt that she was burned much.

"You hate me," she said, and turned her face away.

"That's the way she treats us all the time," Myrt said from the doorway. "Here's a towel."

I lifted her head and put the dry towel on the pillow, and held her hand. Gradually the crazy look in her eyes went away, and she closed her eyelids. With my left hand I eased the chair closer and sat down.

The way her head sunk into the towel on the pillow reminded me of the old story of the death crown. Old-timers used to say that when a really good person, say a preacher that's saved lots of souls or a woman that's helped her neighbors and raised a lot of kids, is sick for a long time before they die, that the feathers in the pillow will knit themselves into a crown that fits the person's head. The crown won't be found till after they are dead, of course, but it's a certain sign of another crown in heaven, my daddy used to say. I've never seen one myself but the old-timers say they're woven so tight they never come apart and they shine like gold even though they're so light they might just as well be a ring of light.

Alice's head sunk into the pillow like it was the heaviest part about her. Her body was so thin it hardly showed through the quilts. You could look at the bed in the lamplight and imagine there was no body in it at all, only the head at the top and the flying white hair. It looked like her body had evaporated and gone, and left her head there with the fear in her eyes. That was the opposite of what happened when she was a little girl, when her mind had gone and left her in a beautiful, healthy body.

My mama said Alice was the beautifulest little girl you ever saw. She had been told by Grandma how fair and blond Alice was, with blue eyes and a sweet smile. Until she had what the old-timers called "the white swelling." I don't know what doctors these days would call it, but back then they named it the awful "white swelling."

What happened was the kids at school, or maybe it was at church on homecoming day, was playing wild horses and cowboys. And one big old boy, Mama said he was a Jones, was wearing these big brogans, and he made like he was a wild mustang and kicked her. He didn't mean to actually kick her, but he did, in the shin. And she was just this little girl with her skin all white and delicate. Where he kicked her it took the white swelling and the whole leg got inflamed.

The place itself swelled up white and she had a fever so high and long it ruint her mind. Her development stopped right there, in the pain of the fever, and never started again.

But the funny thing was her body seemed to get over it. Her leg was swelled up all them months, and they put hot compresses on it day and night, and soaked it in all kinds of things, and put on salves and plasters. And by grannies a piece of bone that had been broke where she was kicked worked its way out through the skin, a splinter off the leg bone. And the place, after about a year, healed up so she could walk again. She limped a little. She always did have a slight limp if you watched her. But she could get around and carry water. And they thought she would be okay, except her mind didn't grow no more. It seemed to go back after the fever to two or three years old, and it stayed there.

I remember bringing Harold over to meet my folks. I was so proud 'cause I was getting married and getting away from home, finally. I was tired of looking after the little kids and Mama was failing even then so most of the work had fell on me.

Harold had this old truck he used for logging. It had a rough bed and all the men he worked with cutting timber up in the Flat Woods rode on it every morning bouncing up the creek road. I don't see how their behinds stood it in the cold. But they laughed and carried on like a bunch of drunk schoolboys. You could hear them banging and hollering miles away.

Anyway, Harold drove me over to see the folks and I was proud he was such a big strong feller. He was kind of quiet around strangers and women, but you could see Myrt and Annie liked him. And Grandma was alive then and he give her a five-dollar bill. Everybody was smiling and Harold stood by the fire with his hands in his pockets. Myrt was making coffee to go with the coconut cake. And Alice comes in with two buckets of water.

She smiled when she saw me. I always brung her something, a dress for her doll, a piece of candy, a little vanity set. She set the water down and come to me smiling.

"Alice, I want you to meet Harold," I said, taking her by the arm. "Me and him is to be married."

And this look come over her face, come over gradually like a stain spreading in cloth, and her lip went crooked and she started to cry.

"Alice, Harold is a nice feller," I said. But she turned and run to her room, leaving the water buckets there on the floor. I had explained to Harold about Alice, but it embarrassed me something terrible for him to see her do that, the first time he visited them.

Alice seemed to be having a bad dream. She said, "No, no," and lifted her arm, knocking away the covers. I put her arm back under the quilt and told her everything was all right.

She was calm for a few seconds, then opened her eyes and rolled them around, and she jerked back like she had seen the devil or a snake.

"What's wrong, Alice?" I said, putting my hand on her shoulder. She was small as a child, but could push with surprising force.

"Oh god, no, no," she hollered and tried to raise up. I bent over her.

"What's wrong, Alice?"

"He's coming to get me," she said.

"Ain't nobody coming to get you," I said.

But her eyes looked like she had seen hell itself, but they was looking nowhere in particular.

"Alice, it's me, Ellen, and nobody's going to hurt you," I said again.

"Oh lord, He's coming. Oh Lord, it hurts," she hollered. There was nothing I could do to stop her but try to hold her down on the bed. Myrt and Annie had come to the door in their nightgowns and asked if they was anything they could do.

"You got any sleeping pills?" I said.

"We ain't got a thing but aspirin," Myrt said.

"Well, bring me that," I said.

They brought me a bottle of aspirins but I couldn't turn loose her shoulder to give her any.

"Bring me a glass of water," I said.

Annie come back with water in a teacup.

"You'll have to put one in her mouth and give her a drink while I hold her," I said.

But Alice kept hollering that something was coming to get her. When Myrt tried to drop an aspirin in her mouth she spit it out, and when Annie held the cup of water to her lips a little spilled on her chin, but none got between her lips.

"We'll have to forget it," I said. I held her down until she started to get tired. I was getting tired too, and my arms was trembling a little. When she finally quieted down Myrt and Annie went back to bed.

"I hate it you have to do this," Myrt said.

"I don't know what we'd a done without you here," Annie said.

I looked at my watch in the lamplight. It was two-thirty. Almost everybody dies between midnight and six in the morning, Mama used to say. Alice had another three or four hours to go if she was to make it to another day.

She had wore herself out and was still with exhaustion. But she had that terrible look on her face, like she was anguished and scared, like she was crazy as people said she was. People will rumor anything. But she never was sick in her mind really, like they told it on her. She was just simple, childlike. People will spread around the worst things they can think of.

But because she was afflicted the family would never take her nowheres, not to school or church singings, or the Fourth of July picnics. Somebody would always have to stay with her, though she begged in her innocence to be carried along. She wanted to go places bad as a little kid does that sees everybody else dressed up and ready to leave. She cried and begged, and they still left her at the house like they was ashamed for anybody to see her. Mama had to go stay with her a lot when she was young, and Grandma before her.

That was how come Grandma and Grandpa got the place, because they agreed to take care of Alice. When Great-Grandma died she left them the house and most of the land for taking care of her and Alice too. That was the way they did things back yonder, leave the place to whoever took care of the old people. Usually it was the youngest that stayed home and done it.

Grandma always hoped Alice would stay in her room when visitors come. That's why the front door was always closed since I was a little girl, cause Alice lived in the front room. I was the only one that went in to see her when we come to visit on Sundays. She'd show me her doll, and talk about play-parties she'd been to, infares and dances. But she made it all up, the way a kid will do.

I remember one time we come over at Christmas in the A-Model truck. That was before I was married. And we carried up a whole sack of presents to the house to put under Grandma's tree. That little room just seemed flooded with presents. I was afraid the house would catch fire there was so much paper scattered around when we started unwrapping. Names would be called out, and there were oohs and aahs and squeals of delight, and "You shouldn't" and "How did you know what I wanted?" I had brought a little box of candy, just a little box of peppermint sticks, for Alice. And I stood up to take it to her room. She never did eat with the family or join in much by the fireplace.

"I'm giving this to Alice," I said.

"Oh the shame," Mama said. "I forgot to bring her a thing." And I could see Mama was hurt to think she had forgot Alice at Christmas. But that was the way things turned out most of the time.

I must have been sleeping because when I looked at my watch it was four thirty-eight. The lamp was still burning, but the room seemed different. It was real still, inside the house and out. It was like something had been there and just gone. Alice was sleeping, but there was a kind of catch in her breath, and a faint gurgling in her throat. I didn't know if it meant anything or not. Her face was relaxed, though it still showed the lines of the earlier struggle.

There was that smell in the house again, the odor I had caught when I first walked in the day before. It was a peculiar old house smell, akin to the scent of coffee soaked into the wood for a hundred years, along with smoke from the fireplace, and mothballs in the big wardrobe, old wool and yellow newspapers. But I couldn't describe the scent itself; it was of age, and dust in rugs. Added to the kerosene smell of the lamp was that other smell, like some electric spark, a warm radio, though there was no radio in the house.

I looked around for Alice's doll, but couldn't see it anywhere. It must be under the bedcovers. She would never have lost it or thrown it away.

In the still every pop and creak of the house sounded like growing pains. I thought of a ship out at sea, the way they say it will groan and creak as the wood gives with the waves.

The skin on Alice's forehead gleamed almost as white as her hair. It was smoother than most old people's skin, and I thought she was lucky in a way to have never growed up, in the times she had lived through. When she was a girl the trains hadn't even come into the mountains, and she lived through the wars with never a worry about them. Now people flew everyplace, and they talked about going to the moon. She had lived through the Depression and didn't know a thing about it while she carried water every day up the hill and set under the pines above the meadow, or sipped coffee in her room. I hated it that her mind was troubled now.

There was a longer gurgle in her throat and her breath come in little jumps and then stopped. I was going to run to get Myrt and Annie, but realized there was nothing any of us could do. Alice's mouth fell open and her head turned sideways a little. Her eyes was closed and there was a long sigh of air coming out of her chest.

It was so still I kept waiting for her to breathe again. But she didn't. "Alice," I said, but she didn't respond. Her face started to relax until it was completely placid. I know people like to talk about how somebody smiles or sees angels or kinfolks that have already passed on when they die, but it was nothing like that. She was dead and her face seemed plain and untroubled. It was a beautiful death.

———————

Robert Morgan was born in 1944 in Henderson-ville, North Carolina, and grew up on the family farm in the nearby Green River valley. He has published nine books of poetry, most recently *Green River: New and Selected Poems*, in 1991. His books of stories are *The Blue Valleys*, 1989, and *The Mountains Won't Remember Us*, 1992. *Good Measure*, a book of essays and interviews about poetry, will be published by LSU Press in 1993. He has received fellowships from the National Endowment for the Arts, the Guggenheim and Rockefeller foundations, and the New York Foundation for the Arts. In 1991 he was given the James G. Hanes Poetry Prize by the Fellowship of Southern Writers, and the North Carolina Award in Literature.

PHOTO CREDIT: ROBERTO CELLI

Years ago I wrote a poem called "Death Crown." Ever since I was a kid in the Blue Ridge mountains I'd heard stories about the feathers in a pillow meshing themselves into a crown around the head of a saintly dying person. But the real beginning of the story, "Death Crown," came when I imagined Ellen talking. I just listened to her voice and let her tell the story. I did hear a relative once describe visiting a great-aunt and, realizing the aunt was dying, staying with her to the end. And I did have a great-great-aunt who had the mind of a child, supposedly because she was once afflicted with "white swelling" fever. People used to describe *death as though it were a work of art, or an ultimate test of character, or both. You could tell something important about a person by the expression on the face of the corpse. Modern medicine has robbed us of some of the drama of the ritual of death which has meant so much to the living. The old ways were not easier, but sometimes they meant more.*

Alison Baker

CLEARWATER AND LATISSIMUS

(from *Ontario Review*)

School had been in session for a couple of weeks when Miss Nancy told us the Siamese twins would be in our class. She said we should be kind. "We want them to feel at home, don't we," she said. I was in love with Miss Nancy, who was large and flat and had browny-gold hair curled up around her face. "We want them to live happy, normal lives." How anyone could expect this is beyond me now, but every six-year-old nodded solemnly, gazing at Miss Nancy's curls as she nodded too.

The next morning the first thing we saw was the double wheel-chair, a frightening object in itself, parked at the end of the second row of desks. A colored boy with a huge forehead sat in it, propped up with pillows, and another one, with a normal-sized head, sat so close they seemed to be hugging each other. This one was grinning, and he had the whitest teeth I had ever seen.

Their names were Clearwater and Latissimus Dorsey, and they were joined at the chest. The doctors said that one heart kept the blood circulating through both bodies, and that it was mostly inside Clearwater. Which was a shame, because Clearwater was the dim one: sweet, always smiling, but never said a word until he was four years old, and that's all that ever came—an occasional word, a phrase, a sigh, a movement of the hands. He was said to have water on the brain, and his head was misshapen; he lay back smiling, weak, perhaps paler than his twin, though they were both chocolate brown, with gleaming black hair.

Latissimus was bright, active, and loud. "I can walk," he said to each child who came in the door. "It's Clearwater who can't. I can walk beside him if I want to." No one answered him. We sat down in our chairs, and tried not to look at the place where the Siamese twins were attached. Binky Pilcher was so nervous he wet his pants. Miss Nancy sent him down to the nurses's office so the nurse could call his mother to bring dry clothes. Nobody laughed at him.

"I wouldn't pee my pants," Latissimus said in a loud voice. "It's Clearwater who never got toilet-trained. If I peed my pants it would break my mama's heart."

Barbara Nixon whispered that Latissimus looked like a baby bird, chirping and blinking and looking around. "Clearwater," she said, "is still an egg."

By the end of the week everyone was a Siamese twin. All over the playground children were smushed up against each other's chests, walking sideways, playing Siamese hopscotch, climbing the monkey bars in pairs. After a while someone decided you could be joined anywhere; then people walked around with their big toes together, or their hind ends, or the tops of their heads. Streams of Siamese twins passed down Elm Street on the way home from school, hip to hip, cheek to cheek, knee to knee. Wherever you were joined, though, was the place your heart was. You always shared a heart with your Siamese twin.

At recess Latissimus held center stage, Clearwater smiling beside him. "I am probably a mathematical genius," Latissimus said happily to the table full of first graders. "It's the one thing my mama has to be thankful for." Clearwater clutched his milk carton, sucking the milk up through the straw; from time to time

Latissimus gave him a piece of graham cracker. Clearwater, his heavy head against the pillow, couldn't lean forward far enough to pick it up himself.

"What's that?" Barbara asked.

"I can do square roots," Latissimus said. He wiped soggy graham cracker off his brother's face.

"Can't you ever be by yourself?" Jack Turnbull asked.

"Can't you even go to the bathroom by yourself?" Ricky Bob Pugh asked; and no one snickered, because we were dying to find out.

"Nope," said Latissimus. He grinned around the table, showing his exotic pink gums. Suddenly he leaned over and kissed Barbara right on the mouth.

Barbara screamed and wiped her mouth ferociously on her sleeve. Everyone else screamed too.

"First comes love," we chanted. "Then comes marriage." We faltered; it was difficult to imagine Barbara pushing a baby carriage *and* the double wheelchair.

"I kiss anybody who want it," Latissimus said happily. "I am the Kiss King."

The Venice Kiwanis paid for Latissimus to take a special class in calculus over at the high school, and Mr. Stevens of Wendell Stevens Fine Furniture let Mr. Prince Albert Franklin, the colored man who worked for him, use the delivery truck to drive the twins up there. Every Thursday two of us got to wheel them out the classroom door and down to the front entrance, and wait there with them till Mr. Prince Albert came.

Mr. Prince Albert was the tallest man in town. His legs were like broomsticks, and he towered above us as he stalked down the sidewalk to the door. He was so black he was purple, like the mulberries the starlings pooped all over the sidewalks in the fall, and your heart just about stopped if he looked at you. "How are these sugarboys?" he said every time. "You have a good day in school?"

"We had music today," Latissimus would tell him. Or, "We did Thanksgiving turkeys."

"Is that so," Mr. Prince Albert would say. Clearwater made his little mewing sounds, and Mr. Prince Albert patted him on the head.

Then he turned to us. "These are your bearers today?" he said, gazing down upon us. "Your servitors of the hour?" We nodded proudly and pushed the chair to the curb where Mr. Prince Albert had put the ramp down from the back of the truck. We pushed it up the ramp, with Mr. Prince Albert giving us a hand, and he lashed it in place with a canvas belt, right behind the driver's seat. "An excellent job," he would say to us in the gloom of the truck. "You will be rewarded hereafter."

And we ran down the ramp, which he pulled up behind us like a drawbridge, and we watched from the sidewalk as they drove away before we went back to the classroom, strangely empty without the Siamese twins.

"I think," my mother said, taking a long drag of her Kent cigarette, "it is a sin."

Auntie Toots leaned over and stuck a new cigarette on the end of my mother's and drew on it till it glowed. On mornings after she'd been there I picked her cigarette butts out of the ashtrays and sucked off the lipstick, pretending I was short-haired and skinny and gorgeous, just like her. "The risk was too great," she said.

"What kind of life can it be?" my mother said. She sounded angry. "They should have been separated at birth."

"Who would have got the heart?" Auntie Toots said. She got up and dropped more ice cubes in their glasses and poured more scotch.

"That's why LaVonda should have done it then," my mother said. "Before she got attached to them."

"Right," Auntie Toots said. "What if it had been Vera and Birdie? And you had to choose one or the other."

I held my breath, but suddenly they looked up, to where I was joined at the waist to the bannister on the landing. "Who's out of bed?" my mother said sharply.

"Nothing," I said, confused. And after Auntie Toots had gotten me a glass of water, and my mother had tucked me back in, I lay back on my pillow and stared into the dark. My head felt funny; I felt like Clearwater. I imagined my sister Birdie beside me, stuck to my chest and breathing asthmatically into my face. I imagined Dr. Wells standing beside us, a carving knife raised over his head.

The Siamese twins were late getting back from Christmas vacation. "I've got my own heart!" Latissimus shouted as they came in the door. They had a new wheelchair; Clearwater was still strapped in among pillows, but instead of sitting on the other side Latissimus walked between the wheels, holding onto a bar and pushing the chair himself.

They had been to specialists in Chicago. "Right here," Latissimus said, pointing to where they were joined. "There's *two* hearts, right together. One for each of us." With their sophisticated equipment the big-city doctors had detected a second heartbeat, faint but distinct.

"Does that mean you'll get separated?" Barbara asked. She was Latissimus's girlfriend now, but she still screamed when he kissed her. I hated her; I had fallen out of love with Miss Nancy and into love with Latissimus.

"Maybe," Latissimus said. He leaned over and checked Clearwater's lap belt. "Look at this chair. I'm supposed to get lots of exercise."

Latissimus not only pushed the new chair, he ran with it, careering down the halls, tearing across the gymnasium floor. He joined in handicap races, with Clearwater as the handicap. When spring came he even played softball with us, under new rules he made up himself: when he was at bat, the pitcher had to be extra gentle, and when he got a hit, the basemen had to count to seven before throwing the ball, to give him a head start. It was only fair. Latissimus made it sometimes, too, racketing into first base, Clearwater bouncing and screaming in delight.

One day during recess I ran inside to go to the rest room, and Clearwater and Latissimus were just coming out of the boys' room. I was suddenly shy; I had never been alone with them before.

"Hi, Vera," said Latissimus.

"Hi," I said. Up close I could see that his eyelashes were actually curly.

"My heart is getting very strong," he said. He and Clearwater came close to where I stood waiting for them to leave so I could go into the girls' room. "Do you want to feel my heartbeat?"

I could not speak, but he took it as assent, a trait I have since recognized in other men. "Here." He took my hand and placed it on their chest, on the seam where their T-shirts were sewn together. "Can you feel it, Vera?" Latissimus asked, looking anxiously into my eyes. "Can you feel which one is mine?"

"I think so," I whispered. I could feel only heat, the heat from their bodies and from my own hot hand, but it was the first gift a boy had ever offered me, and I didn't want him to be disappointed.

"It's getting very strong," he said again. He reached over and kissed my lips, and he smelled like grass that has sat for a day in the sun. "You can be my girlfriend too," he said, and I smiled at Clearwater, who was smiling at me.

What no one had expected was that as Latissimus got stronger, so did Clearwater. One day Miss Nancy noticed that Clearwater was watching her pointer as she tapped it across the blackboard, pointing at new words. "Why, Latissimus!" she said. "Clearwater is paying attention!"

"Oh, yes ma'am," Latissimus said. "He pays attention to everything." We all stared at Clearwater, and before our eyes he changed. Or, rather, we saw that he *had* changed. Instead of smiling at anything, now he smiled at *things*: at Miss Nancy's pointer, at the bell for recess, into the eyes of Jill Redenbaugh when she handed him a crayon. He didn't use the crayon, but he looked at it, and he turned it over to look at the other end.

"I believe his color is a little better, too," said Miss Nancy, and then she blushed and said quickly, "he looks so healthy."

It was true: his skin, which used to hold a touch of gray, a hint of *pale,* was dark and shiny, like his twin's.

By the end of the school year Clearwater was sitting up straight and drawing pictures on manila paper while we practiced printing words. He drew the same thing again and again: a big round head with little circle eyes and stick limbs poking out of it, the kind of people we had all drawn long ago, when we were young. "They look like Clearwater," Jack Turnbull said, but when we laughed and turned to look, we saw it wasn't true anymore. Clearwater was filling out. His head used to look huge above his useless little body, his skinny arms and legs, but now his arms were rounded with muscles from reaching for crayons, and his neck was full and sinewy.

Latissimus looked up from the equations he was working on his own paper. "He wears my same size now," he said, and we saw that Clearwater and Latissimus were more than just Siamese twins; they were identical, the same size, the same color, the same bright and chirpy look. If they hadn't been stuck together, if they could have changed sides now and then, we might never have told them apart again.

On the last day Latissimus told us that he and Clearwater were moving to Chicago. "Mr. Prince Albert Franklin driving us up in the truck," he said. "Us and our furniture and our mama. She got a new job there."

We had heard of Chicago; the only rock 'n' roll station Venice could pick up came from Chicagoland. But none of us had ever been there.

"That's a big city, isn't it, Latissimus?" said Miss Nancy. "It will be different living there."

"We going to school at a university." Latissimus said. "Every-body is smart there."

"Clearwater too?" someone said.

"Might be. Probably." Latissimus grinned.

"We'll miss you, Clearwater and Latissimus," Miss Nancy said. She walked over and hugged them both.

"Will you miss us?" Jack called.

Latissimus leaned his head to one side and shrugged, and Clearwater, grinning, shrugged too. "Might be," Latissimus said. "Mama says we be happier among our own kind."

"I doubt they'll get another girlfriend," Barbara said as we walked home.

"No," I said. "We're it forever." We joined ourselves at the elbow and skipped the rest of the way.

We didn't hear much about them after they left. Auntie Toots heard from someone at work that they were settled in a nice apartment, close enough for Latissimus to walk them to school, and that the doctors were treating them free of charge because they were such an interesting case. When you are young the people you love become blurred in your recollection, because you are adding so many more as you go along. When we went back to school in the fall we were no longer the babies of the school, we were second graders, and we had a new teacher, and new responsibilities.

So we never asked, and were never told, about the operation that would separate Clearwater and Latissimus; the operation that made them healthy, normal boys. Clearwater, on his own, learned to draw more realistic people, and to read, and to run; and Latissimus, free at last, ran faster, and slowly lost his aptitude for numbers, and dropped out of high school and lost himself in the streets; and Clearwater became a janitor.

Or the operation was not a success. It was Clearwater alone who survived, and who lost the little progress he'd made in his few months with us, and sits now, as we all enter middle age, tied alone in the wheelchair, with a vague dim impression in his feeble mind that once he was connected to something bright, something loud, and raced to first base amid cheers.

We never heard. And when they became indistinct, and forgotten, we were left with an impression that had something to do with Latissimus's last words to us: that he and Clearwater would be happy in Chicago, among their own kind. It didn't occur to us that he meant anything besides this: that Chicago was a city of Siamese twins, where everybody had someone who shared his heart.

Alison Baker lives in southwestern Oregon.

PHOTO CREDIT: HANS RILLING

"*Clearwater and Latissimus*" *was not written in the South, nor about the South, nor by a Southerner. But the story's set in Indiana, which is not unlike a southern state, particularly in its small towns; and it has about it a sense of lost innocence, of a lost world, that can be called southern. And the fact is that, from the moment I started writing this story, whenever I stopped to read parts of it aloud—which I often do when I'm working—I read it in an atrocious, inauthentic, but unmistakably southern accent. I can read it in no other voice. So the story knew itself before I ever did.*

THE WINNOWING OF MRS. SCHUPING

(from *The New Yorker*)

Mrs. Schuping lived on a moribund estate that had once been grand enough in trees alone that a shipbuilder scouting live oaks in the eighteenth century had bought the tract for wood to make warships for the British navy. Oak of that sort, when fitted and shipped into six-inch walls, would not merely withstand or absorb cannonballs but repel them a good way toward their source. Mrs. Schuping did not know this, but she knew she had big old trees, and she patted their flanks when she strolled the grounds.

The house had died. So slatternly, so ratty was it that Mrs. Schuping was afraid to enter it again once she had worked up the courage to go out of it, which was more dangerous. She had been hit by boards twice while leaving the house but never when going in.

There was no such thing as falling-down insurance, an actuarial nicety that flabbergasted and enraged Mrs. Schuping. Falling down was what really plagued houses, therefore that was what you could not protect them from by lottery.

She called herself *Mrs.* Schuping arbitrarily. She had no husband nor had she ever found in the least logical the idea of having one man whom you so designated. Wholly preposterous.

She had a good toaster. It was a four-slice commercial stainless square job, missing its push-down knobs, so that you had to depress the naked notched metal thingies to lower the bread. It looked like you'd need a rag to protect your hand, but you did not. Perhaps if you were hustling breakfasts in a good diner you might, but not slowly, at home. Life was winnowing for Mrs. Schuping.

When she bought the house, she had found a huge collection of opera records, of which she knew nothing except that they sounded ridiculous. This collection she played dutifully, over and over, until it was memorized, until it could not be said that she was ignorant of opera. When she had mastered the collection, she wondered why, and she sailed the records, one by one, into the swamp behind the rotting house. She winnowed the collection of opera records until it was a collection of cardboard boxes, and eventually used those to set her first swamp fire.

Setting the swamp on fire was not a winnowing of her life, but it did winnow the swamp. The burnings seemed to her rather naughty and frivolous, and surprisingly agreeable to look at and to smell. She took an unadult pleasure in them, along with an adult fear that she might be somehow breaking the law even though the swamp was hers.

The second time she set the mangy tangled tract on fire the sheriff showed up, and she became sure it was the case that you could not burn your own swamp. The sheriff, whom she had not met before, confirmed her anxiety with his opening remark.

"Your *swamp* is on fire," he said, standing about fifteen feet off her right shoulder and slightly behind her.

She turned to him and said, not knowing what in hell else she might, "Yes, it is."

The sheriff stood there regarding first her and then the swamp and the fire, which gave his face a jack-o'-lantern orange sheen, and said again, "The swamp is *on fire*." The emphasis was meant to confirm his sympathies with having fires, and upon establishing that bond he walked briskly to Mrs. Schuping's side and planted his feet and crossed his arms and cocked back to watch the fire with her in an attitude that suggested he would be content to watch for a good long while. When he breathed, his belt and holster creaked.

Mrs. Schuping could not tell if his affection for the fire was genuine or a trap of the infamous misdirectional-innocuous-talk type favored by country police.

So she said two things. "Sheriff, I set my opera-collection boxes on fire; I confess they were in the swamp." Then, "Sheriff, I do not need a man."

The sheriff looked at the fire, followed it up into the high parts where it licked at the grapevines climbing on the tupelo gums. It was a hot yellow heat in the slack black-ass muddy gloom of a nothing swamp that needed it. He had been taking pure aesthetic enjoyment from the thing until Mrs. Schuping said what she said, which reminded him that they were not free to enjoy this mayhem and that he had to undo her concern with his presence. Concern with his presence was—more than his actual presence— *his job* ordinarily; it was how he made his living. This was the hardest thing about being sheriff: you could not go off duty. A city cop could. They even provided locker rooms and showers for them, and he imagined laundry and dry-cleaning takeout services for the uniforms. But a sheriff was the sheriff, and he was always, always up to something. That is why he had had to talk like a fool to this woman to get her to let him watch her fire with her. How else excuse standing in front of five burning acres and saying "on fire"? But it had not worked. And this *man* thing.

"Mizz Shoop, I just—"

"It's Schuping," Mrs. Schuping said.

"Yes'm. I know. I just like to call you Shoop, though."

With this the sheriff again squared off, with a sigh, to watch the fire, whatever he had been about to say cut off by Mrs. Schuping's correcting him. He hoped he had begun the dismantling of her concerns with his presence, both legal and sexual. He was aware that he had not done much toward either end, but he did not want to babble while watching a good fire. Unless she asked him off the property, he'd hold his ground.

Mrs. Schuping was content, having posted her nolo contendere on the fire and her *no desire* on the man, to let him stand there and breathe and creak if he wanted to. She had been a little hard on the sheriff, she thought. It was the legal part that worried her into overstating the sexual part. Not *over*stating, *mis*stating: she did not need a man, but wanting was another question. And if all you had to do to get a big creaking booger like this one was set your backyard on fire, she was all for it.

Four months later the sheriff and Mrs. Schuping had their second date. He saw the smoke from the interstate, where he was parked behind the Starvin' Marvin billboard at such a ridiculous pitch that takeoff was nearly vertical and he resisted blasting off for speeders unless provoked entirely. What had been provoking him entirely lately was college kids with their feet out the windows of BMWs, headed for Dade County, Florida, with their socks on. That was making him strike, lift-off or no lift-off. He wondered what it was like for a bass. How some lures got by and some did not. For him it was *pink socks*. In the absence of pink socks, there was smoke over the Fork Swamp.

Mrs. Schuping looked even more fire-lovely than she had at the first fire. This time she saw him before he spoke.

"There won't be a problem with the permit," the sheriff said, instead of the idiocies of last time. There was no problem with the permit because there was no permit, but he thought this was a good way to address those concerns of hers.

The sheriff had lost a little weight. Mrs. Schuping had been on intellectual winnowing excursions, and she saw as a matter of vector analogy the trajectory of the sheriff toward her and the swale of her sexual self. He had a swag or a sway—something— of gut that suggested, even if a bit cartoonishly, a lion. This big fat tub could get on *top* of her, she thought, with no identifiable emotion, looking at the crisp, shrieking, blistering fire she had set with no more ado than a Bic lighter jammed open and a pot she didn't want anymore full of gasoline.

The sheriff took a slow survey of the fire, which was magnificent, and loyal—her little swamp was neatly set on a fork of creeks so that the fire could not get away—and turning back he caught a glance of Mrs. Schuping's profile as she watched the fire and, he thought, him a little, and down a bit he saw her breasts, rather sticking out and firm-looking in the dusky, motley, scrabbled light. Bound up in a sweater and what looked like a salmon-colored bra, through the swamp smoke stinging your eyes, on a forty-year-old woman they could take your breath away. He made to go.

"Good cool fire, Mizz Shoop," the sheriff said. "I've got to go."

"You're leaving, Sheriff?"

"It's business, purely business."

To the sheriff she seemed relaxed, legally, and there is *nothing* like a big Ford *pawhoooorn* exit—a little air, a little air and a little time.

Mrs. Schuping had been through every consciousness and semiconsciousness and unconsciousness and raised- and lowered-consciousness program contributing to every good conscience and bad conscience and middle struggling conscience there is. But now she was a woman in a house so falling apart that the children had taken it off the haunted register, and she was boiling an egg on a low blue flame. Outside were the large, dark, low-armed oaks.

Also outside, beyond the oaks, were the smoldering ignoble trees. The white, acrid, thin smoke drifting up their charred trunks was ugly. The swamp had powers of recovery that were astounding, though. It was this magical resilience that confirmed Mrs. Schuping as an avid swamp burner. When the swamp came back hairier than it had been before the burning, thicker and nastier, she found the argument for necessary periodic burning, which was of course a principle in good forestry. She was not a pyromaniac, she was a land steward. The trees stood out there fuming and hissing and steaming. Her life continued to winnow.

Beyond the disassembly of her opera holdings, Mrs. Schuping had gradually let go of her once prodigious reading. She had read in all topical lay matters. She had taught herself calculus, and could read *Scientific American* without skipping the math. She had taught herself to weld and briefly tried to sculpt in metal. She gave this up after discovering that all she wanted to sculpt, ever, was a metal sphere, and she could not do it.

She had dallied similarly in hydroponics, artificial intelligence, military science, and dress designing. She had read along Great Book lines and found them mostly a yawn, except for the Great Pornography Books, for which there seemed to be no modern equivalent. She had stopped going out to concerts and movies, etc., which she had done specifically to improve herself, because it got to where after every trip on the long drive back to the ruined estate she wondered what was so damned *given* about improving oneself. The opposite idea seemed at least as tenable. As her tires got worse, it seemed even more tenable, and she began to embrace the idea of winnowing: travel less, do less, it *is* more. She found a grocery that still delivered, and she picked up her box of groceries on the front porch—as far as the boys would go.

At first she regretted the winnowing, but then she did not: she had had a mind, but nothing had properly got in its way. That happens. The same for bodies: there were good athletes in this world who had never had the right field or the right ball get in their way. It was particle physics when you got down to it, and the numbers of people in the world today and the numbers of things to occupy them made the mechanics of successful collision difficult. So she'd burn her swamp, pat her good trees, cook her egg. She had one old clock radio, a GE in a vanilla plastic cabinet with a round dial for a tuner, which she played at night. If there were storms she listened to the static of lightning.

When the swamp had returned in its briary vitriolic vengeance, reminding her of a beard coming out of a face that was too close to hers, she set it afire a fourth time. The fire went taller than before, so she walked around to the front of the house to see if you could see it from there and, if you could, if it looked like the house was on fire, and there was the sheriff, parking his car.

He rolled down the window and said, "I've got you two puppies." She looked in at the front seat and saw that he did. All puppies are cute, but these seemed abnormally cute. She discarded, immediately, protest. She was not going to be the sort, no matter how holed up and eccentric, to refuse a dog because of the responsibility and other nonsense.

"What kind are they?"

"The kind dogfighters give me just before they have themselves a convention." The sheriff opened the door and let the puppies out and got out himself. They all walked back to the fire. At one point the sheriff misjudged the ground and veered sharply into Mrs. Schuping and nearly knocked her down. He was so big and tight that he felt like the oak walls of the ships that flung cannonballs back, which Mrs. Schuping did not know had made her trees, under which they now walked, attractive to a shipbuilder two hundred years before.

The fire was a good one. There was a screaming, out of human register, as oxygen and carbon clawed each other to pieces, going through peat and leaf and the dirt that somehow stayed up in the leaves, even when it rained, giving the swamp its dusty look that would never be right for *National Geographic*. The dirt in the trees presumably turned to glass, and maybe that was why, Mrs. Schuping thought, the fire always sounded like things breaking. Tiny things breaking, a big fiery bull in the shop.

Without an inkling of premeditation, she turned to the sheriff, who was breathing and creaking there in standard fashion, and balled her fist, and very slowly brought it to his stomach and ground it mock-menacingly into him as far as it would go, which was about an inch. At this the sheriff put his hand on the back of her neck and did not look from the fire. They regarded the fire in that attitude, and the puppies romped, and in the strange orange

light they all looked posed for a family portrait at a discount
department store.

Before going into the house, the sheriff knocked the mud off
his boots, then decided that would not do and took his boots off
and left them outside the back door on the porch. Mrs. Schuping
put two eggs on to boil. The sheriff, who she thought might go
three hundred pounds, should not eat an egg, she knew, but it
was what you ate after a swamp fire—boiled hard, halved, heavy
salt and pepper, and tasting somehow of smoke—and it was all
she had, anyway.

They peeled the eggs at the metal table and put the shells in the
aluminum pot the eggs had cooked in. Mrs. Schuping peeled hers
neatly, no more than four pieces of shell, but the sheriff rolled his
on the table under his palm until it was a fine mosaic. He rubbed
the tiny bits of shell off with his thumb.

When the sheriff came out of the bathroom and stood by
the bed, Mrs. Schuping became frightened beyond the normal,
understandable apprehensions a woman can have before going to
bed with a new man, especially the largest one it is conceivable
to go to bed with. She also had a concern for the bed itself, and
even for the structural capacity of the house—but that was hysterical; the sheriff was safely upstairs, and no matter what he did
he would not get any heavier. Something else frightened her. It
was as if a third party were in the room, a kind of silent presence,
and then she realized what it was. The sheriff, naked, without his
creaking leather, was quiet for the first time, a soundless man. It
gave her goose bumps.

"Get in."

Mrs. Schuping decided it was best to trust a man this large in
the execution of his own desire, and let him near-smother her.
He made a way for air for her over one of his shoulders and
began what he was about, which seemed to be an altogether private program at first but then got better, until she could tell that

the sheriff was not simply a locomotive on his own track, and things got evenly communal, traces of smoky fire in the room, but enough air. Mrs. Schuping thought of winnowing and sailing records and her mother and of how long a gizzard has to cook to be tender, how much longer than a liver, and she lost track until she heard the sheriff breathing, about to die like a catfish on a hot sidewalk, and stop.

"Mizz Shoop," the sheriff said, when he could talk, "this is my philosophy of life and it proves it. Almost everything can happen. Yingyang."

"What would be an example, Sheriff?"

"Well—this," he said, his arms arcing in the space over them and reballasting the bed. "And did you hear about them boys killed that girl for p—excuse me. For sex?"

The sheriff then related the details of a rape case he had worked on. It was not the sort of talk she expected to follow a First Time, but she let him go on and found that she did not mind it. The sheriff had set in motion the pattern of rude and somewhat random speech that would follow their lovemaking in the high springy bed under the ripped ceiling. You would be allowed to say whatever was on your mind without regard to etiquette or setting. Once, it embarrassed her to recall, she declaimed apropos of nothing while they were still breathless, "Listen. I have a father and a mother. I'm a *real person.*"

To this the sheriff firmly rejoined, "I think the whole goddam country has lost its fucking mind."

"I don't doubt it," Mrs. Schuping said.

They could talk like this for hours, their meanings rarely intersecting. The last thing the sheriff said before leaving that first night was, "Fifty pounds in the morning. They'll be all right under the porch." Mrs. Schuping slept well, wondering fifty pounds of what under the house before she drifted off.

The sheriff had initiated a pattern with this remark, too, but she did not know it. She would find that the sheriff was given to talking about things that he did not bother to preface or explain, and that she preferred not asking what the hell he was talking about. Whatever the hell he was talking about would become apparent, and so far the sheriff had delivered no unwanted surprises. She saw just about what she was getting.

In the river of her winnowing life, the sheriff represented a big boulder in the bed of the dwindling stream. It eventually would be eroded from underneath and would settle and maybe sink altogether. Mrs. Schuping, therefore, did not find the facts of her aggressively winnowing life and the solid, vigorous mass of her new man to be in conflict at all.

She had never known a man so *naturally* unrefined. Despite his bulk, the sheriff gave her a good feeling. That was as specific as she could be about it. He gives me a good feeling, she thought, marveling at the suspicious simplicity of the sentiment.

She had a dream of going into the swamp and finding her opera records unharmed and retrieving them and playing them for the sheriff, who, as his appreciation of them increased, began to dance with her in a ballroom that somehow appeared in her house, the operas having become waltzes, and began to lose weight, becoming as slender as a bullfighter; then, in the swamp again, she found the records hung in the trees and melted into long, twisted shapes that suggested, of all things, the severely herniated intestines of a chimpanzee she had once seen in a cheap roadside wild-animal attraction. She woke up glad to wake up. She would look for no records and wish no diet upon the sheriff. "Have my *head* examined," she muttered, getting out of bed.

In a very vague way Mrs. Schuping had decided—before the decisions and lack of decisions that set her life on its course of winnowing—that having her head examined was going to be the certain price if she did not begin to clear a few, or many, things out of it. She saw at the end of theories of consciousness and lay physics and broad familiarity with things topical and popular a wreck of the mind, her mind, on the rocks of pointless business and information. None of that knowledge, good or bad, simple or sophisticated, was ever going to allow her to do anything except more of *it:* drive another eighty miles to another touring concert or exhibition, read another article on the mating dynamics of the American anole.

She decided that a green lizard doing push-ups with his little red centerboard coming out of his throat was one thing, but if she *read* about it anymore, saw any more stylized drawings of "distensible throat flaps" on vectors heading for each other like units in a war game, she was going to be in trouble. This was a petty, flighty kind of fed-upness to reach, and not carefully thought out, she knew, but she did not care. If you looked carefully at bee No. W-128, who was vibrating at such and such a frequency, wagging his butt at 42° on the compass . . . God. Of all her prewinnowing interests, this arcane science was her favorite, yet, oddly enough, it was the first to go. It had looked insupportable in a way that, say, *Time* had not. Yet over the years she had decided, once *Time* etc. had also been abandoned, that the lizards and bees and flow mechanics were supportable in the extreme by comparison—as were the weirdly eclectic opera records more justified than the morning classical-music shows on public radio—but once she had opted for winnowing there was no pulling back. "I'm going *beyond* Walden," she told herself, and soon thereafter began eying the cluttered swamp, which was not simple enough.

So she winnowed to prevent having her head examined. If it were to be, she wanted them to find nothing in it. She knew enough about the process. Her mother had had *her* head examined, many times. Mrs. Schuping did not like her mother, so that was all she needed to know about having your head examined. Not for her.

She looked out the window that morning and saw a man with a white stripe down each pant leg walk away from the house and get in a yellow truck, which then drove off. When she investigated she found a fifty-pound sack of dog food on the porch and the two puppies scratching at it very fast, as if they would dig in spoonfuls to China.

*   *   *

After their first night together, the sheriff arrived without Mrs. Schuping's having to set the swamp on fire. The sheriff had established the two things he would do for or to Mrs. Schuping. One was talk trash in bed and the other was supply her with goods and services that came through his connections as sheriff. After the dog food, which had belonged to the county police dogs until her puppies got it, a crew of prisoners showed up one morning and painted the entire porch, which surrounded her house, with yellow road paint, giving the house the look of a cornball flying saucer about to take off. The sheriff appeared that night—the fluorescent paint more than ever inspectable then— beaming with pride. He did not remark upon it directly or ask Mrs. Schuping how she liked it, but from his face, which in its pride nearly partook of the same yellow glow, it was obvious that he was sure she liked her hideous new paint job. She could not deny it.

She had watched the crew from a lawn chair, drinking coffee while they changed her haunted-looking, unpainted, unannounced house into something like ballpark mustard with mica in it, and never asked them what they thought they were doing. Nor had she asked the man with the shotgun what he was doing. And now it did not seem proper to ask the sheriff. The dog food was done, the porch under which the puppies were to live was done, and something else would be done, and it was in the spirit of winnowing to let it be done.

But in bed that night, before they got to the sheriff's spontaneous trash talking, she did let out one question.

"Listen," she said. "Isn't this, prisoners and . . ." She made a kind of scalloping motion with her hand in the air, where he could see it. "I appreciate it, but isn't it . . . *graft* or something?"

The sheriff took a deep breath as if impatient, but she already knew he would not, if he were impatient, show it; he was a man who could talk about rape in bed, but in other important ways he was a gentleman. He was breathing to compose.

"If you see something I have," he said, "there is something behind it I have given." He breathed for a while.

"Law is a series of *deals*," he said next, "and so is law enforcement." More breathing. "Nobody in law en*force*ment, unlike *law*, makes money *near* what the time goes into it."

They looked at the ceiling.

"If you don't do Wall Street, this is how you do it." A deep sigh.

"That dogfighter I got your puppies from made fifteen thousand dollars the next week in one *hour*, and I let him do it, and I did not take a dime. You have two good dogs he would have knocked in the head."

Mrs. Schuping was sorry she had asked and never did again. But if she saw the sheriff studying something about the place she might attempt to steer him off. He seemed to look askance at her mixed and beat-up pots and pans one night, and, fearful that he would strip the county-prison kitchen of its commercial cookware—perhaps inspired by the odd presence of her commercial toaster—and stuff it all into hers, she informed him casually that broken-in pots were a joy to handle.

She missed his citing for the deck and the boardwalk into the swamp, however. The one clue, mumbled in his sleep, "Ground Wolmanized, that'll be hard," she did not know how to interpret until the ground-contact-rated, pressure-treated posts were being put in the yard behind her house and on back into the swamp by black fellows with posthole diggers and the largest, shiniest, knottiest, most gruesome and handsome arms she had ever seen.

She watched them, as she had watched the housepainters, this time putting brandy in her coffee—something she had tried once before and not liked the taste of. Sitting there drinking spiked coffee, she felt herself becoming a character in the gravitational pull of the sheriff despite, she realized, efforts nearly all her life not to become a character—except for calling herself Mrs. Schuping.

The boardwalk through the thinned swamp looked miraculous, as if the burning had been a plan of architectural landscaping. The handsome, lean swamp, the walk suggesting a miniature railroad trestle going out into it, resembled a park. If you winnowed and got down pretty clean and were normal, she thought, and something happened—like a big-bubba sheriff and thousands of dollars of windfall contracting and a completely different kind of life than you had had—and you started becoming a character, and you paid nothing for it and did not scheme for it, and it reversed your winnowing, and you liked brandy suddenly, at least in coffee, while watching men who put classical sculpture to shame, was it your fault?

Padgett Powell's books include *Edisto, A Woman Named Drawn*, and *Typical*. He teaches in the creative writing program at the University of Florida.

PHOTO CREDIT: GEOFF WINNINGHAM

"*The Winnowing of Mrs. Schuping*" *was written in Istanbul, apparently inspired, if one may presume, by the author's reading of bad, late Hemingway to prepare himself to talk to Turks about good, early Hemingway. The very good Efes Pilsen beer and loud playing of the Fine Young Cannibals and John Hyatt and Robert Palmer also must figure somehow in the birth of Mrs. Schuping, who was known as Mrs. Xylophone until better minds at* The New Yorker *stepped in with cash.*

James Lee Burke

TEXAS CITY, 1947

(from *The Southern Review*)

Right after WWII everybody in southern Louisiana thought he was going to get rich in the oil business. My father convinced himself that all his marginal jobs in the oil fields would one day give him the capital to become an independent wild-catter, perhaps even a legendary figure like Houston's Glenn McCarthy, and he would successfully hammer together a drilling operation out of wooden towers and rusted junk, punch through the top of a geological dome, and blow salt water, sand, chains, pipe casing, and oil into the next parish.

So he worked on as a roughneck on drilling rigs and as a jug-hustler with a seismograph outfit, then began contracting to build board roads in the marsh for the Texaco Company. By mid-1946 he was actually leasing land in the Atchafalaya Basin and over in east Texas. But that was also the year that I developed rheumatic fever and he drove my mother off and brought Mattie home to live with us.

I remember the terrible fight they had the day she left. My mother had come home angry from her waitress job in a beer garden on that burning July afternoon, and without changing out of her pink dress with the white piping on the collar and pockets, she had begun butchering chickens on the stump in the backyard and shucking off their feathers in a big iron caldron of scalding

water. My father came home later than he should have, parked his
pickup truck by the barn, and walked naked to the waist through
the gate with his wadded-up shirt hanging out the back pocket
of his Levi's. He was a dark Cajun, and his shoulders, chest, and
back were streaked with black hair. He wore cowboy boots, a red
sweat-handkerchief tied around his neck, and a rakish straw hat
that had an imitation snakeskin band around the crown.

Headless chickens were flopping all over the grass, and my
mother's forearms were covered with wet chicken feathers.

"I know you been with her. They were talking at the beer
joint," she said, without looking up from where she sat with her
knees apart on a wood chair in front of the steaming caldron.

"I ain't been with nobody," he said, "except with them mosquitoes I been slapping out in that marsh."

"You said you'd leave her alone."

"You children go inside," my father said.

"That gonna make your conscience right 'cause you send them
kids off, you? She gonna cut your throat one day. She been in the
crazy house in Mandeville. You gonna see, Verise."

"I ain't seen her."

"You sonofabitch, I smell her on you," my mother said, and
she swung a headless chicken by its feet and whipped a diagonal
line of blood across my father's chest and Levi's.

"You ain't gonna act like that in front of my children, you," he
said, and started toward her. Then he stopped. "Y'all get inside.
You ain't got no business listening to this. This is between me
and her."

My two older brothers, Weldon and Lyle, were used to our
parents' quarrels, and they went inside sullenly and let the back
screen slam behind them. But my little sister Drew, whom my
mother nicknamed Little Britches, stood mute and fearful and
alone under the pecan tree, her cat pressed flat against her chest.

"Come on, Drew. Come see inside. We're gonna play with the
Monopoly game," I said, and tried to pull her by the arm. But
her body was rigid, her bare feet immobile in the dust.

Then I saw my father's large, square hand go up in the air, saw it come down hard against the side of my mother's face, heard the sound of her weeping, as I tried to step into Drew's line of vision and hold her and her cat against my body, hold the three of us tightly together outside the unrelieved sound of my mother's weeping.

Three hours later her car went through the railing on the bridge over the Atchafalaya River. I dreamed that night that an enormous brown bubble arose from the submerged wreck, and when it burst on the surface her drowned breath stuck against my face as wet and rank as gas released from a grave.

That fall I began to feel sick all the time, as though a gray cloud of mosquitoes were feeding at my heart. During recess at school I didn't play with the other children and instead hung about on the edges of the dusty playground or, when Brother Daniel wasn't looking, slipped around the side of the old redbrick cathedral and sat by myself on a stone bench in a bamboo-enclosed, oak-shaded garden where a statue of Mary rested in a grotto and camellia petals floated in a big goldfish pond. Sometimes Sister Roberta was there saying her rosary.

She was built like a fire hydrant. Were it not for the additional size that the swirl of her black habit and the wings of her veil gave her, she would not have been much larger than the students in her fifth-grade class. She didn't yell at us or hit our knuckles with rulers like the other nuns did, and in fact she always called us "little people" rather than children. But sometimes her round face would flare with anger below her white, starched wimple at issues that to us in our small parochial world seemed of little importance. She told our class once that criminals and corrupt local politicians were responsible for the slot and racehorse machines that were in every drugstore, bar, and hotel lobby in New Iberia, and another time she flung an apple core at a carload of teenagers who were baiting the Negro janitor out by the school incinerator.

She heard my feet on the dead oak leaves when I walked through the opening in the bamboo into the garden. She was seated on the stone bench, her back absolutely erect, the scarlet beads of her rosary stretched across the back of her pale hand like drops of blood. She stopped her prayer and turned her head toward me. Fine white hair grew on her upper lip.

"Do you feel sick again, Billy Bob?" she asked.

"Yes, Sister."

"Come here."

"What?"

"I said come here." Her hand reached out and held my forehead. Then she wiped the moisture off her palm with her fingers. "Have you been playing or running?"

"No, Sister."

"Has your father taken you to a doctor?"

I didn't answer.

"Look at me and answer my question," she said.

"He don't, he doesn't have money right now. He says it's because I had the flu. He boiled some honey and onions for me to eat. It made me feel better. It's true, Sister."

"I need to talk to your father."

She saw me swallow.

"Would he mind my calling him?" she asked.

"He's not home now. He works all the time."

"Will he be home tonight?"

"I'm not sure."

"Who takes care of you at night when he's not home?"

"A lady, a friend of his."

"I see. Come back to the classroom with me. It's too windy out here for you," she said.

"Sister, you don't need to call, do you? I feel okay now. My father's got a lot on his mind now. He really works hard."

"What's wrong in your house, Billy Bob?"

"Nothing. I promise, Sister." I tried to smile. I could taste bile in my throat.

"Don't lie."

"I'm not. I promise I'm not."

"Yes, I can see that clearly. Come with me."

The rest of the recess period she and I sharpened crayons in the empty room with tiny pencil sharpeners, stringing long curlicues of colored wax into the wastebasket. She was as silent and as seemingly self-absorbed as a statue. Just before the bell rang she walked down to the convent and came back with a tube of toothpaste.

"Your breath is bad. Go down to the lavatory and wash your mouth out with this," she said.

Mattie wore shorts and sleeveless blouses with sweat rings under the arms, and in the daytime she always seemed to have curlers in her hair. When she walked from room to room she carried an ashtray with her into which she constantly flicked her lipstick-stained Chesterfields. She had a hard, muscular body, and she didn't close the bathroom door all the way when she bathed, and once I saw her kneeling in the tub, scrubbing her big shoulders and chest with a large, flat brush. The area above her head was crisscrossed with improvised clotheslines from which dripped her wet underthings. Her eyes fastened on mine; I thought she was about to reprimand me for staring at her, but instead her hard-boned, shiny face continued to look back at me with a vacuous indifference that made me feel obscene.

If my father was out of town on a Friday or Saturday night, she fixed our supper (sometimes meat on Friday, the fear in our eyes not worthy of her recognition), put on her blue suit, and sat by herself in the living room, listening to the "Grand Ole Opry" or the "Louisiana Hayride," while she drank apricot brandy from a coffee cup. She always dropped cigarette ashes on her suit and had to spot clean the cloth with dry-cleaning fluid before she drove off for the evening in her old Ford coupe. I don't know where she went on those Friday or Saturday nights, but a boy down the road told me that Mattie used to work in Broussard's

Bar on Railroad Avenue, an infamous area in New Iberia where the women sat on the galleries of the cribs, dipping their beer out of buckets and yelling at the railroad and oil-field workers in the street.

Then one morning when my father was in Morgan City, a man in a new silver Chevrolet sedan came out to see her. It was hot, and he parked his car partly on our grass to keep it in the shade. He wore sideburns, striped brown zoot slacks, two-tone shoes, suspenders, a pink shirt without a coat, and a fedora that shadowed his narrow face. While he talked to her he put one shoe on the car bumper and wiped the dust off it with a rag. Then their voices grew louder and he said, "You like the life. Admit it, you. He ain't given you no wedding ring, has he? You don't buy the cow, no, when you can milk through the fence."

"I am currently involved with a gentleman. I do not know what you are talking about. I am not interested in anything you are talking about," she said.

He threw the rag back inside the car and opened the car door.

"It's always trick, trade, or travel, darlin'," he said. "Same rules here as down on Railroad. He done made you a nigger woman for them children, Mattie."

"Are you calling me a nigra?" she said quietly.

"No, I'm calling you crazy, just like everybody say you are. No, I take that back, me. I ain't calling you nothing. I ain't got to, 'cause you gonna be back. You in the life, Mattie. You be phoning me to come out here, bring you to the crib, rub your back, put some of that warm stuff in your arm again. Ain't nobody else do that for you, huh?"

When she came back into the house she made us take all the dishes out of the cabinets, even though they were clean, and wash them over again.

It was the following Friday that Sister Roberta called. Mattie was already dressed to go out. She didn't bother to turn down the radio when she answered the phone, and in order to compete with Red Foley's voice she had to almost shout into the receiver.

"Mr. Sonnier is not here," she said. "Mr. Sonnier is away on business in Texas City . . . No ma'am, I'm not the housekeeper. I'm a friend of the family who is caring for these children . . . There's nothing wrong with that boy that I can see . . . Are you calling to tell me that there's something wrong, that I'm doing something wrong? What is it that I'm doing wrong? I would like to know that. What is your name?"

I stood transfixed with terror in the hall as she bent angrily into the mouthpiece and her knuckles ridged on the receiver. A storm was blowing in from the Gulf, the air smelled of ozone, and the southern horizon was black with thunderclouds that pulsated with white veins of lightning. I heard the wind ripping through the trees in the yard and pecans rattling down on the gallery roof like grapeshot.

When Mattie hung up the phone the skin of her face was stretched as tight as a lampshade and one liquid eye was narrowed at me like someone aiming down a rifle barrel.

The next week, when I was cutting through the neighbor's sugarcane field on the way home from school, my heart started to race for no reason, my spit tasted like pecans, my face filmed with perspiration even though the wind was cool through the stalks of cane; then I saw the oaks and cypress trees along Bayou Teche tilt at an angle, and I dropped my books and fell forward in the dirt as though someone had wrapped a chain around my chest and snapped my breastbone.

I lay with the side of my face pressed against the dirt, my mouth gasping like a fish's, until Weldon found me and went crashing through the cane for help. A doctor came out to the house that night, examined me and gave me a shot, then talked with my father out in the hall. My father didn't understand the doctor's vocabulary, and he said, "What *kind* of fever that is?"

"Rheumatic, Mr. Sonnier. It attacks the heart. I could be wrong, but I think that's what your boy's got. I'll be back tomorrow."

"How much this gonna cost?"

"It's three dollars a visit, but you can pay me when you're able."

"We never had nothing like this in our family. You sure about this?"

"No, I'm not. That's why I'll be back. Good night to you, sir."

I knew he didn't like my father, but he came to see me one afternoon a week for a month, brought me bottles of medicine, and always looked into my face with genuine concern after he listened to my heart. Then one night he and my father argued and he didn't come back.

"What good he do, huh?" my father said. "You still sick, ain't you? A doctor don't make money off well people. I think maybe you got malaria, son. There ain't nothing for that either. It just goes away. You gonna see, you. You stay in bed, you eat cush-cush Mattie and me make for you, you drink that Hadacol vitamin tonic, you wear this dime I'm tying on you, you gonna get well and go back to school."

He tied a perforated dime on a piece of red twine around my neck. His face was lean and unshaved, and his turquoise eyes were as intense as a butane flame when he looked into mine.

"You blame me for your mama?" he asked.

"No sir," I lied.

"I didn't mean to hit her. But she made me look bad in front of y'all. A woman can't be doing that to a man in front of his kids."

"Make Mattie go away, Daddy."

"Don't be saying that."

"She hit Weldon with the belt. She made Drew kneel in the bathroom corner because she didn't flush the toilet."

"She's just trying to be a mother, that's all. Don't talk no more. Go to sleep. I got to drive back to Texas City tonight. You gonna be all right."

He closed my door and the inside of my room was absolutely black. Through the wall I heard him and Mattie talking, then the weight of their bodies creaking rhythmically on the bedsprings.

When Sister Roberta knew that I would not be back to school that semester she began bringing my lessons to the house. She came three afternoons a week, and she had to walk two miles each way between the convent and our house. Each time I successfully completed a lesson she rewarded me with a holy card. Each holy card had a prayer on one side and a beautiful picture on the other, usually of angels and saints glowing with light or ethereal paintings of Mary with the Infant Jesus. On the day after my father had tied the dime around my neck Sister Roberta had to walk past our neighbor's field right after he had cut his cane and burned off the stubble, and a wet wind had streaked her black habit with ashes. As soon as she came through my bedroom door her face tightened inside her wimple, and her brown eyes, which had flecks of red in them, grew round and hot, and she dropped her book bag on the foot of my bed and leaned within six inches of my face as though she were looking down at a horrid presence in the bottom of a well. The hair on her upper lip looked like pieces of silver thread.

"Who put that around your neck?" she asked.

"My father says it keeps the gris-gris away."

"My suffering God," she said, and went back out the door in a swirl of cloth. Then I heard her speak to Mattie: "That's right, madam. Scissors. So I can remove that cord from his neck before he strangles to death in his sleep. Thank you kindly."

She came back into my bedroom, pulled the twine out from my throat with one finger, and snipped it in two.

"Do you believe in this nonsense, Billy Bob?" she said.

"No, Sister."

"That's good. You're a good Catholic boy, and you mustn't believe in superstition. Do you love the church?"

"I think so."

"Hmmmm. That doesn't sound entirely convincing. Do you love your father?"

"I don't know."

"I see. Do you love your sister and your brothers?"

"Yes. Most of the time I do."

"That's good. Because if you love somebody, or if you love the church, like I do, then you don't ever have to be afraid. People are only superstitious when they're afraid. That's an important lesson for little people to learn. Now, let's take a look at our math test for this week."

Over her shoulder I saw Mattie looking at us from the living room, her hair in foam-rubber curlers, her face contorted as though a piece of barbed wire were twisting behind her eyes.

That winter my father started working regular hours, what he called "an indoor job," at the Monsanto Chemical Company in Texas City, and we saw him only on weekends. Mattie cooked only the evening meal and made us responsible for the care of the house and the other two meals. Weldon started to get into trouble at school. His eighth-grade teacher, a lay woman, called and said he had thumbtacked a girl's dress to the desk during class, causing her to almost tear it off her body when the bell rang, and he would either pay for the dress or be suspended. Mattie hung up the phone on her, and two days later the girl's father, a sheriff's deputy, came out to the house and made Mattie give him four dollars on the gallery.

She came back inside, slamming the door, her face burning, grabbed Weldon by the collar of his T-shirt and walked him into the backyard, where she made him stand for two hours on an upended apple crate until he wet his pants.

Later, after she had let him come back inside and he had changed his underwear and blue jeans, he went outside into the dark by himself, without eating supper, and sat on the butcher stump, striking kitchen matches on the side of the box and throwing them at the chickens. Before we went to sleep he sat for a long time on the side of his bed, next to mine, in a square of moonlight with his hands balled into fists on his thighs. There were knots of muscle in the backs of his arms and behind his ears. Mattie had given him a burr haircut, and his head looked as hard and scalped as a baseball.

"Tomorrow's Saturday. We're going to listen to the LSU-Rice game," I said.

"Some colored kids saw me from the road and laughed."

"I don't care what they did. You're brave, Weldon. You're braver than any of us."

"I'm gonna fix her."

His voice made me afraid. The branches of the pecan trees were skeletal, like gnarled fingers against the moon.

"Don't be thinking like that," I said. "It'll just make her do worse things. She takes it out on Drew when you and Lyle aren't here."

"Go to sleep, Billy Bob," he said. His eyes were wet. "She hurts us because we let her. We ax for it. You get hurt when you don't stand up. Just like Momma did."

I heard him snuffling in the dark. Then he lay down with his face turned toward the opposite wall. His head looked carved out of gray wood in the moonlight.

I went back to school for the spring semester, and because of the warmth of the season, the balmy winds off the Gulf, the flaming azaleas in people's yards, the heavy, fecund smell of magnolia and wisteria on the night air, I wanted to believe that a new season was beginning in my heart as well. I couldn't control what happened at home, but the school was a safe place, one where Sister Roberta ruled her little fifth-grade world like an affectionate despot.

I was always fascinated by her hands. They were like toy hands, small as a child's, as pink as an early rose, the nails not much bigger than pearls. She was wonderful at sketching and drawing with crayons and colored chalk. In minutes she could create a beautiful religious scene on the blackboard to fit the church's season, but she also drew pictures for us of Easter rabbits and talking Easter eggs. Sometimes she would draw only the outline of a figure—an archangel with enormous wings, a Roman soldier about to be dazzled by a blinding light—and she would let us take turns coloring in the solid areas. She told us the secret to great classroom art was to always keep your chalk and crayons pointy.

Then we began to hear rumors about Sister Roberta, of a kind that we had never heard about any of the nuns, who all seemed to have no lives other than the ones that were immediately visible to us. She had been heard weeping in the confessional, she had left the convent for three days without permission, two detectives from Baton Rouge had questioned her in the mother superior's office.

She missed a week of school, and a lay teacher took her place. She returned for two weeks, then was gone again. When she came back the second time she was soft-spoken and removed, and sometimes she didn't even bother to answer simple questions that we asked her. She would gaze out the window for long periods, as though her attention were fixed on a distant object, then a noise—a creaking desk, an eraser flung from the cloakroom— would disturb her, and her eyes would return to the room, absolutely empty of thought or meaning.

I stayed after school on a Friday to help her wash the blackboards and pound erasers.

"You don't need to, Billy Bob. The janitor will take care of it," she said.

She was putting paper clips one by one in a box on top of her desk.

"All the kids like you, Sister," I said.

"What?" she said.

"You're the only one who plays with us at recess. You don't ever get mad at us, either. Not for real, anyway."

"It's nice of you to say that, but the other sisters are good to you, too."

"Not like you are."

"You shouldn't talk to me like that, Billy Bob." She had lost weight, and there was a solitary crease, like a line drawn by a thumbnail, in each of her cheeks.

"It's wrong for you to be sad," I said.

"You must run along home now. Don't say anything more."

I wish you were my mother, I thought I heard myself say inside my head.

"What did you say?" she asked.

"Nothing."

"Tell me what you said."

"I don't think I said anything. I really don't think I did."

My heart was beating against my rib cage, the same way it had the day I fell unconscious in the sugarcane field.

"Billy Bob, don't try to understand the world. It's not ours to understand," she said. "You must give up the things you can't change. You mustn't talk to me like this anymore. You—"

But I was already racing from the room, my soul painted with an unrelieved shame that knew no words.

The next week I found out the source of Sister Roberta's grief. A strange and seedy man by the name of Mr. Trajan, who always had an American flag pin in his lapel when you saw him inside the wire-cage office of the grocery and package store he operated by the Negro district, cut an article from copies of the Baton Rouge *Morning Advocate* and the Lafayette *Daily Advertiser* and mailed it to other Catholic businessmen in town. An eighth grader who had been held back twice, once by Sister Roberta, brought it to school one day, and after the three o'clock bell Lyle, Weldon, and I heard him reading it to a group of dumbfounded boys on the playground. The words hung in the air like our first exposure to God's name being deliberately used in vain.

Her brother had killed a child, and Sister Roberta had helped him to hide in a fishing camp in West Baton Rouge Parish.

"Give me that," Weldon said, and tore the news article out of the boy's hand. He stared hard at it, then wadded it up and threw it on the ground. "Get the fuck out of here. You go around talking about this again and I'll kick your ass."

"That's right, you dumb fuck," Lyle said, putting his new base-ball cap in his back pocket and setting his book satchel down by his foot.

"That's right, butt face," I added, incredulous at the boldness of my own words.

"Yeah?" the boy said, but the resolve in his voice was already breaking.

"Yeah!" Weldon said, and shoved him off balance. Then he picked up a rock and chased the boy and three of his friends toward the street. Lyle and I followed, picking up dirt clods in our hands. When the boy was almost to his father's waiting pickup truck, he turned and shot us the finger. Weldon nailed him right above the eye with the rock.

One of the brothers marched us down to Father Higgins's office and left us there to wait for Father Higgins, whose razor strop and black-Irish, crimson-faced tirades were legendary in the school. The office smelled of the cigar butts in the wastebasket and the cracked leather in the chairs. A walnut pendulum clock ticked loudly on the wall. It was overcast outside, and we sat in the gloom and silence until four o'clock.

"I ain't waiting anymore. Y'all coming?" Weldon said, and put one leg out the open window.

"You'll get expelled," I said.

"Too bad. I ain't going to wait around just to have somebody whip me," he said, and dropped out the window.

Five minutes later Lyle followed him.

The sound of the clock was like a spoon knocking on a hollow wood box. When Father Higgins finally entered the room, he wore his horn-rimmed glasses and was thumbing through a sheaf of papers attached to a clipboard. The hairline on the back of his neck was shaved neatly with a razor. At first he seemed distracted by my presence, then he flipped the sheets of paper to a particular page, almost as an afterthought, and studied it. He put an unlit cigar stub in his mouth, looked at me, then back at the page.

"You threw a rock at somebody?" he said.

"No, Father."

"Somebody threw a rock at you?"

"I wouldn't say that."

"You *wouldn't* say that? Then what are you doing here?"

"I don't know."

"That's interesting. All right, since you don't know why you're here, how about going somewhere else?"

"I'll take him, Father," I heard Sister Roberta say in the doorway. She put her hand on my arm, walked me down the darkly polished corridor to the breezeway outside, then sat me down on the stone bench inside the bamboo-enclosed garden where she often said her rosary.

She sat next to me, her small white hands curved on the edges of the bench, and looked down at the goldfish pond while she talked. A crushed paper cup floated among the hyacinth leaves.

"You meant well, Billy Bob," she said, "but I don't want you to defend me anymore. It's not the job of little people to defend adults."

"Sister, it said—"

"It said what?"

"You were in trouble with the police. Can they put you in jail?"

She put her hand on top of mine. Her fingernails looked like tiny pink seashells. "They're not really interested in me, Billy Bob. My brother is an alcoholic, and he killed a little boy with his car, then he ran away. But they probably won't send my brother to prison because the child was a Negro." Her hand was hot and damp on top of mine. Her voice clicked wetly in her throat. "He'll be spared, not because he's a sick man, but because it was a colored child he killed."

When I looked at her again her long eyelashes were bright with tears.

She stood up with her face turned away from me. The sun had broken through the gray seal of clouds, and the live oak tree overhead was filled with the clattering of mockingbirds and blue jays. I felt her tiny fingernails rake gently through my hair, as though she were combing a cat.

"Oh you poor child, there're lice eggs in your hair," she said.

Then she pressed my head against her breast, and I felt her tears strike hotly on the back of my neck.

Three days later Sister saw the cigarette burn on Drew's leg in the lunchroom and reported it to the social welfare agency

in town. A consumptive rail of a man in a dandruff-flecked blue
suit drove out to the house and questioned Mattie on the gallery,
then questioned us in front of Mattie. Drew told him she had
been burned by an ember that had popped out of a trash fire in
the backyard.

He raised her chin with his knuckle. His black hair was stiff
with grease.

"Is that what happened?" he asked.

"Yes sir." Drew's face was dull, her mouth downturned at the
corners. The burn was scabbed now and looked like a tightly
coiled gray worm on her skin.

He smiled and took his knuckle away from her chin. "Then
you shouldn't play next to the fire," he said.

"I would like to know who sent you out here," Mattie said.

"That's confidential." He coughed on the back of his hand. His
shirt cuff was frayed on his thin wrist. "And to tell you the truth,
I don't really know. My supervisor didn't tell me." He coughed
again, this time loud and hard, and I could smell his deep-lung
nicotine odor. "But everything here looks all right."

Weldon's eyes were as hard as marbles, but he didn't speak.

The man walked with Mattie to his car, and I felt like doors
were slamming all around us. She put her foot on his running
board and propped one arm on his car roof while she talked, so
that her breasts were uplifted against her blouse and her skirt
made a loop between her legs.

"Let's tell him," Lyle said.

"Are you kidding? Look at him. She could make him eat her
shit with a spoon," Weldon said.

It was right after first period the next morning that we heard
about the disaster at Texas City. Somebody shouted something
about it on the playground, then suddenly the whole school was
abuzz with rumors. Cars on the street pulled to the curb with
their radios tuned to news stations, and we could even hear the
principal's old boxwood radio from the open window upstairs.
A ship loaded with fertilizer had been burning in the harbor, and
while people on the docks had watched fire-fighting boats pump-

ing geysers of water onto the ship's decks, the fire had dripped into the hold. The explosion filled the sky with rockets of smoke and rained an umbrella of flame down on the Monsanto chemical plant. The force of the secondary explosion was so great that it blew out windows in Houston, fifty miles away. But it wasn't over yet. The fireball mushroomed laterally out into an adjacent oil field, and rows of storage tanks and wellheads went like strings of Chinese firecrackers. People said the water in the harbor boiled from the heat, the spars on steel derricks melted like licorice.

We heard nothing about the fate of my father either that afternoon or evening. Mattie got drunk that night and fell asleep in the living-room chair by the radio. I felt nothing about my father's possible death, and I wondered at my own callousness. We went to school the next morning, and when we returned home in the afternoon Mattie was waiting on the gallery to tell us that a man from the Monsanto company had telephoned and said that my father was listed as missing. Her eyes were pink with either hangover or crying, and her face was puffy and round, like a white balloon.

When we didn't respond, she said, "Your father may be dead. Do you understand what I'm saying? That was an important man from his company who called. He would not call unless he was gravely concerned. Do you children understand what is being said to you?"

Weldon brushed at the dirt with his tennis shoe, and Lyle looked into a place about six inches in front of his eyes. Drew's face was frightened, not because of the news about our father, but instead because of the strange whirring of wheels that we could almost hear from inside Mattie's head. I put my arm over her shoulders and felt her skin jump.

"He's worked like a nigra for you, maybe lost his life for you, and you have nothing to say?" she asked.

"Maybe we ought to start cleaning up our rooms. You wanted us to clean up our rooms, Mattie," I said.

But it was a poor attempt to placate her.

"You stay outside. Don't even come in this house," she said.

"I have to go to the bathroom," Lyle said.

"Then you can just do it in the dirt like a darky," she said, and went inside the house and latched the screen behind her.

By the next afternoon my father was still unaccounted for. Mattie had an argument on the phone with somebody, I think the man in zoot pants and two-tone shoes who had probably been her pimp at one time, because she told him he owed her money and she wouldn't come back and work at Broussard's Bar again until he paid her. After she hung up she breathed hard at the kitchen sink, smoking her cigarette and staring out into the yard. She snapped the cap off a bottle of Jax and drank it half-empty, her throat working in one long, wet swallow, one eye cocked at me.

"Come here," she said.

"What?"

"You tracked up the kitchen. You didn't flush the toilet after you used it, either."

"I did."

"You did what?"

"I flushed the toilet."

"Then one of the others didn't flush it. Every one of you come out here. Now!"

"What is it, Mattie? We didn't do anything," I said.

"I changed my mind. Every one of you outside. All of you outside. Weldon and Lyle, you get out there right now. Where's Drew?"

"She's playing in the yard. What's wrong, Mattie?" I made no attempt to hide the fear in my voice. I could see the web of blue veins in the top of her muscular chest.

Outside the wind was blowing through the trees in the yard, flattening the purple clumps of wisteria that grew against the barn wall.

"Each of you go to the hedge and cut the switch you want me to use on you," she said.

It was her favorite form of punishment for us. If we broke off a large switch, she hit us fewer times with it. If we came back with a thin or small switch, we would get whipped until she felt she had struck some kind of balance between size and number.

We remained motionless. Drew had been playing with her cat. She had tied a piece of twine around the cat's neck, and she held the twine in her hand like a leash. Her knees and white socks were dusty from play.

"I told you not to tie that around the kitten's neck again," Mattie said.

"It doesn't hurt anything. It's not your cat, anyway," Weldon said.

"Don't sass me," she said. "You will not sass me. None of you will sass me."

"I ain't cutting no switch," Weldon said. "You're crazy. My mama said so. You ought to be in the crazy house."

She looked hard into Weldon's eyes, and there was a moment of recognition in her colorless face, as though she had seen a growing meanness of spirit in Weldon that was the equal of her own. Then she wet her lips, crimped them together, and rubbed her hands on her thighs.

"We shall see who does what around here," she said. She broke off a big switch from the myrtle hedge and raked it free of flowers and leaves, except for one green sprig on the tip.

I saw the look in Drew's face, saw her drop the piece of twine from her palm as she looked up into Mattie's shadow.

Mattie jerked her by the wrist and whipped her a half-dozen times across her bare legs. Drew twisted impotently in Mattie's balled hand, her feet dancing with each blow. The switch raised welts on her skin as thick and red as centipedes.

Then suddenly Weldon ran with all his weight into Mattie's back, stiff-arming her between the shoulder blades, and sent her tripping sideways over a bucket of chicken slops. She righted herself and stared at him open-mouthed, the switch limp in her hand. Then her eyes grew hot and bright with a painful intention, and I could see the bone flex along her jaws.

Weldon burst out the back gate and ran down the dirt road between the sugarcane fields, the soles of his dirty tennis shoes powdering dust in the air.

She waited for him a long time, watching through the screen as the mauve-colored dusk gathered in the trees and the sun's afterglow lit the clouds on the western horizon with flame. Then she took a bottle of apricot brandy into the bathroom and sat in the tub for almost an hour, turning the hot-water tap on and off until the tank was empty. When we needed to go to the bathroom, she told us to take our problem outside. Finally she emerged in the hall, wearing only her panties and bra, her hair wrapped in a towel, the dark outline of her sex plainly visible to us.

"I'm going to dress now and go into town with a gentleman friend," she said. "Tomorrow we're going to start a new regime around here. Believe me, there will never be a reoccurrence of what happened here today. You can pass that on to young Mr. Weldon for me."

But she didn't go into town. Instead, she put on her blue suit, a flower-print blouse, her nylon stockings, and walked up and down on the gallery, her cigarette poised in the air like a movie actress.

"Why not just drive your car, Mattie?" I said quietly through the screen.

"It has no gas. Besides, a gentleman caller will be passing for me anytime now," she answered.

"Oh."

She blew smoke at an upward angle, her face aloof and flat-sided in the shadows.

"Mattie?"

"Yes?"

"Weldon's out back. Can he come in the house?"

"Little mice always return where the cheese is," she said.

I hated her. I wanted something terrible to happen to her. I could feel my fingernails kniving into my palms.

She turned on one high heel, her palm supporting one elbow, her cigarette an inch from her mouth, her hair wreathed in smoke.

"Do you have a reason for staring through the screen at me?" she asked.

"No," I said.

"When you're bigger you'll get to do what's on your mind. In the meantime, don't let your thoughts show on your face. You're a lewd little boy."

Her suggestion repelled me and made water well up in my eyes. I backed away from the screen, then turned and ran through the rear of the house and out into the backyard where Weldon, Lyle, and Drew sat against the barn wall, fireflies lighting in the wisteria over their heads.

No one came for Mattie that evening. She sat in the stuffed chair in her room, putting on layers of lipstick until her mouth had the crooked, bright-red shape of a clown's. She smoked a whole package of Chesterfields, constantly wiping the ashes off her dark-blue skirt with a hand towel soaked in dry-cleaning fluid; then she drank herself unconscious.

It was hot that night, and dry lightning leaped from the horizon to the top of the blue-black vault of sky over the Gulf. Weldon sat on the side of his bed in the dark, his shoulders hunched, his fists between his white thighs. His burr haircut looked like duck down on his head in the flicker of the lightning through the window. When I was almost asleep he shook both me and Lyle awake and said, "We got to get rid of her. You know we got to do it."

I put my pillow over my head and rolled away from him, as though I could drop away into sleep and rise in the morning into a sun-spangled and different world.

But in the false dawn I woke to both Lyle's and Weldon's faces close to mine. Weldon's eyes were hollow, his breath rank with funk. The mist was heavy and wet in the pecan trees outside the window.

"She's not gonna hurt Drew again. Are you gonna help or not?" Weldon said.

I followed them into the hallway, my heart sinking at the realization of what I was willing to participate in, my body as numb as if I had been stunned with Novocain. Mattie slept in the stuffed chair, her hose rolled down over her knees, an overturned jelly glass on the rug next to the can of spot cleaner.

Weldon walked quietly across the rug, unscrewed the cap on the can, laid the can on its side in front of Mattie's feet, then backed away from her. The cleaning fluid spread in a dark circle around her chair, the odor as bright and sharp as a slap across the face.

Weldon slid open a box of kitchen matches and we each took one, raked it across the striker, and, with the sense that our lives at that moment had changed forever, threw them at Mattie's feet. But the burning matches fell outside the wet area. The blood veins in my head dilated with fear, my ears hummed with a sound like the roar of the ocean in a seashell, and I jerked the box from Weldon's hand, clutched a half-dozen matches in my fist, dragged them across the striker, and flung them right on Mattie's feet.

The chair was enveloped in a cone of flame, and she burst out of it with her arms extended, as though she were pushing blindly through a curtain, her mouth and eyes wide with terror. We could smell her hair burning as she raced past us and crashed through the screen door out onto the gallery and into the yard. She beat at her flaming clothes and raked at her hair as though it were swarming with yellow jackets.

I stood transfixed in mortal dread at what I had done.

A Negro man walking to work came out of the mist on the road and knocked her to the ground, slapping the fire out of her dress, pinning her under his spread knees as though he were assaulting her. Smoke rose from her scorched clothes and hair as in a depiction of a damned figure on one of my holy cards.

The Negro rose to his feet and walked toward the gallery, a

solitary line of blood running down his black cheek where Mattie had scratched him.

"Yo' mama ain't hurt bad. Get some butter or some bacon grease. She gonna be all right, you gonna see. You children don't be worried, no," he said.

He smiled with his snuff-stained gums to assure us that everything would be all right.

The volunteer firemen bounced across the cattle guard in an old fire truck whose obsolete hand-crank starter still dangled from under the radiator. They coated Mattie's room with foam from a fire extinguisher and packed Mattie off in an ambulance to the charity hospital in Lafayette. Two sheriff's deputies arrived, and before he left, one of the volunteers took them aside in the yard and talked with them, looking over his shoulder at us children, then walked over to us and said, "The fire chief gonna come out here and check it out. Y'all stay out of that bedroom."

His face was narrow and dark with shadow under the brim of his big rubber fireman's hat.

I felt a fist squeeze my heart.

But suddenly Sister Roberta was in the midst of everything. Someone had carried word to the school about the fire, and she'd had one of the brothers drive her out to the house. She talked with the deputies, helped us fix cereal at the kitchen table, made telephone calls to find a place for us to stay besides the welfare shelter. Then she looked in Mattie's bedroom door and studied the interior for what seemed a long time. When she came back in the kitchen her eyes peeled the skin off our faces. I looked straight down into my cereal bowl.

She placed her small hand on my shoulder. I could feel her fingers tapping on the bone, as though she were processing her own thoughts. Then she said, "Well, what should we do here today? I think we should clean up first. Where's the broom?"

Without waiting for an answer she pulled the broom out of the

closet and went to work in Mattie's room, sweeping the spilled
and unstruck matches as well as the burned ones in a pile by a side
door that gave onto the yard. The soot and blackened threads
from the rug swirled up in a cloud around her veils and wings
and smudged her starched wimple.

One of the deputies put his hand on the broomstick.

"There ain't been an investigation yet. You can't do that till the
fire chief come out and see, Sister," he said.

"You always talked like a fool, Gaspard," she said. "Now that
you have a uniform, you talk like a bigger one. This house smells
like an incinerator. Now get out of the way."

With one sweep of the broom she raked all the matches out
into the yard.

We were placed in foster homes, and over the years I lost con-
tact with Sister Roberta. But later I went to work in the oil fields,
and I think perhaps I talked with my father in a nightclub outside of Morgan City. An enormous live oak tree grew through
the floor and roof, and he was leaning against the bar that had
been built in a circle around the tree. His face was puckered with
white scar tissue, his ears burnt into stubs, his right hand atro-
phied and frozen against his chest like a broken bird's foot. But
beyond the layers of mutilated skin I could see my father's face,
like the image in a photographic negative held up against a light.

"Is your name Sonnier?" I asked.

He looked at me curiously.

"Maybe. You want to buy me a drink?" he said.

"All right," I said.

He ordered a shot of Beam with a frosted schooner of Jax on
the side.

"Are you Verise Sonnier from New Iberia?" I asked.

He grinned stiffly when he took the schooner of beer away
from his mouth.

"Why you want to know?" he said.

"I think I'm your son. I'm Billy Bob."

His turquoise eyes wandered over my face, then they lost interest.

"I had a son. But you ain't him," he said. "Buy me another shot?"

"Sure. Why not?" I said.

Sometimes he comes to me in my dreams, and I wonder if ironically all our stories were written on his skin back there in Texas City in 1947. Or maybe that's just a poetic illusion purchased by time. But even in the middle of an Indian summer's day, when the sugarcane is beaten with purple and gold light in the fields and the sun is both warm and cool on your skin at the same time, when I know that the earth is a fine place after all, I have to mourn just a moment for those people of years ago who lived lives they did not choose, who carried burdens that were not their own, whose invisible scars were as private as the scarlet beads of Sister Roberta's rosary wrapped across the back of her small hand, as bright as drops of blood ringed round the souls of little people.

James Lee Burke was born in 1936 and grew up on the Texas–Louisiana Gulf Coast. He and his wife Pearl have four children and live now outside of Missoula, Montana. He has published ten novels and one collection of short stories. He was a recipient of a Breadloaf Fellowship, an NEA grant, and a John Simon Guggenheim Fellowship. His novel *Black Cherry Blues* received the Edgar Award as the outstanding crime novel of 1989.

PHOTO CREDIT: MICHAEL GALLACHER

"Texas City, 1947" began as a novel about a Texas oil family. However, it just didn't go right and I saved the work I had done by translating it into a short story set in south Louisiana right after World War II. Then I began thinking about a novel again, and the story took on another life. It became the background as well as part of the plot material for a novel entitled A Stained White Radiance, which deals with victimization of both children and adults.

My father was at Texas City when it blew up in 1947, and lost many of his best friends in the explosions that spread from the harbor back through the oil fields. I will never forget the look of grief on his face when he walked into the house late that night. Six years later he and I were fishing out on a bald stretch of prairie in some tanks (ponds) about fifteen miles from Texas City when we walked up upon an enormous water-filled hole that had been scoured out of the earth by a twisted piece of iron the size of a garage door. I couldn't even guess at the force of the explosion that blew it there.

That image of industrial and human catastrophe always remained emblematic in my mind of the dark potential that lies in our midst. Many years later I wrote about it in a novel entitled The Lost Get-Back Boogie. I thought I was finished with the Texas City disaster, but for one reason or another it has had its way of reappearing in my work, perhaps because it represents to me not only our propensity for error but our on-going inability to understand the nature of consequence.

Reginald McKnight

QUITTING SMOKING

(from *The Kenyon Review*)

Jan. 16, 1978
Manitou Spgs., CO

Dear B——,

Happy New Year and all that. Man, are you ever hard to get a hold of. I wrote your ex–ol' lady first, and she said, and I quote, "As to his whereabouts, well, your guess is as good as mine. The last I heard he was still with TWA, but based in London. I do know that he was suspended for six weeks for giving free tickets to London to that girlfriend of his. I'm surprised they didn't flat out fire him." She mainly ranted about how you only write and send money on your boy's birthday. She's still pretty pissed off at you, my man. Anyway, she said that your folks might know and she gave me their new address and phone # in Texas. I didn't even know they moved. Anyway, money's been a little tight lately, and I don't even have a phone at the moment, so I wrote a card. Didn't here anything for a long time, but then your kid sister, Mayra, wrote me, and this is what she said, "We got your letter a long time ago, but we don't know excatly where B—— is My brother has moved alot in the last couple of years because of his job. The reason I'm writing you instead of my mother is because my mother is discusted with B———. But she won't tel anybody why. And she says she doesn't know his adress. I know she does but can't find it any where. But I will look for it and if I find it I will send it to you. My big sister Letonya said if she gets the adress she will send the letter to B——— but I don't think so because she is getting married and is always forgetting to do things. Mamma is discusted with Letonya because she says shes too young to get married. Right now your letter is on the fridge with a magnit on it."

I thought you'd like that, B———.

Then I called TWA. They were kind of nasty, and no help at all. They did tell me you were on leave, though, but wouldn't say where. So, how did I get your address? Letonya came through. She said you were living it up in Madrid for six months, and then you'd be going back to London. I guess she'd be married by now.

I guess you're probably surprised to hear from me after all these years, homes, and I bet you're surprised at how long this letter is, or for me right at this second, how long it's gonna be. This'll be the longest thing I'll ever have written by the time I'm done. I know that already, B———, 'cause the stuff I got on my mind is complicated and confusing. I've been sleeping pretty bad lately, cause I've been thinking about that thing that happened when you, me, Stick, and Camel saw that guy snatch that woman into his car in front of Griff's, just after hoops practice. I'm sure you remember. It bothered me a lot back then, of course, but you know it's been nine years now and you get over things like that after awhile. And for a long time I didn't really think about it all that much. But something happened a few weeks ago between me and my girl friend, Anna, that brought all that stuff up again and has pretty much messed up things between me and her. The stuff I'm gonna tell you, speaking of "between," is just between you and me. Period. OK? but I've gotta tell you the whole thing so you'll understand where I'm coming from and understand why I've done what I've done. I feel bad that I've gotta talk about Anna behind her back like this, but goddamnit, you're the only guy who'd understand what I'm trying to work out in my mind. You and me are pretty much cut from the same tree, you could say. We both grew up in this town, well, I'm in Manitou, now and not Colo. Spgs, but I'll get to that later. We both hung around maybe too many white people growing up. We're both tall and black, but can't play hoops worth a damn. We both have had very weird relationships with redheaded, green-eyed women, only you actually married yours. Anna and I just lived together. Yeah, "live" in the past tense. Looks like it might be over between me and Anna. Over, unless, after you've read all this you think what I've done is wrong, and you say that I should give Anna another chance, or she should give me one. You know, I was gonna try to get in touch with the other "fellas" about this, too. I know where the Stick is. I think I do, anyway. I ran into Coach Ortiz at José Muldoon's and he told me the Stick is teaching Poli Sci at some college in Athens, Georgia. I'd tried his folks' place first, but the old phone number don't work and they're not in the book. The last I heard about Camel is that he joined the service. The army or the airforce, I'm not sure. Can you imagine that big buck-tooth hippie in the service? But anyway, I decided not to write or call those guys 'cause, to be honest, they're white and I don't think they'd understand.

Right now, I'm living in Manitou Springs, like I said, in a place called Banana Manor. A big stone monster painted bright yellow and trimmed in brown. It used to be a hotel, I guess. It's kind of a hippie flop house. Lot's of drugs, sex, rock n' roll, long hair and cheap rent. I got a room here and pay only $65 a month for it. Most of my stuff's still at the place me and Anna shared, and I still go by there and pick up my mail and stuff, but I only go there when she's not around, mainly cause it'd hurt too much to see her. I leave her notes and still pay my share of the rent. Don't know how long I'll do that though.

Before I get to my point (sorry it's taking me so long) I guess I oughta catch you up on me. After all, B——, we ain't seen each other in about six years, or written or called since you split with

Kari. How's your boy, by the way? Good, I hope. Well now, I finally got my certificate in cabinetry at Pikes Peak Comm. Col. Actually, I copped an A.A. in general studies, too. I had the money and the time, so I figured, what the fuck. Besides, Anna kept ragging on me till I did. Graduated third in my cabinetry class, quit this stockBOY gig I'd had at Alco's and got a part timer at Chess King. I sold shake yo' booty clothes to mostly army clowns from Fort Cartoon. (That's what my Anna calls Fort Carson.) Well, I got fired for "studying at work" and "ignoring customers," which all I have to say about is if you remember my study habits in high school, you'll know it was all bullshit. They fired me 'cause I wouldn't wear their silly-ass clothes on the job. My mom always used to tell me, "You ain't got to dress like a nigro to look like a nigro, boy."

So I was out of work for about two months and moved in with Anna, which had its ups and downs (no pun). Anna's got a couple of years on me. Actually five, but she looks about 20. She has a kid, though, and to tell you the truth, I could do without the instant family stuff. But Max, her kid is alright for a rug rat. I mean, he wets the bed sometimes, and he's about as interested in sports as I'm interested in Sesame Street, but he's smart, funny, and likes me, so I could hang with it. To tell you the truth, I miss him a lot.

But like I'm saying, there were some good things about living with Anna, and some things that weren't so good. Good and not so good. The usual. She's divorced, and 31, like I said. We met at the community college about a year and a half ago. It was in the Spring Quarter, and the weather was perfect, in the 80's, sky like a blank blue page. I was sitting on a bench outside the cafeteria, talking to this friend of mine when she walked by in a pink Danskin top and a pink and white flowered skirt. My asshole friend yells out, "Hey! You got the most beautiful breasts I've ever seen." And she blushed and kept walking. I told Steve that was no way to talk to a woman and he told me that broads like that kind of talk, and besides, he didn't say "tits." I told him to screw off and ran after her. I apologized to her and told her I had nothing to do with what Steve'd said. She kind of nodded real quick, mumbled something and kept walking. Then I walked away, and didn't figure I'd ever see her again. I felt like an idiot. Didn't even wanna think about it.

Well, about two weeks later I was in the parking lot and just about to my car when I hear this little voice say, "You have the most beautiful ass I've ever seen." It was Anna, and as they say, da rest is history. She's 5'2" and has a body that would make your teeth sweat. Steve was right about her bust, but he missed the rest. Like I say, she's got red hair, green eyes, but the weird thing is she tans real good. Not like most redheads who sit out in the sun for two seconds and end up looking like blisters with feet, or get so many freckles that you wanna hand em a brown magic marker and go tell em to finish the job. So anyway, she's also about a hundred times smarter than I am, which is no big deal, cause she never jams it down my throat. Besides, since I started at the cabinet mill I make more scratch than she does. (She's on welfare.) Anna's a sociology major at Colorado College, now, and she'd been trying to talk me into going there to get a degree in something, but for one thing I don't have the money, and for another thing, you don't exactly see legions of folks our color over there so I doubt they'd want me. Anyhow, I'm not exactly a genius. I might have done good in cabinet school, but I couldn't pull higher than six or seven B's in general studies. Screw em. Plus, I know the kind of bullshit you had to put up with at Graceland College, amongst all that wheat and corn and cow squat. I still have that letter where you told me about the "joke" (ha ha) Klan party your friends threw for you on your birthday. That kind of thing ain't for the kid here.

Anyway, let me get to my point before I bore you to death. OK, so like one night, about a month ago, Anna and I were in the sack and she wouldn't even kiss me good night. This is strange, I was thinking, cause usually she's more interested in sex than I am, which means she likes it more than a woodpecker likes balsa.

So I asked her what the hell was wrong. (Actually, I said, "Hey, babes, you OK?") And she started crying, real slow and silent. So I got up and burned a doobie. (Yes. I smoke now. Actually, I smoke cigarettes, too, but I'd pretty much quit while I was with Anna. More about that later.) I passed it to her and she took a couple hits. So like I asked her again what was up and she said she got upset cause that day in class they were talking about social deviants (sp?) and her prof said that all of society makes it easy for men to commit rape and that there was no real way to completely eradicate it. So Anna said back to the guy that castration would sure the hell stop it. And then nobody said much of anything for like a minute. Then the prof came back with all that talk show crap that rape isn't sexual, but violent, etc., etc. And Anna just sat there for a while, while the guy kept talking, and she told me that she'd made up her mind not to say anything else. But then, before she knew what hit her, she just sort of blared out, "Then give them the fucking death penalty!" That's exactly what she said. And that started a huge argument in the class.

Well, Anna crushed out the joint in the ashtray. She did it real hard and all I could think about was somebody crushing out a smoking hard-on, which I'm sure she wanted me to think. She's really into symbols and shit. In fact, I think she wanted me to get my A.A. just so I'd get all the symbols she dumps on me. Alright, so I was kind of surprised, cause even though Anna's kind of a women's libber, she's always been pretty mellow about things, and she's always been real anti–death penalty. So I asked her why she'd said that stuff in class. She didn't say anything for about a minute. She was just staring up at the passion plant that we have hanging over our bed. So I asked her if she was ever raped. I asked her flat out, and I was sorry I had. She still didn't say anything. And then she just sort of curled up on the bed. She curled up as tight as a fist and goddamn did she ever cry. Jesus, Jesus, Jesus, B——, I was scared, kind of. I've never seen nothing like that. She didn't make any kind of sound hardly. It was like she was pulling up a rope that was tied to something heavy as the moon. Goddamn, those tears were coming from way, way down. I touched her and every muscle in her was like bowed oak. She was just kind of going uh, uh, uh, her whole body jerking like a heart. Then she threw her arms around me so fast, I thought for a second she wanted to slug me. I couldn't swallow, and I could feel my veins pounding where the inner part of my arm touched her back and shoulders. We held each other so tight, we were like socks rolled up and tucked away in a drawer. I guess I never loved or cared so much about anybody as then.

About, I don't know how long later, she told me about it. We'd went into the kitchen cause I was hungry, and she wanted some wine. Her eyes were all puffy and red. Her voice croaked. And every once in a while she'd shiver, and get this scared look in her eye and look all around the room. She was whispering cause she didn't want to wake up Max, who's room is right next to the kitchen. But the whispering sort of made it weirder or scarier or something. I kept gulping like some cartoon character, and my feet and hands were like ice. I couldn't look at her.

It was this friend of her ex's who'd did it. She says they were sitting in her and her old man's living room. Her old man was at work. He was a medic at Ft. Cartoon. I met him once when he came from Texas, where he lives now, to see Max. Guy's an extreme red neck. So anyway, she says she and this guy were getting high on hash, and just talking about stuff. Anyway, they were just sitting there, getting high, when just like that, this guy pulls a knife and tells her to strip and he rapes her. It made me kind of nervous and sick to hear all that. She told me she'd never told anyone else. I guess it sounds kind of dumb, but I felt honored that I was the only person she'd ever told that to. It sort of made me love her even more. Then just like on some cop show or something, she started telling me that she felt all dirty because of what that guy did. It kind of surprised me that a real woman would talk that way. I pretty much thought that kind of stuff was just made up. But she doesn't even watch TV, except for the news and tennis matches, so I'm sure she wasn't saying it because she'd heard someone else say it. But I hugged her real tight, after she said that, and I told her that she was the sweetest, most beautiful woman I'd ever known. I meant it too. I didn't stop telling her till she smiled a little.

We went back to the bedroom and got back in bed. I never did get anything to eat. Pretty soon she was asleep, but I couldn't sleep at all. It was partly because of what she'd told me, and partly because of what she'd made me remember. That's why I'm writing you, B——. I couldn't and I still can't sleep because of what you and me and Stick and Camel saw that one night when we were standing outside the gym. It was the only time the four of us ever just hung out together like that. I don't even know why we were all there together. Do you? I mean, the Stickmeister never hung with the three of us, cause we weren't real popular. And Camel could have walked home. Usually it was just you and me who'd be out there, waiting for the activity bus. It was colder than Jennifer Lash's underdrawers out there. Remember? You didn't have a jacket, and you offered five bucks to Camel if he'd let you wear his. I remember we all cracked up when you did that.

So, laying there next to Anna it's like I was reliving that night. I kept seeing the blue car, and how the woman kept saying, please, please, please, please, and how she tried to crawl under the car, and how you and me were starting across the street, but Stick grabbed your arm and said, He might have a gun, He might kill her—and then how you just stood there saying, Hey! Hey! Hey! And then they were gone. Everything was just taillights all of a sudden. I can't believe we just stood there. And I was so goddamn embarrassed when the cop asked what year the car was, and we didn't know, what the license plate read, and we didn't know. And I think we were all embarrased when we told the cop our stories. I remember you said she was dressed like a nurse and you saw her on the sidewalk, just walking and then the car pulled up and the guy pulled her in. Then I told them that, no, no, no, first she tried to crawl under the car, then he pulled her in. Then

Camel said, no, no, no, there were two guys, and the guy in the
passenger seat had a gun. Then Stick said no, no, no, no, I think
she was in the car first and tried to get out, and the guy pulled
her back in. Come on guys, Stick said, don't you remember when
the guy kept asking her for the keys? and, no Camel, there wasn't
a gun I just thought the guy might have a gun. And I remember,
you said, B——, God! What's wrong with you, Stick, that was
the woman saying, *please, please, please*; nobody said a damn thing
about no keys! She was crawling under the car and screaming
please!

Jesus. Please, keys, tease, ease, bees, knees, cheese. Jeez, what a
buncha idiots we must've looked like. But the thing that got me
the most, the thing that fucked me up the most that night was
when the cop asked the big money, bonus question, What color
was the guy? You and me said, Couldn't tell. Too dark, Camel and
Stick said, at the same time, Black. Then we started arguing. No,
no, no, too dark to tell. No, no, no, Afro, he had an Afro. No,
butthole, how could you tell? Do you remember if the woman
was black? No? Then what makes you think the guy was black?
The woman was white, you chump. Yeah? Well what color was
her hair? How long was it? How tall was she? Heavy-set, was she,
or thin? Old or young? too dark to tell. Too dark to tell. And
what makes you think she was in the car first, Stick?

God, what idiots we were. And I sat up in bed that night, after
Anna'd told me what she told me and I couldn't get it out of my
head. But I thought about other things, too, B——. I thought
about how I used to fantasize when I was a kid, after I'd seen "To
Kill a Mockingbird." I used to fantasize about how I was on trial
for raping a white woman, and how I knew I was innocent, and
I'd be up on the witness stand with the prosecuting attorney's
hot, tomato-faced mug right up in mine. He'd be spitting crap
like, Didn'cha, boy? Didn'cha? You lusted afta those white arms,
and those pink lips and those pale blue, innocent eyes, didn'cha,
nigger boy?

Objection!

Sustained. Mr. Hendershot, I have warned you about—

Forgive me yo honor—and then he dabs his tomato face down with a crumpled hanky—but when ah think of the way these . . . these animals lust afta our sweet belles, why, sir, it makes mah blood boil. No more questions. Yo witness, Mistah Wimply.

And my defender would get up there and sputter and mumble. The prosecutor'd be laughing into his cuffs, dabbing his face, winking and blinking at the jury. Wimply'd look like a fool, but somehow I'd be able to say the right things, and I'd speak as powerfully as Martin Luther King Jr. himself. And while I talked I'd be looking at my accuser with my big puppy eyes and I'd talk about love and justice and peace, equality, never taking my eyes off her beautiful face. She'd start to sweat and tremble, then she'd pass out. The crowd'd go huzzah, hummah, huzzah. The judge would bang away with his gavel. But soon enough the testimony would end, the jury would come back and basically say, Hang the black bastud. Then we'd come back the next day, and the judge would say, Scott Winters, you have been found guilty by a jury of your peers. You have committed a vile and foul crime, my boy, and this court has decided to make you pay the ultimate penalty . . . But all of a sudden, B——, my accuser would pop up from her seat and say, No! He's innocent! Innocent, I tell you. I accused him of the crime because I love him, but all he did was ignore me every time I tried to talk to him or smile at him. He ignored me. Then she'd cry like a son of a bitch, and the crowd'd start up with the Huzzah, hummah, huzzah. And the judge would be hammering away with his gavel, the prosecutor'd be patting his fat face with his hanky, and the woman would run into my arms. And that'd be that.

Don't ask me why I'd fantasize about that, and I'm not sure if "fantasy" is even the right word. I just played that, whatever it is, in my head, night after night, and I don't know why, exactly, but I think it's because when somebody says rapist, what picture comes to mind? I know I don't have to tell you, B——, it's me and you and your brother and your dad, and my dad, and all our uncles and cousins, and so on. It's like how Anna said at breakfast last year when she was preaching to me like she always does about women's lib stuff. She said, "Scott, if I were to come back from the doctor's today, came home with tears in my eyes because of what the doctor had told me, what would you say?" Well, I didn't know what she was driving at, and I shrugged and said, "Well, first thing I'd ask is, What'd he tell you?" And she jumped up from her chair and spilled her coffee and mine in the process and said, "Bingo! See! See! 'What did He say' that's my point. Do you understand me now? We've got these images imbeded in our heads and they're based on stereotypes!" I'll tell you what, man, I did get her point, but if I hadn't I woulda said I'd got it just the same. Cripes.

Anyway, there I was in bed with her, listening to her breathing, thinking about those old fantasies, and about that day we saw the woman being snatched off the street, and how this beautiful woman laying next to me had to suffer so hard over something she could never, ever forget. I couldn't sleep. I wanted a cigarette bad, the first time I'd really even thought about squares since her and I moved in together. I slipped out of bed and dressed. I was gonna walk up to the 7-Eleven and buy a pack of Winstons, my old brand. I was gonna walk back home, smoking one after another and think about things like why guys are such dogs, and how in hell Anna could love or trust any guy after what'd happened to her. It was cold that night, and snow was falling, but not too hard or thick. They were big flakes, and the sky was pinkish gray. You could see as far as a block or two. Real beautiful. It was dead quiet, no traffic, no voices, no dogs barking. You know how Colorado Springs can be on a winter night at two in the morning. It's funny, but I kept expecting the night to be split in two by screams, and I imagined myself running to wherever the screams'd come from, and I'd find some bastard pinning a woman down on the sidewalk, holding a blade to her throat and hissing, Shut the fuck up you goddamn cunt. And I'd see his big red balls hanging over her. I'd plow my ol' two-ton mountain boots so hard into them sacks it'd take a team of surgeons to pull em out his stomach. I could see myself taking the knife out his weak hands, and making one clean, quiet slice on his throat, and that'd be that. I'd walk the woman home and call the cops, and split before they got there. I was thinking so deep about this stuff, B——, it took me awhile to notice that my fists were clenched, and so were my teeth. And it took me just as long to notice that I was walking, then, in the same goddamn neighborhood where the four of us had seen the woman, the guy, and the blue car.

It really kind of freaked me out. I didn't recognize it right away, because in '69, of course, there'd been a Griff's Burger Bar(f) on that lot. Then they made it into a Taco John's. Now it's some kind of church, but there I was—probably standing exactly on the spot where nine years ago that woman'd stood. Man, I just stood there for maybe five minutes. And then I went and sat on the steps of the church. All them things were going through my mind, all the stuff I was fantasizing about, all the stuff I could and couldn't quite remember. Then I started feeling guilty about being there, on my way to get a pack of squares. I hadn't had a cigarette in eight months. Like I said, it was Anna who'd help me quit them things. It was, in a way, the basis of our relationship. Anna's into health like you wouldn't believe. She used to smoke cigarettes, but quit them, and coffee, when Max was born. She took up swimming and running to get back in shape after he was six months or so. Then when he was like two or three, she quit eating meat. The first couple times we went out we ate at a pizza place, and it was the first time in my life I'd ever had a pizza with no meat on it. It wasn't bad, but I was still hungry. I told her too, but she said, "It's psychological. You're meat-hungry." I paused for a minute and grinned real big. Then she laughed and said, "God, you've got a dirty mind." Well, we went to her place. I'd never even been inside before. It was different, really hippyish. There were plants at every window, and it smelled like incense. There was all this beautiful art on the walls, paintings and prints and lithos. Her bedroom was a loft. It sure didn't look like a welfare house, not what I thought one would look like, anyway. Well, I paid the babysitter, even though she didn't want me to. Then we got high. Then we made love.

I'd never felt so good with a woman. It was all so quiet and natural, but still intense. But when I say quiet, I don't mean she was silent. She made so much noise I thought she'd wake her kid. When I say quiet, though, I mean peaceful, sort of spiritual. She went to sleep, but I stayed awake, and then I went outside and lit up a square. When I went back inside, I noticed how bad I stunk. Tobacco'd never smelled so strong or so bad to me. I went to the bathroom and washed my hands and face, tried to brush my teeth with toothpaste and my finger. Next morning, we got up and she fixed me a fritata. (Don't know if I spelled that right or not). It's this thing with eggs and vegies. We had apple juice and Morning Thunder tea. At first I thought something was wrong with the juice because it was brown, but Anna told me it was natural, and was supposed to look like that. It tasted great. And after breakfast I didn't have a cigarette, which is what I usually do. It wasn't hard. I just didn't want one. We went to school, and met each other during the day as much as we could. I didn't have a cigarette all day. After classes, I picked her up and then we got Max from school, and I took them home. Anna wanted me to stay for dinner, but I was dying for a smoke. When I got home I smoked like a fiend. But the more time I spent with her, the less I cared about cigarettes. It was easy. I quit eating meat, too. I wasn't whipped man. It just didn't feel right anymore.

So, anyway, B———, there I was on the steps of the church feeling guilty about getting cigarettes. I sat there for a long time, but then got up and walked back home. When I got back into bed with Anna, she woke up, and told me how cold I was. "I went for a walk," I said, which was true, but it felt like a lie. I felt guilty about a whole lot of things that night—for wanting a cigarette, for being a man, and for not telling her about that night and what we saw. It was work night, too, even though it felt like a Friday. I knew there'd be hell to pay if I showed up late for work.

Old man Van Vordt is a prick-and-a-½. You show up more than thirty seconds late and he fires you. You cut a piece of lumber as much as ¹⁄₁₆ of an inch too short and he fires you. You take more than the twenty minutes he gives us for lunch and you might as well pack your trash and ride out of Dodge. In the six months I've worked with him, he's fired about thirty guys. He only wants to tell you something once. Fuck it up, and you die. He pays good money, though, and that's why I keep going back to that freckle-headed ol' fart. Besides, I love the smell of wood, and the precision and beauty of what we do. He's the best cabinet maker I've ever run into, and for some reason, he likes me. I'm the only black guy he's ever had working for him. Maybe he believes in affirmative action. But anyway, my point is that I decided to stay up that night, cause I couldn't sleep, and I didn't want to be late to work. That made me want a cigarette all the more.

I started smoking about five years ago. To tell you the truth I like smoking a lot. Cigarettes, I mean. Pot's ok, but I like a cigarette buzz more, for some reason. And I like the way my lungs fill up. It makes me feel warm inside, makes me dreamy, sort of. I like making smoke rings, french inhaling, shot guns. And even though it stinks like hell, I like it when my room fills up with smoke. It's like having indoor clouds. I do go through about a can of air freshener a week, and I gotta run fans and keep windows open to kill the smell, but when the sun's shining through my windows in the afternoons, I'll shut em, fire up square after square, lay in my bed and blow cloud after cloud of blue and yellow smoke. And I hate it when a friend busts into my room on those days and says, "Jeezuz, it stinks in here." Hell, I know it stinks, but you can't smell worth a damn if you're inhaling and blowing. And it's my room.

I started smoking in '73, like I say, when I was still living at my folks' place and you were in college at Graceland. I'd went down to Alamosa to visit with Gary T—— and Dale P——. They were juniors, I think, and were living off campus. Let me tell you, if you think those guys were partiers in high school, you shoulda seen em then. There whole place was set up for partying. No rugs, black lights, strobe lights, lava lamps. They had a refrigerator in the basement that was filled with beer, maybe twelve cases. They had a wet bar upstairs, and this big ass cabinet filled with every type of booze you could name. Then there was this fishbowl in the kitchen that was full of joints, pills, and blotter acid. It was unreal. Serious to God, I wasn't into any of that stuff at the time, and most of it I'm still not. I've never done acid, speed, coke, downers, dust, and I can't stand most booze. I might have a beer every so often, but I just nurse the hell out of em. Man, I can make a can of beer last for a whole party. I did speed once in high school, and once again a couple months ago when I was working twelve-hour days at the mill. Anyway, I went up to check out Gary and Dale cause I hadn't seen them in a year or more. I was really surprised at what they looked like. Both of em had hair down to the middle of their backs. Dale was wearing this big honkin fu manchu and Gary had a full beard. It was incredible. Neither of them was playing hoop anymore. Gary'd quit and Dale'd wrecked his knees.

So, anyway, they weren't having any party that night, but people kept coming by all afternoon and all night to buy drugs. They had quite a nice business. They were each pulling down about 20 thou a year. It's how they paid their tuition. Far as I know they're still dealing.

So like, we shake hands and bullshit, etc, etc, and they show me around their place, etc, etc, and then Gary's fiance comes by, and we go down to the basement and sit on bean bags and then Gary brings out a gas mask and a bag of Panama Red. Oh, Lord, I started thinking. What if the cops bust down the door and start blazing away? What if it's bad stuff and we OD or something? (Yeah, I was pretty naive.) Then Dale said, "You get high, Scott?" And I said, "Oh sure." So when the mask came my way, I huffed and pulled and sucked, but didn't feel a thing. I took about fifteen hits in all, but still didn't feel a thing. Except I did feel paranoid (or as Gary would say, "noid"). I told em I still lived with my folks and they'd kill me if I came home reeking. So Dale reached into his T-shirt pocket and took out a pack of Marlboros, and said, "Smoke these on the way back. You'll smell like cigarettes, and that might make em mad, but you won't smell like weed, which'll make em toss you out." I put em in my pocket, and we hung out for a while longer and talked, etc, etc. Then we ordered a couple pizzas, ate, and then I split back home.

I got back to the Springs about one in the morning and I'd forgot all about the cigarettes till I was almost home, so I pulled off at this junior high parking lot, lit one up. After about five minutes I felt like I was floating. I felt calm. It was weird. I mean, I'd spent the entire evening smoking dope and hadn't felt a thing, but I was getting ripped on a damn cigarette. Well, that was it, man, I was hooked. Into it big time. My mom was pissed off at me when she found out I was smoking, but what could she say really? I mean, both my folks'd started smoking when they were in their teens, and they smoke maybe a pack a day a piece. Things got a little tense around the house, though, so I moved out.

Like I say, I wanted a cigarette, but I didn't smoke. Anna went to school and I went to work. Things seemed pretty normal. I was dragging ass at work, though, and ol' Van de Man was a demon. "Scott! Where's those rabbit cuts I asked you for? Scott! I thought I asked you ta clean that planer. Scott! You building a goddamn ark or what? Thought I asked you for them chester drawer legs a half hour ago!" I saw my career flash before my eyes a half dozen times. It wasn't only cause I was tired, and it wasn't only cause I would have given my left nut for a cigarette, and it wasn't just that I walked around all day with my guts feeling like Jello cause I was afraid every second of what might happen to Anna when I wasn't home. It was because I thought that since she'd told me about the worst thing that'd ever happened to her, that I should tell her about the worst thing that I ever let happen to someone else. But when I got home that afternoon, I made dinner, we ate, she did the dishes, we went to bed and made love for a long, long time. And that was it. It took me four hours to get to sleep that night.

Days went by and days went by and still I didn't say anything. But all I could think about was how that woman was trying to dig her nails into the pavement while she was under that car. And all I could think about was some bastard holding a knife to my woman's throat and breaking into her like a bullet. And I started getting weird and jealous in funny ways, like once when I drove by campus to pick her up from the library, and she was out front talking to this dude. She was standing out on the lawn, holding her books up over her breasts, and this tall blond bearded dude was craning over her, smiling, talking, moving his hands like he was conducting a goddamn band. I could tell they were looking deep in each other's eyes. I thought I could tell she was into this dude. B——, I know this'll sound stupid, but I was sitting there in my car, thinking, You idiot, don't you know what he's got on his mind? Don't you know what he could do to you? I acted like a prick all night long. To her anyway. With Max, I was like Santa Claus. I rode him on my back like a horse, I played checkers with him, I read him a couple stories. Then after everybody was in bed, I slipped out the house, walked to the 7-Eleven and bought a pack of cigarettes, and a bottle of mouthwash. I went to Monument Valley Park and smoked half a pack, washed my mouth over and over till the bottle was empty, and then I split back home. Soon as I got back I smoked a joint to mask the smell.

I thought we should be getting closer. I thought she should mistrust every man, but me. But then I got to thinking that maybe she could sense something about me, knew I was holding something back, which I was. I was holding two things back. I thought she was sensing something, 'cause her attitude was changing at home. She'd gotten pretty rough with Max. Didn't hit him or anything, but she'd go pyro on him if he spilled milk or messed up his clothes. And she only seemed interested in talking to me about stuff she was doing at school. And when all I could say back was something like, ". . . . . . ?" she started giving me all this women's lib stuff to read. Gyno-this and eco-gyno-poly-that. And when I still didn't get it, she'd just click her tongue at me and roll her eyes, sigh real loud and stomp off. She started correcting my English, which is something she'd never done, she started having long phone conversations with people and she'd never tell me who she was calling. And every time I thought maybe I'd better tell her about what you and me and the fellas saw, that night she'd do something else to piss me off, and I'd keep my mouth shut. I think from the time I lit that first square, the base of our relationship started to crumble. But then she was keeping something from me, too. I didn't know for sure, but I could feel it. I couldn't keep my mind off that tall blond son of a bitch.

I started picking up a pack of smokes on the way to work every day. And I started keeping mouthwash, gum, soap, air freshener, a toothbrush, and deodorant in a day sack in my trunk. Some times she'd say to me, "Geez, have you been at work or at a disco?" I'd tell her I just thought she'd like it if I didn't come home smelling like a bear. "You smelled like sawdust," she said, "and I like sawdust." But I couldn't stop smoking. And I started up eating meat again, too. On the way to work, I'd toss my cheese and sprout sandwiches and grab a hoagie, a chillie dog, didn't matter. So I'd play Mr. Tofu Head at home and go to work and let myself get scuzzy as hell. It never occurred to me once to look into other women, but I felt just as guilty. I couldn't sleep for shit, and I was getting kinda soft in bed, if you know what I mean. I couldn't stand myself. And I couldn't stand her. After we'd screw—and it was screwing by then, not love—I couldn't stand the touch of her. It was like every damn day I felt like I was gonna explode. I could see myself dropping to the floor at Anna's feet and begging her to forgive me for all the stuff I was doing, and all the stuff I'd failed to do. I'd beg her to forget that tall motherfucker and come back to me.

B——, I tried and tried and tried to tell her, but I couldn't, and I knew I was smoking a wall between us. I knew that, man, so I'd try every day to quit. I'd crush my cigarettes before leaving work and flush em down the toilet. I'd spray, wash, brush, rinse my ass till I was clean as a pimp. I'd do this every day, and every day I saw them squares, spinning round and round that white water, and going down, I thought that'd be it, that I wouldn't smoke any more. I bought a book on self-hypnosis, and a self-hypnosis tape at this health food place where we used to shop. I tried herbal teas, and hot showers, gum, candy, jogging, prayer. And I'd go home every day with a new idea, or a new way of picking up the subject of rape. I figured that of all the reasons I'd gone back to smoking, that was it. One day, I said, "Hey, babe, why don't we start giving money to one of them women's shelter things?" She was cooking dinner at the time. It was her day to do it. I was kicking back at the kitchen table, drinking some juice. She didn't say anything for like 30 seconds, enough time for me to get nervous, and start looking around. I watched Max tumbling around in the back yard. He looked cute as hell, his hair looked like pure white light the way the sun hit it. Then I looked back at Anna. She just picked up a handful of vegie peelings and flung em in the trash. "I think that'd be a good idea," she said, but she was looking really tight, really serious when she said it. I knew something wasn't "organic" as she would say, so I asked her what was up. Well, she flung that red hair out of her face, wiped away some sweat from her forehead with the back of her hand, dried her hands on a towel, and left the room. She came back in a minute with a little stash box, and I was relieved for a second cause I thought she was gonna twist up a joint and haul me off to bed. I was smiling, I think. She opened the box, reached in and tossed a cigarette, my brand, on the table. "I found it in your pocket when I did laundry yesterday," she said. She just stood there. I just sat there. "Busted," I said.

Yeah, we fought about it, but I didn't have too much fight in me, really. What could I say? It was mine. "I trusted you," she said. "You told me that when you met me, quitting smoking was the easiest thing in the world," she said. Scott Winters, I was thinking, a jury of your peers has found you guilty . . . It really surprised me when she started crying. I didn't think she'd took it that serious. I mean, she never'd asked me to quit smoking. Never said a word about it. And it was easy. When we moved in together, I just didn't buy any more squares. That was it.

From that day on, the day I was busted, is when I started thinking about getting in touch with you, B———. I wanted to ask you how you felt when Kari found out about you and that chick you were seeing. How you felt when you got busted. Kari called me up one day, after you and she'd split, and she was so angry I could hear the phone lines sizzling. She said, "I just wanna ask you one thing, Scott. Will you be honest with me?" And I said sure I would. And she asked me, "Did B——— really tell you he'd dreamt about me six weeks before he and I actually met? Was that true, Scott?" Well, B———, I'm sorry, bud, but I felt bad for her, and I figured that it wouldn't make any difference since you two'd already split. I told her the truth. I told her no, you hadn't told me that. Then she asked me if it was true what your girlfriend had told her, that you'd been picked up for flashing back in '72 when you lived in San Francisco, and I told Kari that's what you told me. Then—and her voice got higher and I could tell she was gonna cry—she said, "And then that bitch told me that B——— had gotten a woman pregnant when he was in college. Do you know if that's true?" I told her that I'd heard about it from a very unreliable source. That's all I knew. But it was good enough for her. She started crying, and God did I feel bad. She kept saying, "Thank you, Scott, thank you, thank you. I'm sorry to bother you, but I just wanted the truth for once. All of it. I just wanted to hear someone tell me the truth." She hung up without even saying goodbye.

That's why you haven't heard from me, B———. I was confused and felt ashamed. In fact, that last letter I got from you a few years back is still unopened. I just figured that Kari had called you up to bust your chops, 'cause of what I'd told her, and you were writing to bust mine. I couldn't take that. And if you don't write back now, I'll understand. Anyway, that time, there at the kitchen table, staring at the cigarette, is when I started thinking about you.

I tried to quit, but I couldn't. Sure, I told her I'd quit again, but I never did. I just got smarter about hiding things. I'd quit smoking so close to the end of the work day, always kept my squares in my locker at work. That kind of thing. On weekends, I never even thought about cigarettes. I'd take Max to the playground. I'd go grocery shopping. I'd go down to Pueblo to fish with my folks, with Anna & Max, or by myself, and I'd never even think about them. But I just couldn't do it this time. Anna was ok after a few days, but I could tell things were kind of slipping. And I got to feeling that she didn't care about whether I smoked or not. I knew I had to tell her about that night. I just never could. It's like she could sense what I was gonna say, and she'd say something, or give me a look, and I'd freeze up. Like this one time when she and I took Max to the "Y" for a swim. She and I got out after a few laps and I asked her what that guy might have done if she cried out for help. I just kind of blurted it out. I don't think she was ready to talk about this thing at a place like that, at a time like that. She just hugged Max's towel to her chest, and looked at the water. She was quiet so long I didn't think she was gonna say anything. "Well," she said, finally, and her answer was pretty much what I thought it'd be except she didn't say, *you stupid asshole idiot fuck,* but I could feel it— "Scott, he said he would kill me. He probably would have." Then she was quiet for awhile, and just slicked her hair back with her hand. Then she said, "There're times I wish he would have." She walked away from me and dove back into the water. That was it. Right then, I knew I was losing her, and I had to tell her. But you know, sometimes I think if I hadn't tried, I wouldn't be sitting up here on the third floor of Banana Manor, listening to the people next door screw their insides out, and hearing some butthead teenager slamming Fleetwood Mac out his speakers for the world to hear. I wouldn't be sitting inside this stinking little cloud of mine at two, now three, now four in the morning, with a terminal case of writer's cramp, trying to lay down something I wish never'd happened.

I was gonna tell her, B——, about everything, the way we all just stood there, and watched a huge piece of that woman's life get sucked away into a car, the make, model, and year of which I guess we'll never know. Man, we watched that piece of her life shrink down to a pair of taillights, and we went on with our own. Yeah, I was gonna tell Anna. I was finally gonna do it, and I was hoping both that she would and wouldn't tell me about that tall blond dude.

I called in sick to work, and ol' Van de Man was pissed because we were behind schedule on a contract we'd had with Pueblo 1st Federal. I'd never took a day off before, though, and I told him that. He pretty much let me slide then, but he did it in Van Vordt style. "You screw me one more time, like this, Winters and ya might as well not come back! Just might as well not come back!" I'm sure that freckled head was hot enough to cook rice. So, anyway, I picked out a great recepie from Diet for a Small Planet, and whipped that up. I ran to Weber Street Liquors and bought her a bottle of Mateus rosé. It's her favorite. I was nervous as hell, and couldn't sit down all day. I went to the Safeway twice and bought a pack of Winstons both times. The first one, I opened the pack, drew one and lit up, but put it out. The next one I opened as soon as I got home, but I crushed em into the toilet and flushed. I cleaned up the house and bought flowers. I was so nervous, I was twitching. I paced around the house all afternoon, trying to think up ways I could tell her, but it all sounded so stupid—*More wine, dear? Oh, by the way, I witnessed an abduction of a woman when I was a sophomore in high school, didn't do a damned thing about it, though. It probably lead to her rape. Maybe even a murder. Just say when!* I was thinking, Scott, you dork. What good is a clean house and rosé wine gonna do? I felt like a bozo.

So, I went to pick up Max from school, since I knew it was

Anna's day to do the laundry. I took the kid into the back yard and I threw him the football for awhile, but I was throwing so hard I just about cracked his ribs. He was ok, though. Didn't even cry all that much, but I hugged him and took him inside, fixed him a snack and let him watch the tube. I really love that kid, I guess. In a way, I guess. At first I was embarrased at all the stares him and I used to get when I'd take him places. I'm sure some people thought I'd kidnapped him or something, but after awhile I didn't even think about it. I think I know how you must feel about being away from your boy.

Anna came home about a quarter to five. Her eyes were all big and she kept asking what the occasion was, and I kept saying, "Cause I love you, that's all." We had dinner, put Max to bed, and broke out the wine. Anna didn't know what was bugging me, but she knew I wasn't very together for some reason or another, and it was like she got nervous, too. She got up after awhile and started putting laundry away. I looked at her—from her little pink feet to her bush of red hair—and I was thinking, "Cause I love you, that's all." She looked gorgeous, and I just knew that what I was gonna tell her'd bring us closer, even if it started off with some hurt. She started to change the sheets on the bed, but I'd already handled that. I swear, the house never looked cleaner, and she kept asking me why this, and why that, but there wasn't, like, excitement in her voice, but it was like kind of an almost irritated tone, like she felt bad that she hadn't helped, or that I was trying to tell her how to *Really* clean house. She kept getting more and more nervous. I think she was figuring I was gonna propose to her, and she's real nervous about marriage. She says she doesn't even wanna think about marriage till she graduates, and gets financially together. You know, just in case the next guy dumps her like the first one did.

So she went back to putting laundry away, and I was following her around the house, just yacking about nothing. Then I just sort of started talking real casual about this essay she'd asked me to read. It was by this woman named Sue Brownmiller. I can't remember the title, and it was pretty tough reading, but it's about how women are better at cooperation and being sensitive than guys, and that's what we need in this world. Maybe that's not all she was saying, but that's basically what I got out of it. Took me forever to read it.

Anyway, I started talking to Anna about the article and she started talking about something we argue about all the time—that if women ran the world, it might be a little bit less organized than it is now, but it would definately be more peaceful. Instead of saying what I usually say, which is, Look, as long as there're men on the planet, there'd still be violence, etc., etc., I figured that here was my chance to get to my point. So I just kind of blurted out, "You know, babe, considering all that's happened to you, I wouldn't be surprised if you hated men." And at first I didn't think she knew what I meant, 'cause she just kept opening up drawers and putting stuff away and closing them back up. I figured she'd just click her tongue at me, and roll her eyes and say, "You missed the point, Scott." But then she kind of turned in my direction, but didn't look at me. She pulled her hair away from her face and flung it back. Then she said, "I'm surprised I don't hate black men. The guy who raped me was black." Then she walked out the room with a stack of laundry in her arms. Then she closed the goddamn door. She closed it soft.

I just stood there, staring at the door, B——. It was like she'd stabbed me in the chest and kicked me in the balls at the same time. I'm not exaggerating, man, my nuts were hurting so bad I had to squat for a minute and take some deep breaths. That ever happen to you, where your blood and adrenelin get pumping so bad it hurts your nuts? It took the wind out of me. It was unreal. I never, ever thought she'd say anything like that to me. It was from Mars, man. Why didn't she tell me that night? I was thinking. Why now? This way. Like a weapon. What the fuck did I do to deserve that? I just sat there, and my hands were shaking and I thought for sure I was gonna throw up. I felt sick and dead and I couldn't breathe right. It was like my veins'd been tapped and were leaking out all over the floor.

Then, after my blood slowed a bit, I opened up the drawers

she'd just shut and I grabbed 3 or 4 of everything, plus a bunch of shit from the closet. Shoes and things. I packed a couple of bags, and I walked into the living room, and to the front door. I looked around the place. It was damned clean, that's for sure. She saw me from the kitchen and she said, "Where do you think you're going?" I just looked at her and shook my head. I wanted to tell her to stick it, but I just shook my head and stepped out. She was on my heels, though, right dead on my heels. She kept pulling on my shoulder and arm, trying to get me to turn around. She kept saying, "What are you doing? Where are you going? What's going on?" Shit like that. I could see her long blue skirt sweeping around and I could see her pink feet. It was cold out there. I felt bad, B——, bad for all kinds of reasons, but I kept moving, jerking my arm or shoulder away from her, you know? My throat was all clutched up tight, and even if I'd wanted to say something to her I couldn't have. I couldn't look at her either. I stuck my car key into the lock, but before I could twist the lock open she grabbed the key ring, and she was flipping by now, practically screaming, ripping at my wrists and hands with her fingernails, "What's going on? What're you doing? Talk to me, Scott, please," and all that. I grabbed her wrist, forced open her hand, took the keys, got in, cranked it up. I never looked back at her face. If I had, I probably wouldn't've split. I mean she was acting completely innocent, like she didn't have any idea of what she'd said. And for a second there, I wasn't sure I was doing the right thing, or if she'd even understood what she'd said or the way she'd said it. By then I was goddamn crying, too. And as I was backing out, she kept saying, "Please, please, please, Scott, please." That's basically why I'm writing you, brother. Do you think she knew what she'd done? I mean, here's kind of the reason why, what I'm gonna tell you now.

I tried not to listen, ok, and I was pulling away. I couldn't see good, because of the tears, but I could see her in the rear-view mirror. She was standing in the street with her hands in her hair, pulling it back like she does when it's wet. She kept saying,

"Please, please, please, Scott, please," but the farther away I got, it started sounding more like, keys, keys, keys, Scott, keys.

Right now I don't know, B——. Sometimes you just don't know. Sometimes you just can't tell what you see or hear or feel. Or remember.

Take care, man,
Love, Scott.

Reginald McKnight was born in Germany, and has lived in New York, California, Colorado, Texas, Alabama, Louisiana, and elsewhere. He is Associate Professor of English in the Writing Program at Carnegie Mellon University in Pittsburgh, Pennsylvania. His stories have appeared in such literary magazines as *The Kenyon Review*, and *Prairie Schooner*, and have been anthologized in *The O. Henry Awards* and *New Stories from the South*. His new collection, *The Kind of Light that Shines in Texas*, was published by Little, Brown in 1992.

PHOTO CREDIT: KIMBERLY PASKO

About my story—why it's southern, and why I wrote it, well both are rather tough to answer. Although both my parents are southern born and raised, my upbringing had been the patchwork of military brathood. I was born in Germany, moved to New York, then to California, to Colorado, Texas, Alabama, Louisiana, and elsewhere. I spent my coming of age, at least the first half of it, below the Mason-Dixon line. In those days, I was beginning to become aware of "my place" in the political context of the times (1965–1969 and 1/2), and there I felt the first *rustlings of sexual attraction. These two factors, more than any others, directly contributed to the creation of "Quitting Smoking" (except for the smoking, which I took up in California when I was a young Marine). In Louisiana, I was old enough to take occasional interest in local and national newscasts. I noted, after a time, that whenever local newscasters reported a crime (allegedly perpetrated) by a black person, the person was referred to as a Bossier City Negro or a Shreveport Negro, etc. Of course, they never noted the color of white criminals. It rather gave one the feeling that only black people committed crimes, or at least that their crimes were more heinous than those committed by nonblacks.*

It must have been that my schoolmates in Louisiana (all white, except for a black kid who came onto the scene a couple of weeks before my family's departure, and another who moved away a couple of weeks after our arrival) had the same opinion. And of course, since we were all steaming and frothing in the broth of new hormones, many of my peers were expressly interested in sexual crimes. It quickly became clear to me that my peers associated black men with rape. After a time so did I. Discovering Soul on Ice *at the tender age of fourteen didn't help much, either. So there I was, in the throes of puberty, attending schools where there were very few, and sometimes not any, black people. I felt embarrassment, confusion, fear, both repulsion and attraction when I saw a girl I thought pretty. I tell you, it was madness. If I exchanged so much as a few casual words with a white girl, some white boy would draw near to listen in, or tease me, or just plain threaten to kick my tail. I didn't know whether the attraction I felt for some girl was pure or prurient. It was weird.*

Susan Perabo

EXPLAINING DEATH TO
THE DOG

(from *The Missouri Review*)

After the baby died I found it imperative that my German shepherd Stu understand and accept the concept of death. The first week wasn't so bad, what with all our friends and relatives around, smothering Stu with affection. And Todd was home from work that week, dumping well-meaning casseroles accidentally-on-purpose onto the kitchen floor for Stu to indulge in. So Stu didn't notice the absence so much, didn't seem to. He trotted around the house happily, oblivious to the fact that the baby, who he had had a big hand in raising, was missing.

Then the party ended. Guests cried the last of their tears at my front door, said "what a waste" for the thousandth and final time, and made their separate ways back to their separate lives, lives that sailed along quite smoothly despite the absence of the infant who they had been mourning for a good seven or eight days.

Todd went back to work; packed up his briefcase and kissed me good-bye. He nearly tripped over Stu in his rush to get out of the house. He wanted away, wanted to get busy again. Stu and I stood at the window and watched him drive away. Stu looked up at me and then back at the empty driveway. He lay down on the floor in front of the window. I sat next to him and rubbed his stomach. He sighed.

What to do with the baby dead? No diapers, no screaming, no feeding. What had I done before the baby? I had been pregnant. Pregnant for longer than she had lived. And what had I done before I got pregnant? I tried to remember. I supposed I had cleaned the house. Cooked. Taken Stu to the park. It didn't seem like it could have been nearly enough to take up a whole day.

In the afternoon I made myself a sandwich from one of the two whole hams that were still in the refrigerator and sat in front of the television. I waited for Stu, waited for him to emerge from wherever he was sleeping, jingling and jangling his way to a possible meal. The house was quiet. Still, very still. The morning the baby died Todd shook me awake to the stillness and said, "Listen, she's sleeping . . ."

I set my sandwich on the coffee table and got up to look for Stu. I called him a few times. Nothing. I walked through the house, from room to room. I found him upstairs, in the baby's room. The room was empty, except for one chair. Todd and the relatives had cleaned it out the day of the funeral because they said it was just too sad to look at. They stashed the crib in the back of a stranger's car and carted it away, hid the dolls and mobiles behind cobwebs in the basement. Then Todd's mother said the room looked so bare, so she had taken a chair from our bedroom and set it by the window. It looked unnatural by itself in the baby's room. Worse than bare. Just awkward.

Stu was lying in the middle of the empty room. His ears were back and his eyes open. He didn't raise his head when I came in. His eyes just followed me.

"Stu," I said. "Stu, what the hell are you doing?"

He looked like he had eaten too much casserole, was what it was, looked like he might toss his canine cookies at any moment. He stood up lazily. He walked in circles around the room. You could tell he was looking for the baby.

"No," I said. I called him to me and patted his head. "No more baby," I said. "Baby's gone."

He looked at me with the universal blank dog look. He had no idea what I was talking about. "No baby," I said again. It was then that I realized the impossibility of the situation. It wasn't even like trying to explain death to a child. The dog simply couldn't understand the language. He had a brain the size of a walnut and all he knew was that the baby wasn't where she was supposed to be. I imagined it must be even worse than knowing the baby was dead. At least Todd had been able to logically spell it out for me that morning to get me to stop shaking her and trying to wake her up, hold the little girl up in my face, point to the chest. NO BREATHING.

It was then I decided that I needed to teach Stu about death, whatever the cost. I figured he had a right to know, being a member of the family.

"Come on, boy," I said. He slunk out of the baby's room behind me. I closed the door.

On the coffee table we had a book. A big *Life* magazine book. *Best of Life*, something like that. I gave Stu part of my ham sandwich to lure him up on the couch with me. I opened the book out on the coffee table, paged through it, looking for the sixties, the best lesson of death on film.

"Lookee," I said. I turned the dog's head toward the contorted face of Lee Harvey Oswald, and the man behind him looking like he might jump right out of his skin from the shock of it. Oswald was holding his stomach, hadn't even hit the floor. "Dead," I said. "Stu, it's dead."

Stu didn't seem to see the picture. He looked at the book, sure, but there was nothing in his eyes that said that he saw the proverbial farm being bought. The way he looked at it, it could have been a picture of a rolling wheat field. I turned the page, looking for something bigger, and found a two-page spread from Memphis, 1968, the man dead on the balcony, people pointing out into the sky. It was big, you couldn't miss it.

"Death," I said to Stu. "No more."

Again Stu glanced at the picture, then back at my ham sandwich. I jabbed my finger on Martin Luther King, held it up in

Stu's face, and still his eyes didn't focus on it. What was I expecting? I don't know. If Todd had been there he would have clapped the book shut and told me the dog didn't know what the hell was going on and he'd be over it in a day and a half anyway. But Todd was gone. Strange things happen when you're alone in the house with pets all day.

In the middle of the night I woke up and heard the baby crying. I sat up and reached for my glasses before I remembered. It was not a staggering thing. It washed over me slowly, the way you remember what day it is when you wake up in the morning. I looked at Todd lying on his stomach next to me, the side of his face pressed to the pillow, his mouth open. The first week it was he who couldn't sleep. I'd open my eyes and he'd be sitting up in bed, his back against the wall, staring into space. The minister had come by and Todd told him about not being able to sleep. The minister said it was probably guilt, thinking that if he'd been awake when the baby died he could have done something about it. After that I guess Todd became comfortable with the guilt, because he didn't sit up nights anymore.

"Todd?" I said.

In the corner, Stu raised his head and looked at me.

"Todd?" I said again. I didn't have the courage to touch him, to wake him up and force him to share the grief, to try to explain to me why I might have heard the baby crying when the baby had been dead for over a week. I lay back down next to him and started thinking about the simplicity of a dog's mind. I tried to think of a way to explain to Stu just exactly what was going on.

The morning was cool and dark. It was May and the natural order of things said it should have been warm and bright. But the natural order of things was wrong, so it was ugly out. Todd sat at breakfast and looked at the newspaper in much the same way Stu had looked at the coffee-table book. His spoon went from the cereal bowl to his mouth without being led by anything but habit. I stared at him and he didn't even notice.

"I think Stu misses the baby," I said.

He looked up from the paper, his mouth open and his eyes empty like he was a vegetable. "What?"

"Yesterday he was lying in her room."

"Close the door," Todd said.

"I was thinking," I said. "I was trying to figure out how to get it across to him that she's not coming back."

Todd put his spoon down. "Why would you think something like that?" he asked.

"I just thought it was interesting. I wondered how dogs understand those kinds of things."

"What are you doing today?" Todd asked. "Why don't you call somebody for lunch?"

"No one wants to have lunch with me," I said.

Todd sighed, looked at me like I was the baby squirming around while he was trying to get the diaper on. "We'll go out tonight, then," he said, but he wasn't even looking at me. He was looking over my shoulder out the back door, out into the grayness that was passing itself off as morning.

The house was clean. Relatives had had their hands in picking up the place before the funeral gathering, and Todd and I hadn't done enough to mess anything up since then. And there was no cooking to do. I decided I would go ahead and take Stu to the park, force him down the slide for a good laugh, spin us both around on the merry-go-round just for a change of pace. There would be no baby carriage to drag through the sand, no need to worry about it slipping from my grip and careering down a hill into the creek. The park was different with no baby. It seemed much safer.

Then we found the squirrel. Stu walked right past it, didn't even notice, but I saw it. It was lying on its side on the grass. Its mouth was open, its eyes empty holes. Other than that it was fine. Perfectly whole, not the work of a cat or a child with a BB gun.

"Stu," I said. "Stu, come here, baby." He stopped, turned back, then trotted to where I was kneeling on the ground. He saw the squirrel and stopped for a second. He looked at me. I reached out to touch the squirrel and Stu took a step back. Its fur was damp and brittle. Stu walked up to the squirrel, then turned his head away and looked at me like I had gotten him into something he wasn't near ready for. A fly landed on the squirrel's head and crawled into the empty eye socket.

"Stu," I said. "This is important." I took hold of his head and turned it toward the rodent. I pushed his nose a little closer to the body. "The squirrel's dead," I said. "You understand?"

Squirrels, I could hear Stu thinking. I chase these things. This squirrel is not running.

Stu backed away from the animal. I tried to hold on to him but he pulled me backward and I fell from my knees onto the wet grass. Stu ran in circles around me, afraid he was in trouble.

So we were going to go out for dinner. Todd came home and sat on the couch in a heap. His tie was askew and his hair mussed. I asked him if he had a bad day and he said he was just a little tired.

"Does that mean we're not going to dinner?" I asked.

"Dinner?" Todd leaned forward and banged the side of his head with his hand, like he was trying to get water out of his ear. "I feel like I'm all clogged up," he said.

"So we're not going out?"

He stopped banging, looked up at me. "I didn't say that," he said. "I didn't say we weren't going out." He paused. "Where do you want to go?"

"We could go someplace fancy," I said. "We haven't been someplace fancy in a long time."

For the first time he noticed the dog, lying on his side on the couch, his eyes staring absently at the ceiling. "What's up with him?" Todd asked.

"I told you," I said. "He's confused."

"He's confused," Todd said. "The dog is confused."

"Yeah," I said. I was trying to think of a way to make a case for how confused Stu really was, but Todd didn't seem receptive to the idea.

Todd stood up and loosened his tie. "Let me change," he said. "We'll go out. I just have to get out of these clothes."

I sat on the couch with Stu and waited. Stu put his head on my thigh and looked up at me. I wanted to do something for him, take him out to dinner with us to get his mind off the mystery of the missing baby. We sat there for a few minutes. I couldn't hear any noises coming from the bedroom, so I got up and went down the hallway. I looked in the door and saw Todd sitting on the edge of the bed. He was banging the side of his head again, but this time he was crying while he was doing it. Actually he wasn't really crying. He was more making little howling noises with his throat. And he just kept whacking himself on the head.

I went back into the living room. I had a desire to get Stu off the couch and give him a push toward the bedroom, so he could stumble upon Todd and see what the death thing was all about, but I didn't have the heart.

I woke again in the middle of the night, but I didn't hear any crying. I got out of bed anyway and went into the baby's room. Stu hopped up and followed me, hopefully, but the room was still empty except for the chair by the window. Still, the dog wandered around, sniffing out the emptiness, the way he had the day before, and the day before that, and the way I realized he probably would for quite a while. I sat down in the chair by the window. Everything was quiet, and I thought of saying to Stu that that was it, that was death, the quiet. But Stu was still sniffing around the room, trying to pick up the scent of the baby, and I realized he would never understand death. All he would come to understand was that the baby was not coming back.

———————

Susan Perabo is a native of St. Louis, Missouri.
She now lives in Fayetteville, Arkansas, where she
is working toward her MFA in fiction. Her work
has appeared in *The Missouri Review*. In 1991, she
received the Lilly Peter Fellowship for fiction at
the University of Arkansas.

PHOTO CREDIT: RANDOLPH THOMAS

I *didn't plan this story. One afternoon I was taking my dog Bones for
a walk and we stumbled across a dead squirrel. Bones stepped right
over it and kept on walking and I couldn't understand why she wasn't
at least interested in the thing. So I pulled her back, made her look at
it, and spent the rest of the walk trying to explain death to her. When
I got home I sat down and started writing. After the title, the story was
easy. I think the world can be broken down into two main groups: people
who hold conversations with their pets, and people who don't. Sometimes,
as the people in the first group know, you make more sense when you're
talking to your dog than you do when you're thinking to yourself. And if
you go one step further and put yourself in the dog's place, things you may
have thought were very complex suddenly seem quite simple.*

Robert Olen Butler

A GOOD SCENT FROM A STRANGE MOUNTAIN

(from *New England Review*)

Ho Chi Minh came to me again last night, his hands covered with confectioners' sugar. This was something of a surprise to me, the first time I saw him beside my bed, in the dim light from the open shade. My oldest daughter leaves my shades open, I think so that I will not forget that the sun has risen again in the morning. I am a very old man. She seems to expect that one morning I will simply forget to keep living. This is very foolish. I will one night rise up from my bed and slip into her room and open the shade there. Let *her* see the sun in the morning. She is sixty-four years old and she should worry for herself. I could never die from forgetting.

But the light from the street was enough to let me recognize Ho when I woke, and he said to me, "Dao, my old friend, I have heard it is time to visit you." Already on that first night there was a sweet smell about him, very strong in the dark, even before I could see his hands. I said nothing, but I stretched to the nightstand beside me and I turned on the light to see if he would go away. And he did not. He stood there beside the bed—I could even see him reflected in the window—and I knew it was real because he did not appear as he was when I'd known him but as he was when he'd died. This was Uncle Ho before me, the thin old man with the dewlap beard wearing the dark clothes of a peasant and the rubber sandals, just like in the news pictures I studied with such a strange feeling for all those years. Strange because when I knew him, he was not yet Ho Chi Minh. It was 1917 and he was Nguyen Ai Quoc and we were both young men with clean-shaven faces, the best of friends, and we worked at the Carlton Hotel in London where I was a dishwasher and he was a pastry cook under the great Escoffier. We were the best of friends and we saw snow for the first time together. This was before we began to work at the hotel. We shoveled snow and Ho would stop for a moment and blow his breath out before him and it would make him smile, to see what was inside him, as if it was the casting of bones to tell the future.

On that first night when he came to me in my house in New Orleans, I finally saw what it was that smelled so sweet and I said to him, "Your hands are covered with sugar."

He looked at them with a kind of sadness.

I have received that look myself in the past week. It is time now for me to see my family, and the friends I have made who are still alive. This is our custom from Vietnam. When you are very old, you put aside a week or two to receive the people of your life so that you can tell each other your feelings, or try at last to understand each other, or simply say good-bye. It is a formal leave-taking, and with good luck you can do this before you have your final illness. I have lived almost a century and perhaps I should have called them all to me sooner, but at last I felt a deep weariness and I said to my oldest daughter that it was time.

They look at me with sadness, some of them. Usually the dull-witted ones, or the insincere ones. But Ho's look was, of course, not dull-witted or insincere. He considered his hands and said, "The glaze. Maestro's glaze."

There was the soft edge of yearning in his voice and I had the thought that perhaps he had come to me for some sort of help. I said to him, "I don't remember. I only washed dishes." As soon as the words were out of my mouth, I decided it was foolish for me to think he had come to ask me about the glaze.

But Ho did not treat me as foolish. He looked at me and shook his head. "It's all right," he said, "I remember the temperature now. Two hundred and thirty degrees, when the sugar is between the large thread stage and the small orb stage. The Maestro was very clear about that and I remember." I knew from his eyes, however, that there was much more that still eluded him. His eyes did not seem to move at all from my face, but there was some little shifting of them, a restlessness that perhaps only I could see, since I was his close friend from the days when the world did not know him.

I am nearly one hundred years old but I can still read a man's face. Perhaps better than I ever have. I sit in the overstuffed chair in my living room and I receive my visitors and I want these people, even the dull-witted and insincere ones—please excuse an old man's ill temper for calling them that I want them all to be good with each other. A Vietnamese family is extended as far as the blood line strings us together, like so many paper lanterns around a village square. And we all give off light together. That's the way it has always been in our culture. But these people that come to visit me have been in America for a long time and there are very strange things going on that I can see in their faces.

None stranger than this morning. I was in my overstuffed chair and with me there were four of the many members of my family: my son-in-law Thang, a former colonel in the Army of the Republic of Vietnam and one of the insincere ones, sitting on my Castro convertible couch; his youngest son Loi, who had come in late, just a few minutes earlier, and had thrown himself down on the couch as well, youngest but a man old enough to have served as a lieutenant under his father as our country fell to the communists more than a decade ago; my daughter Lam, who is Thang's wife, hovering behind the both of them and refusing all invitations to sit down; and my oldest daughter, leaning against the door frame, having no doubt just returned from my room where she had opened the shade that I had closed when I awoke.

It was Thang who gave me the sad look I have grown accustomed to, and I perhaps seemed to him at that moment a little weak, a little distant. I had stopped listening to the small talk of these people and I had let my eyes half close, though I could still see them clearly and I was very alert. Thang has a steady face and the quick eyes of a man who is ready to come under fire, but I have always read much more there, in spite of his efforts to show nothing. So after he thought I'd faded from the room, it was with slow eyes, not quick, that he moved to his son and began to speak of the killing.

You should understand that Mr. Nguyen Bich Le had been shot dead in our community here in New Orleans just last week. There are many of us Vietnamese living in New Orleans and one man, Mr. Le, published a little newspaper for all of us. He had recently made the fatal error—though it should not be that in America—of writing that it was time to accept the reality of the communist government in Vietnam and begin to talk to them. We had to work now with those who controlled our country. He said that he remained a patriot to the Republic of Vietnam, and I believed him. If anyone had asked an old man's opinion on this whole matter, I would not have been afraid to say that Mr. Le was right.

But he was shot dead last week. He was forty-five years old and he had a wife and three children and he was shot as he sat behind the wheel of his Chevrolet pickup truck. I find a detail like that especially moving, that this man was killed in his Chevrolet, which I understand is a strongly American thing. We know this in Saigon. In Saigon it was very American to own a Chevrolet, just as it was French to own a Citroën.

And Mr. Le had taken one more step in his trusting embrace of this new culture. He had bought not only a Chevrolet but a Chevrolet pickup truck, which made him not only American but a man of Louisiana, where there are many pickup trucks. He did not, however, also purchase a gun rack for the back window, another sign of this place. Perhaps it would have been well if he had, for it was through the back window that the bullet was fired. Someone had hidden in the bed of his truck and had killed him from behind in his Chevrolet and the reason for this act was made very clear in a phone call to the newspaper office by a nameless representative of the Vietnamese Party for the Annihilation of Communism and for the National Restoration.

And Thang my son-in-law said to his youngest son Loi, "There is no murder weapon." What I saw was a faint lift of his eyebrows as he said this, like he was inviting his son to listen beneath his words. Then he said it again, more slowly, as if it was code. "There is *no weapon*." My grandson nodded his head once, a crisp little snap. Then my daughter Lam said in a very loud voice, with her eyes on me, "That was a terrible thing, the death of Mr. Le." She nudged her husband and son, and both men turned their faces sharply to me and they looked at me squarely and said, also in very loud voices, "Yes, it was terrible."

I am not deaf, and I closed my eyes further, having seen enough and wanting them to think that their loud talk had not only failed to awaken me but had put me more completely to sleep. I did not like to deceive them, however, even though I have already spoken critically of these members of my family. I am a Hoa Hao Buddhist and I believe in harmony among all living things, especially the members of a Vietnamese family.

After Ho had reassured me, on that first visit, about the temperature needed to heat Maestro Escoffier's glaze, he said, "Dao, my old friend, do you still follow the path you chose in Paris?"

He meant by this my religion. It was in Paris that I embraced the Buddha and disappointed Ho. We went to France in early 1918, with the war still on, and we lived in the poorest street of the poorest part of the Seventeenth Arrondissement. Number 9 impasse Compoint, a blind alley with a few crumbling houses, all but ours rented out for storage. The cobblestones were littered with fallen roof tiles and Quoc and I each had a tiny single room with only an iron bedstead and a crate to sit on. I could see my friend Quoc in the light of the tallow candle and he was dressed in a dark suit and a bowler hat and he looked very foolish. I did not say so, but he knew it himself and he kept seating and re-seating the hat and shaking his head very slowly, with a loudly silent anger. This was near the end of our time together, for I was visiting daily with a Buddhist monk and he was drawing me back to the religion of my father. I had run from my father, gone to sea, and that was where I had met Nguyen Ai Quoc and we had gone to London and to Paris and now my father was calling me back, through a Vietnamese monk I met in the Tuileries.

Quoc, on the other hand, was being called not from his past but from his future. He had rented the dark suit and bowler and he would spend the following weeks in Versailles, walking up and down the mirrored corridors of the palace trying to gain an audience with Woodrow Wilson. Quoc had eight requests for the Western world concerning Indochina. Simple things. Equal rights, freedom of assembly, freedom of the press. The essential things that he knew Wilson would understand, based as they were on Wilson's own Fourteen Points. And Quoc did not even intend to ask for independence. He wanted Vietnamese repre-sentatives in the French Parliament. That was all he would ask. But his bowler made him angry. He wrenched out of the puddle of candlelight, both his hands clutching the bowler, and I heard him muttering in the darkness, and I felt that this was a bad sign already, even before he had set foot in Versailles. And as it turned out, he never saw Wilson, or Lloyd George either, or even Clemenceau. But somehow his frustration with his hat was what made me sad, even now, and I reached out from my bedside and said, "Uncle Ho, it's all right."

He was still beside me. This was not an awakening, as you might expect, this was not a dream ending with the bowler in Paris and me awaking to find that Ho was never there. He was still beside my bed, though he was just beyond my outstretched hand and he did not move to me. He smiled on one side of his mouth, a smile full of irony, as if he too were thinking about the night he'd tried on his rented clothes. He said, "Do you remember how I worked in Paris?"

I thought about this and I did remember, with the words of his advertisement in the newspaper *La Vie Ouvrière*: "If you would like a lifelong memento of your family, have your photos retouched at Nguyen Ai Quoc's." This was his work in Paris; he retouched photos with a very delicate hand, the same fine hand that Monsieur Escoffier had admired in London. I said, "Yes, I remember."

Ho nodded gravely. "I painted the blush into the cheeks of Frenchmen."

I said, "A lovely portrait in a lovely frame for forty francs," another phrase from his advertisement.

"Forty-five," Ho said.

I thought now of his question that I had not answered. I motioned to the far corner of the room where the prayer table stood. "I still follow the path."

He looked and said, "At least you became a Hoa Hao."

He could tell this from the simplicity of the table. There was only a red cloth upon it and four Chinese characters: *bao son ky huong*. This is the saying of the Hoa Haos. We follow the teachings of a monk who broke away from the fancy rituals of the other Buddhists. We do not need elaborate pagodas or rituals. The Hoa Hao believes that the maintenance of our spirits is very simple, and the mystery of joy is simple too. The four characters mean "A good scent from a strange mountain."

I had always admired the sense of humor of my friend Quoc so I said, "You never did stop painting the blush into the faces of Westerners."

Ho looked back to me but he did not smile. I was surprised at this but more surprised at my little joke seeming to remind him of his hands. He raised them and studied them and said, "After the heating, what was the surface for the glaze?"

"My old friend," I said, "you worry me now."

But Ho did not seem to hear. He turned away and crossed the room and I knew he was real because he did not vanish from my sight but opened the door and went out and closed the door behind him with a loud click.

I rang for my daughter. She had given me a porcelain bell and after allowing Ho enough time to go down the stairs and out the front door, if that was where he was headed, I rang the bell, and my daughter, who is a very light sleeper, soon appeared.

"What is it, Father?" she asked with great patience in her voice. She is a good girl. She understands about Vietnamese families and she is a smart girl.

"Please feel the doorknob," I said.

She did so without the slightest hesitation and this was a lovely gesture on her part, a thing that made me wish to rise up and embrace her, though I was very tired and did not move.

"Yes?" she asked after touching the knob.

"Is it sticky?"

She touched it again. "Ever so slightly," she said. "Would you like me to clean it?"

"In the morning," I said.

She smiled and crossed the room and kissed me on the forehead. She smelled of lavender and fresh bedclothes and there are so many who have gone on before me into the world of spirits and I yearn for them all, yearn to find them all together in a village square, my wife there smelling of lavender and our own sweat, like on a night in Saigon soon after the terrible fighting in 1968 when we finally opened the windows onto the night and there were sounds of bombs falling on the horizon and there was no breeze at all, just the heavy stillness of the time between the dry season and the wet, and Saigon smelled of tar and motorcycle exhaust and cordite, but when I opened the window and turned to my wife, the room was full of a wonderful scent, a sweet smell that made her sit up, for she sensed it too. This was a smell that had nothing to do with flowers but instead reminded us that flowers were always ready to fall into dust while this smell was as if a gemstone had begun to give off a scent, as if a mountain of emerald had found its own scent. I crossed the room to my wife and we were already old, we had already buried children and grandchildren that we prayed waited for us in that village square at the foot of the strange mountain, but when I came near the bed she lifted her silk gown and threw it aside and I pressed close to her and our own sweat smelled sweet on that night. I want to be with her in that square and with the rest of those we'd buried, the tiny limbs and the sullen eyes and the gray faces of the puzzled children and the surprised adults and the weary old people who have gone before us, who know the secrets now. And the sweet smell of the glaze on Ho's hands reminds me of others that I would want in the square, the people from the ship, too, the Vietnamese boy from a village near my own who died of a fever in the Indian Ocean and the natives in Dakar who were forced by colonial officials to swim out to our ship in shark-infested waters to secure the moorings and two were killed before our eyes without a French regret. Ho was very moved by this, and I want those men in our square and I want the Frenchman, too, who called Ho "monsieur" for the first time. A man on the dock in Marseilles. Ho spoke of him twice more during our years together and I want that Frenchman there. And, of course, Ho. Was he in the village square even now, waiting? Heating his glaze fondant? My daughter was smoothing my covers around me and the smell of lavender on her was still strong.

"He was in this room," I said to her to explain the sticky doorknob.

"Who was?"

But I was very sleepy and I could say no more, though perhaps she would not have understood anyway, in spite of being the smart girl that she is.

The next night I left my light on to watch for Ho's arrival, but I dozed off and he had to wake me. He was sitting in a chair that he'd brought from across the room. He said to me, "Dao. Wake up, my old friend."

I must have awakened when he pulled the chair near to me, for I heard each of these words. "I am awake," I said. "I was thinking of the poor men who had to swim out to our ship."

"They are already among those I have served," Ho said. "Before I forgot." And he raised his hands and they were still covered with sugar.

I said, "Wasn't it a marble slab?" I had a memory, strangely clear after these many years, as strange as my memory of Ho's Paris business card.

"A marble slab," Ho repeated, puzzled.

"That you poured the heated sugar on."

"Yes." Ho's sweet-smelling hands came forward but they did not quite touch me. I thought to reach out from beneath the covers and take them in my own hands, but Ho leaped up and paced about the room. "The marble slab, moderately oiled. Of course. I am to let the sugar half cool and then use the spatula to move it about in all directions, every bit of it, so that it doesn't harden and form lumps."

I asked, "Have you seen my wife?"

Ho had wandered to the far side of the room, but he turned and crossed back to me at this. "I'm sorry, my friend. I never knew her."

I must have shown some disappointment in my face, for Ho sat down and brought his own face near mine. "I'm sorry," he said. "There are many other people that I must find here."

"Are you very disappointed in me?" I asked. "For not having traveled the road with you?"

"It's very complicated," Ho said softly. "You felt that you'd taken action. I am no longer in a position to question another soul's choice."

"Are you at peace, where you are?" I asked this knowing of his worry over the recipe for the glaze, but I hoped that this was only a minor difficulty in the afterlife, like the natural anticipation of the good cook expecting guests when everything always turns out fine in the end.

But Ho said, "I am not at peace."

"Is Monsieur Escoffier over there?"

"I have not seen him. This has nothing to do with him, directly."

"What is it about?"

"I don't know."

"You won the country. You know that, don't you?"

Ho shrugged. "There are no countries here."

I should have remembered Ho's shrug when I began to see things in the faces of my son-in-law and grandson this morning. But something quickened in me, a suspicion. I kept my eyes shut and laid my head to the side, as if I was fast asleep, encouraging them to talk more.

My daughter said, "This is not the place to speak."

But the men did not regard her. "How?" Loi asked his father, referring to the missing murder weapon.

"It's best not to know too much," Thang said.

Then there was a silence. For all the quickness I'd felt at the first suspicion, I was very slow now. In fact, I did think of Ho from that second night. Not his shrug. He had fallen silent for a long time and I had closed my eyes, for the light seemed very bright. I listened to his silence just as I listened to the silence of these two conspirators before me.

And then Ho said, "They were fools but I can't bring myself to grow angry anymore."

I opened my eyes in the bedroom and the light was off. Ho had turned it off, knowing that it was bothering me. "Who were fools?" I asked.

"We had fought together to throw out the Japanese. I had very good friends among them. I smoked their lovely Salem cigarettes. They had been repressed by colonialists themselves. Did they not know their own history?"

"Do you mean the Americans?"

"There are a million souls here with me, the young men of our country, and they are all dressed in black suits and bowler hats.

In the mirrors they are made ten million, a hundred million."

"I chose my path, my dear friend Quoc, so that there might be harmony."

And even with that yearning for harmony I could not overlook what my mind made of what my ears had heard this morning. Thang was telling Loi that the murder weapon had been disposed of. Thang and Loi both knew the killers, were in sympathy with them, perhaps were part of the killing. The father and son had been airborne rangers and I had several times heard them talk bitterly of the exile of our people. We were fools for trusting the Americans all along, they said. We should have taken matters forward and disposed of the infinitely corrupt Thieu and done what needed to be done. Whenever they spoke like this in front of me there was soon a quick exchange of sideways glances at me and then a turn and an apology. "We're sorry, Grandfather. Old times often bring old anger. We are happy our family is living a new life."

I would wave my hand at this, glad to have the peace of the family restored. Glad to turn my face and smell the dogwood tree or even smell the coffee plant across the highway. These things had come to be the new smells of our family. But then a weakness often came upon me. The others would drift away, the men, and perhaps one of my daughters would come to me and stroke my head and not say a word and none of them ever would ask why I was weeping. I would smell the rich blood smells of the after-birth and I would hold our first son, still slippery in my arms, and there was the smell of dust from the square and the smell of the South China Sea just over the rise of the hill and there was the smell of the blood and of the inner flesh from my wife as my son's own private sea flowed from this woman that I loved, flowed and carried him into the life that would disappear from him so soon. In the afterlife would he stand before me on un-steady child's legs, would I have to bend low to greet him, or would he be a man now?

My grandson said, after the silence had nearly carried me into real sleep, troubled sleep, my grandson Loi said to his father, "I would be a coward not to know."

Thang laughed and said, "You have proved yourself no coward."

And I wished then to sleep, I wished to fall asleep and let go of life somewhere in my dreams and seek my village square. I have lived too long, I thought. My daughter was saying, "Are you both mad?" And then she changed her voice, making the words very precise. "Let Grandfather sleep."

So when Ho came tonight for the third time, I wanted to ask his advice. His hands were still covered with sugar and his mind was, as it had been for the past two nights, very much distracted. "There's something still wrong with the glaze," he said to me in the dark and I pulled back the covers and swung my legs around to get up. He did not try to stop me, but he did draw back quietly into the shadows.

"I want to pace the room with you," I said. "As we did in Paris, those tiny rooms of ours. We would talk about Marx and about Buddha and I must pace with you now."

"Very well," he said. "Perhaps it will help me remember."

I slipped on my sandals and I stood up and Ho's shadow moved past me, through the spill of street light and into the dark near the door. I followed him, smelling the sugar on his hands, first before me and then moving past me as I went on into the darkness he'd just left. I stopped as I turned and I could see Ho outlined before the window and I said, "I believe my son-in-law and grandson are involved in the killing of a man. A political killing."

Ho stayed where he was, a dark shape against the light, and he said nothing, and I could not smell his hands from across the room. I smelled only the sourness of Loi as he laid his head on my shoulder. He was a baby and my daughter Lam retreated to our balcony window after handing him to me and the boy turned his head and I turned mine to him and I could smell his mother's milk, sour on his breath, he had a sour smell and there was incense burning in the room, jasmine, the smoke of souls, and the boy sighed on my shoulder, and I turned my face away from the smell of him. Thang was across the room and his eyes were quick to find his wife and he was waiting for her to take the child from me.

"You have never done the political thing," Ho said.

"Is this true?"

"Of course."

I asked, "Are there politics where you are now, my friend?"

I did not see him moving toward me but the smell of the sugar on his hands grew stronger, very strong, and I felt Ho Chi Minh very close to me, though I could not see him. He was very close and the smell was strong and sweet and it was filling my lungs as if from the inside, as if Ho were passing through my very body, and I heard the door open behind me and then close softly shut.

I moved across the room to the bed. I turned to sit down but I was facing the window, the scattering of a street lamp on the window like a nova in some far part of the universe. I stepped to the window and touched the reflected light there, wondering if there was a great smell when a star explodes, a great burning smell of gas and dust. Then I closed the shade and slipped into bed, quite gracefully, I felt, I was quite wonderfully graceful, and I lie here now waiting for sleep. Ho is right, of course. I will never say a word about my grandson. And perhaps I will be as restless as Ho when I join him. But that will be all right. He and I will be together again and perhaps we can help each other. I know now what it is that he has forgotten. He has used confectioners' sugar for his glaze fondant and he should be using granulated sugar. I was only a washer of dishes but I did listen carefully when Monsieur Escoffier spoke. I wanted to understand everything. His kitchen was full of such smells that you knew you had to understand everything or you would be incomplete forever.

Robert Olen Butler lives in Lake Charles, Louisiana, where he teaches creative writing at McNeese State University. He has published six novels since 1981, and his most recent book is a volume of short fiction for which "A Good Scent from a Strange Mountain" is the title story. His stories have appeared in many literary magazines, including *The Sewanee Review*, *New England Review*, and *The Virginia Quarterly Review*, where he won the Emily Clark Balch Award, and have been anthologized in *The Best American Short Stories* and *New Stories from the South*. He served with the U.S. Army in Vietnam in 1971 as a Vietnamese linguist and is a charter recipient of the Tu Do Chinh Kien Award for outstanding contributions to American culture by a Vietnam veteran.

I have always been intrigued by the early life of Ho Chi Minh. He was indeed a pastry cook under the great Escoffier and he did indeed show up in a bowler hat at Versailles hoping to enlist Woodrow Wilson's help to secure some basic and very modest rights for the Vietnamese in French Indo-China. The story, however, began with its first line, when Ho showed up in my head, obviously straight from the Carlton Hotel's kitchen. Elderly Vietnamese often conduct a kind of formal leave-taking with their friends and relatives at the end of their lives, and once I understood that Ho had appeared in order to bid farewell to a very old friend who knew him from those strange and wonderful days in London and Paris, it was just a matter of letting my narrator speak.

Peter Taylor

THE WITCH OF OWL MOUNTAIN SPRINGS
An Account of Her Remarkable Powers

(from *The Kenyon Review*)

During my long lifetime, even since my early boyhood, there have been groups of girls of a certain lovely kind and character who have repeatedly turned up on my horizon. Again and again, in the variety of provincial places where I have lived, these clusters of charming girls have appeared with seemingly magical regularity. But whether they were little Sunday school girls living in a small southern town or they themselves constituted a sophisticated postdeb set in one of our burgeoning cities or they came on my horizon as nubile young ladies staying at an old-fashioned family summer resort, which once abounded in our southern highlands, still they have always and in every age had the same effect upon me.

I have found them nearly everywhere that I have turned—everywhere from Memphis to Nashville, from Chattanooga to Atlanta, and even on to Birmingham and New Orleans, as well as countless other more obscure points all over and about the countryside. But I may as well say here and now that no other group of girls ever had quite the same devastating effect upon me as did the girls at the summer resort at Owl Mountain Springs, a pretty little sylvan retreat perched high on the bluffs of the Cumberland Plateau in middle Tennessee. It was this superb collection of girls that made their appearance before me—and seemingly for my own special delectation—during the hot Depression summers of 1933 and '34.

I was then indeed a very young man, little more than a boy really, and already there seemed to be girls everywhere. But to get right to the core of my story, and in order to make clear what those girls who summered at Owl Mountain Springs were like and how attractive they seemed to me, I must now make mention of a particular one among them. She was a girl named Lizzy Pettigru, and I suppose she must be called the heroine of this story. Lizzy was very much one of that group of girls at Owl Mountain Springs, yet she did not willingly acknowledge her own likeness to the others. That is the long and the short of it. That was really what troubled me from the beginning. She was a girl somewhat older than I, and in my innocence I imagined that the supreme compliment I could pay her was to say how perfectly integral she seemed to those older girls that I so greatly admired. But she would always reply, "Oh, no, I am not really like them at all!"

It will be easy for almost anyone to imagine what the girls at Owl Mountain were like. Groups of girls such as they, and those at other places before and afterward, seemed always to make their appearances on my horizon in intimate clusters of, say, twelve or fourteen. In my mind's eye their lovely arms were forever intertwined, as it were, and also—so I believed—their young lives. These intertwining postures, both figurative and literal, were ever to my mind the enchanting and captivating thing about them. It was the close and inviolate affiliation, the tender camaraderie itself that I always found most deeply affecting. It was this about them that I in every instance came so passionately to admire. From the outset I *had* to think of Lizzy Pettigru as a girl who was from that particular group. I have to say that altogether the bonding of such girls has constituted one of the chief delights of my entire life. My most vivid dreams have generally been not about some individual female like Lizzy; rather, my dreams have most often been how firmly and intimately such clusters of girls have seemed chemically bonded; I have dreamed about the sense of style they share, about their very evident awareness of their own closeness and congeniality and even their exclusiveness. I believe and hereby acknowledge that it is in this special preoccupation of mine that I am perceived to be in a certain degree different from other men of my acquaintance in our quaint corner of the world.

The girls that I would so much have wanted Lizzy Pettigru to be like came of the precise same stock that she did. The little resort had originally been founded as a gathering place for the principal Protestant sects in our region: Presbyterians, Episcopalians, Baptists, Methodists, and Lutherans. (In early days prayer meetings were held here daily—morning prayers and twilight prayers.) It was natural that no Jewish people would wish to go there. And in the very charter of Owl Mountain Springs Resort it was explicitly stated that the place was founded for the benefit of those of the Protestant faith and it was even stipulated for all the world to read that no Roman Catholic could ever own property inside the Grounds. And since there were of course but few Blacks there in our southern highlands, the summer people had to make do with what was known as Mountain White help.

Perhaps a realistic presentation of the character of the place can best be stated negatively. No one imagined that Owl Mountain Springs itself was exactly a fashionable summer place, not even vaguely so—not in the eyes of the great world, at any rate. It was never thought of as any Blowing Rock or Asheville or White Sulphur Springs. It was never imagined to be a Rye or a Saratoga or a Cape Cod or a Nantucket. It would have seemed laughable to mention it in the same breath with Bar Harbor or Harbor Point. And yet it was quite as much respected for what it was *not* as for what it *was*. And Lizzy Pettigru did seem to represent—or I thought she represented—the very epitome of what outsiders and newcomers envied in the people who summered there always. I suppose those who vacationed there thought of

themselves somehow or other as the special urban remnants of
an old gentry out of another time, out of their remotely agrarian
past. Surely it was the things they did not do that counted most
with them. It was the things they did not have and did not want
that mattered most. It was what they were *not* that made them
who they were. Grandfathers of some had been generals in the old
war, which they tried not to mention too often. They were proud
mostly not of the great battles their generals had won in that
war but of the great battles they had lost. One of theirs had been
blamed or honored for the loss of Missionary Ridge. Another
was held responsible for the debacle at Shiloh. In one family the
Fourth of July was never celebrated because a grandsire had lost
Vicksburg, and Vicksburg fell on the Fourth. At Owl Mountain
we were all the grandsons of someone of a particular distinction
of this kind. All, it should be said, but the Pettigrus! Perhaps
their distinction was that they *needed* no single distinguished forebear. With their name, it seems, one need not ask for more. The
Pettigrus' ancestry stretched back into eternity—through Virginia and South Carolina and Cavaliers and Charles the Martyr.
But the families of all of us at Owl Mountain Springs could be
traced pretty far back. And all of us still owned a good bit of land
somewhere, and all had inherited or had managed to acquire—
even the Pettigrus—a modest cottage on Owl Mountain.

Suffice it to say that when little Lizzy Pettigru was sixteen her
manners were excellent, and withal so unassuming, and her face
had such sweetness, and her charm was so beyond the banal of the
merely beautiful or genteel young lady (of Memphis, of Nashville, and similar cities) that there was no goodness that could
not be attributed to her. And I believe this was apparent to me
without my having to be told of it by my elders. Her charm was
so difficult to describe that, like everything else at Owl Mountain, it was usually said simply what Lizzy was *not*. Her nature
was such that people expected more of her than others, and alas
for Lizzy's sake, as it turned out, they forgave her more than they
forgave others as well. That is to say, they forgave her kindness

to anyone who did not quite fit in at Owl Mountain Springs. It was as though it were only *she* who could afford such kindness because of her goodness and her beauty and her being a Pettigru.

From the beginning it was an annoyance to me that Lizzy Pettigru did not willingly allow me to think of her as being like the other girls in that group at Owl Mountain. My perspective in those days is very clear to me now. I was fourteen in the summer of 1933 and of course fifteen the next summer. The girls I allude to, including Lizzy Pettigru herself, were two or three years older than I. But because boys at Owl Mountain were ever in short supply, these girls were glad enough to have such a youngster as I to "cut in on them" at dances in the Pavilion. I was a pumpkin-headed, freckle-faced boy, my full height barely reaching the shoulder of some of those girls. Still, I was well co-ordinated and a good dancer and fond of hearing myself talk to any girl. And though I had spent all my previous summers at a boys' camp, I was from one of the well-established families of the resort Grounds. "We" had been spending our summers there for three generations. Like everyone else we had our own Con-federate hero as a forebear. Except for my age and my height I was an altogether eligible stag at the weekly Thursday and Satur-day night dances. It was assumed by everyone that I had not yet obtained my full growth upward. (In this they were incorrect, for I would remain of very short stature all my life. As a college teacher I have sometimes sat on a large dictionary in my desk chair to give myself height with the students or even stood on the same behind my lectern.) It was also assumed that within a very few years the discrepancy in our ages would not matter to any girl in the Dance Pavilion. All in all, moreover, no one could have been more reassuring to me about my future prospects than was the beauteous Lizzy Pettigru herself. And as for me, I certainly could not then have predicted the calamity that would befall Lizzy in the relatively near future or the disastrous fate that would ultimately be her lot.

*   *   *

What happened to Lizzy Pettigru the second summer was a calamity not only for herself but quite as much for her family and even, so it seems in retrospect, for the whole summer community at Owl Mountain. Perhaps with the end of the Great Depression already in sight such an old-fashioned resort was doomed to fall into decline. The same people who had once occupied the cottages there in past times began to have the means to go to more distant, cooler, and more prestigious summer places. But because of the sequence of actual events one cannot help associating Lizzy Pettigru's calamity with the decline of the resort, with the approaching end of the Depression, with the preparations for war that were then going on and with its attendant prosperity, which itself made it inevitable that more and more cottages would stand empty at Owl Mountain.

During the war that was to come there would be great changes there. Army officers and their families from nearby military installations would lease and come to live in whatever cottages it seemed possible to heat in the winter. Also certain so-called bohemian artists and writers were ever on the lookout there for a cheap place to hole up in the war years. During this time the old clapboard Owl Mountain Hotel with its tier upon tier of gingerbread verandas was closed down forever, though it did not burn till several years later. It, along with a good number of abandoned cottages, became overgrown with kudzu vine and inhabited by squirrels and by various kinds of rodents. It was just before this significant decline in the place began and when the general exodus of old summer residents was beginning to take place that the Pettigru family felt themselves so demeaned and humiliated by an event in Lizzy's life that they could not return to their old, accustomed seat of residence in the lowlands. And so it was now that they established themselves at Owl Mountain Springs to live the year round. It may seem unlikely and almost inconceivable to young people of the present day what actually were those circumstances that seemed so demeaning and humiliating to the Pettigru family. The event that in the Pettigrus' eyes had altered their position in the world they came out of—altered it beyond all possible repair—was nothing more or less than the public jilting of the incomparable Miss Lizzy Pettigru herself.

Of course from my very first acquaintance with Lizzy I realized that she had a degree of charm and beauty that the other girls in the little resort did not enjoy, that she had an intelligence and kindness in manner toward others that the other girls did not possess. Her beauty and her serenity seemed to me then, when we attended those dances at the Owl Mountain Pavilion, something that could never be changed. And to some extent even in very recent times—so many, many years later—when she had already got to be quite a pathetic old woman and we were still encountering each other now and again every season on the Middle Path at Owl Mountain, I could make out in her sharp old features and jutting chin some suggestion of the delicacy her features once had. By then Owl Mountain Springs had altered so that she and I would sometimes be the only summer residents actually occupying a cottage. But whenever we passed on the Middle Path, the grotesque old creature took no notice of me. In her near blindness it is likely she mistook me for one of the mountain people whom she had come to know so well and who came to sweep out the cottage every so often, or for some stranger who had wandered into the nearly deserted grounds. Or she may, on the other hand, have mistaken me for one of the other rare old-timers like herself, but not one she ever willingly spoke to. Regardless of that, she had long ago, before her cataracts came on, ceased speaking to anyone except those certain mountain people who seemed to be under her spell and were made to do her bidding. In most recent years I might look right into her face as I passed her there and receive not a glimmer of recognition. Old-timers and newcomers—the whole world—had now long since all become one to her. And with her sharp features and her head of wild white hair I could easily see why the mountain people had nowadays come to regard Miss Lizzy Pettigru as something more or perhaps something less than human and would sometimes speak of her as the Witch of Owl Mountain Springs. The disappearance of any vestige of the old resemblance was what would at last seem to me our irreparable loss.

But surely, as I must here interject, surely boys of almost any generation—you, for instance, who are just becoming young men today—will understand the necessity that compelled me to try to identify the incomparable Lizzy as one of the wonderful Owl Mountain Girls. For so perfectly did I invest that band of girls with my ideal of feminine beauty and my ideal of all the higher sensibilities that it was impossible for me to conceive of Lizzy's virtues in any other terms. And this is what is important for any present or future generation of readers to understand: a young man's preconceived ideals of feminine beauty and virtue, if he have such ideals at all, must be reflected in his own beloved— in his girlfriend, if you will. It is true in any generation, I believe, and will always be so. *She* must be the embodiment of all *his* preconceived notions of female excellence.

Why, as much as twenty years later when I would be back on the Mountain and would catch a glimpse of the youngish spinster Lizzy Pettigru across the Mall, I would find something about her to remind me of those other girls whose style or manner I had once so admired. Of course still another twenty years later, forty years after those summers in the thirties, it was quite a different matter. By then her craggy old face and her unkempt hair could remind one of nothing that was human, much less of those long-ago charming girls. And I must say that to an extremely old man it was deeply disturbing and irritating that he could no longer find that resemblance.

But that was only toward the last. When ordinarily I continued to come back home to our family cottage, summer after summer—as indeed I seemed destined to do throughout the rest of my life—I could scarcely have avoided seeing Lizzy there on the Grounds even if I had wanted to. Through those years I would sometimes come great distances just to stay at Owl Mountain

Springs for a week or two during July or August. She was always there. She would have been there even if I had come in mid-winter, because as I have said, Lizzy and her always eccentric parents had very early come to the strange turn of remaining at Owl Mountain Springs the year round. Even after the *first* twenty years of course the father and mother were already dead and buried in the Owl Mountain village cemetery, and her having no brothers or sisters and never having married, she was already very much alone. I can see her when she was just past middle age, trudging alone from her cottage over to the village grocery store and back again. That was the only outing she permitted herself in that period. Or it was so at least whenever we summer people were in residence again—those of us who were still coming back then. Even when she moved along the Middle Path or across the Mall she took no notice of anybody—not of me or of whoever of her other old friends were present—took notice of nobody at all unless she happened to pass one of her special mountain people who sometimes worked about her cottage. At any rate, the point I make here is that whenever I saw her, either in early or in later middle age (sometimes with me staring at her from behind the lattice of the old Dance Pavilion before it collapsed or through the louvers of the closed window blind of my own fast-deteriorating family cottage), I then observed to what extent she still resembled those other lovely Owl Mountain Girls, all of whom had now been scattered, and all of whom, like myself, now lived hundreds of miles away from Owl Mountain Springs, Tennessee. I must add that at this point in middle age Lizzy Petti-gru wore her hair chopped off short like some plain mountain woman and had it pressed tight against her head underneath a wide looped net—a kind of hairnet I never saw otherwise except on mountain women and that I presume must have been sold over the notions counter in the Owl Mountain village grocery store. But even with her hair like that and her face already marked with deep creases and in her plain gingham dress that hung belt-less on her macerated frame, still the sight of her at that age could somehow call up images of girls that my mind had likened to her in the summers of 1933 and '34. It would not be so at a later time. And it was this loss of resemblance that would be the most terrible thing to me about seeing her toward the end.

But when I long ago waltzed and two-stepped Lizzy Pettigru about the floor of the Pavilion, she spoke sympathetically to me about everything concerning myself and spoke generously about girls other than herself who appeared on the dance floor. I believe that from the earliest time she was never heard to say anything critical about those girls with whom she nevertheless did not care to be indiscriminatingly identified. While dancing with her perhaps I talked too much about myself (especially about my various intellectual aspirations and pretensions), but she managed to make me feel that she found the subject as engrossing as I did. Perhaps I also talked too much about the other girls all around us when we danced, but she showed no impatience with my enthusiasm for that subject either. Week after week I could not resist commenting on how very becomingly dressed were the girls who turned up at the dances at Owl Mountain, always including Lizzy herself in my generalizations on the subject.

It has been my observation before and after those two special summers when I was under the spell of the girls at Owl Mountain Springs that bands of such girls will always dress themselves in a fashion that is genuinely artistic in the total or group effect. That is to say, when they are gathered on public occasions there will always seem to be complicated color schemes running through their various forms of attire. To a careful observer like myself, certain shades of blue or green will appear in the hair ribbon of one and in the dainty collar of the blouse of another and on the hem of the skirt of still another, these colors complemented perhaps by reds or yellows in the costumes of yet others. And this is not something I merely imagined on one occasion. I have seen it everywhere, time and time again. There will be patterns of cloth or cuts of dresses in the most sophisticated or the most infantile of them that will seem designed to contrast with or draw attention to the felicitous designs or uses in other garments. And so one *has* to see them as a group if one is to get the beauty of them. One cannot but imagine that the effect has been achieved by one single hand, one eye, one exercise of taste, one sensibility. For instance, I remember observing some little girls who were in the third grade at Miss Fontaine's private school whom I would see skipping out to the little playground at recess with their pretty arms quite literally linked. They formed such a close, human chain across the graveled playground that it was impossible not to take notice of them. The starch in their little shirtwaists, the crinkled ribbons in their heads of carefully curled hair, the very flair of their short little skirts made it impossible not to think of them as all of a piece and to wish to seize them in one all-inclusive embrace or hug. I would be so moved by my own fond feelings for those little girls—and perhaps by the frustration that I felt but could not express—that I would immediately perform some act of badness there on the playground. Afterward when I was punished by Miss Fontaine, the headmistress herself—my act having been so gross for a little boy in the third grade—I would not be able to remember what it was I had done and would hotly deny my act of badness. I was seized by one of those moments of amnesia that have recurred throughout the rest of my life in moments of great stress, and I would deny that I had done the bad thing that I was being punished for.

I am reminded that at a much later time when I was approaching middle age I had another, similar amnesiac attack in connection with another such moment of overwhelming emotion regarding a group of girls who were quite grown up. And I do believe there have been numerous other such attacks in my lifetime following moments of stress, though I suspect I have not always had reason to acknowledge them even to myself (since there was not usually a Miss Fontaine threatening me with corporal punishment). But in that much later instance I do recall that I was by no means any longer a very young man. Nevertheless, I was young enough to be attending the annual presentation ball given at the Country Club. Being a single man still, as I have remained all my life, I was still invited to such events not as an escort for a debutante but as a sort of perennial bachelor or stag. During that period of the evening when the season's debutantes paraded about the parquet as they used always to do at such ritual occasions, I stood with the parents and the other relatives admiring with them the young ladies in the procession. I was acquainted with quite a few of the girls that were being "brought out" that year. A number of them were daughters of some of my slightly older friends. And I knew these girls well enough to recognize that they made up one of those unforgettable special groups with its own style. I watched them pass about the ballroom with considerable satisfaction and pleasure. The evening gowns that year were apt to have somewhat higher hemlines in the front than in the back, and these girls seemed to have adopted that feature as their very own. Their presentation gowns were not so alike, of course, that there was any monotony about them, yet there *was* that particular feature and there were *other* features of design and other complements of colors that suggested that somehow or other there had been some omniscient eye conscious of the total effect to be received. I am not suggesting that the whole affair had been choreographed by one hand or head but that the girls' own ideas of the proper dress and behavior that night was so well understood among them that there could have been no need for consultation beforehand. At any rate when the orchestra had concluded their rendition of "Pomp and Circumstance" and when the procession of new debutantes was ended, I believe that in my state of euphoria I must have broken into an inappropriately loud applause or perhaps even shouted "Bravo" as if at the ballet, or possibly given vent to a prolonged and deafening whistle even with my fingers in the corners of my mouth. I do not remember anything like that, however. For any consciousness of what I did some Merciful Censor drew a curtain across events of the following two hours. The next thing I remember is that upon leaving the party, I know not how many hours later, I was shunned by some of my closest friends on the front steps of the Country Club. The only persons who treated me civilly as I was making my departure that night were certain slight acquaintances who possibly did not realize that it was I who had made the rumpus or scene somewhat earlier up in the ballroom.

That first summer at Owl Mountain Springs it was pleats of every description that were the great vogue among the girls I so greatly admired. Costume jewelry was also much in favor with them. I cannot say whether these fads of fashion were general all over the entire country that year. Perhaps they were. But I am afraid that I was never aware of any ladies' fashions but those that held sway in some special group that had captured my imagination. I remember that one girl that first year wore a little short evening cape consisting entirely of pleats. I found it stunning. There were a number of girls whose full-length pleated skirts swept about the dance floor. It seems to me that all the girls wore such skirts on one evening or another. And the elaborate costume jewelry contrasting with the simple and severe effects of the pleats could almost have been called the general motif of the summer. Strands of pearls and bright colored beads along with pendant rubies and amethysts adorned the milk-white throats of those pure young ladies—gems and pearls that were surely imitative of ornaments intended for harem girls. And on their delicate wrists hung heavy bracelets suggestive also of the harem. The effect upon me of the contrast between those worldly seeming ornaments and the nunlike purity of their pleats was profound. And there was an especial excitement for me derived from the knowledge that so many of the girls' dresses were made by their own hands or by those of their mothers and that the costume jewelry was purchased at the ten-cent store in Nashville or Memphis or perhaps handed down to them from their mothers' collections of keepsakes and trinkets. For this was, it is to be remembered, the depths of the Great Depression when wonderful economies were practiced even by these genteel folk who nevertheless continued to betake themselves to places like Owl Mountain Springs in the hot summer months of the year.

When I repeatedly "broke" on Lizzy Pettigru at the Pavilion dances it seemed to me not that I had selected someone different from those other girls but merely the foremost among them, the crowning beauty, the superior sensibility and intelligence of that remarkable assemblage of young women. But it seemed always to be Lizzy's principal aim to make me understand that underneath and essentially she was cut from a different cloth. "No, I am not like them at all," she repeated. Her general behavior like her dress and her social manner might be indistinguishable from those of the other girls but there was a mysterious essence in her being that she asserted was totally different. However, that mysterious essence was as far as I understood her assertion of difference. And the difference seemed to be one that she purposely withheld from any easy understanding. "You ought to *see* it for *yourself*," she would tell me. And then she would laugh merrily. She declined always to be in any degree explicit about it. I knew only that her attraction for me was infinitely beyond that of any of the other girls, and I did realize that her receptiveness to any charm that might exist in the rather intense and overly serious adolescent that I was exceeded immeasurably any receptiveness from the other girls. They as a matter of fact—whose style and essence I held in such high esteem and regard—were given sometimes to actually patting me on the head as if intentionally to remind me of my shortness of stature and my relatively immature years. I suppose I condoned their behavior with one self-effacing thought: how could they, with all their grace and beauty and their wonderful aplomb in our little social world, their being themselves the elect and the elite of that world that appeared to me then as "our modern world" and appears to me now as an old-fashioned world almost beyond imagining, that is, how could they reveal the least uncertainty or even fallibility? It may seem incredible to someone of the present generation, but I was so enamored of the style and so respectful of the authority of those other girls that I could actually, without taking offense or for that matter without feeling mortally wounded, overhear one of them make reference to me behind my back as "that puny little intellectual." I can almost say I suffered such gratuitous insults gladly in order to be admitted to the weekly company of those girls at Owl Mountain.

But only Lizzy Pettigru treated me consistently with respect and—as I imagined it—with sisterly affection. She would do so even when she had been brought to the dance by someone else. Sometimes she and I would wander off as far from the Dance Pavilion as one of the high wooden footbridges that crossed over the ravine within the resort Grounds. We would stand there leaning on the rail of the bridge, with me talking about what one should do with one's life, but all the while stealing glances at the soft features of her oval face, at her lovely, long throat, at the rich brown hair that then fell about her shoulders and glinted in the romantic play of moonlight, yet neither at those moments nor during our daytime meanderings about the ravine and under the cliffside did I presume to speak directly to her of love. It never once occurred to me that she might have been receptive to my caresses—verbal or otherwise—much less that she might even have welcomed all such caresses. I never once asked her to one of the dances or to go out with me on a formal date—not so much as to attend one of the movies that was shown in the shackly old Youth Building, a structure that along with so many others has long since burned down. I was too conscious always of the two-year discrepancy in our ages and ever conscious also of the older boys—and one in particular—who sought her attention and her favors. But what I was not at all conscious of that first summer was how near Lizzy and the other girls were to being what used to be called a marriageable age. It would not have occurred to me that by the following summer a number of these girls would be officially betrothed to young business and professional men from their hometowns or in some cases to the very boys who this previous summer had escorted them to the dances at Owl Mountain

Springs. And of course Lizzy Pettigru would prove to be among that number. Before the season of the second summer opened her engagement had been announced in the papers. But by the first of August her betrothed had fled from Owl Mountain with a girl whom Lizzy had called her closest friend from back home, a girl incidentally of the Jewish faith who until that night had been present at Owl Mountain only as a houseguest in the Pettigrus' own cottage.

At an early age Lizzy Pettigru chose for her very best friend a girl from next door in her hometown named Sarah Goodrich. That the Goodriches were Jews Lizzy never bothered to learn or care about. Perhaps as a Pettigru she didn't need to care about that. The Goodriches were the Nashville and Memphis Jews who went "everywhere"—or nearly everywhere. (There were no doubt some in Birmingham, too, and in Atlanta and Louisville and New Orleans as well.) It was only to Owl Mountain Springs that the Goodriches generally didn't go. But when little Sarah Goodrich, at the tender age of nine, began to spend a large part of her summers as a guest at the Pettigru family's cottage no one took any notice of it—hardly anyone at all. By the time the two girls were young ladies Sarah was regarded by the Owl Mountain Springs young people as one of the "regular" crowd.

And when it turned out at last that Lizzy's choice for a husband was none other than one Tim Sullivan, everyone might have supposed that more notice would have been taken of that. The Sullivans were the Nashville Sullivans, and they were the richest Roman Catholics in Nashville. Roman Catholics at Owl Mountain were welcome only as visitors or tenants of Protestant cottage owners. In this latter day, under these conditions and for reasons of their own, the Sullivans were willing and content merely to lease someone else's cottage in the Grounds during July or August.

It was thought that the boy Tim Sullivan could be hardly aware of the special conditions of his family's tenure in the Grounds. Certainly he was regarded by the Owl Mountain young people

as one of themselves. And when Lizzy's engagement to Tim was
first announced it caused hardly a murmur on the Mountain. The
idea of a marriage of the Sullivan money and the Pettigrus' gen-
tility was widely approved and even applauded. The announce-
ment of the engagement was featured along with large pictures of
the bride-to-be in the Sunday society section in both Memphis
and Nashville papers, and possibly also some mention was made
of it in the papers of Birmingham and Atlanta and Louisville.
For the Pettigrus had connections everywhere, and the name
Sullivan was becoming increasingly well known. With a Pettigru
connection the Sullivans would no doubt now be a force to be
reckoned with.

It was well after the engagement had already been announced
of course that the awful blow fell. No one had reckoned there
could be any connection between the Catholic boy Tim Sullivan
and the Jewish girl Sarah Goodrich. Least of all could it have
occurred to the Pettigrus. Afterward it would be easy to say that
it came about just because it happened right under the Pettigrus' noses, that it was too close for them to see. But this wasn't
true necessarily. And in part it *was* true that all Pettigrus thought
themselves above any such eventuality.

Lizzy Pettigru herself heard them talking one night—Sarah
and Tim, that is. The two of them were together in what was
known as the "little parlor" in the Pettigrus' cottage. Lizzy was off
in her father's study looking up some disputed point in the fine
print of the *Britannica* there. At first she thought she misunder-
stood what she had heard. She would tell me about it the very
next day before her attitude toward me and toward the whole
world seemed to freeze. Lizzy heard Sarah say the word "Jew"
and heard Tim say the word "Catholic." She could not imagine
the context in which these utterances were made. She believed
she had never before heard either of them speak the words then
spoken except in a most serious vein. But it seemed to her now as
if they were joking. Perhaps they *were* only joking that first time.
Perhaps it began with their merely teasing each other. When pres-

ently Lizzy returned to the little parlor, she found them standing halfway across the room from each other and they *did* seem to be regarding each other with what were clearly teasing expressions on their faces. And yet upon her entering the room, their expressions changed immediately. And what was most disturbing, there was now no continuation of whatever exchanges they had been making.

During this summer at Owl Mountain Springs, and possibly the one before, this same Sarah Goodrich and this same Tim Sullivan, this closest friend and this recently announced fiancé of Lizzy Pettigru, had manifested a common interest in one of the resort's young people's activities. That is, they had taken leading parts in the annual play that was produced in the old gymnasium, which was generally known as the Youth Building. The two of them were the acknowledged stars of the play being "done" there this season. Any number of nights this summer they had been closeted together in the Pettigrus' little front parlor or together out on the veranda practicing their lines. And so it had been on that night when Lizzy heard them speak their revealing words when she was bending over her father's *Britannica*. On previous occasions she had come and gone from the room or from the porch while the lines were being rehearsed. Probably she would never actually know on how early an occasion the personal teasing had begun—if teasing, indeed, was how it began. She knew only that it was Sarah Goodrich who spoke the word "Jew" and Tim Sullivan who spoke the word "Catholic." Lizzy could only imagine or surmise how exactly it had gone. But in the light of what her father would later overhear from his study on this very midnight of their elopement, Sarah would be saying in her youthful resentment and irony, "Oh, I'm only her token Jew," or, "Oh, I'm only Owl Mountain's token Jew," and Tim would have been heard saying, "Oh, I'm only her token Catholic," or, "Oh, I'm only Owl Mountain's token Catholic." Judge Pettigru (for he had once served briefly as judge in chancery court and was addressed ever afterward by that title) coming into his study much later, heard Sarah's and Tim's voices only indistinctly. He was in his study with the door slightly ajar. Probably the young couple didn't know he was there. And perhaps without even knowing it they somehow meant him to hear them. They were together in the little parlor just across the narrow passageway from the study. Judge Pettigru could only make out from their tone of voice that their conversation was of a personal nature, as he said. His own genteel nature and upbringing directed him presently to turn off his lamp and go quietly to the bedroom to which his wife had already retired. He did not mention to Mrs. Pettigru that night what he had heard in the front part of the cottage.

Lizzy waited until she knew her parents were asleep. Then she put out the light in her room and went into the passage that led to the front door. It was totally dark but she knew the position of every piece of furniture and the location of every throw rug, and in her bare feet she recognized the rough pine of the flooring in the passage. When she approached the front of the cottage she could make out that the door to the little parlor was closed. She could see the pale streak of light underneath the door and even the recognizable figure of light in the large old-fashioned keyhole to which there had never been a key. She knew without seeming to think about it and without any pang of conscience what she must do. Yet it took considerable physical effort for her to force herself to act out her part. In her nightgown and without slippers on her feet she forced herself down on her knees, and through the big keyhole she saw them. Afterward she would feel that in a sense peering through that keyhole was the most degrading part of the whole experience. They were on the Brussels carpet and what she first saw were the soles of their feet. She wanted not to see more but she knew that she must, and then suddenly she was distracted from the sight of their actual bodies by their faint animal-like sounds. Now she withdrew almost despite herself. And she retraced her steps down the long passage as silently as she had come. In her room she did not put on a light or think of going to bed and to sleep. She drew a straight chair up by the small bay window and there she sat the rest of the night.

The next morning the young couple was gone. There was no note left behind for Lizzy or for her parents. But sometime during the night Lizzy had discovered that Sarah's clothing and other possessions had been removed from the room they shared. When the girls finally did not appear for breakfast the next morning, Mrs. Pettigru went to their room and found that Lizzy, sitting straight in the chair by the window, was fully clothed and clearly had not been to bed that night. Lizzy heard her mother open the bedroom door and then go away without speaking to her.

The only note left behind by Sarah and Tim was one for the woman who was directing the annual Owl Mountain play that summer. It was a long, earnest, and rather beautifully dramatic farewell note, full of regret that the two leading characters could not go on with the performance. It was thought beautiful, at any rate, by the woman director of the theater, who took their farewell and regret quite personally and declined to show the text of the note to anyone. To other members of the cast and to the managers of the resort's summer program she would allow only a glance—only a quick glance at the elaborate girlish script that would prove it was Sarah's handwriting and would identify the final signatures of both young people. When she announced to the assembled cast early that morning that the performance would be canceled, that the show could not go on without those two, she did so with tears streaming down her very full cheeks. And tears would also very soon be streaming down the young cheeks of all members of the cast. The drama of the moment was so satisfying to all present—that is, satisfying just because it was a young couple's having fallen in love that the show could not go on!—and seemed so satisfying above all to the middle-aged female director that suspicions were aroused among the resort managers. It seemed to the managers that the lady had herself been privy in advance to the plans for the elopement! What she revealed from the farewell note was that the two young people were not only in love with each other but had also fallen in love with the theater itself and that their intentions were to go away and together devote their lives and careers to the great American theater of the future! At the time no one seemed to think of Lizzy and the elder Pettigrus in their cottage, alone with their humiliation.

But late in the morning after the couple went away Lizzy came to our cottage, asking for me. I believe it was the first time she had ever been there, and not knowing her news I was mightily excited when Mother brought word up to me in my attic room. (Boys at Owl Mountain were always quartered in some sort of *garçonnière* up in the attic or in a lean-to in the yard. Boys were not thought highly of there until they were of marriageable age.) I didn't put on a tie but did comb my hair and then came stumbling down the outside stairs to greet her on the front veranda. I can never forget how she smiled at me on the stairs that morning, a pumpkin-headed, freckle-faced, teenaged boy, as though I were some kind of knight errant or an angel descending from the sky. And she never looked more beautiful—or perhaps more vulnerable—to me. My mother was standing in the front doorway of the cottage, and before I was all the way down the steps, Lizzy was addressing me: "I thought you might like to go for a long walk this morning out to Forrest's Steep." I could not help observing the stunned expression on my mother's face. I suppose I glanced at Mother expecting just that. It was unheard-of that a young lady at Owl Mountain of Lizzy's age should call on a boy at this hour—or any hour—and herself invite *him* to go on such an expedition, unchaperoned and even unaccompanied in any manner. Forrest's Steep was situated in a cove way out at the edge of the mountain. It was the passage and steep by which General Forrest was said to have crossed over the Cumberland Plateau on his way from Stone's River to Missionary Ridge. It was not unthinkable, however, for us to take such a walk unac-

companied, and I replied, with another glance at Mother before
we left, that I was in the very mood for such an outing.

I felt it was a decisive moment in my life or almost a decisive moment. At any rate I did accept Lizzy's invitation and did
override Mother's silent protest, which consisted indeed of her
remaining in the doorway until we were out of sight of the cottage. I think Lizzy and I said nothing to each other until we had
reached the outer limits of the Grounds and had come into the
larger undeveloped area known as the Domain. From there we
followed the wagon road under the trees that would lead finally
to Forrest's Steep. It was there that she would begin telling me
all that she had heard and seen last night, sparing me nothing. We
walked under the growth of sourwood and shade trees and I kept
my eyes turned mostly upward into the leafy branches overhead.
I suppose I was too shocked and too embarrassed by what she
related to look directly at her. Then she told me all that her father
had told her that he had heard and also whatever she had heard of
the note written to the woman who had been directing the play.
At the time I could tell she was stealing glances at my face to see
how I would respond to all of this. Still I would not look at her
until she had told me the whole story. When we reached the head
of the cove we sat down automatically on the big flat rock that
is there. Then I looked her full in the face, saying nothing still
but waiting for her to state more than just the mere facts, which
until now I was very much aware she had limited herself to. I
had thought she would have burst into tears at some point. And
if she had done so at this point I believe I would have put my
arms about her and would have known how to comfort her. But
even now she did not. When I looked into her hazel eyes now she
said without emotion, "They have betrayed me and gone away
without so much as telling me they were sorry they had to do it.
And I do suppose they really had to do it. But I can see neither
of them has ever appreciated the love I was able to give them and
did give them."

Then I was able to speak. Whether or not it was from my heart was a question that did not occur to me. "They were neither of them worthy of you," I said. Maybe my logic was only the logic of someone who wishes to reform someone else. "Why did you have to waste yourself on them?" I blurted out. "They were not worthy of you—you of all people."

She looked at me as though she could not believe her ears. And still there were no tears that might yet have undone me. "Who *is* worthy of my love?" she asked.

I must have looked at her with the same logic in my eyes as before. "I can't imagine," I asserted. "I can't imagine." I really was trying desperately to imagine and I suppose I said the first thing that came into my head: "Why, Lizzy, you have had the same wonderful chances that all the other girls have had." I became irritated with her. "You have refused to be what everyone knows you are, the very best of the whole lot. You ought to be glad you have been betrayed by what they are. It proves what *you* are."

Still she looked at me without tears and without belief. All at once she sprang up from the big flat rock and ran back along the wagon road and ran at such speed that it would not have been possible for me to overtake her before we were already inside the Grounds proper. And it would not have done on that day of all days to have Lizzy seen being hotly pursued down the Owl Mountain Middle Path by such as I. And Lizzy would never again through all the years acknowledge any acquaintance between the two of us.

As these years went by the Pettigrus would withdraw more and more to themselves, not only from the world they came out of back home but from the world of Owl Mountain. And as these years went by the old summer resort at Owl Mountain Springs became increasingly less popular with people from such places as Memphis and Nashville. After the Second World War such people as once frequented the place had largely ceased to identify themselves as a separate sort of people, as a separate sort of southerner, as those whose forebears had not lost important battles or minor skirmishes in that old war that was coming to be mentioned less and less. They went "away" during the summer. They too went to Cape Cod and Bar Harbor and the like. For the most part Owl Mountain became a place you only went on a long summer weekend when you didn't want to stay home with the air conditioner and the television. And as those years passed there were fires at Owl Mountain Springs that changed the nature of the place entirely. First there was the old gymnasium. It was there that children and adolescents and even older young people gathered for games and for the rehearsals and actual productions of the annual play in August. It burned one summer night in July just a year or two after Lizzy's mother had died. (She died toward the end of one summer and was buried just outside the Grounds in the village cemetery.) Then there was the fire at the Women's Clubhouse, followed some years later by one at the Men's Clubhouse. And it was one night later that season that we had the fire at the Lecture Hall. That was the year that Lizzy's father died and was buried beside her mother in the village cemetery. At last would come the great blaze that was to destroy the old hotel with its shingled cupolas and its tiers of porches and the lobby with its wide oak staircase and the dining hall in which had centered most of the adult social life. The hotel, too, was burned on a hot night in mid-August, just as the chill of the night air came on. But this was of course twenty years and more after the fire that burned the old gymnasium. During the intervening years nearly all the other places of assemblage had gone up in flames. Only the chapel was spared, and it remains standing today. But many an empty cottage met the same fate as the other, public buildings. And meanwhile, year after year, I continued to return for a few weeks every summer when I was not teaching courses in summer school. And it happened that I was present on the night of the great hotel conflagration.

I saw the flames leap seventy-five and a hundred feet in the clear, cold air above Owl Mountain. I saw those flames light up the charred and scorched foundations of various burned-out cottages that had stood unoccupied both summer and winter for a good many years before the burning. During all these fires, and probably without exception, the now-isolated and aging Miss Lizzy Pettigru had never joined the throng that invariably gathered. Rather, she would be seen by the rest of us wrapped in her plain cloth coat, sitting in a rocker on her front veranda, watching those others who came and went from the fire. If someone approached her cottage to ask if she might know how the fire got started she rose from her rocker before even a foot was set upon her shallow porch steps and silently withdrew inside the front door of her cottage. It was always supposed that she might have seen someone passing in the direction where the fire blazed up. It was always suspected by the ever-suspicious mountain people in the village that she had had a hand in each fire, if only through some magic or witchcraft that they, by this time, confidently believed she possessed. But if Miss Lizzy had made herself available she might have confirmed for them what some of them would already have suspected: that some one of those vagrants who were not from the village but who so often wandered about the Grounds had made a fire to cook his supper in one of the never-used fireplaces and out of carelessness or even malice had set the whole place on fire.

Between Miss Lizzy Pettigru and the mountain people there had developed a history in the years since she had come to live at her summer cottage the year round. This was particularly true after her parents were dead. Whereas the summer residents thought it unbecoming and not fitting for a genteel young lady to live there alone the year round, the mountain people thought it exceeding strange. And as time passed they came to think everything about her exceeding strange. The postmistress in the village, as well as others, became aware of the string of visitors that she turned away from her door. This "string" consisted of many of her old-time summer friends who came great distances to visit her. The postmistress could vouch that there had been letters, probably warning her of their coming. Another criticism they made of her was that she permitted no villager to come insider her front door and hired to do her work only vagrants and so-called covites, both of whom were looked down on by the mountain people of the village.

At any rate, I know that through the years Lizzy Pettigru did have visitors who came knocking at her door. I sometimes recognized them when I happened to be in residence, and I know that she insisted to them that she had had no forewarning and could not receive them. They were often friends from her childhood and came from far-distant places where they had long settled— from Cincinnati, Miami, Chicago, New York. (The mountain people knew from their license plates what great distances they had come.) But Lizzy would not open her door to them. Or if it happened, as it often did, that they caught her rocking on the porch, she would get up and go inside as soon as she saw that they were turning up the footpath toward her place. The mountain people, with their usual imagination, wrongly supposed that she had purposely and magically somehow drawn these old acquaintances to Owl Mountain and then had turned her back on them. They would tell me so again and again when I came to stay for a while in my cottage. And they said she always sent them away again without so much as asking them up on her porch. I knew that in all reason Lizzy Pettigru had never actually sent for those that came back like this. They came uninvited and unannounced. She had no more sent for them than she had sent for me. I knew that they must have come only out of curiosity, in order to discover what kind of being she, Lizzy Pettigru, who had once been so much like themselves, had now turned into. It could not be she who had brought them back, for what need had she now of *their* company more than she had of *my* company? What need had she of their company more than of the company of the miserable mountain people whom she had clearly wounded by preferring to them the covites and the stray vagrants who wandered into the Grounds? Had not the village mountain people found her a mere curiosity in her grief, a monstrosity in her lost life, a total anomaly in their world where one was expected to accept his lot in life and to die in just the same guise more or less that he had come into the world wearing? It was unlikely that she had a need of anyone now. But it was possible that those old friends that she had once seemed so like had a terrible need to see how one who had once been so like themselves could have been transformed into such an unlovely old being as I came to see each summer.

Yet gradually I began to accept that perhaps Lizzy Pettigru had, consciously or unconsciously, made a compact with some dark spirit that her imagination had conjured or perhaps with the very Evil One to whom the mountain people had come eventually to attribute the source of her "powers." But this alteration of my view of the possibilities came gradually over the long years when I saw her turning into the hag, the Witch of Owl Mountain Springs.

I scoffed at them of course when any one of them said she had "powers." "She hasn't got 'powers,'" I told the postmistress more than once when she suggested as much to me. "She hasn't got 'powers'—or not of any sort you mean." Still, she was a solitary old soul, and one saw her sitting there on the veranda of her ramshackle, battenboard cottage, rocking with a certain fury and seemingly a purposeful intensity. There on the porch beneath the wisteria, which was draped all around and about, one saw her talking to herself, her thin old lips moving silently and stealthily as if she might be fearful her thoughts would be overheard by some ordinary mortal passerby. But now and then, as though it were irrepressible, she would give a cackle of laughter, a laugh at once mirthless and breathless yet withal audible in that twilight hour, audible across the wide, weedy lawns of the old resort Grounds and all the way out to the bluff's edge and past Forrest's Steep, perhaps halfway down the mountainside, too. And up there on the wisteria-draped veranda of her ramshackle, battenboard cottage she was like as not laughing at the very thought of whatever it was the mountain people had finally taught me to impute to her.

*   *   *

It *was* the mountain people of course who began all the talk about powers she possessed. But the mountain people would soon enough pass it on not only to me but to whoever of the summer people still came to the Grounds in July and August. We laughed at them at first of course. But they insisted. And they told us how during the dark winter months when there was nobody much to be seen in the overgrown Grounds or strolling along the limb-littered paths and walkways of old Owl Mountain Springs Resort, Miss Lizzy Pettigru would step out on her porch and using a most obvious magic draw nameless men of the vagrant covite sort up the path to her battenboard cottage. Hollow-eyed men they were likely to be, and lean-jawed and chewing on a twig of sourwood. They would have come wandering through the Grounds at that time of year when the last straggling summer resident had gone for the season and they—these hollow-eyed men—had strayed in to pick up the junk—the near worthless junk—that careless summer people would likely leave behind. It was just things on their porches and in their yards—and none of it tied down as it would have been if it were something they valued. It wasn't exactly what you would call stealing that those vagrants did. Such junk was all thought of as fair game for them. And as for Miss Lizzy Pettigru, such fellows were no less than fair game for her. Pretty soon she would be setting them to work in her yard or even inside her old cottage, just as though it were all by agreement. They were the only living souls she would allow on her premises. Generally they were rough mountain men from up the ridge or louts from down in the coves who had probably never lifted a hand in all their lives to provide either bread or keep—not until the unlucky day, so the village people maintained, when they came up against the powerful magic of old Miss Lizzy Pettigru. Of course, said the postmistress and the other ordinary mountain people, it was little that Miss Lizzy cared for such talk about magic so long as she got her leaves raked or her logs chopped for winter, chopped and neatly stacked inside her shed. She laughed in the faces of those solemn village folk who kept a careful eye on all she did. "You had better watch out for such desperate fellows as them!"

Thus they would warn her about those men who came wandering through the Grounds. All the while, I suppose, they were really sounding her out about what powers she exercised over those old vagrants of hers. "They'll cut your throat some night," they warned her. But she would only grin away at them, so the postmistress said. And sometimes the postmistress would wink at me, as though she and I were the only two realistic persons in the world, and say that maybe it was not any "powers" she used to make the old vagrants work but certain cash money she slipped them from under a loose board in her floor or from behind some loose and unchinked rock in her chimney piece that drew them up to her door. It might be the crumpled two-dollar bills, so the postmistress said, that Miss Lizzy had been stashing away there since she was a girl that made the old men turn up her path. It might be the folding money she paid them, the folding money that the old-time summer people never used to pay mountain people. I would listen to the cynical postmistress, but all the while I was beginning to think to myself that there might be a power she had and had always had. There might be something that had kept *me* coming back. There was a power she had possessed always that was a curious strength of mind, a way of thinking, no less, that was different from how other people thought. It might be that she had a power of mind that could somehow prevent any harm that might come from those old men, that could prevent their returning to tear up the boards and dig out the rocks to obtain whatever money that might be hidden there.

There came a point when I began almost to be afraid of her. I listened too much to the mountain people and saw her too much as they saw her. I knew that for half a century now the bodies of the two parents had lain in the village cemetery just outside the gates of the Resort Grounds. I knew that a place was left in their burial plot for the interment of their unmarried daughter. And I had observed that a space was left on their double headstone where the daughter's name could be cut. I was told by the mountain people that all the year round Lizzy Pettigru would be seen visiting the little graveyard. And she would be seen just as regularly in all environs of the village. As the years had passed both the mountain people and the summer people came to feel that she had become more native to the place than any of the natives themselves. It was even said sometimes that when she came out of the woods, after a long walk therein, she would be followed by a deer or a fox or even a bobcat. But as soon as the wild creature became aware of the presence of any other ordinary human being nearby it would straightway turn back and vanish in the woods.

Old Miss Lizzy Pettigru knew where and when the blackberries ripened, and the huckleberries and the elderberries, and where here and there in a mountain recess an unblighted old chestnut tree survived and continued to bear. Most of the knowledge of where things grew she had acquired not from any mixing with the mountain people. (She was quoted by the postmistress as saying she despised folk wisdom. She was quoted as saying folk wisdom was the same as peasant ignorance.) Rather, her information came from certain musty old books on the dusty shelves of what had once been her father's study. And perhaps, it was suspected, her magic powers had a similar source in that darkened room, whose door was kept closed to any rare visitor that somehow gained entry into her cottage. She knew, of course, that that was the thing that made everybody call her a witch—both mountain people and summer people. I think it was that and the obvious fact that she didn't have "inside plumbing." Having no plumbing somehow put the fear of God in the summer people. Then there was also the fact that her battenboard cottage had long since had all its electric wiring removed. When children— mountain children or otherwise—would peer in her windows at dark or at twilight and see only her candles flickering, *that* above all else scared the daylights out of their little beings and made them scurry on home to their folks and report what it was that they imagined they had seen inside.

When the aged Miss Lizzy Pettigru crossed from the Corner in the village, carrying her little straw basket and stooping now and then to gather mushrooms (of a kind even mountain people would never eat), or if she passed through the village street clutching her fresh-garnered herbs (which they would not know where to find), she would laugh to herself, or she would laugh out loud if it suited her, at the suspicious chatter she heard (knowing that all around her thought her to be deaf) and at the ignorant talk she heard very clearly about herself as she kept her eyes straight ahead and went on her way.

When I went to Owl Mountain for the last time, only two summers ago, it was really quite painful to have to confront as an old ogress the girl who once had been the foremost beauty of the place. Yet despite myself I found myself spying her out through the louvers of my own window blind or from behind the still-standing stone chimney of some former neighbor's cottage that had been burned out. I was seized by a new kind of fear, a fear that I would once again have to face the old creature at close range. It was how totally unlike she now was to those other images of her I held in my mind that unnerved me. I told myself she was nothing at all to me anymore. Yet that summer I saw to it that we never again passed each other on the Middle Path. And unlikely as it may seem, for the first time in my long lifetime I found myself locking the outside doors to my old cottage at night. One night I even got up and locked my bedroom door.

It was now more than ever before that I made it my business to listen to the mountain people's superstitious gossip about the visitors who came back to call on Lizzy. And how should I have known whether or not I should have believed them? According to their reports the entirety of that group of wondrous girls had one by one come back to Owl Mountain and knocked on Miss Lizzy Pettigru's door. They came with their husbands and children from the far distant places where events in their lives had taken them. The postmistress told me that she saw letters from them that must have announced they were coming and saw letters go back to them from Lizzy Pettigru that must have told them they would be welcome when they came. (The postmistress was very open about all her observations and shameless in her speculations.) Sometimes it was postcards they would write her and it was welcoming postcards that she would send back. On those postcards certainly it was just as the postmistress suspected it was in the letters. But on the day of her visitors' arrival Lizzy would not of course let them inside her front door. If she was rocking on the front veranda when they arrived she would not let them come up the steps or she would get up and go inside the cottage and close the front door behind her. But there were worse things than that to be told, moreover.

For there were some persons, the postmistress insisted, who did actually come unannounced and uninvited. The postmistress was sure of it. And their coming or not coming was the queerest business of all. She and the grocer and the man who operated the little hardware store had all, at one time or another, seen at least one of those others moving about the village. There was a couple who, even after the death of the elder Pettigrus, had summered in the cottage next door to Lizzy. Sometimes during the season they would send over a casserole or a chicken potpie to Lizzy, though they seldom received thanks or acknowledgment for such kindness. And it was some years after this couple's empty cottage had burned that they were seen in the village one day. They made inquiries here and there about Miss Lizzy Pettigru and about whether or not she was still in residence there. It was while they were still in the village and had not yet entered the Grounds that long-distance telephone calls were put through to both the grocery store and the hardware shop (the operator having first tried to reach the nonexistent number of Miss Lizzy Pettigru) requesting that a message be delivered to that visiting couple. Their son was desperately ill, and it was urged that they return home at once. Without ever entering the Grounds, they hurried away. The poor son was not dead when they got back home and did not die at all. But that couple was never heard from at Owl Mountain again.

There was still another couple who had been close friends of the Pettigru parents and who at a very great age were making one last pilgrimage to the old resort. They had flown from somewhere in the Northeast down to Nashville, and a car and driver had been hired to pick them up at the Nashville airport. The plane had had a frightful collision on the airport runway. Many aboard the plane had been injured. And the old couple, though not injured at all, refused to continue the journey on to Owl Mountain. When the Nashville newspaper interviewed some relatives of that couple, it reported that the two old souls had hoped to visit the daughter of friends they had once had at Owl Mountain Springs. But they had decided that luck was against them and that they had best return home.

There was a ruthless wickedness implied in these two stories— if, that is, one did concede some remarkable powers to the now-aged Miss Lizzy Pettigru. And events conspired that last summer to advance my disappointment and disenchantment with the old resemblance that I had used for so many years to see. My disenchantment was transformed into a kind of fear of Lizzy and perhaps then into something more positive than that. I recognized in myself even a kind of hatred for this creature I once idolized. I think it might have been otherwise than this if I had not happened to be in residence during the last of July and the first days of August.

During the morning of the last day of July Lizzy appeared over in the village blithely buying a box of salt, one small package of nails, even a page of stamps. I had glimpses of her through the windows of the three establishments she entered. I didn't in any instance want to see her, and I turned my face away each time I caught sight of her. But in my swiftest glance even I believe I saw a look of peace and satisfaction on her face that somehow frightened me. It somehow had the effect of repelling me far more than any vacancy of expression or any ignoring of my own presence had done in recent years.

But I didn't feel at all that the expressions I observed through the store windows were really directed toward those with whom she was doing business. In fact I think I observed that when I saw her again—somewhat later and at some distance away on the Middle Path and within the Grounds—she wore the same expression of peace and satisfaction. It was not something I merely imagined. And it seemed utterly bizarre to me that she at this point in her life would take up wearing such an expression. It inspired me momentarily with inexplicable feelings of bitterness. I went to my cottage and must have slept there for a while, which was an unusual thing for me to do in the middle of the morning. Just before noon I went back to the village to do the shopping I had meant to do earlier and had somehow forgotten. It was now, just after I had entered the post office, that the postmistress opened the little frosted glass door that is beside the letter counter across which she does her business. And she summoned me to her by crooking her finger.

"I suppose you have heard," she said in a lowered voice. "You must have heard," she said.

Having no idea of what she meant, I drew closer to her. "I haven't heard anything," I said almost resentfully. I confess I thought it was going to be something that Lizzy Pettigru had told her when I was looking through the post-office window some while earlier. But, anyway, I had heard nothing of what she would tell me. It seems that two persons had been killed in a car that had been catapulted and subsequently capsized on the first of the sharp inclines and curves coming up the east side of the Mountain.

"I am told," the postmistress continued, now speaking almost in a whisper, "that the victims are nobody else but the old movie actress, Sarah Goodheart, so called, and who else but that man she ran away with forty years ago, the man who used his money to make her and himself into movie stars."

Somehow the first, worst shock to me was the news of what had become of that infamous pair. As a former college professor—I had pursued that profession till I was past fifty—I did not of course keep up with what became of old movie stars. I knew—or had once known—that that outrageous couple had actually gone the way of Hollywood and had had some degree of success out there. Probably everyone in this mountain village knew more of their careers than I did. No doubt everyone else knew how long ago they had retired from the screen as well as just how much they were still in the public eye. Certainly I had never seen them once on the screen. I could not have said how great or how little their success had been. But with the shocking news of those old acquaintances' fatal accident I returned once again to my cottage and had once again failed to do the shopping I had intended doing. And once again I must have done the odd thing of falling asleep there—by what must then have been midday.

And queerer than that, I must have slept there on the couch in my sitting room for the whole of the afternoon. When I was awakened by footsteps on my porch, it was already growing dark outside. The Owl Mountain grocer and the hardware merchant, along with two men in dark business suits who were total strangers to me, stood outside my front door. The identity of the strangers was immediately explained to me. One was the coroner from the county seat, ten miles away at the foot of the Mountain, and the other was the county sheriff himself. The two merchants had shown the two other men the way to my cottage. They had come there in order to ask me to accompany them to the county seat and identify the bodies of the two victims of the early morning accident. It seems it was important they be identified before any disposition could be made of their bodies. And it seems that I was the only person still living in the community who would remember them and possibly recognize their faces. The only other possibility of course would have been to call Miss Lizzy Pettigru. Yet knowledge of the long-ago elopement was sufficiently widespread throughout the whole county to make this an impossibility for men with any delicacy of feeling. I had no choice but to comply with the request of the strangers who had come for me. I put on a tie and jacket and went with them.

Before we arrived at the county seat and went straightaway into where the two bodies were stored, lying side by side on two mortuary tables, I had been informed of the circumstances leading up to the accident. It seems that the nattily dressed old couple had flown into Chattanooga by way of Atlanta. Ordinarily any Owl Mountain summer people from the old days would have flown in by way of Nashville. Chattanooga was physically as far as Nashville from Owl Mountain, but culturally and spiritually it was considered to be light years further away. I suppose this was because it was settled as a town only after the Civil War and had been settled by Union soldiers who had taken part in the long siege of Missionary Ridge. It was indicative of how estranged from the scene Sarah and Tim had become that they allowed themselves to be routed by way of Atlanta and Chattanooga. I would read in the newspapers soon afterward that only the man in the airport car-rental service recognized them for the celebrities they were or had once been. And it is likely that that agent only recognized their names on the car-rental forms that he had received in advance.

It was no ordinary car that the agency had managed to hire for the couple. I would also read in the Chattanooga newspaper afterward (for the two were still celebrities enough for the local press to make much of their dramatic end), I would read, that is to say, of a Chattanooga teenager's having observed them at an early morning hour in their dark glasses—their "shades"—and driving a cream-colored Cadillac convertible, moving at incredible speed on a stretch of highway that runs along the foot of Chattanooga's Lookout Mountain and that follows the curve of Moccasin Bend of the Tennessee River. The teenager said he had remarked to himself at the time that the driver and passenger in the car must be a gangster and his moll or perhaps country music singers of some sort. The reporter interviewing the teenager in the *Chattanooga Times* observed that it was wonderful that the car-rental agency could come up with just such a car as the couple had specified in advance they would like to have. And the reporter philosophized further that it was wonderful how much being celebrities enhances people's lives—even such rather out-of-date celebrities as these.

I didn't know any of this, of course, when I went in to look at the two bodies, though in retrospect I have a feeling that I did know all of it. What I actually knew then was only what the sheriff and the coroner had been able to tell me at the time. I knew that it had been a sunny midmorning, and that by the time the exotic pair, Tim and Sarah, reached the ascent up to Owl Mountain they had put down the top to the rented convertible. In that cream-colored automobile and in their dark glasses they must indeed have presented a spectacular sight as they came round the first bend of that winding mountain road. There were a good many people who had been coming down the Mountain at that hour, people who nowadays commuted to work at the county seat. Afterward they would remember the begoggled couple and remember of course the great rate of speed at which they were taking other curves. The thing was, nobody actually saw the car leave the road. The car that was around the next curve above heard the great scream of the tires and heard the series of bumps and crashes as the behemoth went down the mountainside. And occupants of a car on a curve just behind heard it all, too. But no one actually saw the big Cadillac leave the road. As it made its flip upside down through the bright morning air the only witnesses to its fateful move through the air must have been whatever wildlife was present on the wooded mountainside. After other cars appeared, all to be seen were the marks in the tar and some gravel that had recently been put on that stretch of the road—that and some even deeper marks and ruts in the red clay shoulder on the left-hand side of the pavement. From the sound of screaming brakes it could only be surmised that some wild thing must have suddenly appeared from the wooded slopes above the road—some deer or bobcat or fox—and in braking the car at such speed on the newly spread gravel the driver must have lost all control of the vehicle. When the passengers in the next cars to come along stopped and went to the shoulder of the road and looked down, only the underside of the big convertible could be seen. Already a few long wisps of smoke were rising from the wreckage. From the very first there was no question of anyone surviving such a crash. When the police came and the wrecker crew soon after them and the ambulance people not long after, there was some effort made to find whatever wild creature might have distracted and confused the driver and sent the car out of control. Whatever it was must have stopped right in the car's path for a moment and then scampered to safety. But no identifying track could be found. No doubt the turf at the roadside was too ravaged and the loose gravel and the tar too scrambled for any footprints or hoofprints to be distinguishable. Yet surely there could have been no other explanation for the frightful accident.

In the temporary morgue where I was taken it seemed now that one moment I was standing between the two covered bodies and the next moment, by the concerted turns of the wrists of both the sheriff and the coroner, the protective sheets had been drawn back simultaneously to reveal the faces of the two accident victims. And it was almost as though the sudden exposure of the two faces had been coordinated in order to increase the shock I was destined to experience.

I had been told already that in the morning's accident the faces of the victims had not been mutilated or even scarred. All that I had inwardly prepared myself for was how the ravages of time and a life spent in Hollywood might reasonably have altered the faces of my two old acquaintances. But the actual shock I received and that I believe made me literally take a step backward was the sight of the youthfully smooth and untroubled countenances of the two dead people—their dark heads of hair, the unblemished cheeks, the unwrinkled lids of the closed eyes, the serene expressions on their relaxed faces. Before me seemed to be the faces of Sarah and Tim as I had last seen them. Not until later did it occur to me that what I looked upon was the work of dye jobs and face-lifts and perhaps something of a local undertaker's work. But for the moment it was the young Tim and Sarah lying before me. "Yes, yes!" I said, almost without thinking and turning to the men who had escorted me there.

"You have no doubt then," the sheriff said, he and the coroner coming forward at once.

"Oh, no. There can be no doubt," I said. And I could only think to myself, *She* did this to them! It was as if she had done it long years ago on the night they had eloped. As they led me back to the waiting car the two men had almost to support me bodily. And on the road back to Owl Mountain Springs I had not a word to say to them. It was then that I began to realize what was the nature of the work that had been done on those faces. When the men returned me to my cottage they offered to stay with me for a while. But I waved them away. And when I closed the door behind me, I locked myself in my cottage. I had now but one line of thought. Why had I come back to Owl Mountain Springs all these years? Why had I been destined to live so long as to see all vestiges of what I could love in Lizzy's face and figure entirely vanish? And at the last I found myself asking myself: was I ever in her mind any different from the others? And did *she* still have some hideous fate in mind for *me*?

I was awakened once again by the sound of hurried footsteps on my porch. I can only suppose—because I could not otherwise account for the time—that I had fallen into another long period of sleep. The lights were still lit all over my cottage, but certainly I was prone in a sleeping posture on the couch in my sitting room. At some point I had washed myself thoroughly and even got into pajamas. And at some point I had unlocked my front door. And now I was awakened as from a troubling nightmare of the kind you cannot afterward quite remember. Someone on the porch knocked once and then opened the unlocked door. He was a young mountain fellow, a total stranger to me like the two men who had come earlier. I sat up on my couch blinking my eyes at him. Panting for breath and with one hand on the porcelain doorknob, he told me he had been sent to wake me and tell me that Miss Lizzy Pettigru's cottage was on fire. He stared at me for a moment as if to see how I responded. Then he fled across the porch and I heard him calling out to other persons on the path.

I went to my bedroom and pulled on a clean pair of trousers over my pajamas as well as a fresh shirt. Then I hurried out to join the village people who had assembled along the Middle Path and in the yard outside Miss Lizzy's cottage. There were mists of white smoke all about the cottage but there were no flames. Some semblance of an amateur brigade had pulled up a water tank with hoses and already had been at work spraying the shingled roof. In fact, those men were still attempting to spray water on the roof and on the battenboard siding when I arrived. If there had been any appreciable fire it had been extinguished without much effort on their part. At first I began to move directly toward the cottage, but I was restrained by the strong arms of the grocer's wife and the postmistress. "It's too late for you to be any help," one of them said. I could feel their powerful hands taking hold of me, and all at once I became aware of my age. I heard someone say, "They're bringing her out now!" The two women led me toward one of the stone benches beside the Middle Path and forced me to sit down. Other people gathered around where I was sitting and I felt they were all being protective of me and showing respect for my great age. I became aware that a crowd of mountain people were grouping themselves between me and the sight of the body that was being brought out. I knew it was out of consideration for my advanced age and for my well-known friendship with Lizzy Pettigru. No doubt I had grown pale and no doubt the trembling of my right hand had increased and was becoming noticeable, because the grocer's wife now began to urge me to return to my own cottage. When I firmly declined to leave the scene, the postmistress sat down on the stone bench beside me and said in a most reasonable voice, "I think you must be told the whole truth here and now."

And that lady proceeded then to tell me that it was not the fire that had taken Lizzy's life. She told me that the first men to arrive at the fire had entered the cottage, gone down the long central hallway, and found the old spinster lying already dead in her bed. And then for a moment the postmistress looked at the other woman as if to obtain her approval before continuing. "She was already dead when they got here, and there could not have been much of a fire. I tell you just what they told me. Miss Lizzy had had her throat cut." The grocer's wife began to cry in her handkerchief then, but the postmistress sat there looking me straight in the eye. She gave me the very worst of the details. They found blood all over the wall opposite the bed. And clearly the fire had been set as an obvious effort—a too-obvious effort—to conceal the means of death. But the murderer had had no experience in such a business. The postmistress, and everyone else later on, pronounced it most clearly the work of one of the old vagrants from down in the cove. And this of course, as we all remembered, was something that had been predicted years before. Boards had been prized up from the floor and the chimney stones pried loose from the chimney. It was supposed to indicate someone had been in search of the poor old creature's money. But even the search for the money was somehow unconvincing. And there was evidence that the old soul had put up resistance. But there was something unreal about that, too. Chairs and tables were turned over and there were bloodstains on the floor and along the dado of the bedroom. And last of all the murderer's weapon was a knife from

Lizzy's own kitchen. That itself would have been like one of those old fellows from the coves. But the handle of the knife had been wiped dry of all bloodstains and fingerprints, which would not have been like one of those old fellows at all.

I was protected from the sight of the body when they brought the old creature outside. And of course I never looked upon her face again. But the picture described to me of her lying there dead with her throat slit will never leave me. At last I was guided back to my own cottage. I was seen safely to bed by my two lady companions, who sat near me for the rest of the night. I slept not at all and sometimes I remembered that I had not eaten all day. Before dawn it had occurred to me more than once that in all likelihood the body of Lizzy by this time lay in the temporary morgue that had been set up at the county seat. And it was all too easy to imagine that she would be lying there now right alongside the bodies of those who had been victims of the highway accident. I had the impulse to remark on this to whomever I might make listen to me. But of course I found it too grim a thing to mention in the presence of the two ladies who were sitting the night through with me.

In recent days it has seemed almost incredibly ironic, too much of a coincidence to be believed, that Lizzy Pettigru should actually have met her violent end on the very same day as Tim Sullivan and Sarah Goodrich. But if there be skeptics about the truth of my account, they must go sometime and look up the dates beneath Lizzy's name on the tombstone she shares with her parents in the Owl Mountain Cemetery and then travel out to Hollywood and see that the same date is there on the magnificent marble monument that I believe Tim Sullivan and Sarah Goodrich share. And if this be after my death, it might seem worthwhile to go and seek out my own grave in whatever remote place I shall have taken myself off to, and learn just how long I was able to survive the end of such a story as I had to tell.

Peter Taylor was born at Trenton, Tennessee, in 1917. After attending Kenyon College and Vanderbilt University he was in the army for five years and wrote most of his first book of stories there. In later years he taught at such colleges and universities as Kenyon, Harvard, The University of North Carolina at Greensboro, University of Virginia and others. In 1987 he received the Pulitzer Prize for his novel *A Summons to Memphis*. A new collection of his stories, *The Oracle at Stoneleigh Court and Other Stories*, was published in 1992. He is married to the poet Eleanor Ross Taylor. They have two children and one grandchild.

PHOTO CREDIT: JOHN MORAN, *New York Times*

Elizabeth Seydel Morgan

ECONOMICS

(from *The Virginia Quarterly Review*)

Our mother taught us to substitute the word "tiger" for the word "nigger" when the neighborhood gang chose up teams. Sitting here on my brother's porch, watching my nieces play in the yard with their friends, I think how much has changed since he and I grew up in Atlanta—for one thing, two of their playmates are black. Yet children, their summer games, even this ancient choosing rhyme—catch a tiger by the toe—haven't changed at all.

Back then my brother and I said "tiger," but we didn't have much influence on our next-door neighbor, Carson Foster. He poked his finger in our chests as he chanted "eenie, meenie, miney, moe" and emphasized the forbidden word even more. "If he hollers, let him go." He also added codas if "moe" brought his finger to one of us girls. "Eu-gene Talmadge told me so," or "My father said. To pick the. Very. Best. Man."

But then my mother said a variation of the word herself. "Can you imagine a nigra named Queen Esther Parris?" I overheard her say to Daddy, who answered, "Is that her name or her title?"

"Name," said Mama. "Wants her checks written out to Queen Esther Parris."

"Checks?" I heard his low voice repeat.

"Queen Esther wants to be paid by check."

"Strange," said my dad.

This fact, which I now understand to have been phenomenal in the forties, was strange to me, too, because I thought I knew what checks were—money that was not real, the pale blue of Great Aunt Tisha's Christmas check for a million dollars that Daddy stuck in his mirror frame, the many-colored money that stuck out from under the Monopoly board at the Fosters' next door. When we weren't playing softball or strip poker, we'd gather around the board on the Fosters' screen porch and play Monopoly. Though sometimes he let a boy get to the hotel stage, Carson Foster usually won all the money, his pile of gold thousands as big as our worthless pink fives and white singles.

Queen Esther, paid by check (how much, I wonder) on Fridays, worked for us when I was around ten. I remember my age because I can picture and hear the moment in my backyard when Carson laughed at my mother working in her garden and said behind her back, "Your mother's a hoer. Get it?"

I didn't get it, but I was certain he had insulted my mother, and I was sick of him and sick of his games. That day in the garden as my mother hoed the border, I stood, I imagine, with my hands on my hips and told Carson, "Look. I'm almost ten years old and I'm not doin' that strip poker and movie-love stuff with you anymore." I have no memory of exactly what he looked like—except that he was big, and he had long square fingers that he liked to put on me—but today I can hear my own words perfectly: "I'm almost ten years old." And I know I didn't say them until after Queen Esther had been with us awhile.

"Hey Mary Meade . . . your maid's sure some Ubangi," Carson had jeered over the hedge when she first came. Later I saw a movie, *King Solomon's Mines*, I think it was, and there were those six- or seven-foot Negroes—blacks I mean—and true, I guess Queen Esther might have come from such a tall African tribe. She was at least six feet. She towered over me (though now I'm very tall myself); I remember most her pink-palmed hand turned slightly outward at her side, and what would I have been then—maybe four feet tall? We'd walk to Connell's with me skipping at her side to match her long strides, my younger brother and sometimes other children trailing behind, Queen Esther tickling her nose all the while with her triffle.

Queen Esther's triffle was a piece of cotton, frayed into a fringe at the end, that she wound around her forefinger and used to tickle her lips or nose or cheeks. Now I know that it was the same kind of habit as smoking, or fingering a blanket's satin edge, as I do every night to get to sleep; then it was mysterious, like her height and her name.

"Queen Esther, why you have that whatchacallit?" one of us would ask.

"That's my triffle," she'd reply.

"What's a triffle?"

"Your business is to direct us all to this drugstore. My triffle is to help me following you, so we get there."

But she never followed us, and after the first time we walked to Buckhead, she never needed help to get there. I suppose she meant the triffle habit was to help her be where she was.

Queen Esther ironed. She did everything else, too: the vacuuming, the laundry, the beds, the scraping scrambled eggs out of the iron skillet left in the mornings before she came, the picking up of toys and children's clothes and grown-up underwear in the sheets when she changed the beds, the tossing of empty bottles, scraps of hardened cheese on Chinese plates left from Sunday on the screen porch, the emptying trash cans of Modess and deposit slips and green Coca-Cola bottles.

When Queen Esther ironed, she put books under the legs of the ironing board. After she'd tried the Atlanta phone books once, she never used them again. She'd go to the bookshelf in the den or the living room and try a different selection every Tuesday. I was pretty much loving books myself then, so I'd notice, sitting on the floor by the ironing board, just what was raising it up to her arms. I think back now to the selection of books available to her for lifting the ironing board: Reader's Digest novels, *Up Front, Gone with the Wind*, volumes of *Collier's Encyclopedia, Clothes Make the Man, Leave Her to Heaven, The Decameron, Southern Textiles*, and *Warp Sizing*, the last two either written or given to us by our uncle.

She came to use only the brown encyclopedias, eight to an ironing, and I think she and I were probably the first in our house to crack every one open and look at it. We'd find a picture or more often a map she'd be interested in, and while she was sprinkling down the sheets, I'd read about it out loud. After a time, we started reading a little together—I'd read some words, then she'd read some words—"while the iron heats up," she said.

One day before she placed E on the floor, we discovered Esther, the biblical queen of Xerxes who saved her people from destruction. After we read the short column aloud, her namesake read it over to herself.

"Left out the best part, Mary Meade," she said.

"Tell," I said.

"Esther, she knows her husband kicked out his first wife on account of she didn't come when he called her."

"They got a divorce?"

"No. He the king, she out on the street."

"Oh."

"But even so, when time comes to save her people, Esther said, 'Then I will go to the king though it be against the law and if I perish, I perish.'"

She pronounced the quotation slowly, like a teacher.

"That straight out of the Bible . . . from Esther's own book." Then she said quickly in her getting-down-to-work voice, "Now you read your own story for a while."

I remember the brown books under the wooden legs, the scratch of the rug through my cotton underpants, the book in my lap—probably one of the Black Stallion novels—as I sat by the ironing board, reading while Queen Esther intoned the throaty songs that repeated every line with just a little change. *When you get up tomorrow I'll be gone, babe, when you wake up tomorrow, I'll be gone.*

After Queen Esther found out I could charge money at Connell's Drug Store, we walked to Buckhead every Friday, just the two of us. Doc Connell, or Miss Presson, would write my father's name on the pad with carbon paper, write "money" on the first line and "$1.00" beside "total." Then he'd hand me the dollar bill. For several weeks, I'm not sure how long, Queen Esther would stand tall and silent behind me as I made my transaction. After the first surprised look from Doc Connell and Miss Presson, they didn't look at her at all. It was clear she was my maid. "Thanks a lot," I'd say politely. "You're welcome, Mary Meade," he or both of them would answer. If it was Doc Connell, he usually added something about how come I never spent my money in his store, and I always said the same thing, that it was for the Saturday double feature and serial.

I'd pocket the dollar and walk past cosmetics with Queen Esther, out the screen door to Peachtree, down to the corner at Paces Ferry Road where we waited for her bus. "Well, bye," I'd say when the Five Points bus to downtown Atlanta came, "see you Monday." She'd nod her head to the side with this way she had, and I'd start back to our neighborhood to hand over the money to Carson.

One Friday afternoon, standing at Connell's counter, I was surprised by the long black arm extending from behind me, Queen Esther's boney fingers holding out three beige checks to Miss Presson. Miss Presson looked from my face way up over my head and then down at the checks in the black hand. "We don't cash checks," she said to me.

"Those are Mama-an-Daddy's," I said.

"No, sweetie, those are your maid's. And Doc don't allow cashing except for charge customers."

"Mary Meade a charge customer," said Queen Esther.

"What's cashing?" I suppose I asked, because it was then I got a lesson in finance from Miss Presson, learned the difference between my parents' checks and Aunt Tisha's, and watched Queen Esther's arm retreat. As we walked to the bus stop, I asked her how she was going to get real money in place of those beige checks. She stopped still and swiveled her head around on her long neck, looking up and down Peachtree Street. "Somehow," she answered.

Who knows who called my parents, Doc or Miss Presson. "We have to have a talk," said Daddy in his lowest voice, guiding me with a pinch of the back of my neck into the den. "It looks like, Mary Meade, that we need to talk some economics tonight."

"Yes sir," I said.

"Do you know what I mean?"

"No sir."

"Economics is a big word for, uh, hmmm. Uh, money. Things about money."

I remember his hemming and hawing more than his exact words. But Daddy always kept you standing for a long time, getting to the point, and I remember the word "economics" so well from that evening that even today it gives me a catch in the stomach.

"I've been letting you charge a dollar here and there at Connell's—figured it would teach you something—but it looks like you been at it every week. And I would like to ask just why you need so many dollars. I know about the shows at the Buckhead and all, but you also have your allowance, and your money for sitting with Robert."

"Yes."

"Yes what."

"Yes sir."

"I mean yes, what are you doing with the money, Mary Meade?"

I looked at Daddy and opened my mouth. Probably the only two times I've ever been as terrified as that was the time with Carson and the day before my wedding when I told Clifford

Sealew that I could not go through with it. Without planning to, I had lied to Clifford, told him there was someone else.

"Well?" said my father.

From my opened mouth the words slipped easy as a prayer. "I gave the money to Queen Esther."

Unlike Cliff, Daddy didn't explode or break down. He said something along the lines of "I thought so" and went on to question me about Queen Esther going in Connell's with me and trying to cash checks. Then he came back around to my lie. He asked me if she'd forced me to give her money.

"Oh, no, no, no!" I saw immediately what I'd gotten into. I saw his angry look gathering, and I knew it was directed at her. "No, Daddy. I wanted to give it to her. She can't get real money for your checks. She tried, and she can't."

He said something like "So I heard" and changed into being real sweet to me. He praised me that night, which I'll always remember, and my tears subsided. We hugged and kissed and I was sent on somewhere, having learned that lying pays, while Daddy stayed in the den in his leather armchair, smoking a cigarette.

That Friday afternoon I ran to catch up with Queen Esther, who'd already started for Buckhead without me. Even after I caught up with her, breathless, she walked faster than I could keep up beside her.

"What you running for?" she called loud enough to keep from turning her head. "You don't need to go to Connell's anymore. Your charging days are over."

I remember the back of her, its motion—slim thighs, boxy rear end, long, long spine showing through something like jersey, wide shoulders. I think of her in something gray or tan, with a shiny red belt—probably patent leather. I think of her moving, her hips moving smoothly, and me running behind her, eye-level to her red belt.

"How do you know?" I yelled at her shoulders, the long loops of earrings touching them.

"Your daddy."

"He wouldn't tell *you*."

"Oh yes he would. He did." She wore a sort of glittery turban that day, and she turned her head in a flash of shine and swinging earrings. Running, looking up, I saw the profile of her moving lips.

"You are a liar," she said.

"You are a hoer," Carson had rasped slowly at the opening we'd made in the ligustrum hedge.

"Un uh," I said, shaking my head and toeing the soft dirt with my bare foot.

"Yes you are."

"Un UH." I was getting scared. Fear was suffusing my body the way pleasure had when Carson and I had been in the bushes.

"A hoer is a girl who does stuff like you did with me. A bad girl."

"I'm not a bad girl."

"You let me tickle you . . . down there."

"No."

"Come on, you already forgetting movie-love?" He pointed at a bunch of tall azaleas in his backyard. "Under there? Those times you let me tickle you with my finger? A long time. And you said it felt good."

"No."

"Well you can say no all you want to, girl. But I'm telling."

The fear was pushing out at my surfaces. I know my pale white skin was red.

"You liked it," Carson said real low, looking up and down my red skin.

"I said I wasn't . . . I said stop it, you know I did."

"Yeah—later you say, '*I'm ten*.' Big deal. You're still a hoer. You still *liked* it. And I'm telling."

"Ah, Carson. Please don't," I whined. I wonder now why I didn't say "Tell who?" "Tell what?" but to a child "I'm telling" needs no who.

He reached through the opening in the hedge and yanked down the elastic top of my sundress, pulling my bare chest into the pruned branches.

"What'll you pay me?"

"Huh?"

"What'll you pay me to never tell?"

I had no idea what he meant.

"You get an allowance, dontcha?"

I just stood there burning with this new, unbearable feeling.

"Listen!" he spat. "Do you?"

"What?" The backs of my legs prickled like poison ivy.

"Do you get an allowance? Do you get lunch money? Movie money?"

"Movie . . . allowance."

"I want one dollar a week."

"Why?" I'm pretty sure I said. I remember being completely confused.

"Why! To keep me from telling you're a hoer. That's why."

"Okay."

He seemed surprised. "Okay?"

"Okay." It seemed easy that afternoon to stop the burning. Just pay my next-door neighbor one dollar and he would never tell that I let him put his finger between my legs and move it around and make me feel good, and bad.

"Wait a minute, Queen Esther," I yelled, catching up. "Please wait!"

She didn't exactly wait, but she must have slowed her long-legged stride a little because I came up alongside her, puffing.

"Queen Esther, I really wish I could give my dollars to *you*."

Far above me I saw the whites of her eyes as she rolled them. She just kept walking, getting ahead of me again.

"If you can't get cashed."

She looked over her shoulder. "If you knew somethin' beside nothin', you'd be trouble." And then she raised her arm as if to swat me backward, but she only stroked her upraised chin with her triffle.

That slowed her a little and I caught up. My heart was thudding with running and what I was about to do.

"Queen Esther—I have to give all my dollars to Carson!"

"Say?"

"Carson. The charge money. I give it to him."

She stopped. "Wuf fo?" she said in the language I knew as well as I know French now.

What I told Queen Esther as we stopped on the road to Buckhead was surely not the whole story. I never told anyone about feeling the sweet sensation that had spread over my body and made me bad.

I told her we'd played strip poker and doctor and I had to pay to keep it a secret.

"Blackmail!" sang Queen Esther. "Bluemail, man-mail, exto. Strongarm, strong, strong."

It sounded like a chant. Whatever she was saying or chanting, her stride had slowed to let me stay beside her.

We walked together, past my school, past the bungalows smaller than my house, to Paces Ferry Road. Her bus stop was ahead, down at Peachtree.

"Don' pay'm mo'." she said, and I heard this clearly as *Don't pay Carson any more dollars.*

"But how?" I looked up and she heard that clearly as *Without his telling Mama and Daddy I'm a hoer.*

"Say: I'm good. And I know it. And I ain't givin' you a cent. Say: You boy, I am a good girl."

I thought about it. "He'll still tell."

"No. He won't." said Queen Esther.

We'd come to Connell's Drug Store and both tried to look the other way.

"I won't be coming back, Mary Meade. I been let go."

"Where you going?"

"Some other house."

"Where you cashing?"

"I knows a man." She looked down at me. "If I perish, I perish . . ."

"Oh. Can I wait with you for Five Points Bus?"

We waited with the group of maids and yardmen at the corner. Queen Esther was taller than all of them, and the men looked embarrassed to have her standing like a giraffe in their midst. The women seemed ashamed to be dressed so ugly. Every one of them looked drab and dusty. Queen Esther, in her shining turban and earrings and glowing skin, was beautiful. I remember understanding that for the first time.

We watched the bus make its circle around the Buckhead traffic island to head back downtown. Queen Esther looked down and said, with no smile or sadness, no emotion at all, "Tell the boy no mo' dollars, and tell your daddy they never were for me."

Then she took the steps up the bus with one step, ducked her head, and was gone.

All the black people around me moved toward the bus, and I turned toward Paces Ferry Road.

I went home and lied to Carson that my daddy had found out anyway so I couldn't pay him anymore, and I lied to Daddy by never saying another word about it. I never told anyone, then or now, that I am good.

Elizabeth Seydel Morgan was born and raised
in Atlanta, Georgia, went to Hollins College in
Virginia, and lives and teaches writing in
Virginia. Her three children were raised in
Richmond, where they all live now. She has
published two books of poetry, *Parties*, and *The
Governor of Desire* (LSU Press), and only recently returned to where she
started as a writer—telling stories.

M*y father will remember this Atlanta, when Buckhead was a crossroads and his own children could charge money at the drugstore.
The father here is certainly nothing like mine, who will know immediately
that I made up most of this story (just as I used to make up ghost stories
and play scary chords on my grandfather's organ) and that the truth in
"Economics" has to do with race and sex.*

Karen Minton

LIKE HANDS ON A
CAVE WALL

(from *The Georgia Review*)

In a diner north of Little Rock, people were sitting in booths behind plate-glass windows. A garage and a convenience store sat on either side of the diner, and stretches of fields and briar thickets lay beyond. The diner had been built by the same group of developers who, thinking growth was headed that way, had also built the subdivision of wood-frame houses across the highway. Growth hadn't come, and property values stayed low on what the real-estate agents called "great starter homes." Swing sets, clotheslines, and basketball goals stood in patchy yards, and power lines ran overhead.

Some of the homes' lighted windows were steamed up from cooking, but customers in the diner could see into windows where curtains hadn't been drawn. A waitress poured coffee and looked outside, complaining about the cold snap and the early dark of January. A Michigan woman cooled her coffee and said to her husband, "It's a shame they don't have snow to cover it." She looked beyond the brown field—gray, actually, in the light of dusk. Her gaze settled on a green house where, in a lighted living-room window, a woman stood with her arms raised straight above her head, whether in a rage or a stretch, she couldn't tell.

The earthquake started out some six or more miles beneath west Tennessee and twisted the crust of the earth like a lid on a Mason jar. The force that toppled buildings and twisted steel bridges nearer the Mississippi would dissipate like surf at the shore when it reached the rising escarpment of the Ouachita Mountains to the west. It was already losing strength at this distance. When the Michigan woman set her coffee down, it clinked against the saucer and kept clinking. Mailboxes shook. Power poles swayed. Cracks webbed down the sidewalk, split already by time and sporting dead grass and dandelion weeds.

Beside the green house, a walnut tree shook a few dry leaves to the ground. At the other end of the house—the bright south end, where the grass was thin and the paint faded from the summer sun—the mortar in the concrete block foundation began to crack. The outlines of the blocks, smoothed over by layer upon layer of paint, became more defined as cracks traveled up the wall and outward in both directions while the tremor pulsed under the house. The house, sitting on the foundation but not attached to it or connected in any way to the ground, was knocked sideways just a couple of inches off-center to the south side of the wall, struck all those years by the sun and maybe built in the first place by a lazy mason using too much water in the mortar mix to keep it from drying out so fast.

Whatever action continued—barking dogs, pots boiling on stoves, the faraway roar of an airplane overhead—was absorbed by the earthquake. When the rumbling ceased, the contrasting silence seemed louder and longer than the quake, silence broken only by the still-barking dogs and the drumming of hooves in the field behind the house as a white horse galloped toward the unmoving headlights on the highway.

A jagged line of concrete blocks jutted from the foundation, and under the redistributed weight of the house, gave way at the weak south end. And that started more crumbling of concrete on around the front and back of the house until the whole building tilted—not falling, but dropping at one end even as it was held at the other end by the north wall. It simply eased down at an angle on a wadding of broken concrete.

Ginny Robinson pushed her boy and girl through the front door, which had been wedged nearly shut by the porch boards. Then she slipped through the opening, carrying a cardboard box that held the cat she'd had to pry off a window screen. The clouds were still pink where the sun had set before the earthquake began. She negotiated the splintered wood and chunks of concrete to the car in the driveway and put her kids into it. Then, still holding the box, she leaned against the fender and looked at her house.

Concrete dust, caught in the gray light of dusk, swirled around the bottom of the house like a fog bank. Some part of Ginny's mind recognized that other houses were standing, that in fact only fallen bicycles and leaning poles and the slight shifting of sheds and lawn furniture gave witness to the earthquake. Some part of her mind remembered she should have shut off the power and water as the civil-defense commercials warned, but mainly she wondered at her house, upright and solid one minute and canted now as if the ground had risen like an ocean wave beneath one end of it. She paid no attention yet to the cold or to the yowling cat, its claw tearing at her bare arm through the flaps in the box. And some part of her mind marveled that an earthquake sounded so much like a human scream—that within the sounds of the quake and rattling glasses, she had heard screams coming right out of the ground.

Down the street, dark now with a power failure, doors opened and closed, and neighbors called to each other. A collie loped around her house and barked a couple of times at the ground where the north wall of the foundation stood intact. The neighbors drifted to Ginny's house, some carrying flashlights even though the sky was still light. They circled the house, speculating on the integrity of the foundation left standing, checking the power lines and water pipes that ran into the house. One man volunteered to drive to the fire department since the phones were down. Someone said the state patrol was closer, but that depended on what bridges might be out. The yowls of the cat never ceased. It scratched the sides of the box and occasionally darted its paw out to snag Ginny's skin. The collie barked into the opening that gave access to the crawl space. Mattie from next door tried to shoo it off. A boy threw rocks at it. It tucked its tail and crept a few steps away but returned barking at the ground.

Someone said, "Listen"—and underneath the noise of the cat and the dog and children, they heard the man under the house yell for help.

He barely breathed when he gained consciousness this time. He had screamed before, when he first realized the significance of the noise that was coming from beneath him instead of from out there, from airplanes or traffic or from the woman in the house above him. He had heard the rumble and then saw, though it was dark as pitch under there, the house start to lean above him. He heard the scraping concrete and the creaking timbers reverberate in the crawl space. He had darted for the piece of plywood, outlined with light, that covered the opening in the concrete wall. He scuttled toward it—careful even then to stay low on all fours to keep from bumping against the floor and giving his presence away.

When the house fell on his back, he screamed, then passed out. Each time he had come to, he breathed in the dust, and each time he had coughed, passing out again as pain shot through his chest and back. But this time he barely breathed, not deliberately but instinctively fearing the pain. He was practiced at it—breathing slowly to control the creeps of a closed place so similar to a tunnel or a mine shaft, and he knew the closeness of both. His face was pressed into the damp dirt. He couldn't move. He couldn't raise up or roll over or even gather his knees beneath him, and each try almost knocked him unconscious. Outside the dog barked, and his mind began divorcing itself from panic to count the rhythm of barks. Four barks. Pause. Four barks. Pause. Three barks. Finally he caught the drone of voices outside, and he yelled for help.

Ginny hadn't gone crazy during the earthquake. She sat now in the car with the radio on, the way her dad used to sit in his Mercury listening to ball games and smoking cigarettes. Darkness had fallen, but she faced the western horizon where light still fanned across the sky. She had sent her kids to a neighbor's and let the cat loose in the bushes behind the house. Mattie was wrapping her arm with gauze and trying to persuade her to come and sit in her kitchen till the shock wore off. Ginny didn't remember even seeing the cat leave the box, it had darted away so quickly. She just remembered the empty box shredded on the inside by claws. A wet circle of her blood had soaked into the box lid.

She hadn't gone crazy. She had shuffled her mind through insurance policies, through the leave time she'd amassed at the radio station (which was even now broadcasting in her car), and she'd thought of calling her mother in Fort Smith as soon as the phones were working. She thought of the clothes and her purse hanging on the bedroom doorknob, which she needed whenever she could get back in the house. She had forgotten to grab her purse and a coat, so Mattie loaned her John's old coat. Still, she had kept her head. Then they told her there was a man under her house.

She kept potatoes and onions under the floor in a hole dug into the hard-packed dirt. It was cool under there in the summer and safe from frost in the winter—like now, when the temperatures had been in the teens and twenties for too many days running. Her daughter had crawled under the floor last fall after leaving a note that she was running away from home, and exterminators had once spent an expensive day under there when they found termites. She'd also seen a king snake slither through the concrete and thought of it whenever she reached down in the hole for potatoes.

She watched them gather at the end of her house, milling around in the beams of flashlights. She pulled John's coat on and pushed her way over to the house. The sheet of plywood she used as a door to the crawl space was wedged sideways in the opening.

John gripped the splintered top of the plywood as he leaned his head and shoulders into the hole. She heard him talking, but the man under the house was quiet now.

When John backed out of the opening, Ginny asked, "Who is it?"

John said he didn't know and motioned her over to the walnut tree. The neighbors followed. He turned around when he reached the trunk and tried to put his hands in his pockets, even the hand that held the flashlight.

"Ginny, how long's it been since you've been under there?"

"A while," she said. "I keep potatoes and onions under there, but it's been a while since I got any. Why?"

John was a big man, but Ginny stood eye-level with him. His coat fell right on her, just a little too long in the sleeves. She looked into his eyes, but while he looked at her face, it seemed in the dim light he was staring at the top of her head.

"A beam's got him pinned to the ground," he said. "It hit him across the shoulders, and all I could see was his head. It looks like his head is sticking right up out of the ground."

Ginny put her hands in the coat pockets and twirled something, a nail or a hinge pin, in her fingers. It was too dark to read the expression on John's face.

She asked, "How bad hurt is he?"

"He might be bad," John said. "The phones are out, but the state patrol ought to be here soon. We might ought to get somebody else to go. Walt didn't know anybody was under the house when he went to report it."

Ginny said, "What's he doing under my house?"

John took a long time to answer. He looked above Ginny's head where the horizon was lined with light. Stars were out.

He said, "Maybe living there. It looked like he had a damned nest built up under there."

Moonlight shafting through cracks in the crumbled concrete showed like color but didn't light the darkness under the house. The collapsed end of the house sat not on solid ground but on jagged chunks of concrete block. The other end didn't sit on the standing foundation but was tilted against the block wall's inside edge, caught midway in its downward slide. Now, the house pushed slowly, imperceptibly outward against the foundation that was left, seeming frozen there until some cosmic second hand started moving again and the house would finish its fall to the ground.

Pinned between the hard earth and the wooden beam, the man seemed to have served as the wedge that halted the house in its slide. He was conscious now, listening to the voices outside—not to the words, but to the drone of human beings. Dirt was in his left eye, and every once in a while, instinctively, he tried to wipe it, but his arms were somewhere behind the beam looming just in back of his head. His face was cold, both from being pressed into the cold dirt and from the wind that blew in the opening, where he could occasionally see light dart from flashlights or the white paws and snout of the barking dog. He was used to the musty, pervading smell of dirt—even liked it now, as one likes the smell of yeast—but he was barely breathing, taking shallow breaths into a chest that couldn't rise. They would see his bed and the onion skins. The woman would crawl under her house and see her potatoes gone. His nose was running, but his arm didn't pull up to wipe it with his sleeve.

Ginny's receiver had withstood the quake and her backup power system worked. The announcer was broadcasting from the transmitter and had just been joined by a member of civil defense who said in 1811 and '12 it took three earthquakes to release the pressure in the New Madrid fault, so that, at best, they needed to brace themselves for aftershocks. In Mattie's kitchen, Ginny gazed at the transistor radio in the light of a Coleman lantern while Mattie made coffee on a propane stove. No one outside had mentioned the possibility of aftershocks, had maybe not even thought of that yet.

Ginny wrapped both hands around the coffee cup. The oldest of seven kids, she had plowed fields behind a mule and learned the mechanics of a John Deere tractor. She had put herself through tech school waitressing and laying sod, earned her degree in electronics, then helped her brothers and sisters through school. She had worked two jobs after her husband cut out and still got her kids bathed and in bed on time. She had once held a ball bat over her brother-in-law while he packed his clothes and while her little sister nursed a swollen eye. Yet she had fallen to pieces when John described the pillow the man had made from the straw in her potato hole. She had screamed and shaken all over, but in Mattie's kitchen, while she listened to the strong signal on the radio, the shaking stopped. She sucked on a cough drop she'd found in John's coat pocket and tried to remember what she'd heard about aftershocks. They shouldn't wait much longer for help to come.

The state patrol car had pulled off into the grass in her front yard. The siren was off, but the blue lights were flashing around the neighborhood like strobe lights. A couple of neighbors stood by the open car door where a patrolman talked into the radio; she could hear its squawk. The others were grouped around the end of the house. She marched to the house and found John talking to the other patrolman.

"Is he still alive?" she asked.

He was. John didn't see how—mashed in the ground like that. But according to the state patrol, there was a pileup north on Route 67 and a fire at the cotton mill, so the fire trucks and ambulances were tied up. Ginny's ex worked swing shift at the mill. She knew people there.

The patrolman was young. He had a pocket notebook out but wasn't writing anything. Ginny told him to get hold of the city and get a civil engineer out here. He left for the car.

"They're talking about aftershocks on the radio, John," she said.

She remembered driving to work last summer and watching builders put a new foundation under an old farmhouse. The house had sat on jacks for a week, suspended three feet above the new brick the masons were laying.

"The drawback is the house is just leaning against the block wall on this end," John said, "and it could cave in anytime, tremor or not." He was afraid of trying to hoist the house up—any movement or pressure at all would likely cause the house to fall before they could get a stable hold on it. "We might could shore it up somehow, get the house sitting on something besides the foundation. Then if the block gave or if we knocked the house off, there would be something else holding it up. Then we could chance the jacks."

"Would lumber hold it?" Ginny asked.

"It might."

It would take a lot of jacks. Ginny had a generator and a gallon of gas in the shed. She had cranked it over when the cold weather started to make sure it ran all right. She could borrow a circle saw.

"We'll round up what lumber we can," John said. He started across the yard. Ginny called him back.

"Do you have any idea who he is?" she asked. "I mean, does he have anybody we ought to call?"

"I don't think so, Ginny," John said. He stood there a second, put his hands on his hips. "He's been eating your onions."

Ginny sawed two-by-fours, four-by-fours, whatever scattered pieces of lumber they'd found to build the brace. John had said it had to fit right up against the floor of the house; if the house dropped even half an inch, it would be enough to crush him. A man down the road had a gas compressor in his work van, and John ran his nail gun off it. Even the pneumatic force could knock the house off balance, but the rhythmic beat of a hammer would likely have rocked it on down to the ground.

"We'd do better with sawhorses," Walt told Ginny.

Walt had said he'd do the sawing, but Ginny set him measuring boards and bracing them while she ran the saw.

"These cinder blocks are fine, I think," she said. "We don't have time to go find sawhorses."

Walt pressed his hand into the small of his back and laid a two-by-four across the blocks. Ginny set the saw blade against it. A droplight hung from a tree limb, and she had to crane her shadow left then right to see the pencil mark. Sawdust flew out the back of the saw, bright like mica in the cone of light and dissolving in air when it touched the darkness.

Walt took both hands full of boards to John and his crew, who were building the brace just inside the hole. Ginny wanted more boards, wanted to stand sawing endlessly, to concentrate on keeping her fingers clear of the blade and following the dim pencil line. He must have heard her sing. When she was alone in the house she sang with the radio. She sang on Saturday mornings off-key, loud, all the hymns she remembered from church, old songs about the River Jordan and the tree planted by water. Once she had started crying and kept singing while she washed dishes, singing at the top of her voice and crying. He would have heard that.

Walt came back with measurements for cross-bracing. Ginny held the end of the tape measure.

"John's got to crawl under there now to nail these on," Walt said.

He took the pencil from behind his ear and drew a line using an end piece of lumber for a straight edge. The boards didn't have to be cut precisely, they just had to be the right length. No one would ever inspect their woodwork inside the crawl space or check for flush edges and tight joints.

"I ought to do it," Ginny said. "It's my house and my responsibility."

"You'd have to fight him for it," Walt said. He pulled two more long boards from a pile. "They can't tell when any more shocks will come. They don't know how many minutes between them."

"No," Ginny said.

She yelled at her kids sometimes. And the cat. And she had

danced that weekend before having her crying fit. She had put an old record on and danced in the kitchen. He would have heard that. She hadn't danced since high school, so she knew old steps—the pony, stomping dances. She propped a board on the cinder blocks and squatted beside it. The plastic casing of the saw was cold. Her fingers moved slowly. There was enough heat under the floor to keep her onions and potatoes from freezing. He would have heard the television at night, heard the quiet when they went to bed. She couldn't remember hearing him ever. Not even nights she couldn't sleep and lay listening to the creaks or the wind or rain on the roof.

"John said he's mashed flat," Walt said.

"He can't be," Ginny said. "Not and still be alive. The best I can remember, the ground under there's not level. Maybe he's in a hollow."

"That's it," Walt said.

Ginny walked with him to the house. John leaned inside the hole shining his light and talking to the man. John's words were too muffled to be heard outside, but he had a soft voice—Mattie complained about it, said he had to repeat everything he ever said to her. Ginny's voice was loud. Her whole family was loud. Maybe most of the time her voice would have sounded like this to him, a muted hum when she talked on the phone or when she talked to her kids at supper. He would have heard her kids, would know when they fought or made bad grades on homework, would have heard them when they came in crying from falling off their bikes or not getting their way.

The state patrolmen stood with the other neighbors who were still around, waiting to jack the house up. The ambulance still hadn't come. They hadn't gotten hold of a civil engineer either. One of the state patrolmen crossed his arms and leaned his shoulder against the house, then jerked erect. He's so young, Ginny thought. The other one was older—the one who first told them not to do anything until the fire department got there. He had roped orange tape around the front of her yard.

Ginny said, "John."

"It won't take but a minute, Gin. I'll be in and out. Once we get this cross-braced it may hold. A little anyway."

He was too big. He pushed against the plywood and the side of the hole. Someone handed him a board and the air gun. Ginny jumped at the blast of the compressor. He reached out again for another board, just a white shiny hand coming from under the floor.

A wind came up. The droplight swung from the tree, casting shadows of bare limbs in its swinging arc, while the Coleman lanterns fluttered near the house. The moon was higher in the sky now, not quarter or full, just an in-between moon. Down the street houses were lit by candles and flashlights, soft glows in the windows usually bright with fluorescent light. And in the field behind the house, the white horse had returned. This wasn't its pasture—just a place it came to rest after its flight—but in the moonlight the grazing horse was more film than substance. Except for the far-off traffic and the occasional thump of the air hammer, the night was quiet. In summer, the noises of tree frogs and owls would have gone on all night until they gave way to birds at dawn.

A cloud bank slowly spread over the north horizon, covering the stars. The Ozarks lay that way, west a little. It might snow now if the clouds kept moving in. And farther west were the old Ouachita Mountains, so old the trees and even the soil were wearing off them. The caves there were also old, old enough to have sheltered the gatherers who once drew stories on their walls, who made paints of mud and left the marks of their hands behind them. This time the moving earth had stopped short of the caves, short of the bones and diamonds and calcified shards within them. Perhaps the handprints had staved off the violent forces as the early people had believed they would.

He heard her outside. He couldn't make out the words, but he knew the pitch and cadence of her voice. He had heard her sing. There was a lamp now pointing to the braces they had built, the flimsy timbers they hoped would hold up the house. Cribbing would have worked better, maybe. For the first time, he could see the grain running sidelong in the beam on top of him—hickory, he thought. From the angle his neck was cocked, he saw the underside of the floor above him, the dark patch of mold that spread from the concrete wall and the cracked and peeling surface of the plywood. The light struck the straw left in the hole near the door and caused a yellow halo to shine around it.

Ginny crawled through the hole. She was shaking now, chilled from the wind and the night, and worn out from the hangover of reaction. Her hand trembled against the plywood as she slid around it, careful not to knock the new scaffolding, careful not to catch her foot on the cords to the lamp and air gun. The light at her back threw her shadow over the entire space in front of her, casting the man in darkness. She was glad for it. She stayed on her hands and knees, moving more slowly than she had to. Trash was pushed against the wall—wadded paper bags, newspapers, and onion skins shining gold when the light struck them. But there was a neatness to it. She would never have seen signs, likely, if she had ducked her head under the floor to fill a bowl with potatoes. She would have thought it was her mistake if she had noticed at all the potato hole was less full, or would have thought it was rats eating them. She wouldn't have searched the dark corners for a human.

She saw the white of his eye and leaned aside against the beam to let the light hit him. Dirt clung to the side of his face next to the ground where his mouth and nose had run, but he wasn't breathing out blood. The nurse down the street had told her to look for that. His eye next to the ground was swollen to a slit and circled in red. John had washed it out well as he could. The man squinted his good eye shut and frowned with deep furrows between his eyebrows. Ginny moved her shadow over him again. John had left a squirt bottle of water near his head. She squirted water into his mouth, squeezing gently. His mouth didn't close around it but his tongue snaked around the water, holding it in.

"They're putting jacks in place," Ginny said.

His tongue slipped out against his lower lip, and she gave him more water.

"We're going to jack up this end of the house to lift it off of you."

The way his head was turned sideways, he had to look up at her from the corner of his eye. In the darkness, the way the filtered light struck it, his eye seemed all white without an iris or pupil. He closed it again.

"The state patrol said an ambulance is on the way," Ginny said.

She heard the scrapes and clinks through the wall where they set up jacks. She heard Walt holler for something to wedge his jack handle with. She heard Mattie and realized she couldn't make out her words, but recognized some ineffable quality in her voice—its tone or its rhythm. She knew the cough she heard was John's.

Ginny had thought the man would say something. In fact, she had expected him to reveal secrets, to explain what could have driven him to live under her floor.

"I better go now. It sounds like they're set up." She waited. She felt the closeness of space and air and inhaled deeply, but the air smelled musty, confined, not like the full, cold air of outside. He remained silent. She crawled backward, not turning away from him. At the door she said, "It won't be long."

She turned her back to him then and lifted her knee over the light cord.

"Wait," he said.

Ginny froze, straddling the wire. He'd spoken so low she would never have heard him outside the crawl space, or at least would never have realized the soft word was spoken to her. She looked over her shoulder, but her shadow blocked the light. She crawled back and stayed on all fours looking down at him.

He said, "The cat?"

His voice was gravelly, dry. So he had heard the cat, heard through her floor as if it were glass he could see through. Aloud,

Ginny said, "Oh," as she realized it would have crawled up under here. Some nights it didn't come in till daybreak. Some mornings it left mice on the porch.

Ginny said, "I carried it out in a cardboard box." She laughed softly. "Stupid of me—it nearly clawed my arm off. It took off into the bushes, but it'll be back."

She leaned her back gently against the beam that held him down. She had to duck forward, and still her head pushed into the floor above her. Here, she could look at his face, and he could look at her with his good eye without rolling his eyeball too far. She rested her arms on her raised knees. John's coat sleeves covered all but her fingers. The sleeves were filthy now, and the right one had a long tear in it.

"We call it Pansy," Ginny said. "You know that, don't you. My little girl named it. It's a pretty cat, ain't it? Mean, though. It jumps my legs anytime I put hose on."

She pulled at the strings in the torn sleeve. He watched her but didn't say anything.

"I have two kids," she said. "Well, you know that, too. They're down at the Rosens'. My boy, he wanted to stay, but I couldn't be worrying about them. You wouldn't believe how hard it is to find a good jack. Cars nowadays come with scissors jacks. You bust your knuckles using them."

She rotated her fist in circles, showing the motion it took to raise a scissors jack, then brought her fist to her forehead. She laughed shortly.

"I'm talking like you've been frozen in an ice cap."

The man didn't say anything.

"So we went everywhere looking for jacks. We lucked up. There's a shop down the road, and they brought over some big old hydraulic jacks. This end here"—she pointed to the standing concrete wall—"it's too high for most of the bumper jacks. I'll never find out who all these jacks belong to."

She stopped. She'd said it off the top of her head. She hadn't thought actually of returning the jacks when this was all over, or even of its being over. And John's coat. She would offer to buy him a new one, and he'd tell her not to worry, an old coat like that. It was quieter out there now.

"The jacks are in place, it sounds like," she said. John had tried to talk her out of crawling under here, and she'd told him she wouldn't be long. While she sawed wood for the bracing, she'd thought the man deserved it. He'd brought it on himself. But nobody had thought to ask him his name. Ginny had told them she would do it; it was her house and her responsibility.

"We don't even know your name," she said.

She didn't look at him, but picked at her sleeve, unraveling the threads and letting them fall to the ground. Then she glanced at him. His eye was open, looking away from her. She put her hands in her pockets.

"I knew somebody had an Escort," he said.

He paused between words to soak his mouth with his tongue. It took Ginny a second to realize he was talking about cars. Ginny had an Escort.

"A tube comes out of the air filter," he said.

Ginny gave him a squirt of water.

"Carries moisture out . . . drips down on the fuel pump."

John hollered, "Gin." His head stuck through the door. "You better come out now. We're ready."

"I'll check it," she told the man.

Her fingers were busy in John's coat pocket, finding screws and coins while they talked. She found another cough drop, gluey and coated with fuzz from the cloth of the pocket. Her finger touched the inside of his lip as she put it in his mouth. His lips were soft but too dry and cold. It would help a little anyway to keep his mouth from drying out.

"Keep it tucked in your cheek or you'll strangle."

She got on her hands and knees to leave.

"Millard," the man said.

"Millard what?"

"Royle."

At the door, Ginny paused. The cold air stung her nose. She had stopped noticing the closed musty smell under the house, and now the air from outside hurt.

"It won't be long, Mr. Royle," she said and slid out the opening. She almost waved good-bye to him.

They pulled the light out, leaving the crawl space dark and familiar. In the dark the smells, the feel of damp air, and the gray outlines returned—the place he knew. She was larger than he had thought, big-boned, but when he closed his eyes while she spoke, he saw her as he had always imagined her, with long curly hair and high cheekbones. In another few days the cold front would have passed, and he would have moved on. If she had ever found the newspapers under her house, she would have thought kids had left them.

He felt the aftershock before anyone outside did. At first he thought, just for an instant, that the house was falling from the jolt of jacks, but he felt too much the movement underneath, the pulse shooting through miles of earth below his face where he still had feeling. He knew what a wall of underground coal looked like, and he knew the force it would take to move it—through bedrock and ores and roots and subterranean rivers, through the solid ground against which he was pinned—as if the ground were air or water only. All the overpasses and high-rises, museums and hydroelectric dams, were no more than hands on a cave wall in the path of a shifting earth.

The bones in his face tingled with the vibration. The rumble grew louder, closer, like a train roaring toward him on a track. He couldn't have hopped a train or read the secret hobo marks on gateposts—those romantic days were gone before he could have lived them. The waves moved through him, as if he were a conduit connecting the earth on either side of him, as if he weren't separate himself from the earth under the floor. He sucked the candy from behind his teeth and held it with his tongue.

The horse flew again across the field. Dogs barked a few seconds before the droplight hanging in the walnut tree shook with vibrations that grew into a rhythmic sway. The circle of light moved back and forth on the dry grass, catching the steel blade of the saw and moving past it, steadily swinging wider. The half circle of people stepped back from the house, then scattered away from it. Under the house, nails pulled out of the newly built bracing, and boards splintered and split in two. The second hand swept again, and the house, released from time, finished falling.

Ginny tried to run to her car, thinking in the first instant of the aftershock there was some safety there, thinking she had to get to her kids. When she reached her car, she held on to the fender, and those few seconds were enough that the tremor subsided, though she still felt the way she had when she'd stepped off a boat down in the Gulf a long time ago and walked as if the land were the ocean. She turned just in time to see the rest of the foundation give way. The north end of the house pushed the blocks to the outside as it fell slowly, lowered by the crumbling of concrete beneath it. She started to dart toward the house as if she could stop it, but her legs wouldn't hold her up. She slid down against the front tire and watched as white dust flew up from the ground and clung like a cloud touching down.

Maybe they could never have saved him. But when the jacks were all set, and she and John stood at the corners to keep the jack handlers working in sync—right then it had seemed as if it might work. She'd been holding her hand up, ready to drop it as soon as John dropped his to signal the start. There she had been—her hand above her head in the artificial light—when the aftershock hit.

He'd known someone with a car, and Escorts hadn't been out that long.

Her fuel pump *had* been freezing up. She'd put two new ones on since the first cold snap, and the last time she'd cut her hands on the cold metal and cussed and banged her ratchet against the ground. She'd called the parts store and bawled out the boy who answered the phone. Then she had carried a cup of coffee outside wrapped in both her hands, breathing the steam. He would have smelled the coffee.

She knew his name.

The dust took a long time to settle. She could go back in now and get her purse and see how bad the damage was inside.

The clouds were nearly overhead. She wished she had thought to tell him it was going to snow. Snow was rare in this part of Arkansas. The past winter the kids had to haul snow from the neighbors' yards to have enough for a snow fort. They would be glad tomorrow.

Karen Minton lives in northeast Georgia. She received her MFA from Warren Wilson college and has published short fiction in various literary magazines.

PHOTO CREDIT: KATHY PHAGAN

I came up with "Like Hands on a Cave Wall" through the train-wreck process. Ideas in notebook, news on the radio, an old dredged-up memory converge toward a point and something happens. Of course, the wreck is quite contrived. The notes are, after all, in the notebook, and I keep a lookout for something odd, something out of kilter. I did see a house sitting on jacks, raised off the ground, right off its foundation, and the potential energy of it, the sudden obvious possibility of its kinetic energy put a twist on the conventional image of stability. The illusion that all is solid seems to be a long-range theme for me, and since I like a strong sense of place, the landscape often bears the betrayal. A train hurtling through space puts out a Doppler effect and makes us aware of movement, transition, the capacity for danger and grief. But what if we're threatened by those things we count on to stay still? Questions, note-books—we keep pushing scraps of ideas toward a convergence until finally they intersect somewhere and make a story.

A ROADSIDE RESURRECTION

(from *The Paris Review*)

Story opens, Mr. Redding is coughing in a café by the Yocona River, really whamming it out between his knees. He's got on penny loafers with pennies in them, yellow socks, madras shorts, a reversible hat, and a shirt that's faded from being washed too many times. His wife, Flenco, or Flenc, as he calls her, is slapping him on the back and alternately sucking her chocolate milk shake through a straw and looking around to see who's watching. She's got a big fat face, rollers in her hair, and she's wearing what may well be her nightgown and robe. Fingernails: bright red.

"Damn!" Mr. Redding coughs. "Godamighty . . . damn!"

Flenco hits him on the back and winces at his language, sucking hard on her straw and glancing around. Mr. Redding goes into a bad fit of coughing, kneels down in the floor heaving, tongue out and curled, veins distended on his skinny forearms, hacking, strangling, and the children of the diners are starting to look around in disgust.

"Oh," he coughs. "Oh shit. Oh damn."

Mr. Redding crawls back up in the booth and reaches into his shirt pocket for a Pall Mall 100, lights it, takes one suck, then repeats the entire scenario above. This goes on three times in thirty minutes.

Customers go in and out and people order beers and drink them at the counter on stools, but Mr. Redding lies back in the booth while his wife mops his feverish forehead with wetted paper towels brought by a waitress from the kitchen, along with another milk shake just like the last one. The hair on Mr. Redding's forearms is dark and scattered like hair on a mangy dog just recovering, and his sideburns sticking out from under the reversible cap are gray. Twenty years ago he could do a pretty good imitation of Elvis. Now he's washed up.

"Oh crap," he says. "Oh shit. Oh hell."

Flenco mops him and sops up his sweat and sucks her big round mouth around the straw and looks at people and pats him on the back. Truckers come in with their names on their belts and eat eggs and ham and wash down pills with coffee and put their cigarettes out in their plates, stagger back outside and climb up into their sleepers. Flenco looks down the road and wonders what road she'll be on before long.

"Oh shit," Mr. Redding wheezes.

Miles away down the road a legendary young healer is ready to raise the roof on a tent gathering. Sawdust is on the floor and the lights are bright and a crippled boy in a wheelchair has been brought forward to feel his healing hands. The boy lies in his chair drooling up at the lights, hands trembling, the crowd watching on all sides, spectators all piled up along the back and sides and others peeking in the opened opening, some lying on the ground with their heads stuck up between the tent pegs. The crippled child waits, the mother trembling also, nearby, hands clasped breastwise to the Holy Father Sweet Mary Mother of Saints heal my child who was wrong from the womb Amen. The lights flicker. The healer is imbued with the Spirit of God, which has come down at the edge of this cotton field and put into his fingers the strength of His love and healing fire. Outside bright blades of lightning arch and thunderclouds rumble in the turbulent sky as the healer goes into his trance. His fine dark hair is sleek on the sides of his head and he cries out: "Heeeeeal! Heal this boy, Lord! Heal him! Dear sweet merciful God if You ever felt it in Your heart to heal somebody heal this boy! This boy! This one right here, Lord! I know there's a bunch of 'em over there in darkest Africa need healing too Lord but they ain't down on their knees to You right now like we are!"

The healer sinks to his knees with these words, hands locked and upflung before him. Ushers are moving slowly through the crowd with their plates out, but nobody's putting much into the plates yet because they haven't seen the boy get up and walk.

"Lord what about Gethsemane? Lord what about Calvary's cross? Lord what about Your merciful love that we're here to lay on this child? There's his mama, Lord. I guess his daddy's in here, too. Maybe all his brothers and sisters."

"He's a only child," the mama whispers, but nobody seems to notice. The rain has started and everybody's trying to crowd inside.

"Neighbors? I don't believe there's much faith in this house tonight. I believe we've done run into a bunch of doubting Thomases, folks who want to play before they pay. Maybe they think this ain't nothing but a sideshow. Maybe they think this boy works for me. Because I don't believe they're putting in any money to further our work."

The ushers make another pass through the crowd and collect six dollars and fifty-two cents. The boy lies in the wheelchair, legs dangling. This child has never walked before. The mother has told the healer his history. He was born with spinal meningitis, his heart outside his body, and she said God only gave him one kidney. She said on the day she goes to her grave she will still owe hospital bills on him. The healer can see that the congregation thinks nothing is going to happen. He can almost read their faces, can almost read in their countenances the unsaid accusations: *Ha! Unclean! Prove yourself! Make him walk!*

The healer comes down from the podium. The fire of God is still in him. The wheels of the wheelchair are mired in the saw-dust. The mother has already begun to feel what has come inside the tent. She faints, falls over, shrieks gently. An uncle stands up. The healer lays his hands on.

"Now I said *heal*! I don't give a damn! About what's happening over there in Saudi Arabia! I don't care what else You got on Your mind! You got to heal this boy! Either heal him or take him right now! Heal him! Or take him! We don't care! He's with You either way!"

The child wobbles in the wheelchair. The healer digs his fingers down deep into the flesh. More people stand up to see. The mother wakes up, moans, and faints again. The lightning cracks overhead and the lights go out and then come back on dim. The ushers are moving more quickly through the crowd. An aura of Presence moves inside the tent to where everybody feels it. The child grips the armrests of his chair. His feet dig for purchase in the sawdust. He cries out with eyes closed in a racked and silent scream.

"Yeah!" the healer shouts. "Didn't believe! Look at him! Watch him walk!"

The boy struggles up out of the chair. People have come to his mother's side with wet handkerchiefs and they revive her in time to witness him make his stand. He rises up on his wasted legs, the healer's hands octopussed on his head.

"Heal! Heal! Heal! Heal! Heal! Heal! Heal!"

The boy shoves the hands away. The mother looks up at her son from the dirt. He takes a step. His spine is straight. He takes another step. People are falling to their knees in the sawdust. They are reaching for their purses and wallets.

Mr. Redding has to be taken outside because he is bothering the other customers. Flenco lets him lie on the seat of the truck for a while and fans him with a Merle Haggard album.

"Oh shit," Mr. Redding says. "Oh arrrrgh."

"It's gonna be all right, baby," Flenco says.

Mr. Redding is almost beyond talking, but he gasps out: "What do . . . you mean . . . it's . . . gonna . . . be . . . all right?"

"Oh, baby, I heard he'd be through here by nine o'clock. And they say he can really heal."

"I don't . . . believe . . . none of that . . . *bull*shit!"

Mr. Redding says that, and goes into great whoops of coughing.

A lot of money in the plates tonight. The mission can go on. But some helpers have wives back home, trailer payments have to be met, others want satellite dishes. The healer requires nothing but a meal that will last him until the next meal. He gives them all the money except for the price of steak and eggs at a Waffle House and heads for the car. The road is mud. The tent is being taken down in the storm. The memory of the woman is on him and he doesn't feel very close to God.

"Oh shit," Mr. Redding says. "Oh damn oh hell oh shit."

"Baby?" Flenco says. "Don't you think you ought not be cussing so bad when you're like this?"

"Li . . . iii . . . iiike what?" Mr. Redding spews out.

"When you're coughing so bad and all. I bet if you'd quit smoking them cigarettes you wouldn't cough so bad."

She pats him on the back like she saw the respiratory therapist do and feels she knows a little about medicine.

"Oh crap," Mr. Redding says. "Oh *shit!*"

Flenco mops his sweaty head and fans hot air with her hand. She has heard that the healer drives a long black Caddy. They say he refuses to appear on network television and will not endorse products. They say he comes speeding out of the dusty fields in his dusty black car and they say the wind his machine brings whips the trousers of the state troopers before they can get into their cruisers and take pursuit. They say he lives only to heal and that he stops on the roadsides where crippled children have been set up and where their mothers stand behind them holding up cardboard placards painstakingly printed HEALER HEAL MY CHILD. They say that if the state troopers catch up with him while he is performing some miracle of mercy on one of God's bent lambs, the people pull their cars out into the road and block the highway, taking the keys out of the ignitions, locking the doors. It's said that in Georgia last year a blockade of the faithful ran interference for him through a web of parked police cars outside Waycross and allowed him to pass unmolested, such is the strength of his fame. Flenco hasn't a placard. She has rented a billboard beside the café, letters six feet tall proclaiming HEALER HEAL MY HUSBAND. Telephone reports from her sister-in-law in Bruce confirm the rumor that he has left Water Valley and is heading their way. Flenco imagines him coming down out of the hilly country, barreling down the secondary roads and blasting toward the very spot where she sits fanning Mr. Redding's feverish frame.

"Oh shit," Mr. Redding says. "Oh God . . . dang!"

"Just rest easy now, honey," Flenco says. "You want me to go get you some Co-Coler?"

"Hell naw, I don't want no goddamn Co-Coler," Mr. Redding says. "I want some . . . want some goddamn . . . I want some . . . shit! Just carry me . . . back home and . . . goddamn . . . let me die. I'm . . . goddamn . . . burning up out here."

Flenco hugs his skinny body tight and feels one of his emaciated wrists. Hands that used to hold a silver microphone hang limply from his cadaverous arms, all speckled with liver spots. She wants him to hold on a little longer because she doesn't know if the healer has worked his way up to raising the dead yet. She knows a little of his scanty history. Born to Christian Seminoles and submerged for thirty-seven minutes in the frigid waters of Lake Huron at the age of fourteen, he was found by divers and revived with little hope of ultimate survival by firefighters on a snow-covered bank. He allegedly lay at death's door in a coma for nine weeks, then suddenly got out of his bed, ripping the IV tubes out, muttering without cursing, and walked down the hall to the intensive care unit where a family of four held a death vigil over their ninety-year-old grandmother fatally afflicted with a ruptured duodenum and laid his hands on her. The legend goes that within two minutes the old lady was sitting up in the bed demanding fudge ripple on a sugar cone and a pack of Lucky Strikes. Fame soon followed and the boy's yard became littered with the sick and the crippled, and the knees of his jeans became permanently grass-stained from kneeling. The walking canes piled up in a corner of the yard as a testament to his powers. A man brought a truck once a week to collect the empty wheelchairs. He made the blind see, the mute speak. A worldwide team of doctors watched him cure a case of wet leprosy. The president had him summoned to the White House, but he could not go; the street in front of his house was blocked solid with the bodies of the needing-to-be-healed. People clamored after him, and women for his seed. The supermarket tabloids proclaim that he will not break the vow he gave to God in the last few frantic moments before sinking below the waters of Lake Huron: if God would bring him back from a watery death he would remain pure and virginal in order to do His work. And now he has come South like a hunted animal to seek out the legions of believers with their sad and twisted limbs.

"Flenc," Mr. Redding coughs out, "how many goddamn times I told you . . . oh shit . . . not to . . . aw hell, ahhhhh."

The tent is down, the rain has ceased. The footsteps of many are printed in the mud. He's had to sign autographs this time, and fighting the women off is never easy. They are convinced the child they'd bear would be an Albert Einstein, an Arnold Schwarzenegger, a Tom Selleck with the brain of Renoir. Some tell him they only want him for a few moments to look at something in the backseat of their car, but he knows they are offering their legs and their breasts and their mouths. He can't resist them anymore. He's thinking about getting out of the business. The promise has already been broken anyway, and the first time was the hardest.

His bodyguards and henchmen push with arms spread against

the surging crowd and his feet suck in the mud as he picks his way to his Caddy. All around sit cars and pickup trucks parked or stuck spinning in the mud as the weak sun tries to smile down between the parting clouds.

He gets into the car and inserts the ignition key and the engine barks instantly into life with the merest flick of the key. The engine is as finely tuned as a Swiss watchmaker's watch and it hums with a low and throaty purring that emanates from glass-pack mufflers topped off with six feet of chrome. He tromps on the gas pedal and the motor rumbles, cammed up so high it will barely take off.

He hits the gas harder and the Caddy squats in the mud, fish-tailing like an injured snake through the quagmire of goop. The crowd rushes the bodyguards, pushing their burly bodies back and down and trampling them underfoot, stepping on their fingers, surging forward to lay their once withered hands on the dusty flanks of the healer's automobile. Faces gather around the windows outside and the healer steers his machine through the swampy mess of the pasture and over to a faint trail of gravel that leads to the highway. Many hands push and when he guns the big car mud balls thwack hollowly and flatten on the pants and shirts of the faithful left gawking after him in his wake. They wave, beat their chests to see him go. Liberated children turn handsprings in the mud and perform impromptu fencing matches with their useless crutches and these images recede quickly through the back window as the car lurches toward the road.

The healer looks both ways before pulling out on the highway. Cars are lined on both sides all the way to the curves that lie in the distance. Horns blare behind him and he turns the car north and smashes the gas pedal flat against the floorboard. The big vehicle takes the road under its wheels and rockets past the lines of automobiles. Small hands wave from the backseats as he accelerates rapidly past them.

The needle on the speedometer rises quickly. He eyes the gas gauge's red wedge of metal edged toward FULL. He finds k. d. lang on the radio and fishes beneath the seat for the flask of vodka his bodyguards have secreted there. The prearranged destination is Marion, Arkansas, where droves of the helpless are rumored to be gathered in a field outside the town.

He takes one hit, two hits, three hits of vodka and pops the top on a hot Coke while reaching for his smokes. His shoes are slathered with mud and his shirt is dirty, but fresh clothes await him somewhere up ahead. Everything is provided. Every bathroom in the South is open to him. The Fuzzbuster on the dash ticks and he hits the brakes just in time to cruise by a cruiser hidden in a nest of honeysuckle. At fifty-seven mph.

He feels weak and ashamed for breaking his vow, but the women won't let him alone. They seem to know the weakness of his flesh. A new issue of *Penthouse* is under the seat. He reaches over and takes his eyes off the road for a moment, pulls the magazine out. He flips it open and the pictures are there, with nothing left to the imagination, the long legs, the tawny hair, the full and pouting lips. With a sharp stab of guilt he closes it up and shoves it back under the seat. He can't go on like this. A decision has to be made. There are too many who believe in him and he is the vessel of their faith. He knows he's unworthy of that trust now. It's going to be embarrassing if God decides to let him down one night in front of a hundred and fifty people. The crowd might even turn ugly and lynch him if he's suddenly unable to heal. They've come to expect it. They have every right to expect it. But they don't know about his needs. They don't know what it's like to be denied the one thing that everybody else can have: the intimate touch of another.

He lights the cigarette and cracks the vent as a smattering of raindrops splatters across the windshield. He turns the wipers on and passes through a curtain of rain as perpendicular as a wall, crosses over onto a shiny darkened highway with tiny white explosions of water pinging up on its surface. He tromps on the gas pedal and the Caddy's tires sing their high-speeded whine. Small heads on front porches turn like tennis spectators as a black flash shoots down the road. He waves.

Mr. Redding lies near comatose under the shade tree Flenco has dragged him to, and people coming out of the café now are giving him queasy looks. Flenco knows that some good citizen might have an ambulance called.

"Just hold on now, baby," Flenco says. "I feel it in my heart he's coming any minute now."

"I don't give a . . . give a good . . . a good . . . a good god-damn . . . I don't give a shit who's coming," Mr. Redding hacks out. His lips are slimy with a splotching of pink foam and his breath rattles in his chest like dry peas in a pod. He quivers and shakes and licks his lips and groans. Flenco cradles his graying head in her ample lap and rubs the top of his hat with her tremendous sagging breasts. Her rose-tipped nipples miss the passion that used to be in Mr. Redding's tongue. Flenco deeply feels this loss of sexual desire and sighs in her sleep at night on the couch while Mr. Redding hacks and coughs and curses in the bedroom and gets up to read detective magazines or rolls all over the bed. She's ashamed of her blatant overtures and attempts at entice-ment, the parted robe, the naked toweling off beside the open bathroom door, the changing of her underwear in the middle of the day. Mr. Redding appears not to notice, only lights one Pall Mall after another and swears.

She has sent a wide-eyed little boy inside for another choco-late milk shake and he brings it out to her under the tree where she holds the gasping wheezebag who used to belt out one Elvis song after another in his white jumpsuit with the silver zippers. He'd been nabbed for bad checks in Texas, was on the run from a Mann Act in Alabama, but Flenco fell in love with his roguey smile and twinkling eyes the first time she saw him do "You Ain't Nothing but a Hound Dog" at the junior/senior prom. His bat-tered travel trailer had a cubbyhole with a stained mattress that held the scented remnants of other nights of lust. But Flenco, pressed hard against the striped ticking with her head in a corner, found in his wild and enthusiastic gymnastics a kind of secret delight. Shunned by her schoolmates, sent to the office for passing explicit notes to boys, downtrodden by the depression caused by her steady eating, Flenco was hopelessly smitten in the first few minutes with his hunk of "Burning Love."

Now her lover lies wasted in her lap, his true age finally showing, his wrinkled neck corded with skin like an old lizard's as he sags against her and drools. She's not asking for immortality; she's not asking for the Fountain of Youth; she's only asking for a little more time. The hope that burns in her heart is a candle lit to the memory of physical love. She wipes his hot face tenderly with a wadded napkin soaked in the cold sweat from the milkshake cup. Mr. Redding turns and digs his head deeper into her belly. People at the tables in the café are staring openly through the windows now and Flenco knows it's only a matter of time before somebody calls the lawdogs.

"Can I do anything for you, baby?" she says.

Mr. Redding turns his eyes up to her and the pain buried in them is like a dying fire.

"Hell yeah you can . . . do . . . something . . . goddamn . . . do something . . . oh shit . . . for me. You can . . . goddamn . . . oh shit . . . you can . . . just . . . hell . . . by God . . . shoot me."

"Oh baby, don't talk like that," Flenco says. Her eyes mist up and she covers his face with her breasts until he reaches up with both hands and tries to push the weighty mass of her mammary monsters up out of the way.

"Goddamn, what you . . . what you trying to . . . trying to . . . I didn't say . . . smother me," Mr. Redding says.

Flenco doesn't answer. She closes her eyes and feels the former flicks of his tongue across her breastworks in a memory as real as their truck.

The road is straight, the cotton young and strong, and the Caddy is a speeding bullet across the flat highway. The needle is buried to the hilt at a hundred and twenty and the car is floating at the very limit of adhesion, weightless, almost, drifting slightly side to side like a ship lightly tacking on the ocean in the stiff edges of a breeze. The blue pulses of light winking far behind him in the sun are like annoying toys, no more. The healer dips handful after handful of roofing tacks out of the sack beside him and flings them out the open window, scattering them like bad seeds. The blue lights fade, are gone, left far behind. Others of like bent are waiting probably somewhere ahead but he'll deal with them when the time comes.

Fruit and vegetable stands flash by the open windows of the car, junk peddlers, mobile homes, stacked firewood corded up on the sides of the road for sale, waving people, fans. It is these people he heals, these people crushed and maimed by the falling trees, by the falling house trailers, by the falling cars and junk. These innocents carving a life out of the wilderness with their hands, these with so much faith that he is merely an instrument, a transmitter to funnel the energy required to make them stand up and throw away their braces. He thinks of the promise he made going down reaching for the surface of Lake Huron. He gets another drink of the vodka and lights another cigarette and shakes his head as the hubcaps glitter in the sun.

"Lord God I wouldn't have touched her if I was the pope!" he suddenly screams out into the car, beating his fist on the seat. He turns his head and shouts out the open window: "Why didn't you let me die and then bring me back as the pope? Huh? You want to answer that one, Lord?"

He takes another quick suck of the hot vodka. His shoulders shiver, and he caps it.

"I cain't cure everbody in the whole world!"

He slows down and rolls to about fifteen mph and shouts to a God maybe lurking behind a dilapidated cotton pen and guarded by a pink Edsel with the hood on the roof.

"You ought not made it so tough on me! I ain't like Jesus, I'm human! I can't do it no more, they's too many of 'em! They's too many women! I take back my promise, I quit!"

The long low surprised face of a farmer in a 1953 Chevrolet pickup with a goat in the back passes by him in slow motion, his head hanging out the window, a woman looking over his shoulder, seeing, figuring the black car and the haranguing finger poking out at a telephone pole, gathering her wits, her thoughts, her breath, to point back, inhale, scream: "It's HIM! PRAISE WONDERFUL GOD IT'S HIIIIIIIM!"

The healer looks. He sees the old black pickup grind to a halt, the one brake light coming on, the woman hopping out the door, arms waving, the farmer leaning out the window waving. For the first time ever the healer is tempted to burn rubber and leave them smelling his getaway fumes, leave behind him unheard the story of their huge drooling son, prisoner of the basement, chained in the garage at the family reunions. But the faces of these two parents are lit like rays of sunshine with the knowledge that a modern messiah has chosen the road that borders their alfalfa patch to receive His divine instructions.

The woman runs up to the side of the car and lays her hands on the fender as if she'd hold it to keep the car from leaving. Her beady eyes and panting breath and hopeless, eternal, hope-filled face tell the healer this woman has a task of such insurmountable proportions she's scarce shared the secret of her problem with minister or preacher or parson, that this one's so bad he can't quit now. Holy cow. What pining cripple on his bed of moldy quilts with his palsied arms shaking lies waiting nearly forever for his release? What afflicted lamb has lain behind a curtain to be hidden from company all these years? Here, he sees, are the mother and the father, the suffering parents, here with their pain and their hope and their alfalfa patch and cows and fishponds, their world struck askew by the birth or the affliction or the accident that befell their fallen one, with neither hope of redemption nor cure available for what might be eating mothballs or masturbating in old dirty underwear and hiding it under his mother's mattress to be discovered when the springs need turning, might be roaming the pastures by night creeping stealthily upon the female livestock.

"Healer," the woman asks. "Will you heal my child?"

He's not coming, Flenco suddenly decides. In a burst of thought process too deep for her to understand, a mere scab on the broad scar of telepathy that man's mind forgot to remember eons ago, she knows somehow that another emergency has detained him. She knows, too, that they must therefore go find him. She gets up and catches Mr. Redding under the armpits and drags him through the dust toward the truck, where now in large numbers on the other side of the café windows people stand gathered to track the proceedings and place wagers on the estimated time of arrival of Mr. Redding's demise.

"Oh hope, there's hope," she chants and pants. His heels make two trails of dust through the parking lot but his loafers stay on like a miracle or a magic trick. Flenco gets him next to the running board and stoops to release the precious burden of him, opens the door, gives a hefty grunt, and hauls him up into the seat. Mr. Redding falls over against the horn of the truck and it begins to blow as Flenco shuts the door and runs around to the other side. She yanks open the door and pushes him erect in the seat and reaches across him and locks the door so he won't fall out and hurt himself any worse. Those cigarettes have a hold on him that keeps him from eating, from gaining weight, from not wheezing in the early morning hours when she awakens beside him and lies in the dark staring at his face and twirling the tufts of gray hair on his chest around her fingers. But maybe the healer can even cure him of his addiction, drive the blackness from his lungs, the platelets from his aorta, flush the tiny capillaries in their encrusted fingers of flesh. She belts him in.

Mr. Redding sits in a perfect and abject state of apathy, his head keened back on his neck and his closed eyes seeing nothing. Not even coughing.

"Hold on, baby," Flenco says, and cranks the truck. Truckers and patrons stand gawking at the rooster tail of dust and gravel kicked up by the spinning wheel of the truck, then it slews badly, hits the road sliding, and is gone in a final suck of sound.

With stabbing motions of her arm and hand, index finger extended, the mother directs the healer into the yard. A white picket fence with blooming daffodils belies the nature of the thing inside.

"Please, he's a baby, harmless really, come, in here, behind, I just know you, please, my mother she, my brother too they," she gasps.

The healer turns in and sees the black pickup coming behind him, the goat peeking around the cab as if directing its movement, this Nubian. Before he can fully stop the car, the woman is tugging on his arm, saying, "In here, you, oh, my husband, like a child, really."

He opens the door and starts out as the truck slides to a stop beside him, dust rising to drift over them. The healer waves his hand and coughs and the woman pulls on his arm. The farmer jogs around the hood on his gimpy leg and they each take an arm and lead him up the steps, across the porch, both of them talking in either ear a mix of latent complaints, untold griefs, and shared blames for the years this child born wrong and then injured in the brain has visited on this house. The healer is dragged into a living room with white doilies under lamps and a flowerful rug spread over polished wood and a potbellied stove in one corner where a dead squirrel sits eating a varnished walnut.

"Back here, in here, he," the woman rants.

"You know, he, by golly, our field," the farmer raves.

The healer is afraid they're going to smell his breath and he turns his face from side to side as he's dragged with feet sliding to the back room, inside the closet, down hidden stairs revealed by a trapdoor. The farmer unlocks a door in the dark, hits a switch. A light comes on. Gray walls of drabness lie sweating faintly deep in the earth's damp and they're hung with old mattresses brown with spots. The furniture in the room is soft with rot, green with mold. A large, naked, drooling hairy man sits playing with a ball of his own shit in the center of the room, his splayed feet and fuzzy toes black with dirt and his sloped forehead furrowed in concentration. He says, "Huuuuuuuurrrrrnnn . . ."

The healer recoils. The hairy man sits happily in the center of the floor amongst plates of old food and the little pies he has made, but looks up and eyes his parents and the paling youth between them and instantly his piglike eyes darken with total ignorance or, like the darkest of animals, an unveiled hostile threat.

"Hurrrrr," he says, and swivels on his buttocks to face them.

"Sweet Lord Jesus Christ," the healer whispers. "Get me out of here."

"Not so fast, young fella," the farmer says, and unlimbers from a back pocket a hogleg of Dirty Harry proportions, backs to the door behind him, locks it, pockets the key deep in his overalls.

It doesn't smell nice at all in this dungeon and the thing before him begins to try to get up on its knees and make sounds of wet rumbling wanting deep in its throat. The eyebrows knit up and down and together and apart and the healer draws back with his hands up because the man is sniffing now, trying like a blind calf to scent his mother, maybe remembering milk.

Mr. Redding lies back in the seat not even harrumphing but merely jackknifed into the position his wife has seated him in like a form set in concrete while the truck roars down the road. Flenco slurps the sediment of her shake through the straw and flings the used container out the window into a passing mass of sunflowers' bright yellow faces. Her right hand is clenched upon the wheel and her foot is pressed hard on the gas.

"Hold on, baby," she says. "I don't know where he's at but we're going to find him." Her mouth is grim.

Mr. Redding doesn't answer. He sits mute and unmoving with his head canted back and lolling limply on his neck, the squashed knot of his reversible fishing hat pulled down over his ears.

He seems uninterested in the green countryside flashing by, the happy farms of cows grazing contentedly on the lush pasture grass, the wooded creeks and planted fields within the industry of American agriculture thriving peacefully beside the road.

Flenco reaches over and gets one of his cigarettes from his pocket and grabs a box of matches off the dash. She doesn't usually smoke but the situation is making her nervous. Afraid that his rancid lips might never again maul her fallow flesh, she scratches the match on the box and touches the whipping flame to the tip of the Pall Mall 100. Deluged with the desperation of despair, she draws the smoke deep and then worries her forehead with the cigarette held between her fingers. Her eyes scan the fertile fields and unpainted barns for a gathering of cripples miraculously assembled somewhere to seek out the ultimate truth. Somewhere between the borders of three counties a black Caddy runs speeding to another destination and she must intercept it or find its location. The rotting fruit of her romance lies hanging in the balance. The sad wreck of her lover must be rejuvenated. All is lost if not.

Flenco remembers the early years with Mr. Redding. Through him the ghost of Elvis not only lived but sang and whirled his pumping hips to dirges engraved on the brains of fans like grooves in records. He could get down on one knee and bring five or six of them screaming to their feet and rushing to the edge of the stage, the nostalgic, the overweight, the faded dyed ever faithful. Now this sad wasted figure lays his head back on the seat with his lips slightly parted, his tongue drying.

Flenco smokes the cigarette furiously, stabs the scenery with her eyes, roars down the left fork of a road where a sign says HILLTOP 10 MILES. Dust hurtles up behind the pickup as it barrels down the hill. Flenco has the blind faith of love but she panics when she thinks that she might not find the healer, that he might be out of reach already, that he might have taken an alternate road and be somewhere else in the county, doing his work, healing the minions who seek him out, laying his hands on other unfortunates whose despair has eclipsed hers. But as long as there is gas in the truck, as long as Mr. Redding draws breath, she will drive until the wheels fall off the truck, until the cows come home, until they piss on the fire and call the dogs. Until hope, however much is left, is smashed, kicked around, stomped on, or gone. Until Mr. Redding is dead.

Flenco eyes him and feels uneasy over his stillness. She's never known him to be this quiet before. She mashes harder on the gas and her beloved sways in the curves.

"Hold on, baby," she whispers.

The healer stands unmoving with the hard round mouth of the pistol in his back. The man on the floor is growling low and grinding his tartared teeth. His hairy arms are encrusted with a nasty crap.

"Aaaarrrrr," he says.

"Yes, darling," the mother coos. "The nice man has come to help us. You like the nice man, don't you, dear?"

"He likes to play," the farmer says. "He plays down here all the time, don't you, Son?" the farmer says. "We just keep him down here so he won't scare people," he explains.

The parents see no need to recite the list of stray dogs and hapless cats caught and torn limb from limb, dripping joints of furred meat thrust mouthward without mayonnaise. The six-year-old girl still missing from last year is best not spoken of. The farmer now makes use of a pneumatic tranquilizer gun before laying on the chains and padlocks at night. Delivered at home beside his stillborn twin like Elvis, the hairy one has a headstone over his undug grave.

The warped and wavy line of his dented skull is thick with a rancid growth where small insect life traverses the stalks of his matted hair. He sways and utters his guttural verbs and fixes the healer's face with his bated malevolence and grunts his soft equations into the dusty air.

"He wants to play," the mother says. "Ain't that cute."

"Cute as a bug," the farmer says, without loosening his grip on the pistol.

"I can't heal him," the healer says.

"What did you say?" the farmer says.

"Did he say what I think he said?" the mother says.

"I think you better say that again," the farmer says.

"I can't heal him. I can't heal anything like this."

"What are you saying?" the mother says.

"You heard what he said," the farmer says. "Says he can't heal him."

"Can't?" the mother says.

"I can't," the healer says, as the man on the floor drools a rope of drool and moans a secret rhyme and moves his shoulders to and fro and never takes his eyes off the healer's face.

"I bet you'd like to know what happened to him," the mother says.

"Horse kicked him," the farmer says.

"Right in the head," the mother says.

"Turned him ass over teakettle," the farmer says. "Kicked him clean over a fence."

"Like to kicked half his head off," the mother says. "But you've cured worse than this. That little girl over in Alabama last year with that arm growed out of her stomach and that old man in the Delta who had two and a half eyes. You can heal him. Now heal him."

"We done read all about you," the farmer says. "We been trying to find you for months."

"And then he just come driving right by the place," the mother says. "Will wonders never cease."

The man on the floor is trying to form the rude impulses necessary to gather his legs beneath himself and put his feet flat on the floor. He wants to stand and will stand in a moment and the farmer reaches quickly behind him for the coiled whip on a nail.

"Easy now, Son," he says.

A low uneasy moaning begins at the sight of the bullwhip and the bared teeth alternate with that in a singsong incantation as he totters up onto his knees and rests his folded knuckles flat on the floor. The hair is long on his back and arms and legs. His face is transfixed with an ignorance as old as time, yet a small light burns in his eyes, and he has a little tail six inches in length extending from the coccyx bone with a tufted tip of bristles. He slides forward a few inches closer to the healer. Old bones lie piled in corners for safekeeping with their scraps of blackened flesh.

"You might as well go on and heal him," the farmer says. "We ain't letting you out of here till you do."

"He's been like this a long time," the mother says.

"You don't understand," the healer says. "I've never dealt with anything like this."

"You cured cancer," the farmer says.

"Raised the dead, I've heard," the mother says.

"No ma'am. Ain't nobody ever raised the dead but Jesus Himself," the healer says, as the thing begins to look as if it would like to grab his leg. He tries to retreat, but the gun is in his back like a hard finger.

"What you think, Mama?" the farmer says.

"I think he's trying to pull our leg," she says.

"You think he's a false prophet?"

"Might be. Or maybe he's used up all his power?"

"What about it, young feller? You used up all your power?"

"I known it was him when I seen that black car," she says.

"Lots of people have black cars," the healer says dully, unable to take his own eyes off those dully glinting ones before him. What lies inside there will not do to look at, it won't be altered by human hands, probably should have been drowned when it was little. "Don't let him hurt me," he says.

"Hurt you? Why he ain't going to hurt you," the mother says. "He just wants to play with you a little bit. We come down here and play with him all the time, don't we, Daddy."

"That's right," the farmer says. "Hopfrog and leapscotch and like that. Go on and lay your hands on him. He won't bite or nothing, I promise."

"He's real good most of the time," she says. "We just keep him penned up so he won't hurt hisself."

"I can't . . . I can't . . ." the healer begins.

"Can't what?" the farmer says.

"Can't what?" the mother says.

"*Touch* him," the healer breathes.

"Uh oh," says the farmer. "I's afraid of that, Mama."

"You people have got to let me out of here," the healer says. "I'm on my way to Arkansas."

"Wrong answer, mister," the farmer says.

"Definitely the wrong answer," the mother says.

Their boy moves closer and his snarling mouth seems to smile.

Flenco stands in her nightgown and robe and curlers, pumping gas into the neck of the fuel tank located in the left rear quarter panel of the truck. Years ago Mr. Redding took a hammer and screwdriver to it so that it would readily accept a leaded-gasoline nozzle. Flenco pumps five dollars' worth into it and hands the money to the attendant who wiped no windshield and checked no oil but stood gawking at the rigid figure of Mr. Redding displayed in the seat like a large sack of potatoes. The attendant takes the five and looks thoughtfully at Flenco, then opens his mouth to ask:

"Lady, is this guy all right?"

Flenco starts to go around and get behind the wheel and then, when she sees the beer signs hung in the windows of the gas station, thinks of the twenty-dollar bill wadded in the pocket of her robe like used facial tissue.

"Well he's been sick," she says, hurrying toward the door of the building.

"I don't believe he's feeling real good right now," he says to her disappearing back. When she goes inside, he watches her heading for the beer coolers at the back of the store and steps closer to the open window of the truck. He studies Mr. Redding from a vantage point of ten inches and notices that his lips are blue and his face is devoid of any color, sort of like, a *lot* like, an uncle of his who was laid out in a coffin in the comfort of his own home some two weeks before.

"Mister," he says. "Hey, mister!"

Mr. Redding has nothing to say. Flenco comes rushing back out the door with three quart bottles of cold Busch in a big grocery sack and a small package of cups for whenever Mr. Redding feels like waking up and partaking of a cool refreshing drink. She eyes the attendant suspiciously and gets in the truck and sets the beer on the seat between them, pausing first to open one bottle and set it between her massive thighs. She leans up and cranks the truck and looks at the attendant who steps back and holds up one hand and says, "Don't mind me, lady, it's a free country." Then she pulls it down into D and roars out onto the road.

Flenco gooses it up to about sixty and reaches over briefly to touch Mr. Redding's hand. The hand is cool and limp and she's glad the fever has passed. He'll feel better now that he's had a nap, maybe, not be so irritable. Maybe she can talk to him reasonably. His temper's never been good even when he was sober, which hasn't been much these last twenty years. Flenco wonders where all those years went to and then realizes that one day just built on to another one like with a mason stacking bricks. All those nights in all those beer joints with all that singing and stomping and screaming and women shouting out declarations of desire for the frenzied figure that was him just past his prime blend together in her mind and spin like carousel horses in a fun-house ride. They billed him as Uncle Elvis, and he's told Flenco a little about his one trip up the river and how they'd hit you in the head with something if you didn't act right, but those days are long gone and what does it matter now since the cars he stole were transient things and even now probably lie stripped and rusted out in some junkyard bog, a hulking garden of flowers adorning their machine-gunned sides?

Flenco feels guilty for feeling her faith sag a little when she thinks of all the miles of roads the healer could be on and how easy it will be to miss him. She wonders if it was smart to abandon her big billboard sign by the side of the road and take off like this, but she was feeling the grip of a helpless sudden hopeless inertia and there was nothing to do but put some road under her wheels.

Flenco glances at Mr. Redding who is still oblivious to everything with the wind sailing up his nostrils. She takes a hefty slug of the beer between her legs. She nudges him.

"You want some of this beer, baby? You still asleep? Well you just go on and take you a nap, get rested. Maybe you'll feel better when you wake up."

Flenco hopes that's so. She hopes for a clue, a sign somehow, maybe that gathering of the crippled in a field like she's heard happens sometimes. If she can find him, she'll deliver Mr. Redding into the healer's healing hands herself. But if she can't, she doesn't know what she's going to do. She feels like the eleventh hour is fast approaching, and her beloved sits on the seat beside her in stony silence, his mouth open, his head canted back, the wind gently riffling his thin gray hair now that his reversible cap has blown off.

"I think maybe they need a little time to get to know one another, Mama, what do you think?" the farmer says.

"That might be a good idear," the mother says. "Leave 'em alone together awhile and maybe they can play."

The healer looks for a place to run but there are no windows in the airless chamber of what his good work has brought him to and no door but the one the farmer guards with the point of a gun.

"You can't leave me down here with him," the healer says, and he searches for some shred of sanity in the seamed faces of the farmer and his wife. His playmate edges closer.

"You could even eat supper with us if you wanted to after you heal him," the mother says. "Be right nice if we could all set down at the table together."

"He makes too big a mess for him to eat with us very much," the farmer says, a little apologetically, gesturing with the gun. "Throws his food everwhere and what not."

The farmer turns with the key in his pocket and fumbles down deep in there for it. He takes the key out and has to almost turn his back on the healer to get it in the lock, but he says, "I wouldn't try nothing funny if I was you."

"If you're scared of him biting you we'll hold him and not let him bite you," the mother says.

The key clicks in the lock and the farmer says, "I just don't believe he's much of a mind to heal him, Mama. We can go up here and take us a nap and when we come back down they liable to be discussing philosophy or something, you cain't never tell."

"You people don't understand," the healer says. "He's beyond help. There's nothing I can do for him. I don't deal with the mind. I deal with the body."

"Ain't nothing wrong with his body," the mother says. "We just had to slow him down a little."

"His body's in good shape," the farmer says. "He's strong as a ox. Why I've seen him pull cows out of mud holes before. I don't believe he knows how strong he is."

"We'll be back after a while," the mother says, and out the door she goes. "Come on, Daddy," she says back. The farmer backs out the door holding the gun on the healer and then the door closes. There are sounds of the other lock being affixed on the other side. The healer backs hard into the corner and eyes the mumbling being in front of him.

"Jesus would heal him if He was here!" the farmer hollers

through the thick door. "I done read all about what He done in the Bible! What They've done, They've done laid this burden on us to test our faith! Ain't that right, Mama!"

"That's right, Daddy!" the mother shouts through the door.

"We been tested!" the farmer screams. "We been tested hard and we ain't been found wanting! Have we, Mama!"

"You got that right, Daddy! Lot of folks couldn't put up with what we've put up with!"

"Just don't make him mad!" the farmer shrieks. "Don't try to take nothing away from him if he's playing with it! He don't like that! He's a little spoiled!"

"He likes to rassle but don't get in a rasslin' match with him 'cause he gets mad sometimes! Don't get him mad! We'll be back in about a hour! Talk to him! He likes that!"

A rapid clump of footsteps climbing up the stairs fades away to a slammed door above. The healer flattens himself in the corner with his arms bracing up the walls.

"Don't touch me, please," he says, then adds: "I'm not going to hurt you."

The prisoner has made himself a bed of soiled quilts and assorted bedding and he pillows his head with a discarded tire. His nest is knotted with hairs and his lair is infested with lice. The farmer has snipped his hamstrings and Achilles tendon on alternate legs and cauterized the severed sinews while the mother kept the head restrained and the howling muffled with towels rolled and stuffed over his mouth one midnight scene years ago. He moves toward the healer slowly, hard. The healer watches the painful stance, the shifting feet, the arms outspread for balance, and he walks like a man on a tightrope as he makes his way across. Perhaps to kiss? His dangling thangling is large and hairy, swaying there like a big brown anesthetized mole.

The healer watches him come. On the edges of the wasted fields of the South and stuck back in the roadless reaches of timber where people have trails like animals, the unseen faceless sum of mankind's lesser genes quietly disassemble cars and squat underneath trees talking, and back of them lie small dwellings of rotted wood and sagging floors where strange children sit rapt for hours on end slavering mutely and uttering no words from their stunned mouths. Pictures of porches full of them all shy and embarrassed or smiling in delight turn up now and again here and there, but no visitor but the documenter of the far less fortunate comes to visit again. It is not that they are not God's children, but that mankind shuns them, bad reminders of rotted teeth and mismatched eyes, uncontrollable sexual desire turned loose in the woods to procreate a new race of the drooling mindless eating where they shit. He is like them, but even they would not accept him. An old midwife who knew anything would not allow the question. In the first few desperate moments the hand would smother the mouth, pinch the nostrils, still the heaving chest trying to draw in the first tiny breath. The brother and sister above know this. They have known it for years.

The thing comes closer and the healer looks into its depthless eyes, eyes like a fish that lives so deep in the dark black of the ocean and has no need to see. He thinks of the woman's legs in the backseat of the car parked behind a Walgreens in Sumter and the strength of the promise to God. He thinks not of retribution or outrage, and not even fear anymore. He thinks of mercy, and lambs, and he brings his hands out from his sides to suffer to him this outcast. His fingers reach and they touch and he clamps them down hard over the ears. Dust motes turn in the air. They stand in stillness, hardly breathing, locked by the touch of another hand. Their eyes close. The healer fills his chest with air. He prepares to command him to heal

Flenco sits sobbing beside the road in a grove of trees with a cool breeze wafting through, gently moving the hair on Mr. Redding's head. It's a nice afternoon for a nap, but Flenco has no thoughts of sleep. The search is over and he is cold like a slice of bologna, an egg from the refrigerator. The state troopers cluster behind her and slap their ticket books along their legs, heads shaking in utter solemnity or undisguised amazement. The ambulance crew waits, their equipment useless, their ambu bags and cardiopulmonary cases still scattered over the gravelly grass. The sun is going down and the legendary speeder has not appeared, and the roadblock will soon be broken up, the blue and white cruisers sent out to other destinations like prowling animals simply to prowl the roads.

But an interesting phenomenon has briefly materialized to break the boredom of an otherwise routine afternoon, a fat woman drunk and hauling the dead corpse of her husband down the road at ninety, sobbing and screaming and yelling out loud to God, and they wait now only for the coroner to place his seal of approval so that the body can be moved. One trooper leans against a tree chewing a stem of grass and remarks to nobody in particular: "I been to three county fairs, two goat-ropins, and one horse-fuckin', and I ain't never seen nothing like that."

Some chuckle, others shake their heads, as if to allow that the world is a strange place and in it lie things of another nature, a bent order, and beyond a certain point there are no rules to make man mind.

A wrecker is moving slowly with its red light down the road. Doves cry in the trees. And down the road in a field stand three giant wooden crosses, their colors rising in the falling sunlight, yellow, and blue, and tan.

Larry Brown was born in Oxford, Mississippi, and still lives in Lafayette County, near Yocona. His books are *Facing the Music*, *Dirty Work*, *Big Bad Love*, and *Joe*. He is working on a nonfiction book about firefighting, tentatively entitled *Fire Notes*.

PHOTO CREDIT: DOUG HABBERSTAD

This story is as close as I can get to one of my idols, Flannery O'Connor. I wanted everything I could get in here: Jesus, Elvis, faith healers, overweight women, sex, incest, truckers, pickups, goats, pistols, sin and faith and redemption. It took me a week to write it and eight months to get it to where it is now, and it's about as Southern as I can get.

Dan Leone

YOU HAVE CHOSEN CAKE

(from *Black Warrior Review*)

Oscar Tang thinks he is the only one in the world who plays with himself. He is ten years old and he is asleep in the backseat of his father's car, snoring the way kids his age snore.

Dwight Tang, Oscar's father, is at the wheel, trying to keep his eyes on the road. It is three-thirty in the morning and his eyes want to be somewhere else—shooting basketballs or floating over the treetops or looking at a woman named Sarah. These are all things his eyes have been tricked into seeing in the past five miles alone. They are tiny dreams.

Dwight Tang is at the end of his rope. He can't stay awake. His eyelids feel thick and swollen. They get heavier and heavier until his eyes are completely gone and his car leans into the breakdown lane. At this point the sound in his head is a little bit different, which is interpreted correctly by his last remaining thread of consciousness as the sound of his car being off the road. There is an instantaneous explosion of adrenaline, which feels from the inside of his body like an electrical current, beginning behind his eyes (which snap open) and traveling to the back of his head, to his neck, and down his spine to everything else. He swerves back onto the highway, quietly cursing himself for having endangered his life, and his son's. He'll be okay for maybe a mile. Then it happens again.

It happens over and over again.

* * *

"By the time you get here," she said, "I will be dead."

"So why should I bother?"

"Because you still love me, you ass," she said.

"Okay." He sat up in bed, holding the phone in place with his shoulder, and he switched on the lamp. Now he was awake. "Okay, so why are you in Atlanta, and why am I in fucking Arkansas?"

"Because I don't love you?" she said.

He was not in the mood for her games, not at this time of night. His son was sleeping in the other room and the doors, the windows, everything was open, so he couldn't scream. He whispered: "Maybe there is someone you do love, then, who can come over and scratch this itch for you. Maybe he lives less than three hundred miles away. Maybe he lives with you. Did you check your fucking bed?"

"I'm in bed, you idiot," she said. "Don't you know what time it is?"

It was one-thirty.

"Dwight," she said, "I don't live with anyone. I don't even know anyone here."

"Then call an ambulance," he said. "I have to go to work in the morning." And he hung up the phone.

It rang.

He picked it up.

"Are you coming?" she said.

He was already out of bed. "I'm coming," he said. He was putting on some pants.

"Drive safely," she said.

There are no other cars on the road. There are not even trucks. Dwight Tang has his window rolled all the way down and is driving with his head sticking out the window, out in the night. The rush of air is keeping him awake, but it is also making his eyes water. And it's windy inside the car. He's afraid Oscar will wake up.

Dwight pulls his head back in and rolls up the window. He will be okay for a while. It is quiet in the car. He turns around to look at Oscar and Oscar is still sleeping, curled up in his blanket. Oscar is dreaming that someone has handed him an onion. Dwight looks at the speedometer, which says he is going seventy miles an hour. It is another two hundred and fifty miles to Atlanta, so Dwight figures he will be getting there around 8:00 A.M. (He has failed to account for the time change. He will get there around 9:00 A.M., eastern standard time.) Oscar will be waking up around then, Dwight figures.

Dwight will already be late for work. He will miss a day of work, in fact, and then there will be a weekend, and then he will possibly miss more days. Maybe he will lose his job.

"Was that Mom?" Oscar said. He was already awake.

Dwight was standing in the doorway. "No," he said. "Get dressed, okay? We have to go somewhere."

"Where?" Oscar said, sitting up in his bed.

"Atlanta."

"Atlanta?" he said. He furrowed his brow. "Atlanta, huh."

Dwight smiled. "Have you been there?"

"No," Oscar said, "but I think it's the capital of Georgia."

Dwight watched him getting dressed. He liked watching Oscar getting dressed. It was like watching his ex-wife, Oscar's mother, getting dressed, because the boy did it with style. He did it like he cared how he looked, how everything looked. He folded his pajamas and put them away, and he got out everything he wanted to wear and set it on the bed, then sat down next to it and put it all onto his body, one thing at a time. His room was always cleaner than Dwight's.

"How far is it to Atlanta?" Oscar said. He had finished dressing and was making the bed.

"About six hours," Dwight said. "You might want to grab a blanket and a pillow, so you can sleep in the car."

"Whatever you say," Oscar said. He grabbed a blanket and a pillow.

* * *

Dwight Tang is driving without shoes on. He is driving without socks. He has taken his shoes and socks off in the hopes that the vibrations from the pedal will help keep him awake.

It is four-thirty in the morning. Oscar has a blanket and a pillow, and is sleeping in the backseat.

Dwight is impressed with his car, which is a 1975 Pontiac Le Mans. Eight cylinders. The engine does not fall asleep at the wheel, Dwight points out to himself. The engine, too, requires energy to keep going. Where does it come from? Dwight knows. It comes from "explosions" of gasoline that take place in each of the eight cylinders, ignited by a sequence of sparks from the eight spark plugs. It is a self-perpetuating system. All it needs is fuel, and the car will not fall asleep at the wheel.

Dwight tries to apply this knowledge to his own life. Dwight's "explosions," however, are not sparked by spark plugs. They are sparked by his falling asleep for a split second, thereby putting his life in danger, which causes adrenaline to be released. Which keeps him awake for a while longer. Therefore, he must fall asleep and wake up and fall asleep and wake up and fall asleep and wake up in order to stay awake.

Which doesn't make sense, so he takes off his shoes and socks and hopes that being barefoot will do the trick.

It doesn't.

He turns on the radio.

Oscar was sitting in the front seat next to him, asking questions, like: "Was she your girlfriend before or after Mom was?" This was at the beginning of the trip.

"Well," Dwight said, "a little bit of both. But mostly before."

"How come you didn't marry her instead of Mom?"

"Well," Dwight said, "let's put it this way. Let's put it like this: You like cake and you like ice cream, right? Say you're at a birthday party where there are both things. There is cake, which you like, and there is ice cream, which you also like. Which one do you eat?"

"Both."

"Well," Dwight said, "okay, you eat both. But what if you can't? What if you have to choose? Let's say whoever's birthday party it is makes a rule that—"

"They wouldn't do that, Dad," Oscar said. "No one would say that you can't have cake *and* ice cream. Not at a birthday party."

"Okay, you're right," Dwight said. "Let's say you're kidnapped by some bad guys and all they have to feed you is cake and ice cream, which is fine because you like them both a lot. *But,*" he said, "one of the bad guys holds a gun to your head and says you can only have one or the other. Which one is it going to be?"

"Cake."

"Wait, I'm not finished," Dwight said. "Okay—cake. Cake. You have chosen cake. But why? You love them both. Well, let's say that every time you eat cake you love it and you feel good about it. You love eating it. And every time you eat ice cream, you love it just as much as cake but you get sick and throw up."

"I think I see what you're saying, Dad," he said.

"You see what I'm saying?" Dwight said. "I loved this girl, Sarah. I loved her every bit as much as I loved your mother, maybe even more, if you want to know the truth. But she didn't love me. Not quite."

Oscar looked out his window for a while. Then he looked at his father, who was watching the road. "You know what, Dad?" he said.

"No. What?" Dwight said.

"All girls make me want to throw up," he said.

Dwight has his pants undone and it is dark out still and his zipper is down and his son is sleeping in the backseat and Dwight has taken out his penis. He is touching two fingers to his tongue and then rubbing them on his penis, which is getting hard.

Oscar is dreaming that something he can't see is chasing him. He can't see it, but he knows it's there and he can hear it chasing him. He is terrified.

Dwight's penis is touching the steering wheel. He is thinking about Sarah and he is thinking that he is crazy for being out on the road at this time of night. He licks his fingers. He is thinking about being tied to a chair and Sarah has her mouth around him. She is teasing him. She is dressed like a soldier and he is wearing her clothes, her stockings, her lipstick. She has him in her mouth. His eyes are closed.

He is awake. He licks his fingers. He checks the rearview mirror for Oscar, to make sure Oscar is not awake. He watches the road. He's breathing heavy.

Oscar is being chased. He is being chased by bad guys and kidnappers. They are holding a cake.

The light from the dashboard casts an eerie green color on Dwight's face. He is glowing. He licks his fingers. He is a ghost. Sarah is all over him. He is awake.

Oscar is not getting away from the kidnappers. He can't run fast enough. He knows the only way to get away is to wake up, which will turn the whole thing into a dream. He tries to wake up. He has to wake up.

Dwight licks his fingers. He is not asleep. He is crazy to be going back to Sarah, and she is crazy to be dying for him, dying to have him inside of her. He is alive. He moves his fingers, breathing. She was breathing on the phone, like the old days. She said she was going crazy. He is dying to have her all over him. He licks his fingers. He is awake. He is crazy. He is lit up like a ghost and he is crazy to be where he is, doing what he is doing, and he doesn't want his son to catch him, but he is awake. That's the important thing: he is not sleeping.

Dan Leone has published short stories in *Black
Warrior Review*, *The Crescent Review*, *The Paris
Review*, *The Quarterly*, and others. His story,
"Spinach," won the 1992 John Train Humor
Award from *The Paris Review*. In addition to
fiction and poetry, Leone writes songs and plays
ukelele for Ed's Redeeming Qualities, whose two
albums—*More Bad Times* and *It's All Good News*—are available on Flying
Fish Records. He currently lives in San Francisco.

PHOTO CREDIT: YURI ONO

I meant to write a story about a guy trying to track down his ex-wife
in order to regain possession of some carpet samples she has that
rightfully belong to him. I wrote this one instead. It came together in my
head during an all-night drive through Texas on my band's first tour,
and writing it was how I stayed awake at the wheel.

Patricia Lear

AFTER MEMPHIS

(from *The Antioch Review*)

My big brother was the one who had lashed the Confederate flag to the antenna, and so there we were, the four
of us under the blaze of our banner, my brother and I two small
heads sticking up proud in the backseat sucking on Popsicles—
assuming we were ever noticed at all, which probably we weren't
but maybe we were, by a gas-station attendant or something—
and with our dad's big company-president Cadillac tires rubber-
ing us relentlessly north, and with us inside with the car windows
up, and with the car doors locked so that when we fought and
roughhoused we would not accidentally hit the door handle and
fling ourselves out, there was always around us a protective haze
from our parents' cigarette smoke Spanish-mossing into drapey
shapes in the corners.

In the night, after night fell, our parents were mostly just little
red dots darting through the stillness of that hurtling tunnel of
time that was all of us grinding on along on the old highways,
our parents writing circles and S's and slashes with their cigarette
ends that my brother and I could, you know, eye-blinkingly, see
from the back in the dark when we opened our eyes—but also,
and mostly in their murmurings to each other, our parents were
the only things standing between us and the stories they told each
other about, us saying, "What, what, what?" when we couldn't

hear a part, and which stories were to us, of course, what life was about with a capital *L*.

Our mom had stayed on with us to finish the school year, as is often done, and she did the usual things that go with the waiting for the school year to be out—she took us to the pediatrician for our shots and kept being assistant leader for my Camp Fire girls and took us to the swimming pool and put the house up for sale and went to exciting places like to the beauty parlor while we were in school, our dad already having gone on ahead of us across the Mason-Dixon line and taken out bank loans and all, spending a year getting things going such as starting his company and finding us a house, and then coming back to chip us with a chisel out of the South, haul us with a crane out of the country club swimming pool—which is how he said it was for him from the way we were acting.

And with us packed by his own hands into the backseat with the line taped down the middle in red tape, also by him, so that we would not fight or start the next Civil War by touching each other, our dad made a beeline straight through downtown Memphis to get it over with, to speed us as fast as possible across that bridge over the Mississippi River, since my brother and I were suddenly swamped emotionally with a great southern pride-flowering that had started us singing and yelling "Dixie," and me hanging out the windows, screaming.

I had just gotten old enough to care about the South, which was really just as everybody was packing up around me for the move. My brother cared first, of course, and then me. In the car my brother was occasionally shrieking out, "Why, why, why?" between "Dixie" verses, so our mom had to say to us that if we were happy people, we could be happy people anywhere, and our dad, who was landing us in West Memphis, Arkansas, down in the industrial section of town (after a jillion stoplights and direction-readings from our mom, and after the usual gas-station phone calls to the place we were trying to get to) down at the visitor parking lot of the Razorback Ice Cream Company, our dad said it was up to us in this life as far as he knew and not the other way around.

And this was the exact day in West Memphis, Arkansas, right after we left the Razorback Ice Cream Company, that was the last time we ever were as kids to have our born-and-bred Memphian accents, and it was the first time we ever knew we even had Memphian accents in the first place. It was from that day on in West Memphis, Arkansas, from where our dad had threaded our way out of the industrial section of town, it was from lunch of that exact first day in West Memphis, Arkansas, that I think our accents started eroding. I believe it began while we were ordering our Rebel Dogs from the Yankee-looking waitress and while, waiting to eat, we were taking in the speech of everybody sitting around us.

It was just business that we all ate ice cream—Peanut Buster Dairy Queens, little Dixie cups, regular ice-cream sandwiches, Creamsicles, Bomb Pops, Drumsticks. You name it, we probably sampled some of it, as our father went zigzagging us from ice-cream store to ice-cream factory (the Razorback only the first) through Tennessee, Arkansas, and Missouri to teach himself everything he could about the processing end of it and the business end of the ice-cream business and to sit around swapping ideas with the other novelty-ice-cream-company presidents and take us all on long, lengthy tours of manufacturing and production areas, storage and freezer space, shipping dock and on-site lunchroom and convenience vending machines, even snaking us single file through the front office to meet management and to chat with the secretarial and clerk-typist pool. We would drink bottles of pop, and listen to the men talking about sugar prices and overruns, milk solids and packaging, as our mom chatted with one of the employee ladies and drank from a paper cone of coffee that was fitted into a little plastic-handled holder.

At night, though, we mixed business with pleasure by staying only in motels with swimming pools, where water bugs frog-legged around in the water with us. Back on the road, we discussed the Civil War and how they had it all wrong in the history books, especially with regard to what we were up to and what they *really* were up to. They did not care about our slaves and our slaves' freedom and their welfare and all. They were just jealous of how good we were doing. They just wanted our raw materials, is what it was. Us plantation owners were left with nothing, no help to keep our crops and cotton going without our slaves, which we loved and cared for.

And the slaves, hell, they even had it worse free than with us!

I was feeling a deep personal unfairness done to me and was getting madder and madder about wanting our slaves back, as well as the life that went along with us having them, and it was then that my brother brought up with great suspicion, "Hey, how soon is it anyway, or how late is it exactly, that the state of Missouri, where we are moving to, joined in with the Confederacy, and how is it that Kansas never joined in, though it wavered for about a minute, but in the end, what's the deal with Kansas going blue, not gray?"

"Don't know, don't care," our father said, driving us up through the Ozark Mountains at this point and impressing the hillbillies with our company-president Cadillac flying the Confederate flag. "Anyway, all that is over," he said, pointing out a big truck passing us going the opposite way on the highway with his own name emblazoned across its big side. "Anyway, all that is over," our dad said. "Especially the old moldy Civil War." Then he asked our mom to hand us over into the backseat some rolled-up floor plans and a sketch of what our new house could look like once it was finished—although they had yet to decide exactly on which front to put on it from the choices available: ranch, French Provincial, or antebellum.

It was the floor plans and house-front choices my brother and I spread out across us in the backseat that got me to remembering my giant drawing book I carried with me everywhere to draw in, and after fixing the elasticized shoulders on my peasant blouse that had snapped up, I was soon busying myself with my artwork—I was drawing plantation houses with pillars standing across the front, and drawing also cotton fields with slaves. On other pages, tucked away, I have to admit, there were pages and pages of penises, like on my brother and on our dog we used to have, and then on other pages there were also a few very, very stylized vaginas as seen from the front—as in the mirror, and though I did these items in a very, very stylized way, that is what they *were*. So I was humming "Dixie" and drawing and was thinking about all the old times that I would not forget that we were leaving back in Tennessee—such as the lap, lap, lap of the country club swimming pool electrically underlit after dark by a splintery light and top-lit by that magical Memphis moon and floated with a drizzle of fallen cottonwood blossoms (not ten thousand water bugs). Such as Elvis, barbecue pork sandwiches from the Pig 'N Whistle, polo ponies we could ride out in Germantown, the Christmas Cotillion where some day I would be a debutante sort of like Scarlett O'Hara because of not one thing I myself would ever have to have done.

But it was on the road that wends through Springfield, Missouri—the home of the Ozark Big Wheel Ice Cream Delight sandwich—and on up through the Ozark Mountains and around the many finger lakes of the Lake of the Ozarks, which I remember clearly, because it was about there as we were suddenly coming up over a big surprise hill in the road that lifted us up into the air and my brother said, "Is this us? The South rising again?" that the truth of this move-we-did-not-want-to-make began seeping out sideways. I was sitting next to my brother, at first peacefully drawing more of what I said I was drawing in the backseat as the family talked on without me, more about the Civil War that I did not understand or care to learn about just then—since unlike my brother I did have a limit to my caring about the teensiest details, and my brother was droning away with his head stuck up between our parents in the front seat droning names and battles and summits and dates—my brother knew everything, every little detail, his caring knew no limits, so it was about then our dad cut it short finally and began telling us the usual stories about his Uncle Winn (so what) we had all heard all our lives anyway, and about "the farm" (so what) where this Uncle Winn lived. Our mom said, "Oh, Winn . . . ," trailing off, but our dad talked on about this Uncle Winn and this farm where we were in fact going to be living until our house was finished being built, our dad telling us story after story, as he hurtled us evermore deeper and farther into the North, the upchuck of all which was that it was because of this Uncle Winn was the reason we were all riding along so comfy in this Cadillac in the first place (so what), because it was from this Uncle Winn that our dad had learned the meaning of the word "work."

Our dad spoke about Uncle Winn in the same tones, I noticed, as my brother did when he was talking about Robert E. Lee or Jefferson Davis. He spoke about how Uncle Winn was the only one of anyone in our whole family to last through the Depression—no one else did, that is for sure, no one else did. "But how he had a temper!" our dad said. "And when he lost it, watch out! You all remember I told you about the time when the stubborn mule refused to plow and Winn did the darndest thing."

"Mule rocked the wrong boat there," our mom said, smiling back at me.

"It was the darndest thing," our dad said.

Oh hell and so what. We had heard that mule story a million times, and I still never liked it. I was the kind of kid that could be made hysterical by such a story. I thought it was mean to the mule.

But just awestruck was our dad in the presence of this story, I could tell from his eyes glittering up in some approaching headlights, intent as he was with keeping that Cadillac hood ornament plowing a straight furrow north back to where he was going to dip back in to the same "good character" pond for some more of whatever it was that he had gotten back then for us all. And there was to be no way out, what with our mom who I could see in plane-lit profile nodding along with him, her eyes turning velvety and soft, her fingers working up his shoulder to his neck, and whose stories were mostly aimed at me, and were mostly about how not wanting anything was the only way to get anything, while our dad's were mostly aimed at my brother, and were about how you just had to go out there and *get* anything, if you were ever going to *have* anything.

Our dad said, "It was the darndest thing."

I was sad all over again about the mule because I very much wanted a horse and a mule was closer to being a horse than what I then had. I would have wanted to ride that mule. I would have taken good care of that mule, and he would have been pretty decrepit by now and old.

The first thing I remember from when we turned into the driveway of the farm and parked ourselves over by the barn was the rising of the sausage-commercial sun to the crowing of the sausage-commercial cocks, our dad having decided to push on and just get there, even though our mom said she could not sit anymore and had to go to the bathroom so bad she could "pop."

The second thing I remember is my brother in front of the barn, looming through the dawn from a place high up on a ladder, nails bristling from his teeth. I could see a big Confederate flag caped up over his shoulders and his hair ruffling along with the wheat crop in an early morning breeze.

The third thing I remember is that there was an old barn turned dance studio right across the highway from the farm that had a spotlit dancer in a top hat and cane stuck up on the roof.

Uncle Winn was watching us all swarming in on him, watching us advancing up the yard from his rented hospital bed set up in the front parlor, us to him probably like the *Night of the Living Dead* with our suitcases and leftover Popsicle wrappers and comic books and fistfuls of trip garbage we were made to clean out from the floor of the car, and me also with my blanket and pillow from the backseat.

Our dad was soon sitting in the pulled-up BarcaLounger, and those two!—our dad telling Winn—what was it?—something— it was something about butter brickle ice cream back then our dad was all fired up about, just having cut a deal with Heath Bar to supply the butter brickle part.

"Wait until you try it," our dad was saying to Winn. "It was the best thing you will ever eat," as Winn was saying, "What in the Sam Hill is that?" since he was staring out the picture window at my brother up on the ladder above the hayloft nailing in the last nail of our Confederate flag.

Winn sure would not be doing to any more mules what he had done to his own mule, I could see that from when I was made to go over and give him a kiss. The local Missouri mule population was safe.

Next morning it was, "Up and at 'em, you-all!" from our dad who was dressed in his flight suit from the war when he bombed all the Germans, our dad who sang, "Off we go into the wild blue yonder," like my brother and I sang "Dixie," who never slept much, though he would of if he could of, and who never found it in himself to do the thing, to do the sleep method that our mom always said worked for her where you bore yourself to sleep is basically what you do. You lie in bed, and you get yourself and your arms and legs all settled how they feel best—you might want to try out a couple of positions first before choosing because here is the hard part—you *stay* in that same position. *No matter what.* Especially when the urge comes, *and it will,* to move or roll over, you by force of WILL *stay* in that same position. If you do this long enough, you are guaranteed by our mom of going to sleep. Our mom does this sleep method and says it works for her even on the night before Christmas. And the proof is in the pudding because whenever I would go in to check on our mom in bed, such as if I was up going to the bathroom, there she would be, so calm and so asleep. Barely breathing.

Saying, "Work time!" our dad was coming up the stairs to our room and then picking my brother's bed up on its right side legs so it crashed down on the wood floor with my brother trying to stay asleep, no matter what, my brother was going to cling to sleep next to me no matter what was done to him, me, of course watching all this through flittery eyelashes and listening to my brother's breath breathing out Whys and I don't believe thises as our dad was by this time finished with this part of his morning and was tromping on back downstairs to help Winn get going for the day, our dad doing what I know he did all that summer—lifting Winn gently up in his hospital bed, then leading Winn by the elbow over to the Porta Potti he had rolled in from the dining room, and then waiting in the kitchen for him, maybe making toast or reading some of the newspaper business section while he was waiting, or maybe staying in the parlor with Winn but politely messing around with his back turned, spreading the covers over Winn's bed for him, all this while he was waiting, all while my brother would be stomping around my bed pulling all the chains on the antiquey lamps that we had in there and then going into the bathroom, door left wide open, where he would sound like the mule must have sounded to Winn when the mule was going on some solid ground and Winn was stuck behind him, waiting, hanging on to the plow.

My brother would suit up in his work coveralls—his T-shirt underneath peeping the Confederate flag through some un-snapped snaps—and he would sing "Dixie" like he thought if he could wake me up that would mean something, which it in no way meant anything as our mom was in charge of me, so him flinging his arms around and throwing his Eagle Scout slingshot to an end-on-end clatter across the wood floor before slamming out the door was just what I had to live with to get rid of him in those summer mornings.

The men would be packing themselves into the Cadillac; I could hear their voices and see them from the upstairs window as I dragged my bones out of bed to get up and go flush the toilet. I could see out there in the driveway my brother sink-

ing back down into the backseat and settling his boots up flat
against one of the rear windows, hear the engine starting, hear,
I think, "Mack the Knife" playing on the radio, and it was like
this that the men left the farm in the mornings all that summer
before our house was built, while our house was just a hole in
the ground. They left spewing loose gravel from underneath the
Cadillac tires, probably scaring frogs out of the drainpipe sections
along where the driveway met the highway where they would
take a hard left to get out on the highway, passing along the row
of Burma-Shave signs in the Cadillac, passing them by, flying the
Confederate banner, like starting flags.

After crossing the bridge over into K.C., they would thump a
bumper dragging left down on the old road down by the river
flats where, whirling dust, our dad would be driving along and
lifting his hand up off the steering wheel or tapping his horn
at the drivers going the other way, drivers driving trucks of all
sizes with his name stenciled on the sides, our dad all the while
running organizational plans and ways to secure debt and flavor
combination ideas by Winn, and Winn, his whole body pitched
about by the car ride, Winn, not my brother, would be listening
as our dad drove the three of them deep into the industrial section of town to where his ice-cream plant was tucked behind the
Empire Cold Storage Company.

Once, hay mower in the distance, sun a bright butter curl
on the silver butter plate of the midday midwestern sky, two
men from the plant arrived out at the farm with Winn—he
was old and he got tired—and also bringing along with them
an institutional-sized and industrial-quality, top-opening freezer
case with three double lift-up black rubber lids to plug in on
the kitchen porch. They were carrying it up the yard toward the
porch, the very porch where I would usually be lying on the old
tasseled sofa that was moved there from where Winn's hospital
bed now was, our dad having changed the furniture around for
Winn's special needs—rented the hospital bed, hired on some

help, bought the BarcaLounger, moved the tasseled sofa out to where I would lie in a loose Hawaiian shirt I found in the cedar closet left over from the story about when our dad made Winn go on that Hawaiian cruise, forced him to leave the state of Missouri and fly all the way to Honolulu and get on a cruise boat. I wore that shirt all that summer for its comfort, switching off from my Memphis peasant blouse. I even sometimes slept in it at night, and in the hot afternoons after the freezer arrived, me in the Hawaiian shirt lying on the tasseled sofa, I could reach over my hand to the institutional freezer for, say, another ice-cream sandwich as I was reading my comic books or drawing, and being lulled even more into our new life here in the North by the sleepy ironing board creak of "our help," Roberta, the fine churchwoman who was coming to Winn for a few hours each day, who hummed whiney church songs as she ironed Winn's shirts, her ironing board set up in the afternoons between the BarcaLounger and the picture window while Winn would lie in his hospital bed moving his lips along to whatever Roberta was singing.

From time to time, dropping a foot on the floor and elevating my old bones upright to a standing position to see better what kinds of novelty items there were in our new freezer, I would go on into the kitchen and drop down at the kitchen table next to our mom who would be sitting there having a cigarette and some iced Constant Comment tea everybody had started drinking in Memphis, her pockets wadded with Kleenexes and soothing herself with doing her bad habit she never could break; she would be fidgeting and peeling at her fingernails until they peeled off in layers.

So we sat, while the dishwasher chugged and threw the dishes around inside, her with her fingernails and sipping her tea and smoking her cigarette, and me eating a Cho Cho cup with a little wooden spoon, and together we would stare into the parlor at Roberta ironing, watch to find out when it was that Roberta made those iron-shaped scorch marks on Winn's shirts. It was when the carpools came and caused a big honking ruckus in the dancing-school parking lot across the highway.

Even my hostile brother and, most especially, our grinning energetic dad would smell good and manly whenever they came home to call it a day, to seek out some plain old R and R, their clothes and hair and skin dusted over with powdered milk and cane sugar and chocolate mix powder, plus dirt and sweat, and bringing along cartons of new ice-cream items that they had thrown in the back of the Cadillac and brought home packed on dry ice. They were ready to eat chicken-fried steak, pot roast, or chicken, chicken, chicken—that is, if they were home any time close to a dinner hour since our dad worked everything; he worked production alongside his crews, all the shifts our dad worked in the course of a week since they kept the plant running around the clock in the summers for the obvious reasons. And also he did figures and answered phones in the front office right along with the clerical ladies, his fingers virtuoso on the keys of the adding machine processing orders and tallying inventory and doing the payroll. He might slip into one of the quilted freezer-room jackets that were kept hanging on pegs and two-handed pull open the bank vault of a freezer door and disappear into the thick spill of arctic air before the door slammed shut behind him.

And then he might be coming around the back to the loading dock, to load up the trucks, then he was not beyond jumping into the cab of a truck, making the deliveries himself, even driving those great big trailer jobbies, the ones with sixteen gears and a copilot, driving them down to Chillicothe. He was always going to places like Chillicothe back then.

It was the things that did not sell that he brought home to stock our freezer with as much as the good stuff. He would bring home eggnog ice cream in half-gallon cartons and Coconut Xmas Snowballs with the real little wax candles sticking up out of the middle of a holly-berry bunch toothpicked in the top. He'd bring pumpkin-flavored turkeys and green dye #11 Christmas trees. At the plant, there were bags of green dye #11. Roberta would serve more bowls of eggnog ice cream than any other flavor to Winn and my mom and me at noontime with our cold-cut sandwiches. We never saw from her hand an Eskimo Pie or a Drumstick. The vanilla and pumpkin-flavored turkeys she would serve occasionally. The strawberry Valentine hearts once in a while—but it was something about the eggnog ice cream that had Roberta in a thrall.

There were times in the evenings that summer when I would have to go the long way around to get from my room to the kitchen to where my mom would be starting our dinner, maybe grating carrots for our little salads or peeling potatoes, it being too early for her to start on me about my job—pouring the milks for dinner. I would have to go through the dark dining room, slip past the set of sliding oak doors of the parlor where I could hear our dad and my brother in there, with Winn asleep or watching the action in his hospital bed, our dad always sitting in the BarcaLounger and my brother always sitting in the needle-pointed armchair with the arm doilies. Basically what it was was our dad loving my brother so much he could not let him alone, so afraid was he for my brother concerning life, and wanting everything for him to be so proud and good and strong, for him to be strong and good, and my brother just wanting to be left alone to have some one or two of his own experiences just for himself all by himself, to be proud and good and strong and good just all by himself without our dad acting as brilliant, genius interpreter to every little thing, every little time he brushed his teeth, and Winn sometimes even sleeping, who knows how, through those two saying, "Why do you think why?" to each other, or, "Just what do you mean by that?"

Or, "Is that what you think life is?" It could be either one of them saying that.

"What do you think life is? Tell me right now, please, your theories on what life is."

My brother would finally somehow get himself excused, and then he would head outside past the floured chicken parts frying up in the iron skillet and the others waiting their turn on a waxed-paper sheet, past the finished pieces draining on paper towels on the countertop, past the Jell-O mold quivering in our mom's hands as she was maybe walking it over to the refrigerator, past me and the institutional freezer with the black rubber lift-up tops. He would maybe yell something at me, seeing me reading a comic book on the tasseled sofa, "Taylor, you lazy imbecile, go get the dandelion digger," and then he would go on out into the downy evening light to pull out the old rusty push mower from the shed. I would watch him from where I would climb up on the freezer to watch, and I saw him more than once that summer drop down on his knees in some grass beside the push mower to examine something on the mower blades or wheels, some little thing, a mud clot or something dried up and stuck up there in the mower, and my brother would just get down there close next to it and poke it with a stick.

Our dad would stand beside me and watch. "What in the Sam Hill?" he would breathe while he watched my brother doodle around with the stick, then our dad would follow out, not really being able to stay away from my brother, and he would go off across the yard the opposite way from my brother, like he could not watch anymore, but still, so my brother could see him, like maybe he was going on back to work, he would back his Cadillac out of the barn, back it right underneath my brother's Confederate flag, then at this point, our mom would run out in the yard and our dad would hit the brakes and pretty soon he would cut the engine and come on back in the house, going back past me again, me with my bare foot rummaging around in one of the pull-up top openings of the freezer, and he would go on in to sit with Winn where they would together look at the TV evening news or do figures or just wait for the chicken to finally get itself fried.

   Then one night, early on, all of us lying out in the sweet-smelling, just-mown grass my brother was made-to-mow-by-our-dad, we all were lying out after supper having our dessert ice-cream bars in some ratty lawn chairs I found stuck up in the rafters of the barn I had been crawling around in that day, trying to hang out of the hayloft and fix the corner of our Confeder-ate flag where it had come loose. We all were much interested in Creamsicles at that time—vanilla ice cream on a stick covered over with an orange sherbet—something our dad was giving a try that hit BIG, and still is BIG, as you probably know if you frequent the freezer case at the 7-Eleven, but what you would not know was it was my dad that made it that way. We were eating the first Creamsicles on the planet earth and looking around us like you do, and we could see Winn watching TV and eating a Creamsicle, too, lit up in the picture window in his hospital bed. We could see him perfectly, like it looks when you are in the dark outside and somebody is on the inside with all the lights flipped on and funny just because they *are* so totally unaware. The TV noise was blaring far louder out there in the crystalline coun-try air than it would have seemed to be if we were, say, back in the city of Memphis and standing in front of the Peabody Hotel waiting for our car to be brought around front and this same TV noise was blaring out from one of the upstairs hotel windows.
   And with us each shifting our bones around in our wooden lawn chairs, we could see the back of a billboard the Motel 6 motel chain, headquartered around there somewhere, had up there, with electric lights haloing out from around the dark ob-long of its backside, since it was set forward for the oncoming traffic to see, not our way. The Burma-Shave signs we could not see, but there was the perky spotlit dancer on top of the dance studio across the highway outfitted with her top hat and cane, and actually it was she and Winn that outshone by far even the

Motel 6 or the Confederate flag that was nailed up on the barn and lit up ghostlike from all the night neon, and from our pride— my brother's and mine—though that was a shame; the Confederate flag was by far the more beautiful and really meant something important, too. It meant the human spirit and causes.

Our family conversations were mostly round-and-rounds where one person would get on some topic dear to his heart, and then one other person, or persons, would have to get him off that topic ASAP because it was becoming a threat to one or more of the other family members' equilibrium. And then another party would launch off with a topic that soon could not be tolerated by one or more of the others. And around and around it went like that with conversations in our family.

Our mom would say (I know this since this is what she said all that summer), "Houses are never done on time," and our dad would let her run on for a while to get that off her chest, then he would change the subject because what could he do about the house anyway, build it himself? He would change the topic to something like "work"—his work in particular or just "work" in general—and my brother would pretty soon launch into the Civil War and start talking about a battle or a summit even more obscure than the one he talked about the night before since that is what he was talking about all that summer. He might as well have been in the Civil War for all he knew about it. Or he was also saying every other sentence, such as when our mom was going on about the house never being ready, "Let's go back, let's don't do this," and our dad would get us off that topic lickety-split by launching into something like what he said the night I am remembering.

He said, "Oh, family, this place has a history. Oh this place right here and that old man up there in that picture window really have a history. It scares me to think if it weren't for this place and that man."

And how could we not, even my brother, how could we not look up at that picture window and see Winn who, at this point, was holding his popsicle stick in his mouth and drooping it down like I saw the French apache dancers do with their cigarettes on TV, and my brother then said, "What is that he is wearing? Is he wearing my T-shirt? Is that my T-shirt?" and I remember I jumped to my feet to get a better look at Winn.

Our dad then could have said, for example, to get us off that topic, I don't remember exactly but this is close, "Taylor-tater-tot? Do you know how to snap the head off a snake? Winn in there does," which is probably the thing that started my mom down the road I am going to tell about now, because our mom did say one of those drive-in movie perfecto nights, one of those early nights while we were probably all still trip rattled, which is maybe why this thing she told had such a BIG impact on me, why I sucked it up like a damp sponge being wiped across an old kitchen counter, our mom said, "You-all? Oh, I heard this story. Oh, I just heard the most horrible story from home in a letter. Something so sad. Something so terrible."

"Don't tell us," I yelled out at her, attuned as I was to her different tones of storytelling voices, as I was getting myself back in my lawn chair from trying, but not succeeding, in seeing Winn's shirt front. "Don't tell us," I yelled out, wanting but not wanting, I didn't really think, to know her story—all this I had decided just from her tone.

"Snakes reminded me," our mom said.

"Oh boy. Hold your horses right there just a minute," our dad said, working at getting himself up out of his low rickety lawn chair, getting up and then going in the back kitchen door where we could see him stick his head in the electrified parlor where Winn was, then disappear, then come back and toss something in Winn's lap. Then our dad came back out and threw us under-handed, one after the other, a round of spoons and each our own Coconut Xmas Snowball.

"Here's yours, here's yours, here's yours," he said. "Come on. We got to eat these up before they get freezer burn."

"Well, okay," our mom said, as flakes of coconut were drifting down into her lap from the split she had made in the cellophane wrapper with her teeth. I got our dad's Zippo and went around lighting the little candles on everybody's Snowball, staving off the story since I did not need a new story. I had plenty of other stories stored up to get hysterical about. I did not need any more right then. There was the move-story that we were living, so it was not yet really a story; it was our life. There were the kitten drownings. There were penises. I had not yet reconciled myself to penises. There was the mule.

"Well, okay. Here I go," our mom said, gazing into her tiny dancing candle flame. "You know Pete and Jenny Rogers and their little girl from the cotillion, don't you, honey?" she said to our dad. "And it was the Cylinders, the Richard Cylinders, not his brother Benjamin, not the one that you know. John Cylinder married to Linelle, and Patience, her niece, was on the swim team with you, Taylor, at the country club. Peter was a year behind you in Scouts. They were the ones that lent them their cabin over by Pittick Place, down on the Hamlin's road by South Tar Creek. Not Arkansas and not Mississippi."

"What in the Sam Hill are you talking about?" our dad said, just barely ever was he able to tolerate the way our mom went about telling a story, but not daring to shift us off the topic altogether by bringing up the further adventures of Winn or something, as she had her rights, such as to tell an occasional story.

I was working hard on my granite-hard Snowball, also letting the candle drip wax on my fingers as I chipped off little bites.

My brother was staring over at our mom, interested in spite of however she was going to get the story out.

"Okay," our mom said, inhaling a deep breath of honeysuckled air and clearing the decks by setting her Snowball down to melt in the grass by her lawn chair. "I'll try again. There were young newlyweds, the young Pearson couple you all remember from Memphis that were getting married even before we left? Mary Rogers. Mary Rogers Pearson. You saw her picture, Taylor, in the society section a few weeks back. Remember? I showed you? Well they were lent a brand-new cabin for their honeymoon up in the Smokies—and it was the first night right after their wedding party and you know, they were very tired, so they got in bed—"

Here my ears pricked up like the mule's must have done when he saw Uncle Winn walk over to the wood pile and reach his bare arm down.

"On the bed I hear there was one of those chenille bedspreads with the peacock," our mom said, lighting up a cigarette just then, finally relaxing a little into her story, finally having gotten a couple of sentences out unimpeded by the rest of us. The smoke hazed over my way where I smoked it in through my nose.

Now this story our mom was about to tell, I have repeated many times. Over the course of my girlhood, I have told this story, I think, whenever I have spent the night with any one of my many girlfriends, also boyfriends, men, and husbands later, now that I am grown. But this version I am writing here is the most permanent record there has ever been of this story.

Well, the honeymoon couple, Mary Rogers Pearson and her husband, got in bed (sex, penis), and they soon heard things moving around on the floor—slithering noises (snake)—and the husband (penis) said to his beloved, Mary Rogers Pearson, he said that he "must take a small break, my darling, so stay just like that in the bed for just a moment," so he could go and see what was causing those noises (snakes slithering, plus rattles being dragged across the floor) before he continued on with what tender, gentle bliss (penis) he was bringing to his bride for the first time in all her life, and as he hit the floor with his feet and began to feel along the wall for a light switch, he was right then stepping on top of rattlesnake on top of rattlesnake on top of rattlesnake. It was a whole nest of them he was stepping on! Some damn idiot fool had had the stupidity to build that cabin right over the site of the biggest nest of diamondbacks in the whole state of Tennessee!! And those snakes were tangled up everywhere! And the noise level! But the young husband was a southern boy and thought only of his bride, Mary Rogers Pearson—which it would behoove me to be like her, however she was, so I could find someone to think of *me* like that, so our mom's look said to me, our mom with her cigarette smoke ribboning into the natural, plus neon-lit sky—and though the young husband never made it to the light switch in that dolt's cabin (there was a lawsuit), what with those rattlesnakes striking and striking at him as they would of course do, them being wild animals, and him stomping all over them barefooted like a grape stomper, he screamed out to Mary Rogers Pearson, "Oh! My darling! For God's sakes! My love! Stay-in-the-bed! Oh my darling!" as he was, by that time, simply sacrificing himself for her because he could have instead, if you think about it, screamed for her to go and get him some help. But he didn't. He said to her, "My love. Don't move a muscle! Don't move! Don't even breathe! Just-stay-in-bed! Just-please-for-Christ-sake-stay-still in the bed!"

And then he was quiet. And the rattlesnakes even began calming down.

And Mary Rogers Pearson, beautiful, luminous, huddled up on the bed, her bare shoulders marbled in the wedding-night moonlight that was streaming down across those Smoky Mountains and on in through the cabin window, Mary Rogers Pearson, who was armed only with her honeymoon nightgown of Italian lace that was bought for her in Memphis at the Helen Shop, Mary held on.

Now our mom's cigarette tip brightened considerably as she took a deep drag, and we all sat quietly for a while, each alone with our own thoughts.

"She bowed at the Christmas Cotillion," our mom said.

"And they had their wedding reception at the country club," she said.

"The minute we left Memphis, this all happened. The minute we left, or the day after," our mom said.

Oh!

Oh!

Hearing the sounds she had to have heard! Knowing what she

must have known, maybe even seen, because probably she could see shapes and shadows and even more. I mean *really* SEE.

Oh!

I could not imagine that much—being big enough for that much TERROR. And in the morning—as our mom was telling it to us, us glommed on to her every word by now, us at her complete mercy—there was the poor dead husband with too many rattlesnake bites to even count, his WHOLE body a mass of bites, the rattlesnakes by now all gone back down to their nests underneath the floorboards of that cabin like they had never even been there at all. No one really saw them come and no one saw them leave except for what Mary Rogers Pearson said she could see.

"Did that really happen?" I said, wanting my drawing book, my fingers itching to get around a pencil. "Did that happen? Who told you that? When did that happen?" I said struggling underneath the crushing weight of this story.

Now the mule and mule-type stories that were so rampant back then—plus there were others I haven't even mentioned (such as the kitten drownings and the "wild" dog shootings—dogs people did not want anymore, dogs people brought out from Kansas City and let go out on the road by the farm)—maybe, maybe, maybe I could just barely tolerate life knowing those stories happened in the same world I did, and that living things had felt what I had the unique genius to imagine in minute detail that they felt from what I was being told had happened to them, and maybe the violence of us being Rebels forced to live here in the North with the Yankees, that too I could make a semblance of peace with if given a little time, but this story with the honeymoon and the snakes coming up in the dark from underneath and no way out but by getting in with the snakes, and Mary Rogers Pearson in her lace nightgown from the Helen Shop—that story pushed me over the edge, because I was never one who could make peace with things by saying what seemed to take care of everything for everybody else, which was, oh well, that's just the way it goes. That's life for you. *C'est la vie.*

"It happened," our mom said, glancing down at her fingernails.

"You see, listen to me, Taylor!" she said as I was busy balling up my Coconut Xmas Snowball wrapper and struggling out of my chair.

"Taylor-tot!" our dad said, meaning he knew I was sealing over and they were not done with me yet.

"The bride," our mom said, "Mary Rogers Pearson, she stayed right there in the bed and she kept still. She did not allow herself to lose control. She kept *still*. And that was smart. That was her only way out of this mess. And well, how she did it, Taylor, if you are wondering just how she did it—well how she did it was how anybody does anything. She *had* to do it. She *had* to, that's how she did it," our mom said, facing me with eyes as glittery with purpose and adamation as our dad's were when he was driving us up here from our happy home down in the South.

"I saw Winn do a rattlesnake," our dad said. "Winn just grabbed him up by its rattler and cracked it like a whip. Head popped off. Then Winn kept cracking until he had cracked him off into nice little wiener-sized sections for the buzzards."

We all gazed up at Winn's picture window and there was Winn sitting straight up in his hospital bed peering back out the window at us. And he *was* wearing my brother's Confederate flag T-shirt.

"She's okay," our mom said. "Mary Rogers Pearson is doing pretty good now. Went to a Fourth of July brunch at the country club."

Now. I could see no path from that night and those snakes to being anything like "pretty good." None whatsoever. The only path I could make out was the path where I would start screaming my head off and all the snakes would charge up and jump all over me—or maybe, maybe I could make it through the night by accident, by being frozen by fear or something, or by some survival mechanism just built into the species that I did not even know I had, but that would be only to be carted off to the insane asylum the next morning where I would spend all the rest of my life reliving the snake-night honeymoon from the picture screen buried deep in my head.

*   *   *

In the late afternoons at a certain time, I would go and lie down on the wood floor under my brother's bed to wait for him to come back from his day of work at the ice-cream factory. If I had the time right, my brother would stumble in and flop down in his big rubber work boots on top of where I was stowed, and I could hear him up there talking conversations to himself about things he would be thinking about and remembering and trying hard to figure out. He would lie still on the bed and sigh loud enough so I could hear his breath swoosh out. He had not yet really begun to unpack his heart from his over-and-done-with life he used to have back in Memphis where he would do things like take the bus crosstown with his friends and go to the movies.

I was younger and my heart maybe unpacked quicker.

My brother would get up off the bed and kick his boots off and go into the bathroom and get himself a glass of water, then he would come back and lie down and breathe and sigh some more. Sometimes he would get off the bed and ramble down to the kitchen to get a loaf of Wonder Bread, his afternoon food of choice, and sometimes he would trap me by coming back in our room at the wrong time, such as when I was half in and half out from under his bed.

Lots of times when I was lying under his bed, I would find down there beside me a loaf or two of older, forgotten Wonder Bread. I would lie down there, and like he did, pull the crust off slices, then ball up the soft middle part to make bread dough, and I found I liked eating it that way as much as he was liking it up above me. For the most part, I was sympathetic and together with my brother in most ways, but he never knew it. Back then, I would even have been him if I could have.

Like our dad, I had quit sleeping. Like our dad, I found our mom's sleep method was too hard for me. I could not bear the idea of boring myself any more than I already was bored by not being able to sleep.

During the day, I found boards nailed to an oak tree I could climb up in and take my drawing book. I began drawing, along with the usuals you already know about, I drew that cabin in the Smokies and Mary Rogers Pearson in bed with her young husband, I drew the rattlesnakes snarled and snaked around under the floorboards. I drew one of the snakes peeping up through a little knothole in the floor. Then I would look through the tree leaves and draw the silhouette of the dancer in a top hat and cane on the top of the dance studio across the highway. I drew our good old Confederate flag nailed up on the barn, the billboards and Burma-Shave signs, the waving fields of grain and the puffy clouds, the cars that shot by out on the highway. I drew where the mule used to be, where the kittens were drowned as fast as they could get themselves born—and I would draw these things as my brother was pushing the mower around in the grass below me—learning more about the meaning of the word "work."

When I climbed higher in the oak tree, I could see farther out to where the subdivision was with our new house going in, to where the municipal airport was, to where there were turnpikes and interstates all crimped together with tollbooths—the "I-this" and the "I-that," the "I," I suppose, that had brought us here from the South.

I started taking walks. For something to do, I'd lumber down the old cracking highway that went by in front of the farm, and I would go toward the future, toward our subdivision with the special fancy entrance gate, and brand-new sod, and the new flagpole that was flying a regular flag. I would walk along the flat curved streets to where our building site was located, where I would watch the men pour cement for the foundation, where I got to know the carpenters framing out the rooms, where I would mess around in the wood scraps with some glue, a hammer, and some nails. I would walk around on the springy plywood floors and in and out of the framed-out rooms—walk around in the space where my parents said my room would be. Then after a while, I would leave there and go and explore the other subdivisions farther down the highway that had names such as Dundee Hills, Edgewood, Glen Briar, Green Brier, Briarcliff, and

Briarcliff Manor. Briarcliff Manor sat on a bluff overlooking the waterworks and the turnpike and the municipal airport.

At night I would go in by our sleeping mom's bed and drop down on my knees beside her pillow and whisper, "Mom, Mom, Mom. I can't sleep. I can't get any sleep." Then I would sit and wait, maybe get a glass of water from the bathroom, and I would wait and study her. Watch her for how she did it.

Then one night was the last; after that one night I never came in her room that same way again.

She could sleep. I could not.

Things happened. A small plane fell out of the sky and crashed nose-first into the open roof of a half-built split level. I ran and saw the perfect undamaged tail of the plane sticking up higher than the walls, and there was a wing I walked up and down on lying off with some rolled-up sod.

A farmhouse burned down to the ground—ancient electrical wiring—and our mom, Roberta, and I heard the sirens and all came running out of the kitchen, ran across the highway and on back behind the dance studio where we watched as fire trucks jammed up a pasture and boys dragged soggy, sooty mattresses and grimy sofas out into the yard, as a boiling fire took that dried wood house all the way down to the ground. Then below the ground.

There were other wonders. Rains that would snare-drum on the tin roof of the kitchen porch with the sun out, shining and hot. Also heavy, weighty rains that would flood the low spots in the yard, sopping rains where I could run out and dance my-self around right across from the dance studio, then flop down by a ditch and let clear water run over my stretched-out legs, let rainwater paste my peasant blouse to my chest and back and shoulders, to turn it see-through to fine, thin lace, and I would, feeling myself "her," lift my chin up and stick my chest out and just sit there being beautiful.

*   *   *

Our dad and me, we were both of us up at night. If Winn were not so old, he would have lasted all night with us, but as it was, Winn was pretty much a transistor radio pulling a weak signal a long way off and real, real late at night. It was simple old age that saved Winn from that torture you need to be young like our dad and me, young and strong, to take. Anybody else would just collapse. And in the day, if you don't sleep at night, I found you cannot let down either. The whole problem is you cannot let down ever, so you must be able to work up a great jitteryness to get you going up and over your exhaustion in the mornings, and to keep up with a kind of shark-eating, frenzy-type energy throughout the day. Though I was still occasionally glancing in through our mom's door to see her sleep, and our dad did in fact stick real close by Winn in the BarcaLounger even though Winn was often asleep himself and not great company, our dad and I kept pretty much quiet with each other and everybody else about our nights. We would just include within us more and more of this problem, which became like any other thing we could not do a darn thing about. We were on our own, each of us alone, like I was beginning to think we all are anyway.

I would be coming out of my bedroom and pad on down the hall under a wedding veil of drifted cigarette smoke that hung in a swirled wasp nest around the overhead light fixture, and when I had made my way down the steep stairs to the parlor, there would be our dad, beanbag ashtray on knee, sitting in the BarcaLounger next to Winn's bed in the quiet of that old farmhouse where all you could hear was the refrigerator and our institutional freezer and the whole house that turned over from time to time in its deep sleep. He would be dressed in his flight suit from the war and be spooning ice cream out of a mixing bowl, scowling at numbers and figures that were listed out on a big tablet of paper.

At dawn I would finally just get dressed and go out of the house swinging my arms, turning cartwheels, going up and down the tree several times to get the blood going. I would slide under a forsythia bush for a heartfelt prayer (so what) that never changed

one thing, never made the slightest difference, other than unlike
our mom, I was let down every time I tried it. Prayer was only
making me think again and again each time I tried it that I was
the one that nothing worked for.

So carrying along on the side of the highway heading up
toward our building site in the morning-milk-splashing-in-a-
bowl-of-cornflakes sun, in the day-camp-bus-picking-up-the-
little-kids-with-their-lunch-sacks sunshine, I would find Bic pens
and number-two pencils and plastic barrettes lying along the side
of the road. That is not true. That was only sometimes. Mostly
I would find sticks and broken pop bottles and all kinds of wild
flowering weeds that I would pick, the weeds, sometimes having
to get down on my hands and knees and bite off the stalks with
my teeth if twisting and turning and picking at them with my
fingernails or sawing at them with a broken Coke bottle did
not work.

I would see up ahead in the roadside debris a glint or flash, and
I would walk faster; then I would see it was maybe only the inside
wrapper from somebody's cigarettes causing the sun to flash, or
the even thinner foil liner of a Nestlé Crunch bar. Once in a while
it was the foil cover of an Eskimo Pie bar with our dad's name
in small letters under the logo. Once it was a fifty-cent piece that
bought me a small packet of something for my hair at the highway Rexall I had been in seeing what all they had. It smelled like
vinegar when I mixed it with water, and when I rinsed it through
my hair after washing, my hair shined so it was me who was the
one causing the sun to flash.

In his big floaty Cadillac, our dad, with Winn and my brother
packed inside, would sometimes come surging down the highway passing me by on those mornings. Sometimes, I would jump
up and down and wave my bunch of flowery weeds at them, or
throw a stick out in the road. Once I tried to kill them all by
aiming a Coke bottle at their windshield. Once though, our dad
slowed and crunched over onto the shoulder of the highway close

to where I was standing, and as I went up to his side of the car, he made the most charming talk to me. He said, "And how are you, Mademoiselle Taylor?" and he said this in the French manner he learned from when he was in France having R and R from bombing the Germans, and I remember clear as day that "Mack the Knife" was playing on the Cadillac car radio and that our dad and Winn were together and smiling and happy.

No. *Really* happy. *Really, really* happy.

I had myself slung out along a tree branch looking down on top of my brother—I could see his head and the tops of his T-shirted shoulders shoving the push mower up and down the slopes of the yard, his arm reaching down from time to time to throw a stick or a rock out of the way, then hitching himself up again and shoving off to mow more grass, and I was thinking about how I would never want to be mowing the grass—and that obviously neither would my brother.

Our mom, who is in charge of me, I just wait out. I stay in the tree. Like the milk. Pouring the milk at dinner. Pouring milk for dinner is my job.

So slung on the branch overlooking my brother pushing the mower in rusty-blade-rotating shoves, I was busying myself with picking around and collecting acorns and small branches, things to drop down on his head as he would shove under my tree, things to ping off his flag-shirted shoulders, as I listened to him say, "Why? Why? Tell me why? Why is this such a big deal? I would just like to know what you think."

He was out across the yard in the dandelions and I could see the wheel nut fell off again or the mower was jammed up with a stick again. He tried getting it going by assuming different positions—like one foot braced up on the mower for extra push force, and then the other foot up on the mower and his shoulder braced on the handle and then picking up the entire mower and turning it over upside down, saying, "Why, why, why?" I watched him through a kaleidoscope of oak leaves as I was changing around my position in the tree, going from one side of the tree to the other, the arms flapping on my Hawaiian shirt, my hair, I suppose, flashing in the sun, and then I noticed him coming stolidly up the little slope, passing right under my tree, where I froze on my branch and took aim and bombed down on him a couple of the acorns. He headed into the garage where there are the tools.

Asking for more, my brother walked back under my tree (more acorns, twigs, some spit) and on back down a way to the push mower where he kneeled and dropped his ass low in the dandelions. "Get me a Bomb Pop, Taylor," he said over his shoulder. "Get out of the stupid tree and go get me a Bomb Pop, or a Popsicle is okay."

I held still in the tree, flattened on my branch, my hair with the drugstore stuff hanging down to where even I could see the different growing out lengths, to where the ends thinned to a translucence from the sunlight that was laced in through the leaves.

My brother pulled off his Confederate flag T-shirt. He pulled it over his head and used it to wipe across his face, then glancing up at the bigger Confederate flag nailed on the barn, he worked at tying his shirt up around his head so it would flop down his back, flag out. Turning, he looked up at me. I flattened flatter.

"Popsicle, Taylor," he said. "Or I will come up there and kill you."

Grasses rustled from the little suppertime breeze. I was about ready to just go and get it for him, to get him his Bomb Pop or Popsicle. The sun, I noticed, was an egg yolk drooped over the fields as I shifted around on my branch, then monkeyed over to another branch, the back of my Hawaiian shirt floating out behind me, as my brother was watching and saying, "Go get me a Bomb Pop now, Taylor."

Then it was what I think must be sleep, that I was dreaming. The automatic reaction of, say, Mary Rogers Pearson happening in me; I froze. I was so quiet beside that delicate slipping through, a delicate slipping through is what it was, that I must have been sound asleep (finally) and dreaming this thing, this moving stillness up there beside me, which after a brief pause set off my shoulders to press back, my rib cage to part wide for air, my lungs to grab for reaches of sound that I grabbed hold of, dug my heels in, and wrenched from my heart. Arm on its own volition reached out and grabbed hold of the moving stillness, and we fell, the two of us together, moving stillness now a garden hose with the water turned on full (but no water), we fell tangled around in the Hawaiian shirt that flew up around my neck, we fell through the air together to land on my back out of the tree to there where my brother was standing with us rolling around, me screaming out, the garden hose all muscle now with trying to get away, undulating, coiling, and wrapping on me, my shoulders pressing forward, legs trying to stand up.

I got hold of, not the tail, but the whole rear third and unwound it off my body. Up in the air my arm went and straight up it went, but nothing. Nothing. So I did this, pretty calm too, I held it in one hand and found a better grip with the other, and then I did it, I cracked it again, but all that happened was it looped. It sketched a U shape in the air, so I did it again and let her fly, or he got away, or he got himself, herself, up in the air where she gave a bronco lunge and charcoaled several W's in the air and landed a way off deep in the dandelions over by where my brother was standing by the push mower. He, she, swished through the grasses, or she—she went—back to her babies. Or she *was* a baby and her mother was a mule-eating, Missouri-wheat-crop python waiting out there in the field for me when I went looking.

The picture window was a crowd of faces looking out, Winn in the middle sitting straight up in his hospital bed.

I fixed my shirt down from around my neck and went up the yard to get my brother his Bomb Pop. I got a couple of Bomb Pops out of the institutional freezer, our mom and dad calling out my name from the parlor, and then I ran back outside to my brother before the sun dropped its yolk completely into the field and the day was all over. We sat down together by the push mower and tore the wrappers off our Bomb Pops.

No one is in charge of me.

Patricia Lear was born in Memphis, Tennessee, and now lives in Kenilworth, Illinois. She has published stories in *The Quarterly* and *The Antioch Review*. Her third published short story was anthologized in *The O. Henry Awards, 1991* and her story collection, *Stardust, 7-Eleven, Route 57, A&W and So Forth* was published in the spring of 1992 by Alfred A. Knopf, Inc.

PHOTO CREDIT: BILL HAYWARD

So far "After Memphis" is my most autobiographical story. We did move to Kansas City from Memphis, and no one much wanted to go other than my father. My brother had a hard time because he was in high school and quite rooted in Memphis. I wanted to get down on paper the difference between the female lives in our family and the male lives— my father and my brother working and working, and me, because I was a girl, just kind of wandering around, loose, depressed, floating, taking in the sights, yet free in a way my brother would never be allowed to be.

The story is a collage of real episodes and whole cloth invention. The snake episode was something I overheard my mother repeat to one of my aunts one afternoon in Memphis. I always thought it was something that happened to someone she knew in Memphis. After "After Memphis" came out in the The Antioch Review, *I learned that my mother had seen that rattlesnake story in an issue of* Reader's Digest *and was telling my aunt about something she had* read!

As far as writing goes, I work so hard, you just can't imagine. I chisel, I rack my brain, I die a thousand deaths. I do fifty, a hundred drafts. I wonder how I can keep it up, but really it's all I have ever wanted to do.

Oh, yes, my father did own a novelty ice cream factory and he was the one who invented the Bomb Pop. Try one. They're still around.

APPENDIX

APPENDIX

A list of the magazines consulted for *New Stories from the South: The Year's Best, 1992*, with current addresses, subscription rates, and editors.

Alabama Literary Review
253 Smith Hall
Troy State University
Troy, AL 36082
Semiannually, $9
Theron Montgomery, Editor-in-Chief, James G. Davis, Fiction Editor

The American Scholar
Phi Beta Kappa Society
1811 Q Street, NW
Washington, D.C. 20009
Quarterly, $21
Joseph Epstein

The American Voice
The Kentucky Foundation for Women, Inc.
332 West Broadway, Suite 1215
Louisville, KY 40202
Quarterly, $12
Frederick Smock, Sallie Bingham

Antaeus
The Ecco Press
100 West Broad Street
Hopewell, NJ 08525
Semiannually, $30
Daniel Halpern

Antietam Review
82 West Washington Street
Hagerstown, MD 21740
Once or twice a year, $5 each
Ann Knox and Susanne Kass

The Antioch Review
P.O. Box 148
Yellow Springs, OH 45387
Quarterly, $25
Robert S. Fogarty

Apalachee Quarterly
P.O. Box 20106
Tallahassee, FL 32316
Three times a year, $15
Barbara Hamby

Artemis
Artemis/Artists & Writers, Inc.
Roanoke, VA 24010
Annually
Dan Gribbin

The Atlantic Monthly
745 Boylston Street
Boston, MA 02174-0022
Monthly, $15.94
William Whitworth

Black Warrior Review
The University of Alabama
P.O. Box 2936
Tuscaloosa, AL 35486-2936
Semiannually, $9
Glenn Mott

Carolina Quarterly
Greenlaw Hall CB# 3520
University of North Carolina at
    Chapel Hill
Chapel Hill, NC 27599-3520
Three times a year, $10
David Kellogg, Editor, and Claudine
    Murphy, Fiction

The Chariton Review
Northeast Missouri State University
Kirksville, MO 63501
Semiannually, $5
Jim Barnes

The Chattahoochee Review
DeKalb College
2101 Womack Road
Dunwoody, GA 30338-4497
Quarterly, $20
Lamar York

Cimarron Review
205 Morrill Hall
Oklahoma State University
Stillwater, OK 74078-0135
Quarterly, $12
Gordon Weaver

Columbia
404 Dodge Hall
Columbia University
New York, NY 10027
Semiannually, $11
Stephen Morrow, Editor, and Paul
    Gediman and Elizabeth Thomas,
    Fiction

Concho River Review
c/o English Department
Angelo State University
San Angelo, TX 76909
Semiannually, $12
Terence A. Dalrymple

Confrontation
Department of English
C. W. Post of L.I.U.
Greenvale, NY 11548
Semiannually, $10
Martin Tucker, Editor-in-Chief, and
    Julian Mates, Fiction Editor

Crazyhorse
Department of English
University of Arkansas at Little Rock
2801 South University
Little Rock, AR 72204
Semiannually, $10
Judy Troy

The Crescent Review
1445 Old Town Road
Winston-Salem, NC 27106-3143
Semiannually, $10
Guy Nancekeville

Crosscurrents
2200 Glastonbury Road
Westlake Village, CA 91361
Quarterly, $18
Linda Brown Michelson

Crucible
Barton College
College Station
Wilson, NC 27893
Terrence L. Grimes

CutBank
Department of English
University of Montana
Missoula, MT 59812
Biannually, $12

Peter Fong and Dennis Held, Co-
editors, and Claire Davis,
Fiction

Epoch
251 Goldwin Smith Hall
Cornell University
Ithaca, NY 14853-3201
Three times a year, $11
Michael Koch

Fiction
c/o English Department
The City College of New York
New York, NY 10031
Three times a year, $20
Mark J. Mirsky

The Florida Review
Department of English
University of Central Florida
Orlando, FL 32816
Semiannually, $7
Russell Kesler

The Georgia Review
The University of Georgia
Athens, GA 30602
Quarterly, $12
Stanley W. Lindberg

The Gettysburg Review
Gettysburg College
Gettysburg, PA 17325-1491
Quarterly, $15
Peter Stitt

Granta
2-3 Hanover Yard
Noel Road
Islington
London
NI 8BE
ENGLAND
Quarterly, $29.95
Bill Buford

The Greensboro Review
Department of English
University of North Carolina at
Greensboro
Greensboro, NC 27412
Semiannually, $8
Jim Clark

Harper's Magazine
666 Broadway
New York, NY 10012
Monthly, $18
Lewis H. Lapham

High Plains Literary Review
180 Adams Street
Suite 250
Denver, CO 80206
Three times a year, $20
Robert O. Greer

Indiana Review
316 North Jordan Avenue
Bloomington, IN 47405
Three times a year, $12
Allison Joseph

The Iowa Review
308 EPB
The University of Iowa
Iowa City, IA 52242
Three times a year, $15
David Hamilton

The Journal
The Ohio State University
Department of English
164 West 17th Avenue
Columbus, OH 43210
Biannually, $8
Michelle Herman, Fiction Editor

The Kenyon Review
Kenyon College
Gambier, OH 43022
Quarterly, $22
Marilyn Hacker

The Literary Review
285 Madison Avenue
Madison, NJ 07940
Quarterly, $18
Walter Cummins

The Long Story
11 Kingston Street
North Andover, MA 01845
Annually, $5
R.P. Burnham and A. Patricia
  Jaysane

Mid-American Review
106 Hanna Hall
Department of English
Bowling Green State University
Bowling Green, OH 43403
Semiannually, $6
Ken Letko, Editor, and Robert Early,
  Fiction Editor

Mississippi Review
Center for Writers
The University of Southern
  Mississippi
Southern Station
Box 5144
Hattiesburg, MS 39406-5144
Semiannually, $15
Frederick Barthelme

The Missouri Review
1507 Hillcrest Hall
University of Missouri
Columbia, MO 65211
Three times a year, $15
Speer Morgan

Negative Capability
62 Ridgelawn Drive East
Mobile, AL 36608
Three times a year, $12
Sue Walker

New Delta Review
English Department
Louisiana State University
Baton Rouge, LA 70803
Semiannually, $7
Kathleen Fitzpatrick, Editor, and
  David Racine, Fiction Editor

New England Review
Middlebury College
Middlebury, VT 05753
Quarterly, $18
T. R. Hummer

New Virginia Review
1306 East Cary Street, 2A
Richmond, VA 23219
Three times a year, $15
Mary Flinn

The New Yorker
20 West 43rd Street
New York, NY 10036
Weekly, $32
Tina Brown

Nimrod
Arts and Humanities Council
  of Tulsa
2210 South Main Street
Tulsa, OK 74114
Semiannually, $11.50
Francine Ringold, Editor, and
  Geraldine McLoud, Fiction Editor

The North American Review
University of Northern Iowa
Cedar Falls, IA 50614
Quarterly, $14; Six times a year
  starting in 1992
Robley Wilson

Northwest Review
369 PLC
University of Oregon
Eugene, OR 97403
Three times a year, $11

John Witte, Editor, Cecelia Hagen,
    Fiction Editor

Ohioana Quarterly
Ohioana Library Association
1105 Ohio Departments Building
65 South Front Street
Columbus, OH 43215
Quarterly, $20
Barbara Maslekoff

The Ohio Review
290-C Ellis Hall
Ohio University
Athens, OH 45701-2979
Three times a year, $12
Wayne Dodd

Old Hickory Review
P.O. Box 1178
Jackson, TN 38302
Semiannually, $12
Dorothy Stanfill and Don Phillips

Ontario Review
9 Honey Brook Drive
Princeton, NJ 08540
Semiannually, $10
Raymond J. Smith and Joyce
    Carol Oates

Other Voices
820 Ridge Road
Highland Park, IL 60035
Semiannually, $16
Lois Hauselman and Sharon Fiffer

The Paris Review
Box 8
541 East 72nd Street
New York, NY 10021
Quarterly, $24
George Plimpton

Paris Transcontinental
Institut du Monde Anglophone
Sorbonne Nouvelle
5, rue de l'Ecole de Medecine

75006 Paris
FRANCE
Semiannually, 130F
Claire Larriere

Pembroke Magazine
Box 60
Pembroke State University
Pembroke, NC 28372
Annually, $5
Shelby Stephenson, Editor, and
    Stephen E. Smith, Fiction Editor

The Pittsburgh Quarterly
36 Haberman Avenue
Pittsburgh, PA 15211-2144
Quarterly, $12
Frank Correnti

Ploughshares
Emerson College
100 Beacon Street
Boston, MA 02116
Three times a year, $19
DeWitt Henry, Editor, and Don Lee,
    Fiction Editor

Prairie Schooner
201 Andrews Hall
University of Nebraska
Lincoln, NE 68588-0334
Quarterly, $17
Hilda Raz

Puerto del Sol
Box 3E
New Mexico State University
Las Cruces, NM 88003
Semiannually, $6.75
Antonya Nelson, Editor, and Kevin
    McIlvoy, Fiction Editor

The Quarterly
201 East 50th Street
New York, NY 10022
Quarterly, $40
Gordon Lish

350   APPENDIX

Quarterly West
317 Olpin Union
University of Utah
Salt Lake City, UT 84112
Semiannually, $8.50
Regina Oost and Tom Hazuka

Redbook
The Hearst Corporation
959 8th Avenue
New York, NY 10019
Monthly, $11.97
Ellen Levine, Editor-in-Chief, and
    Dawn Raffel, Fiction and Books

River Styx
14 South Euclid
St. Louis, MO 63108
Three times a year, $20
Jennifer Atkinson

The Seattle Review
Padelford Hall
GN-30
University of Washington
Seattle, WA 98195
Semiannually, $8
Donna Gerstenberger, Editor, and
    David Bosworth, Fiction Editor

Shenandoah
Washington and Lee University
Box 722
Lexington, VA 24450
Quarterly, $11
Dabney Stuart

Snake Nation Review
110 #2 West Force Street
Valdosta, GA 31602
Semiannually, $15
Roberta George, Pat Miller, and
    Janice Daugharty

The South Carolina Review
Department of English
Clemson University

Clemson, SC 29634-1503
Semiannually, $7
Richard J. Calhoun

Southern Exposure
P.O. Box 531
Durham, NC 27702
Quarterly, $16
Susan Ketchin, Fiction Editor

Southern Humanities Review
9088 Haley Center
Auburn University
Auburn, AL 36849
Quarterly, $12
Dan R. Latimer and Thomas L.
    Wright

The Southern Review
43 Allen Hall
Louisiana State University
Baton Rouge, LA 70803
Quarterly, $15
James Olney and Dave Smith

Sou'wester
Southern Illinois University at
    Edwardsville
Edwardsville, IL 62026-1438
Three times a year, $10
Fred W. Robbins

Southwest Review
307 Fondren Library West
Box 4374
Southern Methodist University
Dallas, TX 75275
Quarterly, $20
Willard Spiegelman

Stories
Box Number 1467
East Arlington, MA 02174-0022
Quarterly, $18
Amy R. Kaufman

Story
1507 Dana Avenue
Cincinnati, OH 45208
Quarterly, $17
Lois Rosenthal

StoryQuarterly
P.O. Box 1416
Northbrook, IL 60065
Quarterly, $12
Anne Brashler, Diane Williams, and
    Margaret Barrett

The Threepenny Review
P.O. Box 9131
Berkeley, CA 94709
Quarterly, $12
Wendy Lesser

TriQuarterly
Northwestern University
2020 Ridge Avenue
Evanston, IL 60208
Three times a year, $18
Reginald Gibbons

Turnstile
Suite 2348
175 Fifth Avenue
New York, NY 10010
Semiannually, $12
Mitchell Nauffts

The Virginia Quarterly Review
One West Range
Charlottesville, VA 22903
Quarterly, $15
Staige D. Blackford

Voice Literary Supplement
VV Publishing Corp.
36 Cooper Square
New York, NY 10003
Monthly, except the combined issues
    of Dec./Jan., and July/Aug., $17
M. Mark

Weber Studies
Weber State College
Ogden, UT 84408-1214
Semiannually, $5
Neila C. Seshachari

West Branch
Bucknell Hall
Bucknell University
Lewisburg, PA 17837
Semiannually, $7
Karl Patten and Robert Taylor

Wind Magazine
RFD Route 1
Box 809K
Pikeville, KY 41501
Semiannually, $7
Quentin Howard

ZYZZYVA
41 Sutter Street
Suite 1400
San Francisco, CA 94104
Quarterly, $20
Howard Junker